PRAISE FOR SOUNDRISE

"Lynn Voedisch's *Soundrise* is a fast, fun run through the strange and mystical, with a unique cast of characters who keep things jumping, and more plot twists than you can count. Put it all together and you have a great read!"
— Renee James, author of *Seven Suspects, A Kind of Justice,Transition to Murder,* and *Coming Out Can Be Murder*

"*Soundrise* by Lynn Voedisch is a compelling mashup of a post-modern *Mr. Robot* and the search for an ancient scientific breakthrough that could change the world. It's also the story of a young man who finds himself by facing the physical and emotional dangers of that search. Part sci-fi, part romance, part mystery, *Soundrise* delivers a well-written, exciting, and surprisingly poignant story that will leave you thinking about the characters well after you've read the last page."
— Libby Fischer Hellmann, author of *Jump Cut*

SOUNDRISE

LYNN VOEDISCH

The Story Plant
Studio Digital CT, LLC
PO Box 4331
Stamford, CT 06907

Story Plant hardcover ISBN-13: 978-1-61188-286-5
Story Plant paperback ISBN-13: 978-1-61188-311-4
Fiction Studio Books E-book ISBN-13: 978-1-945839-45-0

Visit our website at www.TheStoryPlant.com

First Story Plant hardcover printing: September 2020
First Story Plant paperback printing: October 2021
Printed in the United States of America

Dedicated to my husband, Brad Blumenthal

CHAPTER ONE

Clicking echoed into the early morning, a persistent clattering of plastic bones, a death rattle of a dream. A tap dance of an unseen gremlin. Crisp, staccato clacks issued coded commands into the bowels of electronic machinery. Tap. Open a new screen. Click. De-bug. Rat-a-tat-a-tat. Compile. Beep. Execution fault.

Rhythm was all, and Derek Nilsson was in the zone, the space where concentration is pure and tensile, buzzing with neuron electricity. His hands flew so quickly across the keyboard, he had almost no conscious awareness of their movement. The fingertips were hot-wired to the brain. He punched in lines of code, read the computer's response, then tapped some more. Line by line, command by command, the program took shape, with Derek only one step ahead in this elaborate tango of two minds. He clicked, and the machine pulsed patterns on the screen. He tapped, and the program fanned out in strength and breadth, surging toward completion.

Yet today, the clatter rang hollow, the taps reverberating off the apartment walls, enlarging the cavities of the room. The rattle was the sound of old ladies leaving a museum, striking a vast hardwood floor with sturdy heels and well-used canes. The chatter of dentures. The sound of nothing more to say, nothing more to see. Amid blinking lights and whirring disks, Derek felt a loneliness that threatened to swallow him whole.

Before, The Project—the all-encompassing, all-absorbing decryption effort—had commanded Derek's attention into the tiny hours of the night. When he sat down at his keyboard, home after a long day of boring programming, the Project infused him with a fresh new challenge. It was a puzzle to piece together, a tantalizing tangle of encrypted code to unwind. Derek loved the challenge of looking for clues that led to a key, which then revealed the first few lines of readable code. He was often amazed at how the process would take over, build, create a net that waited to catch the characters when the code finally broke.

Now, however, he sat at his patched-together array of two desktop computers and one laptop, toggling between windows on the screens, keeping track of multiple programs running simultaneously. One screen displayed nothing but black characters on a white screen, the nuts and bolts of Charles—a language Derek had developed specifically for encryption analysis. The cascade of letters, numbers, slashes, tildes, brackets, carets, dashes, hashes and bangs, all as familiar to Derek as a kindergartner's ABCs, marched in presto across the screen. The parade of blinking letters reminded him of too much effort, too many hours spent in front of the screen.

Derek stopped. He listened to the silent night, turning to look at the books, papers, disk drives, printers, empty soft-drink cans, fast-food wrappers, that filled his home office. A bookshelf that had become a warehouse of skip drives and old computer parts. The analog clock on the wall counted out the seconds. Two thirty-seven in the morning. An overhead light sizzled with high-pitched vibrations. Derek's cat, Foo, dreamed on in his lap, sending up soothing, rumbling waves of contentment. Outside, a tire squealed and an engine let out a gasp of exasperation before roaring into the distance. In the midst of Chicago's twenty-four-hour whirlwind, there was emptiness, as if the night were begging Derek to fill it.

He threw his head back onto the padded leather of his desk chair, wondering if there was any sense in going to bed. At seven, he would have to rise anyway to make it to work by nine. Would four hours of sleep matter? The Project had eaten up so much of his time, he might as well surrender completely, pull an all-nighter, and stumble through his day job on autopilot. It wouldn't be the first time.

Derek's finger poised over the keyboard, ready to pull up the code-breaking program to see what had been accomplished lately with brute-force encryption-cracking tactics. Thousands of hackers (proud computer wizards and not the criminals derided by the press) worldwide had voluntarily signed on to Derek's little "contest," a gauntlet tossed on a popular website before the computer community: "See if you can break this code first and it's the key to something big." Derek was astonished three months ago when computer nerds worldwide downloaded the data and started code busting. People were bringing computer resources from everywhere, and they were all working on Derek's puzzle.

While the machines slashed away in the dark, Derek and his partner George Esterberg guided the larger decryption enterprise. Right now, small blocks of data were readable, and Derek was figuring out where they fit in the broader scheme of a coherent data set. Like Jean-Francois Champollion, the man who cracked the Egyptian hieroglyphics inscribed on the Rosetta Stone, he was looking for a cartouche, a meaningful arrangement of characters that would serve to organize the rest of the material. When Champollion found the cartouches, royal names of the pharaohs, he learned that hieroglyphics were representations of sounds. By working out the syllables and then applying them to other words, the master code breaker made a silent language begin to speak for a new age. Derek was looking to do the same thing; only he was attempting to make discarded data talk—and he wasn't even sure what subject they would speak about.

The bit that he'd retrieved last night was tantalizing. This obviously was the work of a magician, a real master coding with signature flourishes. Derek nodded in appreciation of the mathematical elegance of it all. If he could patch together just a few more of these readable blocks of code, he might be able to feel the rest of the data fall into a pattern. It would take more late nights, intense concentration, a dollop of intuition, and spades of luck. He chorded on the keyboard, attempting to bring up his e-mail client. Time to see what George thought of the gem. Time to read missives from all those number crunchers working alone in the cyber-Outback.

"Derek," an electronic voice announced. "I am Ra-jah. Here to help you."

Derek's feet shot to the floor, Foo rocketed off his lap in a flurry of fur and scrambling claws, and Derek was on his feet, staring at the screen. Where had that come from? Was there someone in the apartment? Derek spun around, checking out his tiny home office. Nothing there. No, wait, check the process list. There were only the usual programs running.

Sound files. Of course. Check for sound files. Derek clapped a shaky hand over his heart and slid inch by inch down into his seat, examining the screen for any signs of a recently downloaded file. Easy, boy. It's probably just something damned clever. Take a look.

Derek scanned the screen several times before he realized that nothing new was running. No new files. No new processes. In his mind, he replayed what had just happened. He had clicked on the e-mail program and some bizarre voice popped up. A message had come in recently, maybe at the exact time he heard the voice. A quick run through the intrusion-detection routines was in order. He tapped a number of keys and set a program running. It would take a good twenty minutes. This was as good a time as any to take a break.

Ra-jah, indeed. Or was it Roger? Did he know any Rogers? Derek shrugged his shoulders and shook his head with irritation.

He shuffled off to the kitchen and found Foo hovering over her water dish, looking none the worse for wear. He stroked her silken fur, a delicious patchwork of calico patterns, and felt his neck and shoulders relax. For four years he had shared life with Foo and never needed another roommate. Through graduate school, through the summer internship with George, through the job hunt, and during his shaky first months at BitJockey.com, Foo had been a steady companion. Cats, unlike people, didn't provide commentary about Derek's irregular hours, burrito-and-delivery-pizza eating habits, towering piles of laundry, or lack of friends. As long as there was a warm lap to lie in and a fragrant bowl of tuna or cod puree twice a day, Foo was a happy companion. At night, Foo would jump on his back, lie down and give him a neck rub, purring at high decibels the entire time. No judgments and no criticism. Not everyone understood him so well.

Geek. Nerd. Misfit. Socially challenged. Derek had heard it everywhere; from the time he first programmed a little microprocessor in high school, all through college and grad school, people had been snickering at him. Childhood buddies took banking jobs, wore pricey watches, joined country clubs, and smirked if they passed Derek on the street. Girlfriends—who never seemed to hang around longer than six weeks—found his cyber-world lifestyle initially amusing, until they began to realize that he was serious about shrugging off the real universe. His mother, Astrid, never stopped reminding him that if he didn't "get out more," he'd end up alone like her. Friends, such as Trevor Chen, the graphic artist who made BitJockey's game software shimmer with realism, would scrutinize Derek's long, gaunt frame, sunken chest, scraggly goatee, and threadbare clothes, and shake their heads.

"Get a real life," Trevor would say, his dark eyes shining. "Or your closest relationship will be with your computer."

Well, George understood. But then, George was like Derek—a computer jock, a bit boy, a true code gladiator. George knew why it was possible to forget about eating for twenty-four hours, what it was like for an evening to morph into dawn in no time at all. He understood why dating stopped being fun once women started making demands on your precious computing time. George knew that there was no kick in the world that matched the adrenaline rush of stringing together the right commands and having a mighty computer, or fifty, or five hundred, at your disposal. All those millions of bytes thinking for you, traveling the world for you, and, if need be, breaking and entering for you.

No night of drinking or drugs or sex could ever compare to a long evening of productive hacking. And not script kiddie stuff, either. None of that cruising into other machines using someone else's code and seeing how many you could tamper with and "pwn" (or own). No, Derek and George were turned onto the big game: finding hidden secrets, creating new datastreams for artificial intelligence to chew on, breaking into the most closely guarded codes in the world.

The Project was as close as Derek had ever come to pure computer opium, hacker junk, the total ride. If George and Derek could break down and make sense of the cleverly encrypted data they had stumbled onto, they most likely could retire at the tender age of twenty-five. And then think of the carefree hours they could spend playing with computers.

Foo's ears began to twist around like radar dishes, and Derek turned to see what she had heard. A moment later, a beep from his computer signaled that the intrusion scan was finished. He glanced at his well-used coffeemaker, set to start brewing at 6:45 a.m., and decided against messing with the mechanism to get a shot of caffeine and pulled a cold caffeinated Power Jolter out of the fridge. Coffee could wait.

He padded back into his office—really a tiny changing room between the bedroom and the bathroom—and leaned over his computer screen. The scan showed no break-ins. Derek stood bent over with his lower back screaming, scrutinizing the screen. If there was no sound file and no virus, what was going on?

He clicked the e-mail program again. This time there was no eerie electronic voice, just a long list of unread messages. Five of them were from George. Derek tapped the keys to open the first one, then the next. Each note was more boring than the last, automated reports detailing mundane specifics of what George's students were working on at the University of Chicago. As a doctoral student, George had a small cadre of undergraduates and masters students at his disposal, all eager to help George in his program. The trouble was that they needed constant care and feeding, a chore that Derek would rather avoid.

He stood up and gazed toward his bedroom, catching a glimpse of the full moon outdoors. Like a gaping eye, it focused on him, soaking him with an unsettling light that seeped across his body like running mercury. Derek shivered, and the feeling of loneliness returned.

Okay, maybe a few hours of sleep was a decent idea after all. The day job did pay the bills. Can't be crashing and burning at the office. He crawled onto the unmade bed and found the pillow with his cheek. He closed his eyes and watched a manic slide show unfold, replaying scenes from his day, images of system crashes, and overdue bills, microwaved pizza rolls for dinner, and tons of messages. He rolled over onto his stomach and tried to stop the parade of unwelcome thoughts, tried to think of nothing more than his breath, tried to forget the ringing in his ears. He felt the soft feet of Foo land on his sheets. With deft precision, she maneuvered herself onto his back and began kneading his knotted neck and shoulders with her paws. The vibrations of her purrs sent Derek into a soft haze. And Derek's roving mind created the image of a bird.

It was a peregrine falcon, a statue that his father gave him long ago. Carved of wood and darkened with age, the bird of prey still stood in Astrid's living room. Derek hadn't thought of the bird for years, but now it stood out in his mind with astonishing clarity. Proud and erect, the bird sat on its perch, eyes trained on some unfortunate animal in the distance, wings tucked back but poised for instant unfurling, beak lifted at a cocky angle.

"One of the finest specimens on earth," Charlie had said, the day he presented the falcon to Derek. "The ancient Egyptians recognized that. They associated the bird's qualities with those of their god, Horus."

Derek was only ten and couldn't understand what his dad was trying to tell him. He'd gotten some pretty strange presents from his dad, but he'd come to expect that. Charlie, usually red-eyed and breathing alcoholic fire, ranted on and on about subjects that puzzled Derek. This fascination with birds was a new one. When Derek asked his mother what to do with the sculpture, she sighed and suggested its current home on a high shelf.

"Why couldn't he get me a PlayStation, Mom?"

"Why indeed?" she said and bit her lower lip so hard it looked as if it would swell up.

Derek burrowed his face deeper into the pillow and the bird reappeared. But now, the falcon was alive. It flew silently, its stiff wings hardly twitching, riding air gusts higher each second. Its eyes targeted on a pinpoint in the dark night. The beak, a hooked and pointed instrument of lethal possibilities, pierced the air as the feathered warrior swerved and circled its prey. An enveloping, mechanical buzzing, almost musical in its regularity, surged, then cleared.

"Derek. I am Roger. Here to help you."

The bird slipped through the crisp April air, parting the rich landscape of dreams. As pure spring sunlight prodded the trees, forcing withering frost to withdraw, exposing the sweet green buds and sprouts to a wash of emerging light, the bird rode on the singing rays of dawn. He began to spin, rotate, and whirl into something dark and deep. Derek felt unseen eyes that were moving, probing, penetrating his innermost thoughts. His brain began to howl.

"Derek. I am Roger. Here to help you."

The bird regarded him, staring into Derek's open eye. Unable to move, a synthetic voice bleating in his ears, caught between a dream and reality, Derek did the only thing he could. He filled his lungs with a desperate breath and screamed himself awake.

CHAPTER TWO

The streets were wrapped in a slick coat of rain, shining with a dull glow. Derek Nilsson thought the pavement looked bound in shrink-wrap, tidied up and readied for mass-market sales. But Derek knew that under the slick surface lurked grime. Layers of dirt and spit and bird feces lay just below the shimmering glaze. Derek knew not to trust appearances—especially in downtown Chicago.

This part of town, the sparkling Near North Side neighborhood of Streeterville, was built on swampland. Landfill solidified the bogs and wetland marshes to create a newer, firmer, tidier landscape. Yet, Derek wondered, what if the marshes threatened to return, lapping at the concrete and steel pilings that drove straight down to the bedrock? He wondered if the primitive soul of "chee-ka-gou"—an American Indian tribe's word for "wild onion"—could bring all those towers crashing into the mud.

The bus lurched a bit, nearing Derek's stop. He inched forward in his seat, preparing to rise, straightening his windbreaker. At nearly 9 a.m., the air was already moist and warm. For the first time in many years, the Great Lakes states were enjoying a real spring. That meant no snow in April, not even bone-chilling rain and ankle-deep mud. Flowers had been blooming since March and now, in mid-April, Chicago looked as postcard pretty as it usually does in June. The day showed promise of comfortable breeziness.

Derek stood up and pushed toward the exit, trying to gauge his balance as the driver rolled and rocked through rush-hour traffic. As he hung on to a metal handrail, trying to keep from bashing into the large woman in front of him, Derek considered taking his lunch outside today. Maybe he'd sit in the plaza two blocks away and watch the women walk by—women who were always too busy to smile or wave, women who had no time for a tech-head like him. Derek let out a small sigh as the bus door opened, the hefty lady moved out of the way and he hopped into the pulsating throng of pedestrian traffic.

He joined the trench-coated brigade, letting the cadence of his steps take over all thoughts, preventing him from remembering something that happened overnight. An event he'd rather not dredge up now, not with a full day's work on the docket. Something disturbing.

"Lost in space?" asked a soft voice.

Derek looked up and spotted Kyra Van Dyck, the small, spirited redhead from BitJockey.com's marketing department, fixing him with a quizzical look. She cocked her head to one side as if she had been considering him for some minutes. Derek stumbled and stopped, allowing her to push through the revolving door first. As the sweeping combine expelled them into the lobby, Derek gazed over at Kyra. Some answer was required of him, he was sure of that. But try as he might, Derek could think of nothing to say. He mumbled something incomprehensible and smiled.

Kyra moved toward the elevators, her brow furrowed a bit, juggling her briefcase and shoulder bag to free a hand. Derek reached over to push the call button. Her finger was already there. The two bumped hands, hers graceful and manicured, his sweaty and shaking. She smiled and looked at the ground, seeming to study the floor tiles.

"I'm not really a space out," Derek heard himself saying, as lighted numbers tracked the elevator's descent.

"What?"

"You know, what you said when we were out on the street."

"Oh yeah. Well, you didn't see me looking at you."

"Too little sleep. Occupational hazard."

"So I've heard. Code warriors, we call you guys."

Kyra started to smile, but her happy glow disappeared in an instant. Derek followed her gaze to the elevator lights. They had stopped flickering. Kyra stretched out an arm, freeing her wrist from the sleeve of her trench coat, and peered at her watch—a plastic sports watch.

"That's not the image," Derek said, at once regretting the fact that he had opened his mouth. What made him do that?

"What's not?"

"The watch. It's not Rolex." Derek silently cursed the elevator for its tardiness and tried to keep his disgust of BitJockey.com's management under control.

Kyra dropped her head and let out a soft laugh.

"No, and I don't blare on a cell phone in fine dining rooms, either."

"Sorry. I don't know what came over me. You seem like a nice person."

"We're not all corporate clones. Is that what you nerd boys think?"

Derek shook his head and reached to touch his hair. Portions of the light brown do-it-yourself coif were sticking up like spikes of fur on a water-soaked puppy. The elevator emitted a muffled bell tone and the doors swept open. Derek hurried in before he could get himself into more trouble. He and Kyra took a few steps inside before a crowd of workers smashed them into the back wall of the car. Pinned next to the paneling and pressed next to Kyra's arm, Derek felt her wavy, auburn hair, still damp from a morning shower, touch his skin. He inhaled her clean scent and was ready to stand next to her for hours, but the ride was over in seconds.

"Look, I'll see you later," Kyra said as she pressed out onto the seventeenth floor. "The prediction is beautiful for today. Maybe we could take our lunches outside?"

Derek froze. He clutched his stomach, but could not master his anxiety.

"No time," he said with more force than he intended. He grinned a feeble apology as the doors closed on Kyra's deflated expression—then he caught the door in a frenzy, unsetting other passengers. "Another day, OK?" The door closed on Kyra's confused look.

Derek stiffened as he felt the elevator ascend to floor eighteen, programming. That was damn stupid. A woman, smart and a real fox, was making an overture and he just nearly shut her down. He thought about how many times his mother explained that shyness can be mistaken for arrogance. Did he just act like another over-amped techno boy or a pathetic hack with a total lack of social skills? Kyra might not waste any more time finding out.

≈

Derek's desk was covered with odd bits of paper, some commanding him to various meetings throughout the day, others cataloging hundreds of software codes. Derek moved enough paper to make room for his coffee cup on a five-by-five-inch patch of bare desktop.

Today was a core crunch day. If Derek finished writing a major part of the Herriges software upgrade, he'd be in fine shape by the end of the week. If he could just keep going with only four hours of sleep a night, he could get this project finished and move that extra-curricular gig off the ground at the same time.

A sudden wave of drowsiness made Derek feel as if he were slipping in mental quicksand, losing footing, feeling solid land turn to mush. A thought lurched forward into his consciousness. This morning, he had heard a dream voice in the back of his mind. It was calm and sharp, interested and curious. It had called itself "Ra-jah." Or maybe it said "Roger."

Derek opened his eyes as if he had seen a great, furry spider walk across his computer screen.

Hearing voices. One of the first signs of insanity. Derek seized his computer mouse in a death grip. A voice had lodged in his brain, there was no doubt about that—and it wasn't his own mind chattering away. Or was it that sound file—that undetectable sound file—playing repeatedly through the early hours of the morning? He did leave the computer on, didn't he?

"Shitty night, huh?" A hand clapped Derek on the shoulder, and he shuddered with a tense, involuntary jerk. He looked up to see Trevor Chen staring into his eyes.

"Oh God, man. Don't do that, not first thing in the morning." Derek laughed and winced at the same time, wiping the drops of coffee that had spilled onto the papers on his desk.

"You look like you've seen a ghost," Trevor said, moving back from Derek. He reached behind his head to adjust the elastic band that secured his long ponytail. Derek looked at Trevor's hair—an obedient sweep of black—artistic and businesslike at the same time. Derek put his hand to his head and fingered his messy tangle of thin fringe, still damp from his earlier, nervous encounter with Kyra.

"Ghost, yeah, maybe I have," Derek said half to himself. "Weird things happen to you when you don't sleep."

"Saw you talking to Kyra down by the elevators," Trevor said, cocking one eyebrow. "I think she's got it for you, boy."

Derek allowed himself to smile as he straightened the myriad memos on his desk.

"Yeah, maybe. I don't know," Derek said, thinking of some way to change the subject. Trevor wasn't about to comply.

"There are women who find hackers irresistible, you know. It's that pallor, that lack of sunlight and fresh air."

Derek let out a breathy laugh that sounded almost like a sigh of relief. He thought about his appearance: his long, skinny frame, pale skin, thin hair, bloodshot blue eyes, languid manner. Derek knew he was hardly a ladies' man. He had no idea what Kyra could see in him.

"Yeah, surrounded as she is by all those suits, those guys with BMWs and platinum credit cards, she would naturally be drawn to a guy with a full set of designer software t-shirts," Derek said. Trevor fixed his dancing black eyes on Derek.

"Seriously, why don't you ask her out?" Trevor said, a bit of longing peeking out from beneath the inky surface of his irises. "She's awfully pretty ... and she's got brains, too."

Derek wanted to tell Trevor to try his own advice. Trevor had the image that a public-relations girl would fall for. Trevor, with his Fiat two-seater and his apartment full of Calder prints. Trevor, the graphic designer with a head full of ideas that were simply too avant-garde for BitJockey.com.

"Nah," Derek said, looking toward his screen, edging his hand toward the mouse. "Still getting over the last one."

"Don't get over it too long," Trevor said as he took steps toward the art department. "Or your only intimate relationship will be with your computer." Derek repeated the familiar line along with him. By now, it had turned into a joke.

Derek attempted to let that parting shot slip between the pixels on the screen, but it echoed in his throbbing head. Had Trevor pronounced a curse or did he see the future? Derek wondered if his computer really had started talking back.

≈

The phone wouldn't stop ringing. Although Derek programmed it to "do not disturb" mode, it continued to slice through the air with its chirping interruption. Derek looked over at Patty, the receptionist. She was the only one who could override the phone codes. She shrugged her padded shoulders.

"Your voice mailbox is full," Patty said with an apologetic tilt of the head. "And she said it's important."

Derek lifted the handset, stated his name, and barely heard his mother's wispy voice rushing over the static. He breathed deep into his gut and looked at the clock. He'd gotten three solid hours of work done—and now this.

"You remembered tonight, right?" his mom was saying. Derek knew from the perky artificiality of her voice that she had entered the aching, black gloom of depression, again.

"What's tonight?" he asked, his throat tightening as he anticipated her hurt.

"No! You didn't forget did you? The Merles are coming into town. They haven't seen you since you were twelve."

"Mom, I have an extremely important project on the line here."

"At eight in the evening?"

"At all hours. I'm working constantly. By Friday, I'll make one deadline and I can lighten up a little."

Derek felt a dull blow hit his stomach as silence sat on the telephone line. He waited for his mother to let out that light, heart-breaking exhalation of air that she had used on him ever since he was small. But the cruel sigh didn't come. White noise crackled on the line. Derek couldn't stand it any longer.

"Mom, are you still there?"

There was a breath and then a weak "yes."

Derek felt his eyebrows pinch together. He hated this trap she set, yet he also knew that any argument he tried she would shut down in seconds. Yes, he knew he had promised. Yes, he was neglecting his health. Yes, he was making her worry. Yes, it was only a couple hours out of his busy day.

"Okay, Mom," Derek said, massaging the bridge of his nose, feeling where the tight muscles jammed into his skull. "I'll be there at eight. Do you want anything?"

"No," Mom said, her voice cracking at the edges. "Just you."

≈

Astrid Nilsson, Derek's mom, was pouring wine when he pushed through the back door. She measured a prescribed dollop for each glass, moving the bottle with mechanical precision. She tipped her cheek up for a kiss when Derek placed a bundle of tulips on the counter top.

"For the table," Derek said with a slight cough, trying to push his presence through the haze of Astrid's semi-awareness. Astrid put the wine bottle on the countertop with painstaking slowness. Then she looked up at Derek with eyes full of regret—fifty years full of longing. When Astrid went into her own private hovel of pain, Derek noticed that her eyes changed from blue, the exact color of Michigan blueberries, to a twilight shade of purple.

Derek used to imagine that Astrid's eyes were bloodshot, adding an illusory, pinkish cast to her blue irises. But, over time, he discovered that this wasn't true. Astrid's eyes actually changed, became lavender-hued, as her body chemistry altered. Missing a salt here or an enzyme there, Astrid metamorphosed into something lethargic and immovable, something that sent vibrations of tension and pain to the corners of every room.

"Hello, son," Astrid said, offering a wineglass. "The Merles are in the living room. Would you like to go in and say hello?" She gave him two wineglasses to offer.

Derek nodded, noticing a raspy sensation in the back of his throat. Derek felt his shoulders sag as he stepped into the living room. As he passed a bookshelf, he saw that blasted statue of a falcon hovering over the room. He thought of Roger and shivered.

The bulky figure of Jim Merle advanced. Nothing had changed in twelve years, except for the fact that Jim packed even more heft into his tightly clenched belt. A large paw clubbed Derek on the shoulder.

The heavy thud took Derek back to his boyhood, when he often flinched under Merle's clumsy touch. He remembered standing at the kitchen counter when he was eleven, watching his dad slug down a can of beer while Jim announced that Derek was one of the boys. He remembered the bruising slap on the back, an unwanted initiation rite. Derek's dad, Charlie, eyes red and unfocused from an afternoon of chugging brews, would just chuckle. Derek always wondered why his dad put up with Merle.

Derek straightened his shoulders, shrugged off the memory, and presented the wine glasses to Jim and Sandy—she, too, more outsized than before in her polyester tent dress. Pleasantries exchanged, the interrogation started.

Yes, he was twenty-four years old now. Yes, Derek was doing well in life. No, a liberal arts education hadn't limited his career choices. A computer programmer. Pretty decent money.

Derek shifted from foot to foot as he considered seeking refuge in the kitchen, back with his bleak, detached mother, back where emotional cloaking baffled all sensation. Better that than this middle-class status report.

Leroy. Leroy Merle. He had to come up in conversation sooner or later. The memory of Leroy emerged from Derek's unconsciousness like a Leviathan from the deep. Leroy, the laughing little fat boy, the one who used his heft to pin Derek to the floor; the kid who never returned toys. Leroy was now a banker.

"Married," Sandy said, her sparkling little marble eyes bobbing above her cheeks. "And they are working on kids."

"Any special girl there, Derek?" Jim questioned, his left hook coming dangerously close to contacting Derek's ribs. Derek opened his mouth to change the subject, when Astrid announced dinner. Derek escaped to the kitchen, where he stood a long minute at the sink, trying to get back his bearings. He blinked back sleep as he helped his mother bring dishes of pork tenderloin and red cabbage to the dining room. He heard Astrid continue the conversation in her low voice.

"Oh, you know Derek. It takes him a while to find a girl. He's just as picky as I am," Astrid said with a slight giggle, one that might have sounded girlish had it not been so shrill. Derek knew that Astrid only started talking about her status as a lonely divorcee when her moods were really bad. He sat down, praying the conversation would veer away from Astrid's love life.

"Charlie was my best friend but I think he was a nutcase for taking off to Indian country and leaving you behind," Jim said, a leer peeking through the syllables. "I should think that someone would have found you by now, Astrid."

Derek hated this part. If they were going to go over his dad's drinking and the way he took the Geographic Cure—moving to New Mexico to start over—Derek didn't want to hear it again. He tried to focus on the dinner, but he was drifting. His brain became soft and soggy as his skull imploded. He kept imagining that his head was made of butter. In the background, he could hear Jim reminisce about the great times in the old Andersonville neighborhood, before it had been "taken over by minorities." Derek looked at potatoes au gratin and saw a vision of his piles of unwashed dishes waiting for him in his own kitchen. He heard Astrid, moaning about how bad the news coverage had gotten at the *Chicago Independent* ever since she retired.

"You were a damn good entertainment editor," Jim bellowed. "You left too early. You let them railroad you out of there."

"And we always appreciated all those free tickets," Sandy added, folding and refolding her linen napkin as she spoke.

Mom was looking misshapen, Derek realized. In his mind's eye, she was always trim and eagle-eyed in the days before she retired—or was forcibly retired. She headed out every day as if she were going to set the world aright as she edited the perfect story, assigned the perfect feature, won the best journalism prize. Tonight, she looked lumpy. Her gaze was askew. Derek wondered what chemicals went amiss in Astrid's brain. Or was it him? He tried to focus his left eye. It didn't respond.

Derek considered the red cabbage, swimming in a pool of purplish ooze, and thought someone might be asking him a question. He might have heard Jim mention Leroy again. But Derek was unable to answer. His brain fastened onto the computer puzzle that lay before him, the one that kept him up nights, searching and experimenting. In his head, he thought he could see the code, snaking its way through the bowels of interlinked computers. The lines of binary information slithered from machine to machine, turning on bits, turning off others. Somewhere in this multitude of minute clues lay Derek's answer. He almost could see the tail end of his key code, disappearing into a motherboard, giggling with delight as it eluded Derek, just as he reached out to grab the tail.

"Derek!"

He sat up in this chair and felt his brain roll around inside. He could swear there were pillows stuffed inside his temples.

"What?"

"Mr. Merle is asking you about your career plans," Astrid said, gritty irritation roughening her words.

"I'm working too hard, Mr. Merle," Derek said, pushing his pork around the plate, sliding it into a pool of white gravy. "I'm not getting enough sleep, I guess."

Merle laughed with that old, derisive bark that Derek hated as a kid. It sounded less like good humor than a prelude to a lecture.

"Sleep! Yes! Underrated!" Merle said, his voice gaining too much urgency. "But if you want to get ahead, I suppose it's the one thing that has to go!"

Sandy patted her husband's hand, reminding him that she always made sure he got eight hours of sleep every night. And look how well they did: a winter house in the Keys, a Land Rover, money in mutual funds.

The code was calling again, and this time Derek caught its tail. He started pulling it out, bit by bit, allowing element after element of the numerical sequence to reveal itself, backward. If he could only remember this, write it down. As he grappled, the code's head popped into view. It was laughing and spitting at him, the body retracted into a curling lash of electronic energy, whipping about like the body of a cobra.

"Roger!" the code said, grinning with mad glee. "Roger! That's who I am. I'm talking to you!"

"Roger, for God's sake! Leave me alone!"

Scalloped potatoes, silver forks, Gewürztraminer in a crystal goblet, a red polyester tie, a voice rasping in one ear. Cold hands pressed to his forehead. Mom's couch. Aunt Emma's afghan, knitted in 1962. Soft stuffing. Deep need for sleep.

"Derek? Who's Roger?"

CHAPTER THREE

FIVE YEARS IN THE PAST

Charlie Nilsson's feet touched the tarmac with a solid, crisp sound, the soles clicking on the pavement like magnets adhering to a sheet of steel. Even before he gazed at the horizon-hugging Sandia Mountains, he knew he had come to a place where he couldn't slip.

The air smelled of dust and grit, completely dry, alien to Charlie's Midwestern soul. He felt a twinge and looked at the back of his left hand, veins popping from the effort of carrying the overstuffed duffel bag, and saw how the sun lit up the tiny hairs where the wrist began. The rays, even in the early morning, felt as if they were singeing his skin. He knew it would be no time at all before the white spot on his ring finger was tanned over, obliterating twenty-five years of mistakes. His mistakes.

Charlie walked to the baggage retrieval area, not sure where he was headed next, only sure that he needed a safe haven. It shouldn't be hard, he thought, in a wide-open state like New Mexico. In town, when the skies had barely clouded over, Charlie bought a used car with half the money he brought from Chicago. He drove away in a little Mazda car with plenty of zip, aiming straight east on the highway that follows the general path of old Route 66. Halfway to Tucumcari, white flakes began to swirl around red cliffs and mesas, frosting the rocks with a phosphorescent sheen. By the time Charlie got close to Santa Rosa, snow had nearly erased the landscape.

Charlie could barely keep his eyes on the road, for the snow was unlike the deadened, gray debris that fell from the Chicago skies from November to April. This was illuminated, dancing dust, like talcum powder adrift in the sunlight. Falling and then billowing up, puffing skywards before spiraling in a vortex toward the earth. The rugged red strength of the mesas and cliffs offset the delicate impermanence of the crystals.

The hills were almost whited out when Charlie pulled off the highway at the Santa Rosa exit. He inched down the main drag, pulling up in front of a row of motels. When he opened the car door, the wind socked him in the jaw, burrowing up his sleeves and startling the hairs on his nape. Snow flew into his eyes, ears, and hair. The cold was shocking and pleasing at the same time, almost like the sensation of jumping into a cold swimming pool on a ninety-degree day. Charlie swallowed, hearing the wind play a sweet, barely audible whistle in his ears, hinting at something to be revealed.

He drew his arms across his chest and ran into the office of an old lodging, the Santa Rosa 66 Motel. He chose it because it was close by, and also because of the decrepit, stuffed "jackalope"—a mythical half-antelope, half-jack rabbit—that stood on a log pedestal on the office porch. The poor animal, with antlers jury-rigged onto its head, seemed to call out to Charlie. Here was someone in worse shape than he was.

He pulled open the door and stood by the entrance, brushing white fluff off his thin denim jacket, peering back at the desert outdoors, a vista painted white.

"Got a few rooms left," said a husky voice.

Charlie turned to see a woman in her fifties, with a face hardened by the sun and a voice seasoned by long bar-room nights. It was the sort of speech he was used to—a whiskey voice. Charlie shivered.

"Sorta got caught," he said.

"Dontcha listen to weather reports?"

He shrugged and gazed at the whiteout beyond the front window.

"I guess I didn't think it snowed in New Mexico," he said, lowering his eyes to count out forty dollars, the stated room rate on a sign on the wall. He slapped the money on the counter.

"They all say that," the woman said, taking his cash and tossing a key across the desk. "We're up high, see? Mountain elevation. When the drought hits, it hits hard too. Nothin' easy in the desert."

Charlie nodded and fingered the worn plastic tab on his dented key.

"Name's Marge," the woman said, tossing back her bouncy blonde hair, her only healthy feature. "First room on the right. Hope the rowdies next door don't keep you up."

By the time the sun set, casting an orange glow on the sugar-dusted hills outside, Charlie had sampled every TV channel, read the *Albuquerque Journal* twice, and was nearly ready to leaf through the ripped Events Guide he pulled off the wobbly nightstand. He put a quarter in the Magic Fingers machine instead and flattened out on the hard mattress, ready to surrender to the salvation of electronic vibrations.

A knock at the door interrupted his little experiment. Unwilling to rise, he leaned on one elbow.

"Who is it?" he called out.

"It's Marge. Wanna see how you're doing."

For a second, Charlie thought of sending her away. But, somehow, the idea of listening to Marge's foghorn voice seemed more interesting than staring at the ceiling tiles, so he rose with stiff limbs and made his way to the door.

Marge stood with her yellowed teeth glinting in the dimming light. She held up a whiskey bottle as if hailing him. Charlie stumbled backwards two steps and felt both fists tightening at his sides. He studied the green carpet, noticing how it had frayed where someone trimmed it to meet the doorframe. He tried to think of breathing, just breathing.

"Whatsa matter?" Marge said, sounding more curious than offended.

When Charlie didn't answer, Marge put her free hand on his tense shoulder, tacitly commanding him to meet her eyes. When he couldn't stand the force of her gaze anymore, Charlie looked up. She looked at his face for a long second and nodded.

"Okay, I get it. You don't drink. Mind if I do?"

He shook his head. She pushed past him and perched her skinny, angular body on the footboard of his bed, after putting the bottle and two plastic cups on the nightstand. She placed her bony hand on the vibrating mattress and smiled. Charlie pulled out the old wooden desk chair and sat astride it, backwards, leaning his long arms on the ladder back.

Marge drummed her pink nails on the pilling polyester quilt.

"Geographic Cure?" she asked.

Charlie felt electric current shoot up his back, wondering if the Magic Fingers were plugged into the wooden chair.

"Yeah, I guess you could call it that."

"Seen a lot of it, you know," she said, her eyes trailing over to the whiskey bottle, then fastening onto the window. "Quite a few folks I know did the same."

"I hear it never works. But I had to give it a try."

"Wife toss you out?"

"No. I left her. I was a pain to live with. She's probably glad."

"All drunks are pains to live with."

Charlie looked outside at the Christmas-like scene, watching Indians in cowboy hats shuffle through the deep slush that coated the streets.

"I was the biggest pain of all."

Marge looked at the whiskey bottle again and Charlie nodded. She poured herself a glassful of bourbon and swallowed it in two gulps. Charlie felt a rolling nausea start to fill his gut, but he looked away and practiced his breathing again.

"Sometimes it works," she said, wiping her mouth with the back of her hand. She reached into her jeans pocket and produced a mashed pack of unfiltered cigarettes. She held the pack out to Charlie, who extracted a smoke with shaky fingers.

"Sometimes it works," Marge repeated, lighting Charlie's cigarette, then her own. "But it's got nothing to do with the geographics. It's got to do with you."

Charlie took a long puff and watched the snow whirl outside his window. He'd been wanting to quit smoking, too. But he realized now that he was going to have to contend with one demon at a time.

Nothing was moving on the street outside. Charlie watched a red pickup truck transform into an alien object as the snow piled high on its roof, wedging between the outside mirrors and the door, building a small, narrow mountain on the top of the antenna.

"Truth is, Marge, it's no fun anymore. I'm sick of it."

"I am, too, honey, but I ain't there yet. I just ain't there."

She took another long drink, this time out of the bottle, and winked.

He watched a cockroach waddle into a corner crack of the room. Charlie's insides, moments ago tightened for the fight of his life, now felt formless, without substance. He was like a balloon tethered to a pole—wandering, flopping randomly with the wind.

"If I'm not there now, I'll never be," he said and flicked his cigarette butt after the retreating pest.

≈

There wasn't much of a plan to Charlie's journey, just as he had no plan for his recovery. He was going to drive and he was going to do it sober. That was the extent of it.

When the snow stopped, two days after he checked into the Santa Rosa 66 Motel, Charlie pointed his car west and retraced his tracks through the lonely bluffs of red-rock country.

As the Eagles blasted on the CD player (he liked the part about Winslow, Arizona), Charlie thought about Marge's bourbon kisses. For two nights, she had crawled into his bed and Charlie, too shell-shocked to object, found himself enjoying her enthusiasm. She was certainly more energetic than Astrid, even though he missed the slow pleasures of Sunday mornings in Chicago.

But he knew he had to get away, for Marge breathed an alcoholic blaze he was too weak to resist. The taste on her lips made him want to leap out of bed and raid her office bar, draining every bottle of Jack Daniel's and Cuervo Gold, rendering his mind blank and memory-free. And that last night in Santa Rosa, that's what he did. Comatose was how Charlie longed to exist: free from regretting the past, free from worrying over the future.

Charlie's mind had said no to booze but his body was still ready and willing for a killing dose. So now he had to start over again. The shakes would start soon, and he didn't want to appear in public when they did. He gripped the steering wheel so hard his knuckles ached and he breathed again, thinking clearly of each breath, of the lane markers on the solitary road, of nothing but driving and existing on a New Mexican morning.

He pulled off the road at a gas station south of Santa Fe. He looked for the gas cap on his new car and inserted the pump nozzle. As the tank filled, Charlie kicked at the red earth, gazing northward into the scrubby hills.

"Melting up there," said a boy hanging out the window of a dilapidated van. "Lots of sun melting the snow."

Charlie nodded, paid the cashier and bought a Dr Pepper. Caffeine for the road. He planned to have his eyes wide open when he found dry land. At the end of the snow lay Charlie's promised land, his geographic cure.

≈

Patterns etched a chiaroscuro picture, bold dark blotches dotting the white fields of snow, in the retreating frost somewhere between Los Alamos and Bandelier National Monument. Charlie wasn't sure where he was, since the map blew out of his window as he paused to inspect the area near a reservation. And the Mazda was not equipped with a GPS feature. Up there in wild, desolate country, he had pulled over on a two-lane highway to investigate the sun-drenched earth. The patches of dirt were larger than the patches of snow. Soon, he figured, the snow would disappear, the buds would shoot out of the trees, and a normal April would return to mountain country. Or at least he hoped so.

He walked a bit, out to a giant stump of a piñon tree, and breathed in the cleansing scent of scrub pine and sage. He thought about the Anasazi, the ancient Indians—who disappeared before the Europeans came to seize the land. They had settled in cave dwellings throughout the region. Charlie, a long Swede with thinning blond hair, felt like one of them as he plopped on the stump, surveying ancient hunting grounds.

Beyond a fallen tree, Charlie spied a pattern so fine it looked as if lacemakers had woven it. The patches of red dirt were free-form, yet seemed to resemble objects. Charlie looked at the ground and then, to get closer, crawled over to the sunny area on his hands and knees, looking into the melting snow the way a child regards the clouds, searching for signs. Here was a running coyote, there a grazing bison. A hunter stood hovering nearby, watching the trails of his prey, waiting for the time his spear would be released from the frost.

Charlie squatted and wondered if the Anasazi looked for signs in the melting snow. He wondered if the earth revealed to them the path they should take for spring hunting. Did their gods talk through these blotches on the ground? Charlie knelt down and touched the grainy soil. As he rubbed the moist dirt between his fingers, enjoying the feel of the grit, Charlie spotted a reddish blotch that wasn't like the others. It seemed to glow, for it was a sheet of ice that had frozen, melted, and re-frozen. Now it was melting again, reflecting the sunlight, giving off a pulsating sheen. He bent down and saw a picture there. Not a real picture, but a visual exploration of a sensation: equilibrium, calm, yin meeting yang. He began to breathe deeply as he took in his personal vision. He saw himself free, in a state of blissful surrender. He closed his eyes, looked again and saw nothing at all. His mind was utterly clear. He sat back on his heels and felt, for the first time in his life, the desire for nothing. No urge to achieve, no drive to force things his way, no impulse to slap his brain silly with drugs and drink. No craving to do anything at all but sit back in the melting snow and cry.

≈

The cabin appeared on a slight incline near a grove of low trees. It looked more like an outhouse, but when Charlie got close enough he saw it was big enough to live in—after a fashion. Creaky and full of gaps, the shack looked as if it had been abandoned a few years ago. The outside had been painted deep red, that same brick color that Charlie used to paint the trim on his old home in Chicago. Inside, the elements had reduced the flooring to a pile of dust and the windows to near opacity.

There was room inside for his down sleeping bag. A chimney and ancient wood-burning stove still stood in the corner. They didn't look as if they had been used for a long time.

It would do. Charlie had no idea how far he was from a town or a trading post. He only knew he hadn't seen a liquor store for miles. This would transform into his hospital, his recovery clinic. He was going to sweat out the poison right here.

If someone came back to claim the place, he'd be happy to move on. He went out to open the car to retrieve the sleeping bag, food and sundries he had bought on the way out of Santa Rosa. He peered into the west, watching the sun near the horizon. Soon it would plunge behind the mountains and light this silhouette on fire.

In the filtered twilight, Charlie looked through the trees and thought he saw something blinking in the distance. A red light, pulsating, sending a staccato code to the stars.

CHAPTER FOUR

Derek tapped his fingers on the mouse pad, waiting for graphics to load on the computer screen. His foot jabbed against the leg of his desk, first a delicate touch, then a constant, rhythmic prodding. The download didn't respond to Derek's physical goading. He stood up in irritation, forcing the chair back with a loud squeal. He walked down the hall, reached the end and walked back toward his desk again.

Waiting was hell and he'd had enough of it today. The commute had been slow, the day job boring, and now his computer wasn't cooperating. Derek paced back down the hall, kicking absently at the baseboard that was coming loose from the wall. Patience was essential to the Project. He needed forbearance to let the coders chip away at the decryption side of things, to stay calm when the data came in late, composed when hardware was falling apart. The Project required a cool head. Derek tried to make his muscles relax.

At least that eerie voice had gone away. Ever since that first night, when that mysterious sound file infected his computer, he'd been hearing it at odd moments: when he stared out in space thinking, when he got dressed in the morning, when he loaded paper in the printer. He hadn't heard it in his dreams again, but he was always on guard. For weeks, Derek came awake with a wince, pulling his blankets over his head as he anticipated another unwanted message. Every morning, he would let out a happy sigh, thinking that maybe there was nothing wrong with his mind.

The truth was, Derek was half convinced the voice he had heard was a product of his overworked brain. Maybe the darn voice wasn't a sound file. Maybe he was certifiably insane. He must have checked that hard drive a hundred times, but he never found a sound file or virus there. So he must be crazy, a screaming Loony Tune, a whacked-out geek head.

But one day, he realized the voice had stopped talking to him, stopped repeating that haunting sentence. Roger had shut up. Still, Derek remained vigilant, going through his Project routines in a state of high anxiety. By evening, he would tumble into bed, exhausted by work but relieved by the idea that he got through the day sane.

So on the scale of life's problems, this little download snag he was facing was no big deal. Derek shuffled back to his desk and looked at the screen. "Network error," said a box on the screen. He broke the connection and turned his attention instead to his e-mail—one hundred fifty new messages, automatically filed in dozens of folders. The Project folder held seventy-five of them. That's where he looked first.

George sent greetings and the usual jokes. This time he provided an attachment with a little dancing cartoon figure that swooped across Derek's e-mail, tossed a stick of dynamite that "blew up" the screen, and disappeared in a wisp of smoke. Cute. The actual message had no news.

The coders sent varying reports of success. Some guys down in Cham-bana—better known as the University of Illinois at Champaign-Urbana—had found common structures in several of the encrypted code blocks. They were only days away from finding a pattern, they said. The guys in Austin at the University of Texas hadn't gotten anywhere, but were contributing a lot of horsepower. A couple of MIT dweebs reported incompatibilities. Wonderful.

Derek grabbed for his stone-cold coffee, hoping for some better news, only to be stricken by an electrically charged rush of intuition that told him things were going to get a lot worse. He hated this feeling. It was completely irrational, a sensation that would shoot over him without warning. When it was bad, the impression hung like a baseball bat overhead, ready to knock him silly. Derek shook his head, pretending the cudgel wasn't there. The next message popped into view. The sender was unfamiliar. The back of his neck began to itch as he leaned forward to read.

To: D.Nils@bitjockey.com
From: Roger@uchicago.edu
Subject: need help?

Derek: I've been trying to reach you re: d.c. project. George recommended I get in touch.

Roger

Derek read the message several times, focusing, trying to figure out what made this message seem so menacing. A guy wanted to help decrypt code. He'd gotten a dozen of these requests in the last month. He looked at the name "Roger" for a few long minutes and typed the two-button code for "reply." He tapped rapidly, his fingers moving over the keyboard with intimacy.

To: Roger@uchicago.edu
From: D.Nils@bitjockey.com
Subject: Re: need help?

Roger: George hasn't mentioned you. What's your background? For some reason, your name is familiar. Do you have a last name?

D.

The itching had stopped, only now replaced by a high-pitched whine in his ears. Time to lay off the caffeine. He started forwarding the message.

To: G.Esterberg@uchicago.edu
From: D.Nils@bitjockey.com
Subject: Who's this?

G-man: Who the heck is Roger? Background?

D.

Derek began rocking back in his chair, trying to decide if he should go to the kitchen and find something to eat. Food was a big problem. There was never any in his apartment and never time to go grocery shopping. A body can't live on delivery pizza forever, and Derek's own body was testing the limit. He'd been home from work for three hours now and he couldn't put off dinner too much longer. It would only take half an hour to pop over to the Fast Forward mini-mart.

A message from George zipped back from the ether. The guy was always online.

> To: D.Nils@bitjockey.com
> From: G.Esterberg@uchicago.edu
> Subject: Re: Who's this?
>
> Nilsson: Dunno, I guess I talked to some Roger guy. Working with Clancy. I'm sure he's okay.
>
> G.

Derek closed his eyes and tried to still his mind. George was always meeting grad students, promising them a pie in the sky, and promptly forgetting the whole thing. This wouldn't be the first time some eager kid from the suburbs figured he'd hitch his wagon to George's star.

Derek walked into a pair of unlaced sneakers and shuffled toward the door. Fast Forward's famous microwave-ready burritos were calling. *Roger. Roger. Wasn't that the same name? Hell, there were zillions of Rogers in the world.*

≈

It was five in the morning when Derek had last looked at the clock. He pulled his head off his desk and massaged the dull ache that was beginning to pool around his left cheek and the side of his forehead. At least it was a Saturday. The computer screen cast a benevolent, soft radiance throughout the room, its filtered glow complementing the gray morning light. Derek felt pain shoot from his forearm as he pulled himself to an upright position.

The overcast morning suited Derek. The recent string of fine, sunny, spring days, replete with loud tulips and brash daffodils, had been a distraction of the worst sort. During the usual bleak, damp-to-the-bone Chicago spring, Derek could keep his mind on his work. This spring he was noticing too many flowers.

Time must have passed, because he turned an unfocused eye to the computer screen and made out the time: 9:25 a.m., Saturday, May 10. Saturday, thank God! Derek slumped into his chair, feeling a curious sense of relief tinged with anxiety. He felt the familiar gas pain from eating cheap burritos. He picked up the telephone and punched buttons. After a few rings, George answered, his voice thick and untested.

"Sorry, man," Derek said. "I just woke up myself."

"Thanks for letting me share the joy," George said, his voice swathed in cotton.

"I just wanted you to know that I put your new man on part of our project."

"What new man?"

"Some guy from your U. You know, Roger something."

"Yeah, sure, I guess. Lots of willing students. Lots of computer time there."

Derek laughed. The biggest chore in the Project was not finding volunteers—they were crawling out of the networks. If you had enough money you could buy data hounds on the cloud. Grad students with research projects never raised an eyebrow. Someone like this Roger fellow would be perfect.

"For some reason that name Roger is familiar," Derek said. The hair on his arms stood to attention. He swallowed.

"I dunno, man, there are so many of those grad students, I can't keep 'em straight. Are you done so I can go back to sleep?"

"Yeah, one more thing and I'll let you go. Going to Trevor's bash tonight?"

"If you are."

"Wouldn't miss it. The man has serious food at his parties."

After George hung up with a grunt, Derek couldn't sit still. Four and half hours of sleep didn't give him any relief from the overwhelming fatigue that gripped his body. He was devoid of energy but his nerves were trembling. And he realized, that despite last night's burritos, he was desperately hungry.

He slipped on some khakis and a clean t-shirt and stepped out of his two-flat building into the moist and windy spring morning. The trees were covered in leaves the color of new asparagus—a soft, baby green, tender and not yet hardened by the elements. Derek saw a large oak reaching toward the blue sky like a black hand gloved in delicate green velvet.

Derek breathed the air, full of weight and promise, scented for a second or two by the lilt of cherry blossoms. He headed down Rockwell Street to Devon Avenue, where his favorite Indian restaurant served up gourmet saffron rice and those wonderful dumplings called samosas.

Devon Avenue was Derek's favorite place in the city. It had none of the snootiness of the Near North Side, where all his friends lived. Here on Devon, Indians, Orthodox Jews, Pakistanis, Greeks, and Russians walked the streets in their saris, black frock coats, and loose-legged trousers. Sari shops shared space with kosher delis and Islamic reading rooms. In the street, languages collided as the traffic rolled by at five miles per hour.

Derek especially loved the smells of the avenue. East of his apartment, he'd walk past the Jewish bakeries and ride on the intense scent of freshly baked challah. On Central Devon, he'd catch a whiff of the olive oils and herbs of Greek dolmades and moussaka. From there on, east nearly to the lake, ambled an endless olfactory parade, a veritable amusement park of exotic scents, all oozing out of Pakistani diners and Indian restaurants. Coriander and masala mixed on the breeze like incense, taking Derek to a higher sense of himself, lifting him above the bus fumes and gray skies.

When he got to Indira, a plain little storefront with clean windows and a hand-lettered sign, Derek pulled the door open and raised his hand in the direction of a young Indian man who was wiping down a countertop with a fluffy rag.

"Come on, sit down, skinny boy," said a familiar voice, bubbling with its multi-toned accent, one that found too few notes in English to settle into comfortably.

"Ravi, it's been way too long since I was here last," Derek said, sliding into a counter seat. He nodded at the Indian men at the counter who gulped their cups of chai. They bobbed their heads in gravity.

"No eating, huh? I can tell," Ravi continued, setting a steaming cup of coffee in front of his guest.

Derek could never fool Ravi. The New Delhi native was barely older than Derek himself but he radiated a calming sense of wisdom. Ravi knew all, Derek figured, so he didn't pretend otherwise.

"Give me some samosas with lots of hot sauce . . . and chutney," Derek said. "And no coffee, Ravi. I want some chai today."

Derek loved the aroma of chai, the Hindi word for tea, served with a blend of masala spices and warm milk.

"Ah, chai is good for the soul," Ravi said, replacing the coffee with an aromatic cup of tea. He poured milk into the brew until it looked and smelled like liquid caramel. "Coffee is, how do you say . . . ? Coffee is like pure oxygen, you know? Chai is air mixed with spring rain."

Derek smiled and took the cup in his hands, feeling the warmth work through his palms and up to his forearms. The spices teased his nose as he took a sip of his favorite ambrosia.

"So what's my aura look like today, Ravi?" Derek said, peering into the mystical depth of Ravi's soft brown eyes. "Tell this Swedish boy what's going on."

Ravi stepped back a few inches, letting his focus soften just a bit. Derek always thought Ravi's eyes took on the look of a camera aperture adjusted to let in just a bit more light than normal. Ravi gazed and nodded. It was a familiar game the two played: Ravi the sage, Derek the seeker.

"Too much thinking," Ravi said, nodding his head as he looked back down at the counter. "Swedes always have too much thinking."

Ravi plopped the samosas, rich potato puffs filled with spiced meat and peas, in front of Derek. He tipped his head sideways as he regarded his customer.

"When have you been going walking? Looking at Lake Michigan?" Ravi said. "When are you sitting in nature?" His voice bobbed up and down, accenting random syllables.

"You sound like my mother."

"Mother is right. Your energy is all in your head. Very bad. You need to ground yourself to the earth."

Ravi unfocused his eyes again before continuing.

"Something else is in your head, you know?" He was looking at the air to the left of Derek's ear. "You hearing someone?"

Derek swallowed his samosa as if he had taken a bite of gravel.

Ravi seemed not to notice Derek's discomfort as he continued to stare, tracing lines of an imaginary strand from the area near Derek's head out toward the door. He stroked the air, which made Derek's head tingle. The itching returned.

The Indian men at the counter watched with no particular interest, as if they saw this sort of thing every day. And maybe they did. One grumbled and stood up.

"Bad things with that guy," an older man said to his partner, as he slipped some bills on the counter.

Derek swallowed again and looked at Ravi. Someone surely was in his head—or had been. And now there was that strange new e-mail from a guy named Roger. Derek felt vulnerable, but there was no way he was telling Ravi. Derek figured the minute he shared his fears with someone would be the minute they all became true.

Ravi continued to stroke the air near Derek's ear before answering. He looked as if he were brushing the atmosphere, soothing fine strands of invisible electricity, unsnarling tangled wires.

"Your chakras are unbalanced," Ravi said, grinning. "I know a guy; he'll balance for you. Cheap. Or he'll do it if you fix his computer."

"I'm that messed up, Ravi?"

The young Indian placed his hands back on the counter and shrugged.

"It's weird, you know," Ravi said, his eyes dancing. "I've seen nothing like it." He reached over and touched Derek's shoulder. "You go in nature, Swede boy. You lose this head thing."

Derek gave Ravi a five-dollar tip, stumbled home and slept more deeply than he had in months—because he was in mortal terror of staying conscious.

≈

Derek had been staring at the picture on the wall for at least fifteen minutes, tracing the red lines that ran from the center blob to the wavy external perimeter. The painting, indeterminate at first, now reminded him of a computer language, stretching out in all directions, delivering the same commands repeatedly. The artwork drew him in, until Derek felt he knew the texture and gradation of every painted surface. Derek's eyes were trying to enter the canvas.

"No one else likes this one," said Trevor, clapping Derek hard on the shoulder. "My mother told me to throw it into the trash." Trevor flipped back his black sweep of hair, worn loose. In his own domain, surrounded by his artwork and favorite furnishings, Trevor stood solid and sure, rooted to his reality.

Derek, ruffled, turned from the painting and shifted his drink from hand to hand.

"Well, it reminds me of code," Derek said, swallowing a mouthful of beer.

"You *have* been working too hard," Trevor said, rolling his eyes. "I just talked to George and he said you hadn't slept in a week."

"Well, it's not that bad, certainly not as bad as the time I took a swan dive into the scalloped potatoes at my mother's dinner party," Derek said. "I crashed all day today. Right now, I feel as if I crawled out of a spaceship, encountering humanity for the first time."

"And you immediately fastened onto my worst painting. What a way to examine humanity," Trevor said. "Come on over here and I'll show you what I've really been up to."

Trevor tugged him by the sleeve, leading him over to a red wall covered with art canvasses. Next to the biggest picture—a giant abstract filled with geometric shapes and vivid colors—stood Kyra. She hadn't seen the men approach and stared into her drink, one foot playing with the heel of her shoe, her shoulders slumped a bit. Dressed in a purple cocktail dress, which exposed her slim neck and shoulders, Kyra looked tiny and vulnerable. Derek stared. He watched the way she looked into her highball, as if she were viewing a heartbreaking movie inside the glass. He looked at her red hair, upswept to expose the nape of her neck. That slender stem looked so pure, so kissable. Derek started imagining what it would be like to run his tongue next to the tendrils that lay behind Kyra's ear. He felt warmth shoot through his thighs.

Kyra jerked her head when she sensed Derek looking at her. Derek, sure that she had read his thoughts, felt a flush pressing up his cheeks.

"Kyra," he said, the word nearly exploding from his lips. "Nice to see you. It would be nice to have lunch."

Kyra put her hand to her chest for a second, then she plucked at her dress as if trying to improve how it floated over her body. She nodded and looked as if she wanted to say something, but no sound came out of her throat.

"Derek is seeing computer code in my paintings," Trevor said with arched brows. "So I thought I'd show him more. Maybe he'll see whole software packages come alive on canvas," Trevor said. He seemed to find great sport in Derek's discomfort, not only needling him about his code obsession but also using subtle body movement to nudge Derek closer to Kyra. Derek hadn't enough willpower to resist.

"This," Trevor continued. "Is 'Tao Stream.' The title is the only clue you get."

Derek and Kyra looked up at the canvas, softly glazed with a sheer red paint, which partially obscured a blue underpainting. Deep beneath the blue, a black thread trailed from edge to edge, snaking its way through the various image planes.

"Red is earth and blue is spirit," Kyra said, not taking her eyes off the picture. "And the Tao—the Now, the What Is—runs through it all."

Trevor smiled with quiet appreciation. Derek was dumbfounded.

"How . . . ?" he began.

Kyra waved a hand to cut him off.

"I was an art history major," Kyra said. "You know, one of those useless liberal arts degrees."

Derek turned to her and tried to look past the makeup and the jewelry and the bravado. Here stood much more than an apologist for a high-tech software firm.

"You should have been an art critic," Derek said, his eyes glowing with interest. "That was quite ... sensitive."

"Art critics are sooo in demand," Kyra said, shrugging her slender shoulders.

Derek recognized the emotion. Self-deprecation was a popular feature in his own mind too. How odd that Kyra, who looked so put together each day in her expensive suits and salon-fresh haircuts, could have doubts. Maybe she wasn't the self-assured marketing princess he imagined her to be.

"So you went into public relations," he started to mumble.

Kyra's eyes opened wide as the sarcasm slid off her gentle features.

"It pays the bills, and I can do the job well," Kyra said. "I sold out. At least you're doing what you love."

"Sorry," Derek said. "I didn't mean to criticize . . . "

Screwed up again, Derek thought. Why can't I speak to this lovely woman without making a horrible faux pas?

Derek noticed that Trevor had long since disappeared, guiding more of his guests toward the food and drink. He asked Kyra where she grew up, finding himself growing increasingly interested in the elegant way her long neck met the sweep of her jaw.

He closed his eyes and his body stirred. He felt shimmers of excitement as Kyra spoke of art and compromise. In her purple dress, cut just tightly enough to skim her lithe, athletic body, Kyra was tiny and fierce, a compact dynamo, a sun compressed into a neutron star.

Kyra spoke his language. She didn't know a thing about computers, but she understood the misery of being an outsider. In a sentence or two, she made a connection with Derek's isolated world.

Derek remembered that happening only once or twice in his life. Once it hit him when reading James Joyce's *A Portrait of the Artist as a Young Man* for his high school honors English class. No one else in his class had any idea what Joyce was talking about. But Derek gravitated to the story of a youth who thought too much and dreamt too much for crude Dublin society to understand. Joyce, he thought, had peered into his mind, into his upbringing. It was the first time Derek had felt a deep connection with another human being—even if it was a dead Irishman.

The long talk with Kyra was like that, like a communion with a vaunted author. The conversation didn't last long, an hour at most. But she looked at life the way Derek did and he stood amazed.

"You've got what you want at BitJockey," Kyra had said, her eyes lowered, studying the untouched drink in her hand.

"If you consider writing code for nifty websites to be worthwhile, I guess so," Derek answered, daring to bring her eyes up to meet his. Her eyes were green, touched with gold flecks on the rims. The irises seemed to pulsate.

"I thought you were getting the big projects. On your way up," Kyra said.

"There's nothing more to those projects than getting bigger projects," Derek said, throwing a hand into the air. "It's empty. It goes nowhere. I'd go nuts if that's all there was to my career."

Kyra had gazed back at Trevor's painting and wet her lips with her tongue. Derek felt his stomach tighten.

"You want more too."

"A lot more."

≈

Since the party, he'd run into Kyra at work. He sometimes looked for her, just happening to find himself wandering around on the seventeenth floor, near the marketing offices. They shared sandwiches at the bank plaza nearby when Derek took a rare lunch break. He'd park himself on the granite bench near the windswept plaza next to Kyra, laughing at her jokes as they watched the irises bob wildly in the urban planters. The sun sometimes made Derek dizzy, for he never remembered sunglasses. Or perhaps this was something other than sunstroke.

He was on the verge of asking Kyra on a real date. The time had arrived, surely. A good two weeks had passed since Trevor's party. Yet, the Project interfered at every turn.

The Project. In bed for once, Derek opened his eyes and stared at the light outside his window. Memorial Day weekend. Already!

He jumped out of the covers, didn't bother to pull his jeans over his boxer shorts, and slipped into his office. Within seconds, he logged onto his computer. While it was coming up to speed, Foo slipped in, announcing her need for breakfast. Derek dashed to the kitchen to open a can of Captain's Choice seafood blend and refilled the water dish. When he came back, e-mail awaited. Plenty of it.

Most messages were from programmers who were making some sense of their code blocks. The underlying data became more complex than any Derek had ever seen. Soon the next tranche of code blocks would be arriving and he and George had to arm themselves for the onslaught.

Derek pecked and tapped at his keyboard, answering mail, evaluating answers, organizing files, lost to the progress of the morning sun. Noon blazed overhead as Derek clicked on a message from Roger. His empty belly trembled.

> Derek:
>
> Greetings. Code broken and data to follow. I'm wondering if I can ask what more you are looking for? I can be useful to you.
>
> Roger

Derek shuddered. Something about the message seemed less than innocent. Roger, he figured, was smarter than the average programmer. He knew something. Derek replied.

> Rog:
>
> Stay put where you are. We need to assess all data. Thank you for your assistance.
>
> Derek

The answer shot back within seconds.

D:

Love to help you further. This goal was too simple.
Give me something to really sink my teeth into.

Roger

Roger wouldn't take no for an answer. Roger wanted a piece of the action. Derek couldn't get him to back off. Exasperated, Derek picked up the telephone. He didn't wait to exchange pleasantries with his partner.

"George, it's Derek. It's about your man at computer science. That Roger. What does he know?"

George didn't answer for a second or two. Derek's stomach was in freefall. Finally, George coughed.

"I don't know any Roger in my department."

"What? A few weeks ago, you said he was okay, so I put him on the job."

"Well, I remember the conversation and I remember not being sure. I was half asleep, remember? One day, I went over the list of U. of C. participants. No Roger."

"Well, this nobody cracked a code block with lightning speed, George. Now he wants more. He knows we're onto something else. I've got the creeps here, buddy."

George, his voice emotionless, promised to look into the matter. He'd ask the university's systems operator if Roger's e-mail could be identified. Right now, Derek's attempts to "finger" him, locate him via electronic means, were not working.

Derek shook his head as if trying to dislodge reality from his brain. An intruder was lurking at the heart of their operation. Because he was unknown and unseen, this interloper was unverifiable and Derek sensed, illogically, that he was potentially disastrous.

The cursor blinked again on the screen. Another note from Roger. Derek's solar plexus squeezed as he clicked on the message. He felt his insides turn to ice as he read.

Derek:

There is no longer any reason to pretend.
You might be feeling by now that I am watching
you. In a manner of speaking, I am.
I can help you, if you will allow it.

Roger

CHAPTER FIVE

The phone sent a shrill call through the foggy air at four in the morning. Derek knew it was four o'clock, because he had hit the mattress a few minutes beforehand. It had been two days since Roger's e-mail and he'd rarely seen a pillow. Now this.

"Derek," said a weak voice.

"Mom, what's wrong?"

It sounded at first as if Astrid was going to mutter "oh, nothing." Something about the way she made that clicking sound with her tongue hinted at one of those nonsensical tossed-off comments. But the line rasped with static instead.

"Mom?"

"Oh . . . I don't know, Derek."

Derek waited for his mother to continue. He stared at his digital clock.

"Mom. It's four-oh-three a.m. You didn't call to chat."

"No. I didn't."

"You want me to come over?"

"Maybe . . . "

"I'll be right there."

Derek tossed off his covers, gave his cat a quick few strokes behind the ears, and watched enviously as the cat snuggled back to sleep. He put his still-warm clothes back on. He knew that sound in his mother's voice. She was depressed again. Clinically depressed. It sounded as bad as the time she was forced out of her job. As bad as the phase she went through when Dad left for Indian country. Derek didn't have time for this, but she had no one else to turn to. It was the curse of being the only child.

On the drive to Evanston, Derek wondered how to convince Astrid to go back to the nice old therapist she use to see, the one with the Old Country accent and the watery hazel eyes. Derek tried to imagine how to get her to take the anti-depressant medications again. They put the blue back into her eyes and gave life to her voice. He wondered if she was going to turn into a Problem Mother instead of just a plain-old everyday clingy mother. He wondered why he didn't have the patience to take the bad times in stride.

When he arrived at her two-story Victorian home, all the lights were off. He let himself into the dark living room and discovered Astrid sitting by candlelight on the hardwood floor, with all the family photo albums strewn about her. The house was so silent he could hear his mother's shallow breathing.

"I did it to him, you know," Astrid was saying, sitting in a crossed-leg position, her head bent low on her chest.

"Did what, Mom?" Derek said, kneeling next to her, removing a half-full glass of wine from her reach.

"Made him drink," Astrid said. She pointed at the pictures in the books, photos of the family at weddings, on vacations, at Derek's high school graduation. In most of the pictures, Dad held a beer can aloft. It was his personal salute.

"Exactly how was that your fault, Mom?" he said, sitting next to her, putting his arm about her rigid shoulders.

"Well, look." She pulled up an album with photos of Derek's fifth birthday party. The family gathered around a cheap linoleum table—Dad made little money then and Astrid hadn't gone to work yet. Derek held a new toy fire truck in his hands. The Nilsson grandparents were there, Mormor and Morfar as they were called in Swedish. So was Uncle Henry, Astrid's brother, now dead of lung cancer. In the background were the Merles, looming like phantoms.

"Nice picture," Derek lied, wondering what she was getting at.

"See the look in my eyes? I was furious at your dad that day. Furious. The house looked so bad, the furniture was so awful. We had no money, and all those people were coming over."

"That's not why he drank. He drank because he drank."

"He was getting away from me. He always was getting away from me." She tossed the book in the direction of other albums strewn on the floor. "And he finally did, for good."

Derek leaned his head on Astrid's shoulder and felt her muscles harden. Usually when he hugged someone, he'd feel a warmth, a heart beating, a breath of life. Astrid was cool like a granite boulder. There was no one inside.

He looked closer at her head in the candlelight. There were bruises on the side of her face like the last time they went through this. He had walked in on her one night banging her head against the posts of her bed. He'd have to call the doctor in the morning. Someone was going to have to talk her into getting back into treatment. Maybe it was time to call the relatives in Sweden. They were the only ones she ever listened to.

"Let's get you in bed, Mom," Derek said, urging her to her feet. To his surprise, she obeyed. She sagged a bit as she walked, leaning her leaden, zombie-like weight on his shoulders. As he led her up the stairs to her bedroom, she stopped on the staircase and turned to look at him.

"Will you find him?" Astrid asked, her eyes growing large in the dim light. For a second she looked small, like a tiny girl, ready to cry if no one checked for monsters in the closet.

He found himself nodding, although he knew that finding his father, the man who had transformed his mother into this living specter, was the last thing he ever wanted to do.

≈

George sat on a rusty swing, pushing his skinny frame backwards and forwards as Derek walked onto the playground. Derek reached the swings, a sad affair of half-rusted steel poles and squeaky chains, and scuffed his basketball shoes on the woodchip mulch. George didn't look up. Derek heard the roar of cars on the nearby expressway. There weren't any kids playing. The park was just too damn loud.

"The noise. Is that why you picked this place?" Derek said, talking to George's back.

"Yeah," George said as he swung back into sight. He was smiling, with that strange impish smirk that appeared when he had the upper hand. "No one can overhear us. No one can even record us. The background noise would make it extremely difficult."

"Jeez, George, have you been watching too many movies? Who the hell is going to record our conversation?"

"You're the one who's paranoid," George said as he stopped swinging, dragging his tattered deck shoes on the ground to slow his movement. Derek fitted his backside into the neighboring swing. As he sat down, the canvas gripped his hipbones in a painful cinch.

"You mean about Roger."

"Roger, yeah."

The two sat side by side for several long minutes, not looking at each other but staring at suburban traffic. In the distance, Derek heard a police car's siren. It was coming closer, possibly coming their way via the expressway. It sounded like the car exited the highway and was heading their way.

He'd asked for an emergency meeting with George, away from e-mail, telephones, cellular phones, or any technological equipment. He needed to talk without the danger of anyone overhearing them. George took the precautions a little too seriously, perhaps, but Derek, jittery from nerves, was grateful.

George stood up and removed his windbreaker.

"Look, Derek. I checked and checked. The guy doesn't exist. I know his e-mail trail exists. But the actual guy? No one can trace him."

"You're saying he's not real? That I'm hallucinating?"

"Of course not. But maybe he's not really a threat. Just a damn good code cracker who had a lot of fun playing with us."

And playing with my head, Derek thought. He scratched his goatee and wondered whether he could possibly make logical, steady George understand that this Roger guy could be far more dangerous than any gonzo hacker.

"George, I think he knows everything."

"What could he know? There's not one thing that we are doing that's illegal. All anyone can see is that we are using a lot of grad students to analyze encrypted code blocks. That's not illegal. People do it all the time."

"The feds are gonna wonder."

"Since when are they going to care?"

Derek listened as the siren came closer to the park. He watched cars pulling over to the curb on the busy suburban street. Pedestrians on the sidewalk started to crane their necks, looking for some excitement on this normally dull May day. Derek shivered in spite of the warmth in the air.

George jumped off the swing and walked along the grass that grew along the periphery of the swing set. He leaned over, plucked some dandelion puffs and blew the seeds into the warm wind. He frowned as he watched the tiny little flock of paratroopers disperse.

"Derek, do you want out?"

Derek jutted his jaw and swallowed. "No."

"What do you want me to do then? I swear to you he can't cause any more harm. All he wants is a new adventure. We can use a guy like that."

"George, he wrote that he wants to help me. He made it sound personal. What the hell is that about? He's either with the feds or he's a nutcase."

George merely bent over to pluck a few more dandelions. He radiated calm reassurance. George was never one to give up, even if the FBI itself was breathing down his neck.

George could be as Zen-like as he wanted, but Derek knew the dangers were high. Ever since the celebrated Seth Stonegate case, black hats and white hats knew the chilling effect of the government hovering over network computer operations. Last year, Stonegate, a seedy little data wizard from New Jersey, had hacked into credit-card codes and telephone accounts all over the globe. By the time he was done, Stonegate had millions of dollars of sensitive data in his hands. When FBI agents came to arrest him one day, he asked for a few minutes to call his lawyer. No cell phone available. He rushed off to a phone in another room. When the agents got tired of waiting and burst into his space, they discovered he had nothing but spam on his hard drives.

Yet Stonegate now sat in a federal penitentiary, because the FBI combed the country, eventually discovering vans loaded with Stonegate's computers—one in South Dakota, the other in Oregon. Stonegate had fed them data from the East Coast via his cellular phone. Although it seemed that the case was solved, the Stonegate mystery was still up in the air and the FBI was still inventing new criminal charges. Hackers everywhere knew there was more of Stonegate's data to discover—and the rumor was that the hidden data contained much hotter property than stolen credit-card numbers. So far, the FBI was hunting for the treasure, along with almost every computer nerd on the planet, including Derek and George.

They were trolling for hidden data too, but they had not stolen a thing. They were trying to piece together a puzzle they happened upon during a fortuitous summer internship at a large telecommunications business.

"I think we were nutcases to get involved in the first place," Derek said, as George, now sitting on the grass, looped the stem of one dandelion around the blossom of another.

"It's not crazy to track anomalous data." George tied another dandelion onto the chain.

"George, it wasn't our data to track," Derek said. "We were just interns."

"Damn smart interns."

As the dandelion chain grew, Derek thought back to the summer job. Schlepping out to the far northwest suburbs in Derek's vintage VW Beetle, sitting in a freezing, overly air-conditioned office analyzing long-distance calling patterns. That's when they found the "noise." One day, there was a huge spike in the numbers for one of the cellular-to-long-distance switches. At first, George thought all it represented was a long phone call, but then he realized the call had the pattern of digital data transmission. This was no ordinary phone call. This was not a voice conversation. Plus, the data moved almost completely in one direction.

After searching through piles of logs, George found similar spikes every month on a regular schedule. George put a pen register on the number. It was an illegal wiretap, but George never bothered much with niceties. He took the data to Derek for analysis. It turned out the information was computer data sent by cellular phone to a remote location in the southwest.

"You never should have tapped that line," Derek said, as the daisy chain splayed across the grass like a carelessly discarded piece of jewelry.

"And deprive you of the fun you had?" George said, tossing the flowers into the wind. "You're the one who practically opened a bottle of Champagne when you found out that it was computer data."

"Yeah," Derek said, remembering the elation of finding a pattern in the white noise, discovering binary code that led straight from the cellular phone switching station to somewhere in the desert. "Yeah, I guess that was pretty amazing."

"So, no more regrets, right?"

Derek barely moved his head from side to side. The sirens raced past them, on to another block.

"Look, Derek. Don't get mad. But I wrote to Roger. I put him on a new job. He's happy to help."

Derek didn't say anything. He peered down the street to see where the sirens had gone.

"I sent him to find where all that code went to," George continued. "I sent him to find the proverbial shack in the woods."

Derek let a steady stream of air out of his pursed lips.

"Before you go ballistic, think. Derek, it's a wild-goose chase. It will keep him busy for months. Meanwhile we can finish busting the code. Then if Roger has made any headway at all, we can use his info when we look for the data's terminus."

Derek felt the sun baking his skull right through the thin hair on his head. He looked at George and could see only sunlight reflected from his pal's sunglasses. Derek felt the landscape spin and grabbed the metal chains of the swing.

"You crazy bastard," Derek said, closing his eyes. "Why the hell do you have to be the best friend I've got in this world? Why the hell are you my partner?"

"Because I'm slightly smarter than you. Someone's got to be."

CHAPTER SIX

Derek opened one eye and stared at the green screen of the schefflera leaves, which nearly obscured his living-room window. It was the plant that wouldn't die, no matter how badly he mistreated it. He figured that the cups of half-spent coffee he threw on the soil had actually nourished this alien life form, which now filled his front window like a runaway tree.

A chirping sound sailed through the air, summoning Derek up, off the couch, into a standing position. He picked across the room, stepping over magazines and computer cables and box drives, over to answer the pleading, incessantly bleating cell phone. He wondered why the call wasn't just going to voice mail.

"Hello." Derek held his breath, willing this silent millisecond of static to bring good news. Please, no more of his mother's antics. No more news of Roger. No more annoyances from the office.

"Hey, Derek. It's Kyra."

Derek shuffled back to the couch, telephone in hand. He instinctively reached down with his free hand to feel if he was wearing pants. He was. And the fly was zipped.

"Kyra," Derek managed to mumble, the words forming clumsily on his thick lips. He felt a spit bubble form on the side of his mouth. "What a surprise."

"Were you asleep? It's two in the afternoon."

"Oh, well, another late night. You know. . . ." his voice trailed off.

"Working on your project." Kyra's voice hinted at curiosity, the edges of her phrases lilting.

"Yeah, the Big Secret One," Derek said with a shrill laugh, nearly a ten-year-old girl's giggle, far too loud for the circumstances. He cleared his throat and continued, this time keeping his voice level. "It's good you called, Kyra. What's up?"

"Well, if you want to know . . . " Kyra's voice became weaker for a moment, then gained urgency. "Since you wouldn't call me, I decided to just barge in. I want to know if you want to get coffee or something after work next week."

Derek noticed a familiar sizzle in his heart area—adrenaline rush. Action was demanded, right now. He forgot how to breathe.

"Oh . . . yeah," was all he could force through his paralyzed lips. How Kyra kept talking, in such well-modulated tones, was a mystery to Derek. She had obvious communications skills.

"Of course, I'm asking you out," she said. "If that's okay with you."

"Oh, yeah," Derek said, wishing he could find the rest of his vocabulary. "It's great."

They settled on Wednesday after work at McCracken's Brew House, which was only a few steps from the office. Derek realized that some of the programmers might see him with Kyra. He smiled to himself.

As they continued chatting, Kyra sounded increasingly smooth, her voice becoming more mellifluous every minute. Her voice was strong and controlled. Derek was having trouble keeping his vowels from trembling. By the time he hung up the phone, Derek realized he was awash in his own sweat.

"Oh, my God," he said to Foo, who dashed behind the schefflera, making it swirl. He scooped up his pet and began cradling and petting her. The cat's purrs helped him think. The last time he had seen Kyra was almost a week ago. They ate takeout corned-beef sandwiches in a crowded plaza off Michigan Avenue. An old lady, dressed in heavy winter clothing—expensive items that were trimmed with real-looking fur—tossed breadcrumbs to the pigeons and seagulls. The birds skulked and bobbed their way among oblivious diners as they pecked for the food. Derek surprised Kyra by calling the birds "pigs of the air."

"It's a translation of a Swedish phrase, flygg grisor," he said as she narrowed her thin eyebrows. "My mother always said that after my trip to Stockholm."

"Mmm, Stockholm." Kyra threw back her lovely, fair-complected face, the sun washing over her freckled nose, long eyelashes and open lips. The sun in her hair revealed a wild tangle of colors, from gold to russet red to pumpkin orange. "Let's hear it."

Derek had been thirteen and on vacation in Stockholm, visiting his maternal grandparents. They didn't really live in the big city, but were eager to show Stockholm off to their American relatives. It was Midsummer Day, the longest day of the year, and a time of great frolic in this northern country. On Midsummer, the days could last eighteen to twenty hours in the lower part of Sweden. Up in the Arctic Circle, it was the time of the Midnight Sun. For a land that spends the winters in near darkness, Midsummer sparkled as a treasure for cherishing. Throughout Sweden, revelers dressed in traditional garb and danced around a May pole (although why it was not a June pole was never explained to young Derek). Neighbors laid out lavish smorgasbords. Festivals were everywhere. If this weren't a Christian nation, you'd expect a tribute to a sun god on every street corner.

Derek and his family had been dining al fresco on the wharf, and Derek held a giant hot dog aloft, poised in front of his mouth and ready to eat. In a rush of air and a blur of white motion, the hot dog was gone and a seagull sailed bay-ward with its meaty prize.

"Flygg gris!" his grandfather yelled, shaking his bony fist. But it was too late. Young Derek felt a sinking in his stomach, but not because he wouldn't receive another hot dog. Of course, his grandparents would buy him another one. But Derek felt betrayed, as if nature was just waiting for him to slip up. The seagull played him for a fool. Probably it snatched dozens of wieners from unsuspecting tourists all day long. Derek had felt like a chump back then, and now he felt his frustration return as he told the tale.

Kyra listened and laughed in a sweet manner, looking into Derek's eyes with round, green irises, as delicately colored as spring leaves shot through with sunlight.

"Sucker!" she said, her voice gentle, despite the word. "That's what the seagulls were thinking: American sucker!"

"Exactly." Kyra had nailed the feeling. He smashed his paper bag into a neat little ball. To his surprise, he had started to laugh. Of course, that's all it was. Just another trick the birds played on an unsuspecting tourist. It wasn't as if the whole world were laughing at him.

Derek looked through his open window, the memory so clear that he half expected a gull to sail straight into his apartment. It was a good thing Kyra had called him. He'd have waited months to make a move. Maybe he never would have picked up the phone. He knew why. The constant squalor of his living quarters made it impossible for him to bring a date home. Bookshelves were double-stacked, with volumes nearly falling onto the floor. Books that didn't make it to the bookshelves lay stacked on the floor. Dry cat food was ground into the carpet. Boxes that the movers dumped in the dining room sat unopened. There were papers piled to eye-level on the dining room table. No woman would put up with this filth. He knew that from experience. The last woman he dated refused to set foot in Derek's apartment again. She accused the shower curtain of making lewd advances at her.

He stomped off to the kitchen. The coffee he had brewed hours ago now languished in the glass decanter. Sludge, stewed and gone cold, had settled at the bottom and oil floated on the top of the aged brew.

He shook his head and rubbed at the stubble on his cheek. Why had he spent last night on the couch? Although he went out for beers after work with Trevor, Derek never got drunk. That was the burden of growing up with a lush for a parent. There's too much paranoia that he would end up just like Charlie—and Derek had seen too many blotto Swedish relatives to know that genetics weren't on his side.

Damn depressive, drunken Nordic blood. Only good for suicides and Bergman movies. He vaguely wondered where the common view of wild, carefree Swedish libertines had come from. Not from his family. Not from anyone he ever knew.

After digging through the back of a cabinet with a sticky wooden spoon, Derek found his dusty jar of instant coffee. It was awful stuff that probably tasted worse than the sludge in his coffeepot. Derek decided against it and dropped the dusty jar in the trash can. He pulled a shirt—hanging over the back of a kitchen chair—over his head and started off for the Donut Shoppe. There was good coffee there and lots of happy cops.

≈

The corner of Rockwell and Devon was pounding with energy. Cars rumbled by, some pulsing Mideastern music that left a wail hanging over the street. Men and women strolled by in caftans, dashikis and saris, putting on a United Nations fashion show. Derek watched the side curls bob on an Orthodox Jewish man who bounded across the street, as the light changed from yellow to red. An Iranian woman argued with a black man in African dress over a parking space. Neither spoke English but they gestured well enough for even Derek to get the meaning. He walked on.

The doughnuts were in a storefront sandwiched between a jeweler—a twitchy little guy who looked to Derek like a man who sharpened knives in his basement—and Ravi's samosa shop. Without thinking, Derek lengthened his steps and pushed past the doughnut stand, straight through Ravi's door.

The young proprietor stood, white rag in hand, leaning on his counter and watching a sports event on television. Derek squinted to see what held Ravi's interest: guys running around in white outfits, but not playing tennis.

"Cricket," Ravi said, beckoning Derek forward, eyes still on the screen.

"I didn't even know they had that on TV," Derek mumbled, pulling up a counter stool.

"Oh, satellite," Ravi said, crisply enunciating the Ts. "Landlord has it. I pay a little extra."

As he spoke, the Indian man pushed a mug of coffee Derek's way.

"I thought you were always trying to get me to drink tea," Derek said.

Ravi pursed his mouth and raised his eyebrows toward his scalp. Derek figured Ravi had his ways of knowing what made customers happy. He sipped at the hot coffee, which rivaled anything he could have gotten at the Donut Shoppe. As he delighted in the rush of caffeine that started to play at the edges of his frayed neurons, Derek felt a strange twinge near his left temple. He looked up to see his friend holding one brown hand near his head. Ravi stood this way for a long minute, his eyes unfocused.

"Good," he said at last, bringing his hand down to the counter, as if he had been doing nothing more unusual than straightening silverware. He nodded. "You lost that thing in your aura."

Derek only nodded. What was the use of trying to fool Ravi?

A steaming plate of samosas came sliding over the counter without waiting for Derek's order. To Derek, the scent of dough, meat, vegetables and spice was as alluring as that of the finest jasmine flower. He fell upon the food with gusto, drenching the delicacies with hot sauce and chutney. He ravaged his way through the dumplings before he even thought to look up.

Ravi was grinning, alternating his attention between the cricket match ("well bowled!" the announcer declared) and Derek's ravenous behavior. Derek dabbed at his mouth with a napkin while Ravi watched with twinkling eyes.

"Ravi, that Thing you were talking about," Derek said, letting his gaze stray to the cricket game, where a man dressed like a Roaring Twenties yachtsman whacked at a ball with a flat bat. He noticed that all the players were black. "Well, it didn't actually go away."

"Well, it's not in your head, Swedish Boy," Ravi said in his singsong voice. He jerked his thumb at the TV. "Jamaican team. They're hot."

Derek gestured for another cup of coffee.

"Ravi, what if I told you that it's in my computer, sending me e-mail?" Derek pulled at his short hair with his fists as he spoke. He wondered if he sounded mad. But he knew he'd go even crazier if he didn't talk to someone about the Roger problem. "I don't know what it is, but it won't leave me alone. Have you ever heard of such things? Can something like this exist?"

Ravi poured another cup and let out a snort of exasperation as the Jamaican team dropped the ball. Derek couldn't follow the play but it seemed to resemble a throwing error in baseball. Ravi shook his head and refocused his intent eyes on Derek.

"It all depends on how you see the world, Derek," he said, no longer joking, no longer dividing his attention between Derek and cricket. Ravi leaned his hand on the counter and bent down to Derek's eye level.

"There is this world and there are other worlds. You have studied physics?"

Derek nodded.

"Alternate universes?"

"They exist only in theory."

"So does relativity, my friend," Ravi said. Derek saw his point and nodded.

"Rarely do the universes intersect," Ravi continued. "But the rishis found that they do. Did I ever tell you about the rishis?"

Ravi was a Hindu, that much Derek knew. But he had no idea that the chef standing before him had studied the holy men of India. The rishis, who lived thousands of years before the birth of Christ, were the writers of the Vedas, holy texts of the Hindus. They, Ravi explained, were so adept at meditation that they were, according to the tales, able to step out of our world and into others.

To understand the travels of the rishis, it was important to leave logic behind, Ravi said. Logic is part of the world of Maya, the illusion of the everyday world. Beyond Maya lay a reality totally untouched by Western thought.

Ravi drew a circle on his shining counter top using water spilled from a drinking glass.

"This," he said, jabbing at the inner part of the circle, "is how Western people see the world. You are in here and the divine is out there." His finger moved to the outside of the circle.

"To Hindus, there is no Out There," Ravi said, blurring the watery ring until it was spread into a fine sheen. "It is all a part of one reality, one being, one consciousness. So how can there be an In or an Out? We just need to learn to really see."

Derek remained speechless.

Ravi peered into the distance, as if looking for a translator. He picked up a rag and began to polish the countertop, first with languid swipes, then with increasingly energetic swirls.

"How many senses do you have?" Ravi said, pursing his lips. "Five, of course. But what does it mean when we see or hear or feel something no one else can sense? That it doesn't exist?"

As Ravi threw the rag on his pile of soiled cloths, his voice picked up urgency.

"Animals—dolphins, for example—can sense the magnetic fields. We can't. Does that mean that dolphins are crazy? Making it up? We can't see ultraviolet light, but a machine can see it. If the machine didn't sense it, would that mean the ultraviolet spectrum didn't exist?"

Derek swallowed. There was a strange logic to Ravi's disjointed outbursts. He thought he could see where it was heading, but he still wasn't sure.

Ravi blew air out of his mouth, puffing his cheeks.

"You see, just because we can't see it doesn't mean it's not out there. In our normal, waking state, we may never see the other dimensions. But the rishis went to another plane, a place beyond dreaming. In that moment before you sleep, when you are not awake any longer, you stand at the threshold. A tiny window opens. The rishis popped through it. They went to the place where all things are one."

Ravi stopped to gauge Derek's reaction. Derek's attention was riveted on him.

"Maybe that is what you are picking up, a place where the planes intersected. You have an opportunity here. Learn from this visitor."

"But e-mail, Ravi? Would such a teacher use e-mail?"

"Technology is nothing more than Maya."

≈

Digesting his samosas and Ravi's tales, Derek returned to his computer, scrolling through the hundreds of e-mail messages that popped up overnight. Two hundred messages a day was nothing. Some days he had five hundred. Thanks to aggressive filtering and an exhaustive filing system, the mail wasn't overwhelming—unless he didn't stay on top of it; then the mail could build up dangerously. Derek wondered what would happen if he ever took a vacation. He considered switching his mail to a mail server with elastic storage. But when was he going to get to that?

Derek thought back to the conversation he'd had with Ravi. Rishis and meditation. E-mail from alternate dimensions. It all sounded so seductive when Ravi spun his tales. Mystics! Maybe Ravi had been making sense to him because he was so sleep-deprived.

Derek's eyes, scanning the screen for something to distract him from the Roger mess, stopped straightaway as he perceived a new correspondent, someone with a single name. Sekhmet. She was using a domain name he didn't recognize routed through a service provider he didn't know. The subject header made his heart jump.

Derek put the message on screen, chugging his lukewarm coffee, which he had brought back from Ravi's in a Styrofoam cup. He read, cringing with anticipation. He remembered what happened the last time he got e-mail from a stranger.

> To: D.Nils@bitjockey.com
> From: Sekhmet@ra-egypt.com
> Subject: I've been watching
>
> Hello, there. I've been reading your postings on the Hacker Haven chat room on Reddit and found myself intrigued with the telecom code conundrum. Attached is a proposed solution.
> Want to trade bits some time?
>
> Sekhmet

Derek pulled up the attachment, something he didn't do often when the sender was unknown. He scanned it for viruses. It checked out. He called it up on the screen. What he saw made him drain the last drops of coffee with sudden urgency. This was killer code: elegant, simple, stylish in its logic, streamlined in its precision. Mathematically graceful, the code solved one of his peskiest scheduling problems in the fewest possible steps.

Who could this Sekhmet be? It was a mythic name, that much he remembered. He did a quick Web search on her name. Within five minutes, he knew that Sekhmet was an Egyptian deity who was the lion goddess, the flip-side of the benevolent cat angel Bastet. Sekhmet was a potent female divine being around whom mystery schools were devoted. She was pure feminine feline energy. You've got to have guts to take on a user name like that.

Derek blinked a few times, trying to figure if Roger had struck again. Roger didn't have much of a sense of humor, but it wouldn't be beyond him to become Sekhmet.

There weren't too many women on any of Derek's chat rooms—all coder's sites for trading updates on hardware and riffing on the latest technology. It wasn't that there weren't women who could crunch code as beautifully as he could. It's just that women were a minority in the computer field. The women he knew were nothing like Sekhmet; they tended to make pronouncements as no-nonsense as the guys did. Yet, here comes someone with the sultry name of Sekhmet, practically leaning against a streetlight and cooing Derek's name.

She probably weighs 350 pounds and lives on romance novels. If she's really a she. Derek turned back to his e-mail and ran through a dozen missives from his coding companions. The Project, as he and George envisioned it, was narrowing down to one focus. And that darn piece of code that Sekhmet just delivered could sharpen the view even more.

This helped, because Derek was making significant progress on this little treasure hunt. Sitting in his living room, nearly buried under piles of data printouts, Derek had pieced together what looked like the key block of the telecom code, which he had done without the aid of Sekhmet's additional information.

Buried in the data was what amounted to a table of contents. There was a subtle but logical arrangement to the pile of digital sequences. They probably weren't credit-card numbers, bank accounts or stock certificates. There was too much organization here for a routine list of numbers. Derek was willing to bet the data made up a compilation of engineering formulas—a book of recipes. There were encoded headings and then various formulas that followed. There were numbers that looked like three-dimensional measurements, consistent sequences that could be interpreted as three-dimensional matrices representing points in space. Numbers detailing actual, physical objects. Then other measurements followed. It was impossible, without piecing all the data together, to figure out what the numbers meant. But somehow, Derek knew that this was more than a kid's pet science project.

If he really had discovered pointers to a compilation of formulas, why would someone need to send them via cellular phone on a telecom line? The need for secrecy must have been great, because normally a coder would just send code by e-mail. Or why not simply mail the data, or even fax it? Why the need to encode it and send it off to some godforsaken place? It only made sense if this was highly secretive material, something experimental that couldn't be published. Yet.

If that were the case, the need to find the terminus—or the "bit basket" as he and George dubbed it—was essential. Who was uploading all this information? And what use would they have for it?

And Derek was certain only of one thing. They better find that landing spot before the CIA did, or some rogue foreigners. There could be anything there: maps to the security setups in museums, instructions to the world's first cold-fusion machine, a method for suspending the law of gravity. Derek let his imagination go wild. This could be Stonegate's motherlode.

CHAPTER SEVEN

FIVE YEARS IN THE PAST

The moon was still up when Charlie pushed open the heavy timber door to his new home. The lunar disc hung in the western sky, hovering over the mountains, pale and tissue-thin, bleached to near transparency by the dawn. It was full and looked as if it would put up a fight until the end—a fight for its very existence. It hung where it ought not be, in a brilliant blue sky, over the red rocks of Indian country.

Charlie counted it as a good omen. Heck, he figured everything in every new day was a good sign, now that the toxins and devils and evil spirits had run screaming from his body. For two weeks, Charlie lay in that tiny room, sweating and swearing, chewing strips of beef jerky and drowning himself in endless cans of Dr Pepper. When the madness ended, he'd found his new Indian blanket—the one he bought on the road from a gold-toothed Pueblo woman—torn to tatters and rags. He was damned if he could remember how he did it. Must have been those intruders in the night. Those little hands that plucked and jabbed at him as he slept, asking and begging and pleading for something Charlie couldn't give them anymore.

The moon glowed like an after-image, like a headlamp in the fog. He breathed the dry air and heard squirrels racing up tree trunks, their little claws clicking against the piñon bark. Here reigned peace, a hard-earned one, but there was emptiness too. Charlie felt the void in his gut and wondered if it ever would be filled.

A leaf cracked and Charlie looked to his right. A tiny wisp of tobacco smoke tinged his nostrils. Charlie peered into the woods and made out a man, tall and solid, planted amid the trees. The figure began to move, striding into full view, cigarette glowing in one hand.

Charlie said nothing, nor did he move. He was a squatter and would yield his little sanctuary if challenged. But somehow this man didn't look like an enforcer. The man stood at least six-foot-six, tawny as the pine bark, black hair in a pigtail tied by a leather thong, a cowboy hat jammed on top of his big head. He appeared muscled as a lumberjack and was dressed as if he had just ridden in from the mountain ranges.

Charlie raised his hand in greeting. The man did not reciprocate but stood his ground for several long minutes. Finally, he took his cigarette, lifted one cowboy boot, bent over, and ground out the ember. Then he pried open the butt, sent the shredded tobacco sailing on the wind, wadded up the tiny bit of paper that remained and put it in his jeans pocket.

"Nicely done," Charlie said, leaning against the door frame.

"Who are you?" the man asked. His black eyes were flat, neutral, impossible to read.

"Charlie Nilsson."

The man blinked for a second and let out a laugh that rumbled through the light breeze. Charlie figured something must be funny, so he managed a throaty chuckle.

"Not the man I was expecting," the Indian said.

"Well, who exactly were you expecting?"

The laughter stopped and the big man returned to his neutral gaze.

"The man who made the cabin of lights." The Native American man pointed off into the distance and Charlie just made out a tiny house much like his new home, sheltered by a crag of rock. He'd thought he'd seen a few twinkling lights off in that direction, but chalked it up to more visions of aliens and bogeymen.

"Come on, I'll show you."

Charlie walked over and held out his hand. The Indian shook it with a solid grasp, full of vigor and warmth. Charlie felt his own hands cold and lifeless in comparison.

"Nilsson, huh? I'm Elk Horn."

The Indian's eyes looked as old as the chalky boulders. Charlie blinked again, feeling as if he were seeing the world through this man's steady gaze.

≈

The hut was a twin to Charlie's, but it wasn't built to house people. The heavily padlocked door—outfitted with an electronic locking system as well—showed a narrow gap or two between planks of wood. By looking between a crack someone had widened with a hunting knife, Charlie could make out some of the contents of the interior. It looked like a room full of electronic equipment. A few of the devices had blinking red or amber-colored lights, which probably were what Charlie had peered at in the distance.

"How the hell?" Charlie said, stepping back and shaking his head. He looked up at the roof to see a cable snaking down from the electrical lines that ran through this desolate land. No wonder the cabin was where it was. There surely was no other electrical source for miles. Staring into the bright sky began to make Charlie's eyes hurt. A wave of dizziness came over him and he stumbled backward. Elk Horn's hand caught him by the elbow.

"It's been this way for a year. There's a man who shows up now and then to tend the machines, but no one has ever seen him close up."

"And you thought I was . . . . "

"Well, not really. Just an off-chance hope. You see, the guy stopped coming."

Charlie kicked at the cabin walls and thought of how someone might secure so much expensive equipment in the wilds of New Mexico. But who'd even think to look in this deserted piece of land anyway?

"What was the guy up to?" Charlie said, squinting as he gazed at Elk Horn.

"You tell me." Elk Horn took his knife and scraped another sliver from the chink in the door. "You tell me."

≈

When Elk Horn suggested they hunt up some food, Charlie half expected his strapping new friend to haul a rifle out of the truck and stalk a deer in the woods. He stood next to Elk Horn's rusty red pickup, shifting from foot to foot, unsure what to do with his lanky body.

Elk Horn grabbed a door handle and pulled the driver's door open. He squinted at Charlie before he ducked his head to get inside. "You comin'?"

Charlie reached for the handle to the passenger door, then snatched his hand back immediately, palm smarting. The handle was red hot from the unfiltered mountain sunlight that blazed on Charlie's side of the car. He gingerly opened the door, as if he were getting a hot pan out of an oven. When he got inside, Elk Horn was laughing again.

"I pegged you for a city boy, but I didn't know you were as big a weenie as all that." He slapped the steering wheel in amusement as he turned the key in the ignition. "You look really pale, though. Sorta half on this earth. What were you doing in that cabin all by yourself?"

Charlie was silent, rolling down his window and feeling the spring sunlight roast his white skin.

"Aw, you don't have to tell me," Elk Horn continued. "I've seen it all before anyway."

Charlie pointed toward the cabin "That looked like fifty-thousand dollars worth of computer equipment over there. Is this reservation land?"

Elk Horn reached over to push in the lighter. An unlit cigarette was already hanging from his lips.

"That's the hell of it. It used be classified as Indian land but somebody bought about five acres off the elders. That's just a tiny bit of land for people around here, but they must have paid a fantastic price for the Nation to give it up."

"Navajo?"

"Yeah, Navajo."

Charlie's lips were deeply cracked and the effort of smiling brought blood to his top lip. It had a salty tang.

"We don't want you Anglos to buy up the small amount we've got left," Elk Horn continued.

"I'm not an Anglo," he said, studying the markings on the road. A sign pointed toward Bandelier and the ancient dwellings of Native Americans long gone.

"Yeah, how's that?"

"I was born in Sweden. Came over here in 1979."

Elk Horn nodded as he drove, smoke streaming through his sharp, pinched nostrils. His pigtail had strands of gray entwined in it, yet the skin on his high cheekbones betrayed not a crease.

"That's good. We'll have no arguments."

Charlie didn't see any reason to contest that.

≈

"Don't get me wrong," Elk Horn said, pushing away his plate of meatloaf and baked beans, the daily special at Mesa Bill's Diner. He rested one arm on the scratched tabletop. "We aren't stupid or backward or any of those things you people think of us."

Elk Horn's eyes were tiny slits but Charlie saw the amusement peeking out. He waited for the Navajo to continue. He had learned this over the past few hours: if he waited long enough, Elk Horn would finish what he started to say.

"Nope," Elk Horn said, rubbing his smooth chin. "But some are young and political. They have returned to the old religion and find signs, omens. The shack has meaning to them." Charlie continued to look into Elk Horn's black eyes. The big man swallowed his coffee and continued. "It's built on sacred ground, no matter who owns it now. They believe it's a bad omen. When the lights go on, bad things happen."

"And you think they are crazy?"

"I think nothing."

"But you know it's only an array of computers, put there by whites."

"The gods can speak any way they choose, through the throat of a crow or through a computer screen. We have no way of knowing how the messages are sent."

Charlie waved off a waiter, who stood poised with a pitcher of beer, ready to pour a glassful.

"It's dime-a-beer day," Elk Horn said, his voice carefree but his eyes beady and sharp as those of a blackbird. Charlie said nothing and concentrated on his hand, still a bit tender from his encounter with the white-hot car-door handle. He opened it and closed it into a fist. Elk Horn shook his head at the waiter, who wandered off to another table.

"You know where the gods reach us? In the voids, the vacuums," Elk Horn said, his voice descending half an octave. It became a murmur, hypnotic and slow. "The black hole in your spirit is nothing more than a space for the gods to enter."

Charlie merely nodded, not looking up, still studying his fist.

"We Navajo have a tradition of using sand paintings for healing ceremonies," Elk Horn said. He spread a fine layer of salt upon the table.

"Traditionally, sand paintings were made on the floor of the tepees or hogans. The ailing person sat in the middle of the painting and a medicine man would start the healing. Soon the sand would absorb the sickness."

Elk Horn took the salt shaker and placed it on a sunny spot on the table.

Then he began to spin the shaker as he talked.

"When the sand pulls out the illness, the sick are completely drained, not only of energy but of emotion, of thought, even of a system of belief. They are fragile as spring leaves, weak as old men."

He moved the shaker around in the sunshine. Then he let it fall over on its side, clanging on the table. "And then they are given the power to heal themselves."

Charlie uncurled his fist. He felt a warm surge in his belly.

"You're a survivor too. Aren't you?" he asked Elk Horn.

Elk Horn nodded.

"Has your empty space been filled?"

"I've been constructing my sand painting for twenty years." He tossed a ten-dollar bill on the table. "Sometimes you gotta wait for the payoff."

CHAPTER EIGHT

To: Sekhmet@ra-egypt.com
From: D.Nils@bitjockey.com
Subject: Re: I've been watching

Sekhmet: Whoever you are, you are a genius. I used your algorithm and it solved my problem perfectly. You have my heartfelt thanks.

Best,
Derek Nilsson
Programmer, BitJockey.com

To: D.Nils@bitjockey.com
From: Sekhmet@ra-egypt.com
Subject: You silly boy

My dear Derek: You don't have to use that dweeb .sig file on me. I know you're a programmer. I know all about you, Swedie pie. As I said, I've been watching . . . . And I think I could be a big help . . . if you want me.

Sekhmet

To: Sekhmet@ra-egypt.com
From: D.Nils@bitjockey.com
Subject: Re: You silly boy

Sekhmet: I don't want to get paranoid here, but how have you been watching me? You wouldn't happen to know a guy named Roger would you?

D.

To: D.Nils@bitjockey.com
From: Sekhmet@ra-egypt.com
Subject: Re: Re: You silly boy

Ah, now it's D. That's so much better. I can see myself cooing "D" to you as I slip you some devastating bits. Mmmmm, D.

Roger doesn't ring a bell, baby. I focus on one man at a time.

Sekhmet

≈

The crowd was so thick at the bar that Derek could barely recognize a soul. The bartender kept staring at him. He was a big brute of a man, with a wide nose with enormous nostrils—the kind that looked big enough to plug up with wine corks. Derek shook his head with a wrenching twist to get the cartoonish image out of his head.

"Beer?" the bartender croaked, his voice ravaged by the acrid air and constant need to yell across the crowd.

Derek shook his head.

"I'm waiting for someone," Derek said. But the big barkeep kept staring at Derek as if to say "So what?" Derek finally nodded his head and motioned for a mug of whatever was on draft. Derek wondered why beer was considered a necessary prop for guys at watering holes like this. What would be wrong with a mixed drink or a coke? Was it less macho to ask for a Rob Roy? Derek wondered what actually went into a

Rob Roy as the bartender brought over the mug of pale, surely tasteless brew. Derek peered through the crowd, looking for a petite redhead.

The place was full of high achievers, all looking for a suitable match. Men in power suits leaned on the bar, jingling keys to Ferraris or inspecting five-thousand dollar watches on their wrists. Women with troweled-on makeup flipped their hair as they talked to their friends and kept their eyes trained on the men. No one was looking Derek's way. For this he was grateful.

"Hey, spaceman," said a familiar voice at his back. He whipped around to see Kyra, dressed in her business suit, holding a glass of white wine.

"Where were you? I was looking everywhere."

"Thought I stood you up, huh?"

"No, of course not." Derek grinned to hide his anxiety. He had been worried that he got the time wrong, or the day. Mostly he was afraid that one of the luxury-car drivers had already whisked Kyra way.

"Well, I found us a table. No easy feat in this madhouse."

Derek picked up the sweating beer, which looked even less inviting now that the foam had disappeared, and shuffled after Kyra. She picked her way through the boisterous crowd like a sherpa climbing a mountain. Each step well placed, each shift in direction deft. Derek stumbled behind her and stepped on some woman's shoe that looked expensive. He apologized without looking up.

They reached a secluded spot marked by Kyra's trench coat and briefcase. It was far enough away from the bar to afford a sense of seclusion. The noise level had also dropped off to a low din. Kyra collapsed into her seat as if she had finished an exhausting workout. She fanned her forehead.

"Wonder if anyone from work is here?" Derek asked, secretly hoping that Trevor or someone else he knew would help him break the ice.

"Oh sure, that would be pleasant," Kyra said, rolling her eyes.

Derek looked into his beer and twisted his mouth. The wrong thing to say again.

Kyra took off her blazer, revealing a neat, pink silk blouse that skimmed her slim torso. Derek gulped some beer.

"I'm getting really sick of BitJockey, Derek," she said, grabbing a few beer nuts from the tiny dish on the table. "I don't want to think about that place."

She paused and tossed a nut into the air a few times before eating it. She chewed with a solemn expression and continued.

"Ever since we had that conversation at Trevor's party, I've been thinking of why I'm in marketing at all," she said. She drummed her coral-polished fingers on the table for a few long seconds. "I'm thinking of getting out."

"Out?" Derek said, and again swallowed the watery, bitter beer. He coughed. "But you're good at it."

"What difference does that make? I'm trying to sell products I don't understand. I'm putting on happy faces for people like that cretin Schermer."

He laughed as he pictured Dwayne Schermer, a powerful client who contracted BitJockey for forty percent of their software output. He was a jerk from the word "go"—an apelike goon who was a tight fit in his shiny suits. The kind of guy who thought that manners were for sissies. A guy who would pat the women on the butt, if given half an opportunity.

"Well, *I* could help you understand the products," Derek said. He felt that warmth start to fill his lap again as he imagined Kyra and himself leaning into a computer screen together, heads nearly touching as he explained how his code made the screen come alive.

"That would be a pleasure," Kyra said, tilting her head for a sly smile. "But it's still not going to solve the problem."

"We could try," Derek said and did his best to mirror her smile. Kyra took her left hand and fluffed back her hair. Derek knew this sign. It was a good one. He hadn't screwed this date up so far.

≈

To: D.Nils@bitjockey.com
From: Sekhmet@ra-egypt.com
Subject: code breaking

My dear little D: I haven't heard from you yet regarding my offer to shed light on your code-cracking conundrum. I know that's why you've got all those grad students churning away on the university hardware.

I'm better than they are, you know that. I also dress better. You like lace?

Sekhmet

To: Sekhmet@ra-egypt.com
From: D.Nils@bitjockey.com
Subject: Re: code breaking

I like lace just fine. I just don't know too many programmers who wear lace. I have to find a reason to trust you. You have to understand that.

D.

To: D.Nils@bitjockey.com
From: Sekhmet@ra-egypt.com
Subject: Re: Re: code breaking

My Swedish meatball: Of course, you can trust me. Honey, I know all about you. I know about George, about the terminus you're looking for, about the worldwide network of nerds you've got hacking away for you. Do I tell anyone? No, never. I never kiss and tell.

Sekhmet

To: Sekhmet@ra-egypt.com
From: D.Nils@bitjockey.com
Subject: Kiss?

Sekhmet, you are presuming a great deal here. I'm not interested, okay? I don't know how you know what you know, but from now on, I'm assuming that you are Roger. And I'm not answering any further messages from you.

Derek Nilsson
Programmer, BitJockey.com

To: D.Nils@bitjockey.com
From: Sekhmet@ra-egypt.com
Subject: Re: Kiss?

Roger, huh? Roger this, sweetheart.
(attachment: lace.jpg)

≈

"Well, this isn't so bad." Kyra stepped over a pile of technical journals and perched herself on the edge of the living-room coach. "And look at that plant. It's enormous."

"I live in a hellhole and you know it. And the plant is from some other planet, threatening to take over Earth."

Kyra laughed and kicked off her shoes. Dinner had been a casual affair, but Kyra was dressed in a sexy sheath that left her toned arms bare. Her pumps must have been uncomfortable, but they certainly had complemented her well-defined calves. Derek figured that Kyra must exercise in earnest. He looked at his own scrawny arms and felt an inner cringe.

"Do you think I expect *Architectural Digest*?"

"No. But you might expect general sanitation."

Kyra motioned for Derek to sit next to her. Ever since the night at murky and loud McCracken's, when Kyra admitted her disenchantment with BitJockey, Derek didn't feel quite so fearful of her. He plopped down on the couch, reaching over to give Foo a reassuring pat. The cat leaped off the couch and ventured forward to sniff at Kyra. Within minutes, the feline was curled in her lap, purring like a Sopwith Camel that needed a tune-up.

"A little loud, isn't she?" Kyra laughed with delight.

"Oh yeah, she's always loud, especially at 6 a.m., when she wants to eat."

Kyra continued to pet the cat but then stretched out her hand and fingered the computer printouts stacked near her legs.

"The Project?"

Derek nodded and averted his eyes. He hated keeping it secret from her, especially since she had shared the details of her new job hunt with him. If BitJockey found out that she was looking for an art museum job, Kyra would be out on her ear. She had trusted Derek with the knowledge. Why couldn't he have faith in her?

"I won't ask," she said, petting the cat. A tiny crease appeared in her forehead.

So much for getting to know her better. She's not likely to even kiss me in this mood.

"Hey, I'll get us some chips," Derek said as he started to jump up.

"I don't want any chips," Kyra said with a touch of a growl. She pulled Derek down by the belt so he was sitting almost in her lap. "And right now, I don't want to pet the cat either."

≈

To: Sekhmet@ra-egypt.com
From: D.Nils@bitjockey.com
Subject: your picture

Sekhmet:

Well, I'm impressed. I guess you are a goddess. Unless, of course, that's someone else's picture you sent me.

D.

To: D.Nils@bitjockey.com
From: Sekhmet@ra-egypt.com
Subject: Re: your picture

My long, tall Nordic boy: Cut the crap. You know it's me. I know what you look like, too. Love that goatee, Derek. I love the way nerds don't understand how sexy they are. Lose that bitch you're seeing.

I want you and I want you to myself.

Sekhmet

To: G.Esterberg@uchicago.edu
From: D.Nils@bitjockey.com
Subject: who's this?

George: Do you know someone named Sekhmet at Ra-egypt.com? She sent me this stunning bit of mathematics (attached). It solves our last coding problem perfectly and I'm thinking of bringing her in. Do you know any reason why I shouldn't? I can't get her identity on Ra-egypt.com. I think it's an alias, but she's covered her ISP trail beautifully. It looks like it's plugged into two major backbones.

It's risky, but George, her help might be too good to pass up.

D.
(attachment: RACode.tar.Z)

≈

Weeks passed and he was continually harassed by Sekhmet, but he managed to keep seeing Kyra with no problem. One morning,

Derek reached over to stroke Kyra's thick hair, but instead found Foo next to him grooming noisily on the next pillow. His heart sank as he began to fear that Kyra had run off, leaving him to face the morning and his jumpy emotions alone. A noise in the bathroom calmed him down. Before long, Kyra appeared, smiling and fully dressed. She sat on the edge of the bed, dressed in a sleeveless polo top and a white tennis skirt, kicking her athletic shoes against the bottom mattress. Derek leaned on his elbow and tried to pull himself into a sitting position.

"I suppose I ought to ask why you look ready for Wimbledon," Derek said, admiring the short white skirt that showed off Kyra's trim legs.

"I told you last night that my tennis league starts today. That's why I brought the change of clothes in my backpack." She looked at her watch and jumped back off the bed. "I've got to run off."

"I thought . . . "

"I know what you thought, tiger man. But I've got to go."

Kyra stretched across the bed and kissed Derek with gentle lips. Derek closed his eyes and remembered last night. He felt the sweet sense of release surge through his veins. He'd finally stopped letting Kyra do all the work. Weeks after she had grabbed him on the couch, Derek had found the nerve to lure Kyra to his bedroom. He had picked her up and carried her through the door, caveman style. And Kyra, he discovered, loved playing Cro-Magnon.

As Derek leaned forward to make the kiss last longer, a shrill noise blasted in his ear. The telephone call at eight on a Sunday morning. Citizens—at least those who slept—needed legislation against that. Derek considered ignoring it, but set his jaw and picked up the phone anyway. A familiar voice came booming over the handset.

"Hey, Derek! Good day to you!"

"*Farmor! Hej*!"

He put his hand over the mouthpiece and whispered, "Long distance—my grandfather from Sweden" to Kyra. She jumped off the bed, blew him a kiss and headed for the door, as Derek sat up to continue the conversation. Derek prepared for a rough talk. His grandmother spoke fluent English, because she had spent many years in the United States when she was young, single, and working as a nurse. His grandfather thought he could speak English, but it came out as a strange amalgam of Swedish and English—Swinglish as second-generation Swedes called it.

Before he could get his grandmother on the phone, he had to make small talk with Farmor. Unfortunately, Swedish was a language that only lurked in his subconscious, with odd words that were gleaned in childhood stored willy-nilly in odd pockets of his brain. He told Farmor that yes, the weather was lovely, yes, Midsummer was nearly here, and yes, he was well. And could he possibly speak to his grandmother?

After what seemed an endless exchange of trivialities, Mormor's sure voice came over the line and Derek felt his brow relax.

"So what's happening, Derek? Why did you leave a message last night?"

"It's Mom. She's bad again."

Derek heard his grandmother breathing. *Darn if those Swedes don't have a fantastic telecommunications network. The sound quality is unreal.*

"Well, Derek, you said she was having some problems. We were concerned but I thought things would even out."

"It was okay for a while, but last month I found her completely distracted, weeping and going through photo albums. She hadn't been eating or sleeping. She tried to hurt herself."

Derek gulped as he tried to think of ways to describe the severity of Astrid's depression without sending his grandparents into a panic.

"She got better for a few days, but yesterday was bad. I went over there and she's completely uninterested in caring for herself. I think she needs to be hospitalized."

"And she won't go."

"No."

"And you're afraid she's going to do harm to herself."

"Well, Mormor, that's what happens sometimes. I have tried and tried to get her to take some medication. But she won't do it."

Derek's grandmother drew a sharp intake of breath. It was a sound that's often alarming to Americans, but it's the Swedes' way of stalling for time, akin to the American habit of stammering "hmm" or "well." She held her breath for an agonizing length of time. Finally, her voice came across, steady and firm.

"Well, would it help if I talked to her? She never listened to me much. Especially when she married your father."

Derek was ready for this turn of the conversation. He knew darn well that Charlie wasn't to blame for clinical depression, but he didn't help Astrid's mental state when he ran way. For years, Mormor and Morfar detested Charlie and his drunken carousing. They always figured that Charlie married Astrid, who was born in the United States and a dual national, so he could become a US citizen. It was true that as soon as Astrid and Charlie eloped for a Stockholm wedding, they were on a plane headed for America. Derek never knew the truth of the matter, but he did know that Mormor and Morfar saw Charlie as the errant ne'er-do-well who took their daughter away. How convenient to blame Astrid's current mess on him now. Derek, deep in his heart, wanted to blame Charlie too.

"Well, he's out of the picture these days."

"I tell you what, Derek. I'm going to collect every book and article I know on the problem and send it to Astrid. She'll trust the written word, even if she won't trust us. And then I'm going to send Boone to visit."

"Boone? We haven't seen him in ten years. What makes you think . . . ?"

"Boone owes us all some big favors. Besides, he's Astrid's favorite cousin."

"He'll help?" Derek was trying to pull the memory of Boone Sandstrom from his foggy brain. Nothing was coming up. Nothing but memories of loud laughter, Christmastime, and some lethal *glögg*—a Swedish hot toddy that Boone was a specialist at concocting.

"You betcha," Mormor said, pronouncing the all-American phrase with her delightful Swedish lilt.

Derek felt the mood lighten as he began to laugh.

They chatted about the weather again—a favorite Swedish pre-occupation—and then Derek hung up. He went to the kitchen to discover that the coffeemaker hadn't turned on yet. Kyra got him up too early. He grabbed an Ultra Wham caffeinated drink from the refrigerator and chugged it down, waiting for the caffeine to enter his bloodstream.

He plodded back into his office and logged onto the computer to pick up his e-mail. Since he'd been dating Kyra, he'd been spending less time on the Project. The e-mail must have been sitting on his server for twenty-four hours now. Five hundred twenty messages filed into his hard disk. He waited for the filters to assemble it all and then started scanning.

One message grabbed his eyes as he dropped the empty beverage can on his desk.

> To: D.Nils@bitjockey.com
> From: Roger@uchicago.edu
> Subject: Re: Found it
>
> Derek: Please read the encoded message that follows.
>
> (attachment: defcom.gd)

Shaking, Derek called up the attachment and discovered it was encrypted. Roger, that creepy bugger, used a code that George and Derek once concocted in school together. How Roger could have known about that little collegiate lark defied all logic. Derek ran a program over the data and, within seconds, he revealed a small but powerful message:

> I have found the terminus of the transmissions. They are being sent to a small cabin in the southwest, 1,517 miles from here. I have exact co-ordinates, which I will send to you over a more secure network. It appears the data is untouched and no others seem aware of the cabin's existence. I will keep this information entirely confidential.
>
> Still your friend,
> Roger

CHAPTER NINE

Sun broiled the pavement at the little park near the expressway. The blacktop of the basketball courts wore a sheen, and Derek could see a shimmery haze rising from the tarred surface. An acrid smell irritated his nostrils. A crow called in the air, ragged and exhausted, but no other birds sounded on this hot, humid day. As mid-June kicked into high gear, spring was gone and muggy heat covered the area like an invisible soggy blanket.

Derek didn't really mind, however. Like many other long and lanky people, he tolerated heat quite well. He stretched on the grass to bask in the sun. A tiny breeze rippled across his face and riffled the pages of the computer printouts he had tucked under one arm. The smell of hot asphalt mixed with the subtle fragrance of flowers.

"Everyone else is hiding in the air conditioning and here you are—a sun god."

Derek opened one eye to see the fuzzy image of George coming into view. The traffic roared in the background. The sun was so bright that Derek could hardly get both eyes to focus.

"Well, this time you're late," Derek said, sitting up and cradling the papers in his lap with care. "While I was waiting, I thought I'd get my beauty rest."

"Couldn't you at least find some shade?"

Derek shrugged and got to his feet. He ambled toward a tree on the perimeter of the basketball court. As he walked, he stared at George, barely recognizable in his huge Australian hat, sunglasses, tank top, and cutoffs. He looked like some ranger from the Outback rather than a computer expert from the South Side of Chicago.

When they reached the shade, George produced a couple of soft drinks from the cooler he carried. The man was prepared for any heat emergency. Derek opened the can of pop and realized he was dehydrated.

"So whatcha got for me?" George said, a cipher behind his mirrored sunglasses.

"Well, first of all, I wanted to tell you that Roger found the proverbial shack in the woods."

"I know. He sent me the same message."

Derek looked at George and couldn't think of a response. A crow called from a tree across the way. He seemed to have his black eyes fixed on Derek.

"What code did he use?"

"He didn't. He was rather elliptical. But I knew what he was getting at."

Derek didn't say a word but merely handed George a printout of Roger's encrypted message, "He used our sophomore encryption." George studied it for a long time, before lifting his head and smiling with the self-satisfied smirk that never failed to annoy Derek.

"So you broke the code?"

Derek nodded.

"And Roger knows the code, too?"

Derek lifted his shoulders a bit. That much was obvious.

"Oh this is beautiful. Beautiful. Now we just have to find out what the data is all about."

"That's what this is," Derek said, patting the huge stack of paper in his lap. "I'm really going out on a limb, but this is what I've got."

Derek handed the pile over to George, who began poring through the data like an automaton. While he read, Derek's memory of this morning's message returned, looming larger in importance than Roger's stunning find. Sekhmet wrote with a proposal. She wanted to meet with Derek in Milwaukee to impart information that couldn't go over the Net. She wanted to see him face-to-face. Derek sensed in his gut that meeting her was a terrible, perhaps dangerous, idea. He still had no reason to trust her—and her brilliance made her a potential threat. But that picture.... Could she really be that much of a bombshell? Sekhmet the Net goddess? He really had to know. She was getting harder to shake than a tick.

"Derek!"

He looked up with a jerk in the direction of the crow. The bird stared back at him and let out a mocking laugh. Derek thought this time that it looked like a falcon, the bird from that horrible dream in the spring. He shook his head with force and turned in George's direction.

"Get over here! This is brilliant!"

George was holding the printouts and jumping up and down under the tree. He looked like an explorer who had found a new passage to a land of gold and spices.

"Millionaires. We're gonna be millionaires!"

Derek decided not to bring up Sekhmet again. Not now. Things were going too well.

≈

In ten minutes, the post office was closing for the weekend. Monday would be too late. Derek raced downstairs, hanging on to a freshly wrapped parcel—a birthday present he was sending for Astrid to Great-Aunt Annabritta in Minneapolis. Bursting into the vestibule of his apartment building, he found the way blocked by a large man who leaned forward reading the different names next to the doorbells. He kept running his wide finger over the names. Normally, Derek would have offered to help him out, but instead he tried to maneuver his thin body around this large, fleshy obstacle. When he was just about to clear the man's backside and sprint to the door, the big guy straightened up and turned around.

"Excuse me," he said, a light, familiar accent trailing from his words. "I'm looking for someone who lives here . . . . "

The man stopped talking midstream and squinted his blue eyes. He was about six foot three, taller maybe, and weighed a good two hundred fifty pounds. He was blond and sunburned, with the look of a man who doesn't mind sleeping outdoors. His age was indeterminate: he had the healthy heartiness of the thirties, but the eye creases and receding hairline of the forties. He wore blue jeans and a t-shirt that said "Fred's Feed" on the front. The shirt had a caricature of a smiling pig with a bib around its neck.

The interloper, who was beginning to emit a distressing odor of perspiration and coffee, leaned forward and gazed into Derek's face. His thin lips were set in a straight line but the ends began to bow upward.

"His name is Nilsson, boy, and I guess you're him!" The man put out a ham hand and offered it to Derek, who stood pinned by the glass-paneled front door.

"Boone!" the man thundered. Derek took a huge breath and shifted his package, which would never make the mail deadline now, and offered his right hand. Boone's grasp swallowed it.

"Well, Mormor said you were coming . . . . " Derek started to say, staring at Boone, whom he hadn't seen since he was fourteen years old.

"You bet. Aunt Emma was on the phone faster than a rabbit in a celery patch. I hear you got some trouble."

"Come on up, Boone. We'll talk." Derek sighed a bit and turned to unlock the inner door and head back up to the third floor. It was just like Boone not to notice that Derek was on his way out. Boone, if memories were working correctly, was one big, self-absorbed guy. At his size, he didn't need to pay attention to the world around him. Boone had the same attitude that beautiful women often affected. The world would come to him, and it usually did.

As they trudged upstairs, Derek began to see little movies in his mind, foggy replays of family events that had included Boone. There were a few picnics in Indiana, where Boone presided over a pig roast or a sack race. Derek remembered his loud voice calling through the dense, pollen-rich summer air. "Get a move on, boy, you're gonna come in dead last!" Boone had a way of laughing that made Derek feel like a mere microbe.

Christmas sparkled as Boone's special time. As Derek unlocked his apartment door, he recalled when Boone had arrived in Evanston for Christmas Eve—the day that Swedes celebrated Christmas *jul*—with a shopping bag full of presents in one hand and a bag of booze in the other. Boone would make his way to the kitchen, kissing the women and slapping the men on the back, and begin to make the *glögg*.

Glögg is the most potent of Swedish concoctions and the chef who can make a true fire brew is revered at any *julfest.* Derek could never get his non-Swedish friends to pronounce *glögg* correctly ("Not 'glahgg.' You have to make your mouth say 'ewh,' sort of like 'ew' but in the front of your mouth. No, not 'gluhgg.' ") but he could see that they appreciated it. Anyone could love it. A sort of mulled wine, spiced with cardamom and cloves and flavored with raisins, *glögg* was fortified with brandy and sometimes vodka to give it a requisite kick. Heated and served in a punch glass, it was the fuel that fired many a volatile holiday evening.

Boone concocted the best *glögg* anyone had ever tasted. That's because the man was a connoisseur of fine alcohol. Unlike poor Charlie, Boone could hold his liquor and never left a party unsteady on his feet or slurring a word. He was, as Astrid often put it, "a functioning alcoholic." Derek learned in years afterward that some alkies could continue like Boone until they die, others would hit bottom eventually. Whether Boone was lucky or not was a subject up for debate.

"Well, you didn't have to clean up for me!" Boone said as the front door opened. He slapped Derek hard on the shoulder. Derek winced. "A real bachelor, I can see. Well, I can respect that, being one myself."

Boone started walking around Derek's place without being invited on a tour. He was gone for a few long minutes. Derek finally found him in the kitchen opening the refrigerator.

"Got any beer?"

Derek's mind spun. It was before noon. And he never kept beer in the house.

"Well, Boone, not really. We could go out . . . . "

"You're sure not Charlie's boy," Boone barked with a big grin on his face. "Well, then again, you are, aren't you? He couldn't drink right, either. Good idea to stay away from it if you can't handle it."

"Well, Boone, it's not that I can't handle it," Derek started to say. He wanted to explain the fear, the social pressures, the fact that he could have two and just not want anymore, but Boone interrupted.

"Okay, let's talk about my cousin."

"Astrid."

"That's still her."

They retired to the living room, where Derek made room on the couch by pushing over a stack of computer manuals. Boone hadn't asked a thing about Derek's life and career, even though he hadn't seen him since he was a shy teenager. Derek let the bitter thought pass and plunged on with the business at hand.

"Mormor told you about the problem," Derek said, finally putting down the package he had never mailed.

"Oh yeah. Deee-pression. Seen it before in the Sandstrom family. Can't be helped, you know. It's in the genes."

Derek shifted his weight on the lumpy cushion. He couldn't imagine how Boone was going to help. This big oaf of a feed salesman from central Indiana was a far cry from a mental-health professional. What was his grandmother thinking? This nutty family.

"Uncle Tomas had it, and Oscar and Ingvar too," Boone continued. "It's everywhere. And I've dealt with it before. Like when I had to put my own dad in the hospital." Derek searched his mind desperately to place Boone's father, but came up empty. Boone rushed on. "Anyway, you know and I know that I'm Astrid's favorite cousin. And I don't bullshit around. I'll come straight to the point with her, and pencils-to-pushpins she'll listen to me. *Ja så!*"

"Ja så," Derek answered, using the Swedish equivalent of "yup" almost instinctively. "How do you plan to do it?"

"Do what? I'll ring her doorbell, talk her up a while and then lay down the law. No problem."

Boone leaned forward, putting his hands on his knees. One of his thighs was the size of Derek's entire torso.

"Let's get a move on to some bar around here. I had a long drive up and I'm thirsty." Boone punched Derek in the ribs with a playful look on his face. Derek took in a quick breath. "You can have a coke."

Boone's laugh roared down the stairs as they left.

≈

Howard Street was a pot-hole-ridden thoroughfare blemished with old-man bars and discount package-liquor stores. The Castaway was perhaps the seediest bar of its kind, decorated with wood paneling that Derek guessed housed colonies of cockroaches. It was the kind of place that Derek only made jokes about. But here he sat with Boone, nursing his second beer while Boone stacked dead soldiers around him like ten pins. Derek wondered how this Swedish immigrant, a guy who didn't learn English until he was twenty, managed to act like a good old boy from White Bread, USA.

Boone's original name was Bo Sandstrom, with Bo pronounced "boo" in Swedish. When he immigrated to America, Bo didn't take kindly to people who tried to dub him "boo-boo," nor did he like the sound of Bo pronounced with a long O, so he changed his name to one that retained the original sound, but was unimpeachably macho. The name fit the man so well that even the Swedes back home started calling him Boone. Here was a man who could reinvent himself any time he pleased. It was no wonder he could pass for an Iowa trucker as he sat at the bar pouring out tales of pigs, gully washers, and duck hunting.

"So where are you headed tonight, good buddy?" Boone asked, with only the barest trace of a Nordic lilt to his phrasing. Derek could still hear it, buried under Boone's bravado.

"Milwaukee."

"What the hell's in Milwaukee?"

Derek heard himself answering. He could have blamed the beer for his loquacious mood, but he really just needed a bit of male simpatico. He just couldn't help himself. He told Boone about Sekhmet. Not about the code, just about wanting to meet her.

"Is that the broad in the picture by your desk?"

Derek fogged. Was he talking about the picture of Kyra he had tacked over his monitor—Kyra, looking wholesome, freckled and posing in front of the Grand Canyon? Or did he mean that printout of Sekhmet that he meant to hide, but still left on top of the file cabinet? Sekhmet in her black lace, her untamed black hair spilling over one well-shaped breast.

"The one in the lingerie?" Boone continued.

"Man, you did get around my apartment in a few short minutes."

"I only took in what was essential, buddy boy. Nice bachelor, computer guy, probably doesn't get out much. Nice girlfriend's photo on the monitor and a sexy bitch stashed over in the corner for future reference. Do I have it right?"

Derek could only manage a nod.

"Listen, how about if I go up to Milwaukee with you? You said you think she's dangerous, right? Probably hooked up with someone spying on you? If she's got goons with her, I can take care of them." Boone nodded, sticking out his lower lip with assurance. "And, if you don't mind me saying so, I'd like a look at this Sekhmet myself." He emitted a giggle more suitable for a little child than a king-sized man. "I want to see if she's really a man."

≈

To: D.Nils@bitjockey.com
From: Roger@uchicago.edu
Subject: Please read

Derek: I think, by my past actions, that I have proven my reliability and sincerity to you. The terminus is quite real and I will be happy to point you there if you wish to visit it. In the meantime, I will continue to monitor the telecom transmissions to this location. They are so infrequent and so heavily packed with data that they must be significant.

But on a larger issue, Derek, I want to establish a bond of trust between the two of us. I admit that I made mistakes in my first dealings with you. I am not a graduate student at the University of Chicago and I'm sorry I pretended. It seemed necessary at the time to take on this persona to get you to listen to me.

The task you have ahead of you requires much more than mental brilliance and quick wits. You will need to think with your whole mind, your emotions, your soul. For this, Derek, you need a guide. And I am here to help direct you in the best way that I can.

Please, fear me no more, for I am here for your aid and support. Trust that I am genuine.

Ever your servant,
Roger

CHAPTER TEN

The dark red VW Beetle sloshed through the main thoroughfare of downtown Milwaukee, parting thin planes of shimmering rainwater. Above the glassy streets, the city looked deserted. Not a cab or a pedestrian moved against the bleak landscape. Boone sat in the front seat of the car, his knees almost to his chin, peering through the raindrops at street signs.

Derek always felt slightly off-kilter when he ventured to Milwaukee. Because it was a Midwestern city much like Chicago in mood and style, Derek expected to know where he was going. Yet, invariably, Derek would think a street looked familiar, take a sudden detour and end up on a one-way avenue with no outlet. Milwaukee teased him with its pleasant German neighborhoods and nineteenth-century architecture, full of the same turrets and gables that peppered Chicago's North Side. Yet, Milwaukee was distinct. It was a beer town gone south, a once-proud manufacturing site that lost jobs and opportunities to St. Louis and Gary, and, of course, Chicago. It was a city that had imploded into a small town, and Derek couldn't get the feel for its illusive emptiness.

"Where the heck did she say she'd be?" Boone thundered, pressing his huge face up to the windshield. "This looks like Dodge City after a gunfight."

Derek held the steering wheel as if it were a life preserver. There was a Victorian-festooned three-flat on his right-hand side. Or was it? A man sauntered down the street wearing a Milwaukee Bucks jersey and a red Chicago Bulls cap. At least Derek wasn't the only one who was confused.

"Where'd a boy from Malmö learn to talk like that?" Derek said, trying to keep the mood light, in spite of the fact that he was horribly lost.

Boone showed his straight rows of white teeth. "Just talented, I guess." He returned to peering out the window. The scenery began to change as they headed toward downtown. Buildings became square, more industrial. Baroque curlicues gave way to Bauhaus modernism. "Some kind of spy bar, she said?"

"Yeah, the Countersign. It's sort of a Milwaukee tradition. A little bar devoted to the secret agents of the 1960s. The only problem is that I can never remember how to find it."

Boone whooped, making the loose passenger-side window rattle. "Good planning! Only spies can find it!"

"I think that's what Sekhmet had in mind."

As they crisscrossed the grid of streets that made up downtown Milwaukee, Derek began to feel a jumpy bolt of panic in his stomach. He might not find this place. Or maybe it was out of business and Sekhmet had lured him into a trap. He concentrated, trying to recall her last message.

> To: D.Nils@bitjockey.com
> From: Sekhmet@ra-egypt.com
> Subject: Let's do a face2face
>
> Hey, Hon: Things are getting a little too hot here to handle by e-mail. Glad someone decrypted that last bunch of goodies. I can tell you what they mean.
>
> Let's reconnoiter in Milwaukee. You know the spy place? I'll be there Saturday at 10.
>
> I'll be wearing black.
>
> Sekhmet

No address. No telephone number. Not even the place's name. When he tried to pry specifics out of her, she only gave flirty replies having to do with lace teddies and spike heels.

"Damn, I feel stupid," Derek said, pounding a fist with lackluster force on the steering wheel.

"Well, boy, you should. We spend an hour and a half driving up here and you don't know where you're going."

"Not about being lost. I feel stupider about the way she lured me up here."

Boone nodded. Boone knew almost nothing about Sekhmet, nothing about her amazing computer skills or gifts of logic. But Boone knew a come-on when he saw one and he said as much to Derek before the Milwaukee journey began.

"She's playing you for a fool, boy," Boone said, opening the window a crack as the rain let up. Skyscrapers loomed outside and the streets seemed to narrow into trenches. "That's why I'm here, to keep you from making a total idiot of yourself."

"I have a girlfriend," Derek said, his sweaty hands slipping on the steering wheel. "At least I will if I play things right."

"Not if Sekhmet has anything to say about it." Boone giggled again. "If she ain't some overweight, pimply-faced man named Irving."

Boone was pepped up now. He sat up tall in his seat and gripped the dashboard with both hands.

"I heard about some online babe named Tania who was making it—in the cyber sense—with half the hackers in this techno chat room. Not one of those kiddy chat rooms, but a real high-tech place for nerds like you."

Derek shot him a dark look, but Boone rambled on.

"She said she was an eighteen-year-old lesbian who could just possibly be convinced to switch hit if the right man came along. She said she was an Asian/Caucasian mix, which for some reason turns on guys like a string of Christmas lights."

Boone clearly was enjoying himself. He nodded with a sly smirk on his paper-thin lips.

"Oh, yeah. She had 'em lined up, slobbering, 'Tania, Tania, do me.' And then some guy fingered her, you know . . . "

"Traced the account, I know."

"And she was a guy! A pathetic, lonely guy who could only get a life by pretending he was a bisexual bimbo. It's too rich."

Derek coughed.

"Boone, have you ever been online?"

"Hell, no. I'm a feed salesman."

The car came to an abrupt stop, the pavement squealing under the rubber tires. They were at another dead end. Foggy clouds drifted past gray slabs of concrete that surrounded him on three sides. Derek was sure that Milwaukee was full of nothing but dead ends.

"For Christsake!" Boone yelled.

"Look," Derek said, snatching the map off the floor. "It's on Taylor Street, which should be just down there."

He pointed down another narrow roadway that ran parallel to the river. Hulking warehouses stood on either side of the street. The road didn't look as if it went anywhere.

"Let's just get out of the car and walk there," Derek said.

"Oh, this is good. Walk into what amounts to a dark alley off a deserted street."

Derek shrugged and stepped out into the fine mist that shrouded the city in a gentle haze. The streetlights shone through the fog like fireflies in a bayou. It was hot and night stuck to his skin, but Derek pulled his windbreaker against his neck, closing the Beetle's door, feeling vulnerable and unsure of his bearings.

"Come on," he said to Boone and started towards Taylor Street to the hidden bar he thought he remembered in the town he thought he knew.

≈

"Whattya mean you don't know the password?"

Derek stood in front of a massive red door, holding a telephone receiver to his ear, staring straight ahead as Boone repeated his question. The two of them had trudged up and down Taylor Street for fifteen minutes until they found the entryway of Countersign. They had passed empty warehouses and seedy bars, all of which filled Derek with foreboding. This building was no different from the rest—a crumbling brick storehouse with black paper covering the windows. When he had knocked on this locked door, a wall-mounted telephone began to ring. There was nothing to do but pick up the receiver. A voice on the other end wanted tonight's password.

Derek tried to keep his expression blank. Some time in the past, he'd been to Countersign. He remembered that there was a video camera above the entryway. It transmitted pictures back to a huge screen over the bar area, where the crowd snorted and laughed at the predicament of people struggling to figure out the entry code. Derek knew they were all looking at him right this minute and he didn't want to gape like a clown. He didn't have to—Boone was doing that for him.

"Sekhmet," Derek mumbled into the phone. Static crackled and he heard shrieks of laughter in the background.

"No dice. Try again," said the voice of his invisible inquisitor. Derek gazed at the bric-a-brac mounted all over the walls and doorframe: condom wrappers, bumper stickers promoting a heavy-metal band, a Milwaukee Brewers pennant, an ancient wooden tennis racquet. He knew the clues were there. Some nights the password was the name of a package of cigarettes tacked in a corner. Some nights it was the name of a rock group on a newspaper headline. Last time Derek was here, the password was "Dolly," the name of the first cloned sheep that had been everywhere in the news.

While he was deliberating, a finger jabbed him in the ribs.

"Sekhmet. That's right."

Derek jerked to his left and saw a skinny man with a hairstyle that seemed to spring from his head like a wild cactus. Braids stuck out at impossible angles, big, puffy plaits the color and shape of cigars. It might have been the hairdo of a Jamaican Rastafarian, but this man looked vaguely Arabic.

"Did you say something?" Derek said, still holding the phone in his hand. He felt Boone's massive gut press close to his other side.

"Yeah, Sekhmet. Right?" The man said as he nodded. The hair moved like an annoyed animal sitting atop his head.

"Yeah," Derek said, replacing the receiver on its hook. Rasping laughter spilled out of the earpiece until the connection broke off.

The Hair Man jutted his sharp chin toward the street. "She's not in there. We're supposed to meet you down this way."

Derek turned to look at Boone, who merely pounded one fist into his other hand. Boone didn't look worried.

Derek nodded and followed his guide, who bobbed along the sidewalk in an up-and-down lope, hair bouncing with each step.

The guy was a geek if Derek ever saw one. He looked as if he had found his clothing at a church bazaar. A red plastic belt held up baggy jeans and a threadbare navy shirt was worn nearly white at the seams.

They heard their destination long before they saw it: pounding bass drums, thundering laughter, an occasional high-pitched scream of hilarity. It was a neon-lit bar that Derek and Boone had hurried by in their zeal to find Countersign. Hair Man must have picked them out and followed their path.

"Is Sekhmet here?" Derek asked, trying to read any kind of expression in his guide's face, now an alien shade of blue in the reflected bar light. Hair Man smiled, his black eyes barely visible below the mass of braids.

"No, man, she couldn't make it." A trace of an accent leaked out. Derek tried to place the nationality, but felt lost. Someone pulled the door open and the smell of whiskey and aftershave tinged with sweat hit Derek in the face.

"Come on," the guy continued. "We work with her. We know what she knows. And we got something she wants to give you."

Derek and Boone exchanged a silent look and made their way to a table in the back. It was covered with playing cards, for a neat game of solitaire was in progress. A bald-headed guy, not more than twenty-one, heavyset and wearing black sunglasses, pulled a card off the bottom of the deck and slapped a red ten on a black jack. He wore black leather and was sweating as if he were in the sunlight. He looked up and giggled when Derek and Boone stopped in front of him. An earring, in the shape of an ankh, the Egyptian symbol of life and fertility, dangled from one ear.

"Oh, yeah, yeah. It's the Swede. Sit down, sit down." The bald man pulled out two chairs.

Boone plopped into the wooden seat, threatening to condense it into sawdust. Derek balanced on the edge of his perch. Derek saw Baldie size up Boone. The corners of the young man's fleshy lips twitched for a millisecond. Just being near him made Derek feel overheated. He pulled back a few inches.

"We just want to talk," Baldie said, answering the unasked question. He pulled out an envelope and smoothed it the way one might pet a cat.

"Might help if we knew who we were talking to," Boone said. He narrowed his eyes.

Baldie shrugged. "Ra."

Derek felt a laugh sputter out of his mouth before he could stop himself. Baldie arched his hairless brows.

"I guess this over here is Osiris?" Derek said, jerking his thumb at the man with the wild coiffure. "Anyone else in this Egyptian fantasy that you want to introduce us to? Bastet, the cat goddess? Thoth, the god of wisdom?"

Baldie stroked the envelope again. "It's easy to see why you would find it humorous. I'm Ra because I own Ra-egypt.com—a small company. We import Egyptian products. Sekhmet likes to call me Ra." Derek felt his eyes roll heavenward, but Baldie didn't seem to notice. "This is Salim." Hair Man nodded. "We have data for you."

A fluorescent-orange-haired waitress slammed a pitcher of beer and plunked jug-sized mugs on the table. She winked at Baldie before slapping a check in front of him. Boone reached for the pitcher and poured himself a cool one, no jitters apparent. The bald man slid the manila envelope toward Derek.

"Don't read it now. Sekhmet says its gonna take some time to digest."

As he pulled the packet across the table, Derek felt the paper crinkle under his fingers, tantalizing him. Damp puddles of spilled beer and water soaked into the envelope's paper and slowed the progress. He was about to lift the parcel off the table when a giant hand slapped onto the prize.

"Whadda we hafta do in return?" Boone said with a grunt, his hand trapping Derek's.

Baldie tilted his head like an animal hearing something unexplained and new. "Well," he said, his shaded eyes reflecting the bar lights into Derek's gaze. Baldie peered at Salim, and Derek could see that twitch again on his upper lip. "We just need a little help with some data of our own."

"What kind of help?" Derek said, his fingers wriggling for freedom. He began to sweat because the idea of touching the package was almost as repulsive as maintaining contact with Boone's bear paw.

"The flow. The datastream has a flow."

"You want the terminus?"

"You know where it's going. We know what it is."

The air became dry and itchy. Derek's tongue glued to his upper palate. He grabbed for the beer. It tasted like swill, but at least it was wet. He felt Salim's dark eyes pushing him back. They almost seemed to reflect light, like a dog's. Or a jackal's. Baldie cleared his throat. The earring danced, and a plume of cigarette smoke wafted over from another table. Boone sat poised on his tiny, insubstantial chair like an elephant on a circus stool.

"Well, that would be a problem," Derek said. He felt out of control, a robot on automatic settings. He stood up, freed his hand, and looked down at the guy who called himself Ra. *What a poser. Ra, indeed.* He tossed a ten-dollar bill on the table for the beer, too jumpy to care that he was overpaying. Boone rose too, sending a large shadow across the table. "Goodnight, then."

Derek turned to walk out the door. He expected a scene. Perhaps Baldie would make a lunge for him. Maybe Salim was armed. Possibly half of the hulking, blue-collar workers lining the bar were in cahoots and would give chase at any moment. Derek tried not to notice how large and muscular the other patrons were.

Boone opened the door and they broke into a dash down the rain-soaked street. Nothing happened. Derek craned his neck, looking down the street for a gang of toughs. The way was deserted, lined by nothing but lonely stockrooms with yawning, empty windows. Derek and Boone hurried to his car, Derek jogging and Boone huffing to keep up. When they reached the red Beetle, Derek spied a large manila envelope wedged behind one of the windshield wiper blades.

"No," Derek muttered, walking over to the hood and gently poking the package with a finger.

"Can't be the same damn package," Boone said in an uncharacteristic hushed tone.

Derek grabbed a stick lying in the gutter and pushed the soggy envelope away from the wiper's grasp. It didn't explode. With a delicate touch, he picked the package up, held it far from his torso, and opened the flap with care. He saw a pile of documents, topped off with a piece of parchment paper. Inside, the paper was dry and crisp, meaning the envelope couldn't have been sitting on his windshield for long. He looked up and down the street, but there was no one visible.

Derek reached into the envelope and fished out linen-colored stationery, which he held up to the streetlight's gleam. The small square was made of rough fibers, crisscrossed to form a lattice pattern. It looked like flax or––alarm bells rang in his head—papyrus. On top of the note was the image of a large scarab beetle holding a disc. The sun disc. A letterhead said Ra-egypt.com.

Swirling handwriting filled the paper. He read aloud to Boone: "I knew you'd leave. So, I took precautions. I see you did too. You're smarter than you look, Derek. Read this stuff and we'll talk. And next time we'll chat without our buddies around. Sekhmet."

Derek dropped the note onto the hood of the car and stared into Boone's slitted eyes. A sudden movement, a nocturnal bird dive-bombing from a high tree to the river, made him look past his cousin. His line of sight rested on the warehouse across the street. In the third-floor window, a figure gazed down at him. Dimly lit by a nearby streetlamp, the figure was almost impossible to make out, but Derek could see long, wavy, black hair. The wind blew and he thought he could just detect a soft, mocking laugh winding like a serpent through the night air.

CHAPTER ELEVEN

Four hundred e-mail messages awaited. Three hundred ninety-eight were from the Project hackers. One was from Kyra. One was from Roger.

Roger. Derek wasn't sure he could stand any more surprises tonight, not after reading Sekhmet's amazing document by flashlight on the car ride home. While Boone drove, complaining the whole while of having to use a stick shift, Derek poured through Sekhmet's data. What he discovered made him feel like a bewildered kid caught standing next to a class slugfest. He hadn't participated in any way. He merely gawked. But now he was just as culpable as anyone else. His stomach felt sour and he realized that he hadn't eaten a thing, even after Boone had stopped for a burger at a fast-food drive-through in Kenosha.

Kyra. Derek felt his forehead flush. Why did he feel as if he had hurt her? He thought of Kyra lying on his couch in the late morning, reading her new résumé to him, asking for edits or suggestions. She had been resplendent with her legs over the sofa arm, holding the sheet of paper straight over her head. Sun shone through the sheet, making it glow with fluorescence. Her hair had spilled onto the upholstery, resting like a red starfish under her head. The light flicked over one freckled arm and Derek wondered why the freefall sensation in his stomach felt so good.

All he knew was that mentioning Sekhmet or the trip to Milwaukee might upset the sweet relationship that had grown between them. He felt as if Sekhmet were some ugly, heavy secret he lugged around from day to day, something he had to keep locked away from Kyra.

Roger, then. He opened the message.

Derek:

I know about Sekhmet. Reveal nothing to her. Reality is nothing more than a habit. To see further, we must be shocked, amazed. Do you see anything new?

Roger

For the first time, Derek didn't close Roger's message in a panic. Ever since Roger's last message, when he promised to function as a guide and a friend, Derek was conflicted but reassured. Sure, the message was strange. Why did Roger promise a passage to self-knowledge? What could this disembodied messenger know about Derek's life? But somehow, Derek was now convinced that Roger was on his side and no longer felt lost in a funhouse when he read the epistles. They were so obviously beyond the scope of the average Net prankster that Derek had to believe they didn't come from an evil source. And heck, anyone who warned about Sekhmet seemed on the right track. Right now, Roger looked innocuous—safer certainly than Derek's own family, his confused romantic aspirations, and his ever-worsening professional trap. He deliberated and then clicked open a return message. He typed, not spending any time to edit himself.

Roger:

Okay, tell me what to do now.

Derek

He pushed "send" and, fearful of the answer, decided to take a breath before reading it. He stopped only to check on Boone who snored loudly on the couch with Foo curled innocently on his crotch. Derek locked the door, ran down the stairs, and kept jogging down the street, turning east to meet the dawn. It was only when he left that he realized Kyra's message was still unread.

≈

The chai tasted wonderful. Ravi sweetened it with honey this time, and the frothy milk rivaled anything that could have come out of an espresso machine.

"So what does she look like?" Trevor asked, pulling his long hair back from his half-opened eyes. He lurched as if to keel over into his coffee, but leaned on one arm instead.

They sat in the back of Ravi's shop at one of the little booths. Derek could scarcely have found a better sanctuary.

"You mean what does she really look like?" Derek replied and took a long sip of his tea. It had been a long night without sleep.

Trevor nodded. When Derek went to find him at dawn, Trevor had been pacing, sleepless in his studio. He couldn't work and couldn't sleep. He said that listening to Derek's tale of cyber vixens and mysterious data was infinitely more interesting than finding the right shade of terracotta red. Derek wondered about an artist's torment, wondered if it were as frantic as the hacker's mania. Creative urges blocked by indecision and self-mockery. Derek decided it was all one and the same.

"Well, she's hot," Derek said, feeling his face starting to burn. "You know, black lace, leather, the Penthouse crap. A stereotype, I know."

"And you believe that."

"Well, no. Well, maybe. I mean I saw someone in that warehouse window. And the hair matched."

"Oh, come on, Derek," Trevor said, collapsing back into the squeaky vinyl booth. "Even your cousin could put on a wig and stand in the dark. Would you believe he was Sekhmet too?"

Derek stirred his chai again, cooling it. He had to admit he sounded insane. Yet confiding to Trevor was the only thing he could do to keep from cracking up. With George, expressing any vulnerability was risky. With Kyra, the subject of Sekhmet was out.

"Well, it was damn weird." He heard Ravi mopping the floor in the kitchen and leaned forward a tad. Was Ravi listening? Did it matter if he did? "But the data, Trevor. The data. It's acoustical information."

Trevor just stared. Derek tried again.

"It is a list of various dimensions and corresponding acoustical instructions."

"For what? A sound system?"

"That's the thing. It has nothing to do with audio equipment. It's a precise formula based on the physics of acoustical movement." Trevor's eyes drooped. Derek had a feeling he'd lost him. He pressed on. "What Sekhmet explained was that this formula is beyond ancient. It's a lost technology. Something people have been trying to find for centuries."

Trevor's eyelids separated a few millimeters. "Now *that's* different."

"And Roger . . . "

"The gremlin in the computer?"

"Yeah. The ghost in the machine. Roger knows where the data has been sent."

"I'd say you better go find it."

Derek looked up to see Ravi arranging chairs around the remaining tables. Coffee was beginning to brew and the scent of cardamom-spiced rolls lifted into the new morning air. The young Indian never looked Derek's way, honoring his friend's privacy. Derek felt secure.

"But I owe Sekhmet something now. What kind of bone am I going to throw her?"

"That's an interesting metaphor." Trevor smiled for the first time that morning. "I'd send her on a merry chase, the same as the one she popped on you." Trevor looked at his watch and scrunched his mouth. "Listen, hacker boy, it's now Sunday morning and neither one of us has seen any sleep. I think it's time to pack it in."

Derek nodded, fishing in his wallet for dollar bills. He thought of reading Kyra's message when he got home and started to bite his lip. What if she was beginning to wonder about Saturday night? It was usually their evening for Chinese food. He had backed out with some elaborate story of Boone's sudden arrival and needing to get him settled in Chicago. Would she be petulant, curt, too busy to see him ever again? Worse yet, was she going to ask to see Boone? He couldn't imagine what embarrassments his cousin would present for him then.

Trevor shook his head, pressed the single back into Derek's hand, then walked over to Ravi to pay the bill. Derek snatched his windbreaker off the back of his chair and hurried after his friend.

"Call Kyra, will you? Today?" Trevor said, waving off the change that Ravi offered. "Go out on a real date with a real woman and start living a genuine life." He shook his head. Derek knew he wasn't kidding, despite the mocking tone.

As they moved to leave, Ravi beckoned to Derek and leaned toward his ear. Derek inclined his head.

"You look much better," Ravi whispered. "I think now you see beyond Maya."

Derek nodded, muttered something resembling thanks and forced himself to meet the daylight on Devon Avenue.

≈

"Don't slip."

Kyra looked up, her eyes questioning. Derek pointed to the treacherous staircase that wound away below them, trailing like a coiled snake into the basement of the old museum. Kyra narrowed her brows as she regarded the dark entryway. Derek placed his hand on her arm, ready to guide her steps.

"Well," Kyra said, an embarrassed laugh overcoming her scowl. "I expected a staircase, but not a descent into the underworld."

"It's an Egyptian tomb, you see," Derek said, as they stepped down into the murky stairwell. "It's *supposed* to be scary. But believe me, the effect is quite different when dozens of screaming schoolchildren are racing down the steps in front of you."

"Maybe that would give you a better picture of Hell," Kyra said.

"Not what the Egyptians had in mind, I'm sure," Derek said.

They navigated the steps in the unnatural stillness, arriving at the bottom of the museum's "tomb" in a somber mood. Derek could have kicked himself for coming up with this idea for a date. George had connections at the Field Museum of Natural History and snagged an invitation to a "Behind the Scenes" night. The exhibits were closed to the public, but open for big-shot donors, nosy journalists, and hangers-on, such as George and his pals. Derek hadn't considered the creepiness factor.

A stone sarcophagus stood in a niche, barely lit by a tiny track light.

"Is this supposed to be where the mummy was laid to rest?" Kyra said, making no move toward the box. Derek kept his hand on her arm. At least he had an excuse for continued contact. He read the inscription on the wall.

"It's supposed to represent an example of a robbed tomb," Derek said. "You see, it's empty." He surveyed the rest of the corridor. "Let's pass up some of the creep-show props and get to the good stuff."

Kyra nodded, relieved. The spook-show atmosphere was getting to her. He could tell by the way she pursed her lips, so tightly they looked as if they were white. Or maybe they weren't; in this muddy light, even the most beautiful face could look freakish.

They regarded a few mummies, one unwrapped. Derek couldn't stop thinking about how he'd feel if his dead relatives were on display for hundreds of people to gawk at each day. No wonder the current Egyptian government was asking for mummies to be returned and re-interred in hillside mastaba tombs.

"I heard they used to have mummy-unwrapping parties in England early in the twentieth century," Kyra said, eying the flattened nose of one wizened, dried-up body. "Can you imagine that?"

"I'd rather not," Derek said. He grabbed her hand and pulled her out into the bright display area, away from tombs and bodies. They wandered among mystical carvings of the cat goddess Bastet, cases of intricate jewelry, and stopped before a display of a huge building block. Next to the block, which sat on a model sledge, was a description of how the Egyptians pulled a massive sculpture. Dozens of men pulled together, dragging the statue of a pharaoh.

"If you'll notice," Derek said, pointing to the picture, "this is a New Kingdom illustration. The pyramids were ancient by the time they were pulling this statue."

"What's your point?" Kyra said, trying to move the sledge, which didn't budge.

"They are trying to say that this is how they built the pyramids, with thousands of men pulling blocks like this," Derek said. "But, really, they don't have any idea how they did it. Most of the buildings and techniques of the New Kingdom were inferior to those of the Old and Middle Kingdoms. So possibly a secret was lost along the way."

Kyra looked up at him, eyes dancing. "Since when do you know all this about Egypt?"

"I've been researching something."

"The Project?"

"It might have to do with the Project. Yes." Derek felt uncomfortable again, wanting to spill all he knew right there in the quiet Egyptian room. But he couldn't. Kyra didn't seem to mind. She wandered over to a model of an Egyptian woman. She lined her own face up with the reflection. Derek came up behind her and watched as she turned into a priestess of the Nile. Then Derek did the same with the male image. He looked like a black-coiffed rock star.

"You always ask me why I was attracted to you," Kyra said. "Well, it should have been obvious. It's because you're so darn smart."

Derek laughed, unsure of how to respond. Kyra turned around and gave him a kiss.

"Tell me more about Egypt," she said. "Its art is so intricate."

Derek, more of a technical expert than an artiste, regaled her with stories of the precision of the pyramids and other Old Kingdom structures. Although the popular theory is that they were built using ramps and levers, most engineers cannot see how the ramps could have worked. The weight of the ramps alone would have collapsed before the pyramid attained any height. Archeologists continued to argue for the ramps-and-hauling-workers theory, but some renegades contend that the ancients must have possessed a secret technique that was lost over time. Not all civilizations progress, he said. Sometimes they regress.

They exited the exhibit, making their way to the gift shop, conveniently open for this special exhibition. Kyra immediately gravitated to the display of Egyptian jewelry. She pointed to rings of gold and beads of lapis lazuli. But, in the end, her heart was set on a pendant of a falcon, its wings outspread, holding ankh symbols in each clawed foot and bearing the sun disc on his head.

"Tell me about this symbol," she asked Derek, as the clerk pulled it out of the glass display case and laid it on the counter for Kyra to examine. "What does it mean?"

"It's Horus, appearing as a falcon and bearing the sun on his head," Derek said. His father's words from long ago began to ring in his head, but he pushed them down, out of his consciousness. "Horus is an important god, because he was the miraculous offspring of Osiris and . . . " Derek's voice caught, but he forced himself to continue. "Of Osiris and Isis." He hoped he wouldn't have to say any more about the gods or Sekhmet's name might pop out.

"Who are they? Isis, yes, I heard of her before her name became the title of a terrorist organization," Kyra said, modeling the colorful pendant, which found a home just under the crest of her collarbone. It was made for her.

"They were Egyptian gods," Derek said. "Osiris died and Isis brought him back to life. From this miraculous union, Horus was born."

"Oh, you *are* a brain," Kyra said as Derek took out his credit card to purchase the falcon. "I wonder how many books on Egypt you've read."

"Sometimes I think I'm too smart for my own good," Derek said, watching the son of Isis bobbing delicately on Kyra's pure ivory neck. He felt something when he watched her, something new and delightful. She became beautiful in his eyes and his gift was a token of—*why not say it*—love. Derek pulled her close and promised himself to give her more of himself, as much as she needed.

≈

The sun reflected off Kyra's painted toenails as she wiggled them in the breeze. Kyra had propped up her feet on the railing that separated the bleacher seats from the ivy-covered walls of Wrigley Field. Derek noticed that each toenail was painted a different iridescent color, giving her small feet a shimmering, rainbow effect.

"Do you think I could have the scorecard back?" Derek asked, watching as Kyra scribbled in the players' names.

"Just let me do this," she said, filling in the batting order for the Cubs and then for the Pittsburgh Pirates.

Derek bought the scorecard, as he always did before every baseball game, as a focusing tool. Whenever he went to games, he found his attention wandering—baseball is a slow game, after all—and scoring the game forced him to keep his eyes riveted on the field. He hated missing things. Now his date had swiped the card.

"I didn't even know you knew how to fill in a scorecard," Derek said, trying to sound cheerful. "And how did you know the Pirates' batting order? They didn't announce it yet."

"Typical thing for a guy to say," Kyra said, handing back the card to Derek, as if it were a wet napkin. "My brother is a baseball player. Triple A. Anyway, I know their usual lineup."

"You never told me about him."

"You never asked."

When the first pitch shot through the air, snapping hard into the catcher's mitt, Kyra grabbed the scorecard back. One, two, three, the Pirates went down, and Kyra penned a large K in the third box. She chewed on the end of the pen as she watched each pitch, squinting as she analyzed the flight of each ball, and announced "sinker," "changeup," "split-finger fastball" more to herself than to Derek.

"They are only going to keep Davis in for a few innings, because he has a sore elbow," Kyra said. "But watch them work Torres in the bullpen. He's a lefty and it'll throw the Pirates off for an inning or two. You watch."

"Talk stats to me, baby," Derek said, feeling a wide grin spreading across his face. "This is better than sex."

"Better?"

"Well . . . "

The Cubs battled on, falling behind by three runs. Kyra was alternately cheering and moaning with each change in baseball fortunes. Derek felt his senses wandering. He heard the beer vendors barking and the organ urging on the calls of "defense." Peanut shells cracked underfoot, hot-dog vendors clacked their metal box lids, and the scent of sunblock alerted him to the presence of his new neighbor, a woman in a halter top with an enormous blonde hairdo.

He shifted closer to Kyra and watched her yell as Colon slugged a fast line drive. She slumped back into her seat when the Pirates' first baseman snagged it with the tip of his glove.

"So close," she said, scribbling on her scorecard. Hers because Derek would never get it back.

"Well, that was only the first out, three on base, so we'll do okay," Derek said. He reached over and grabbed her hand. Kyra looked up at him. Her eyes were green. Green like the ivy. Green like the well-tended turn near home plate. She squeezed Derek's hand.

"Thanks for bringing me here," she said, her voice losing, just for a second, the sports announcer's tone of authority.

As Derek returned the squeeze, the crowd inhaled as one great being. It felt as if all available air lifted off the ball field. A tiny, pale baseball shot away from the earth, sailing in an arc that stretched from home plate, over left field, and straight into the blue heaven over Derek's and Kyra's heads. They stretched their necks and gazed as Abbott's perfect homer—a grand slam in the making—moved like a shooting star over them. Derek pulled Kyra close, shut his eyes and felt her delighted laughter tickling his ears. He wished for a second, wished on this baseball miracle, that he could always find this moment. No matter the state of the outside world, this moment he could find, slip inside, make his only lasting reality.

CHAPTER TWELVE

"And so we are ceasing operations on July 1."

Derek stared at the speaker, a tiny man in a large suit. BitJockey CEO Bushnell ("Bushy") Green stood behind the podium, craning his neck to reach the microphone, stretching his neck from side to side as if he were in pain. BitJockey had just been acquired by a larger firm, Bushy had told them. Now he was answering questions. A crowd of angry, suspicious co-workers pushed close to the dais.

"Who will stay?" The speaker was a small red-faced man who had never done a lick of work since Derek started at BitJockey. He wondered if a mistake was made in payroll keeping this guy busy at his sinecure.

"Lots of you," Bushy said, yanking at his shirt collar with an index finger. "Most of you. The rest will get a generous severance check."

Moans filled the room. Derek looked over at Kyra, who was beaming. Nothing better could have happened for her—severance pay and plenty of time to find a new job. Trevor stood silent as a leopard spotting prey. Derek wondered if there was a bright sign Trevor recognized that Derek couldn't see. Bushy was mumbling into his microphone, trying to assure his troops that things would be the same under the leadership of TechStar Industries, but everyone knew the score. TechStar was the Death Star of software businesses: well-run, spotless, and ruthless. Deviants like the BitJockey techno-nerds would be weeded out at the first opportunity. Shoulders sagged. Mouths drooped. The meeting was over.

As the workers shuffled out to return to work, Derek felt a hand on his sleeve. He started when he saw Bushy, a full six inches shorter than he was, staring up into his face.

"Sir?"

"You're our lead programmer, Derek," Bushy said, his pale blue eyes wandering around the room, barely focusing on Derek's face. "You will stay. No transition is possible without you."

Derek felt alarm zinging through his insides. What the heck did that mean? They didn't want to make him management, did they?

"Sir?"

"The thing is, we need a hiatus here." Bushy looked over at a man across the room. Eyes met and Bushy jingled some change in his pocket. "We have to re-evaluate all the products and . . . "

"You'd like me to stop working on them."

"Yes." Bushy frowned, creating a deep dimple between his brows. "Sounds odd, I know. But, anyway, until you are vested in the new company, you've got a month off. Paid."

Derek kept staring at the dimple. It faded. Bushy was attempting a smile.

"Well, go on, boy. We like you. Get some sleep." The CEO clapped him on the back and hurried off.

Derek half-walked, half-jogged back to his desk to call George. Patty, the secretary, tossed Derek a large box as he dialed the number. He shot her an inquiring glance.

"Pack up," she said. "You lucky dog."

George answered as Derek stared at the mountains of documentation on his desk. Where to start?

"So you're history," George said. Smart man. He must have heard inklings of this on the business wire days ago. He should have been a reporter.

"Well, they aren't being that gentle with me," Derek said, piling official BitJockey memo pads in his box. "They like me."

"Uh-oh."

"Thing is, there could be no better time for a vacation, George."

" I hear you. Quite relaxing. Maybe you can find a little cabin out west somewhere."

≈

St. Louis, MO. Latitude, 38 degrees, 37 minutes. Longitude, 90 degrees, 11 minutes. The arch, barbecued ribs, jazz.

Derek stretched out his cramped legs and dumped the atlas onto the couch cushion. *Never been there. Well, I've been through there.* That was the first stop for the phone signals, too. According to Roger's carefully recorded data, the code was transmitted via the cellular relaying station in St. Louis. On the way to where?

Derek stared at the piles of documents and printouts on his coffee table. The paper had spilled off the table and all over the floor, spread out all the way to the mutant houseplant next to Derek's front window. Derek gazed past the leaves, past the glare on the glass and into the night sky. He pushed his brainwaves west, trying to pulse his thoughts through the telephone wires, moving like electrons, squeezing through molecules.

Roger was right, of course. Reality *was* a habit. A boring and stupid habit when you got right down to it. What use was a cosmos that set up barriers, when you can touch a reality that responds to different rules? What did Roger say again?

It was in the e-mail. "Thought is energy. Energy is matter. What can be achieved by a single thought?"

Derek resumed his meditation and thought small. He cogitated in quanta-sized bits, flew at light speed.

Kansas City. A mere bump in the fiber-optic highway. Derek barely slowed gears as the signals switched, rotated a bit. Heading . . . heading . . . south, southwest. No landscape here, no sense of geography or even space, but Derek's mind was moving closer to Earth's middle. South, south.

Dallas. Latitude, 33 degrees. Longitude, 97 degrees. *I went to Austin once. With Dad.* Derek saw the music festival clearly in his mind's eye. People in the streets. Guitar players in every bar and corner restaurant. Newspaper and magazine reporters walking around with their credentials strung around their necks like huge Army dog tags. Charlie tapping his feet to country music. Derek nearly bursting out of his teenaged skin with self-doubt. *Why did he take me? Did he even care if I was alive?*

Derek's eyes flew open. He grabbed the atlas. Yes, Dallas. It was a likely telecommunications transfer point. It matched the data. From Dallas, the communications line flew off in various directions: San Antonio, Oklahoma City, Little Rock, Albuquerque. The electrons were buzzing in his head now. Albuquerque, NM. Land of

Enchantment. License plates with Hopi sun gods on them. Latitude, 35 degrees, longitude, 106 degrees, 30 minutes. No need to refer back to Roger's notes now. This matched. Derek could see the lines converging in his head. North a tad, near Santa Fe.

Santa Fe. Town of art, fashion, the Santa Fe Trail, the Wild West. Charlie dead drunk at some dive called the Cactus Spine, knocking back tequilas with a local lush. Astrid in the hotel crying. Hospital, electrolytes unbalanced. "He had better get off the hooch or his liver's gonna fail." An Indian sitting in the downtown plaza, peddling turquoise and silver rings. He held a bauble up and the stone began to pulse. Signals, streaming, throbbing like the heartbeat of the earth, moving northward still. Into the reservations.

Derek stopped and jabbed his finger on the map of New Mexico. Latitude, just shy of 36 degrees. Longitude, 107 degrees, almost dead even. Indian country.

Derek picked up the phone and punched numbers, his fingers seeming to act independently. He heard a voice mail message and waited for the beep.

"George. I know where I'm going for my vacation," Derek said, feeling his head begin to pound. "I'm leaving in three days."

≈

"Santa Fe!"

Astrid sat like a queen at the breakfast table, with a spoon poised midway to her open mouth. Her eyes were wide open, staring, bluer today. Definitely bluer.

"Yeah, Santa Fe. Or the area nearby."

Astrid let the spoonful of yogurt settle in her mouth and she seemed to consider the flavor rather than Derek's announcement. Boone leaned forward, his heavy arms tipping the table a fraction, jingling the silverware and rattling the coffee cups.

"You hate Santa Fe," she said.

"Mom! *You* hate Santa Fe. I just hate what happened there all those years ago. Anyway, I'm not going for pleasure."

Astrid looked down at her yogurt bowl. It was empty, but she scraped the edge with her spoon as if she were retrieving flakes of gold dust. Waste nothing.

"What the hell do you hate about Santa Fe?" Boone said, his voice making the crockery rattle anew. "Everyone I know says it's great! Spicy food, nice dry weather, Indian stuff, cowboy stuff . . . "

His voice trailed off as Astrid gave him a measured, chilly look. Although Boone had done a little psychological magic—that much was clear by Astrid's ability to make a fine breakfast—Astrid clearly resented Boone's meddling. When she wasn't lost in depression, Astrid ran a tight ship. Boone did not behave the way she wanted.

"Santa Fe represents some rather bad memories for Derek and me," she said, pushing away her coffee. She glanced at Derek, who was chasing runny yolks around the plate with a bit of cooked egg white. "What do you mean, 'not for pleasure'?"

"Love?" Boone said, winking.

"No, not love," Derek blurted with more force than was necessary. He cleared his throat. "It's got to do with business."

"Business? But you're on leave, a man of leisure," Astrid said, beginning to stand up, ready to clear the dishes.

"That's why I have time to do this. It's research for a side venture. I can't really explain."

"It's all hush-hush, Astrid," Boone said, putting a big, fat finger to his lips and widening his eyes. "Cloak and dagger, secret agent stuff." He let out a whooping laugh. "Hot damn, Derek! I want to go! My partner can run the feed store."

Derek, helping his mother gather dishes, held the egg platter high in the air, forgetting what to do with it.

"Why?" Derek asked, platter poised just above his forehead. It felt like a UFO hovering there, unexpected, out of place.

"Well, my cousin here doesn't want me hanging around bothering her anymore," Boone said, nodding at Astrid. She shrugged. "And now that she's taking them Happy Pills again . . . "

"Boone!" Astrid snatched the platter from Derek's uncertain hands.

"Well, damn, Astrid, you *are.* Nothing wrong with that. Best thing in the world for you. In two weeks, you'll be whistling 'Suwannee River.' "

"That's whistling 'Dixie,' " Derek said. Boone often got his American idioms all twisted around. Derek secretly found pleasure in finding chinks in the Good Ole Boy armor.

"Yeah, 'Whistling Dixie.' Wonder why you can't whistle 'Suwannee River'?" Boone asked.

"You could, Boone, you could, but that's not what they say," Derek said, scratching his goatee. Astrid disappeared into the kitchen.

Derek couldn't think of a good reason to tell Boone he couldn't go on the trip to New Mexico. Boone's mission with Astrid was over. Lord knows what went on between them, but a change did come over her. Derek knew for certain that Boone could make Astrid laugh when everything else in the world set her crying. But Boone's charm also had a way of wearing off.

Derek often had the same reaction; Boone was a refreshing change at first, an oppressive annoyance later. Yet, Boone could be useful on the road. Big, burly, and a form of security. He certainly came in handy in Milwaukee.

"Boone, how can you take so much time off from the feed store?" Derek asked.

"Aww . . . it's a long story. Fred went and got cancer a few years ago and I took over the shop completely while he was in treatment. But he did recover and he's cancer-free. So, he told me anytime I want to take off for a while, he's happy to let met do it."

Derek reached down and grabbed a sliver of coffeecake from the last plate. He chewed and thought. Boone also could get in the way. And what were his motives? But he was free.

Boone grinned like a cartoon character, all teeth, and took one last slug of coffee. He stood, accidentally shoving the table forward and nearly knocking over the vase of flowers. He had a strange look on his face, as if he were anticipating some secret delight.

"Gotta get there before Sekhmet," Boone said, reading Derek's mind. "Of course, I wouldn't mind if we did run into her."

At least Derek had Boone's motivation clear. Now if he could only get him to learn discretion.

"Who's Sekhmet?" came Astrid's voice from the kitchen.

≈

The clouds surged overhead, blackened and tinged with violet. Winds picked up speed, lifting trash and spinning it about the feet of spectators. A woman on the tennis court caught her service toss mid-air and scowled. She waited until there was a lull in the breeze and then set up her serve again. This time, she walloped the ball with a resounding thwack. Derek felt his stomach sink as the yellow-green projectile rocketed right past Kyra.

"Ace!" yelled some beefy kid in the crowd.

Derek had decided to take in more of Kyra's activities and picked this doubles match. She was delighted to have him there, but Kyra's doubles team was already one set behind. Now, they were tied 3-3 for the match and this game wasn't going well at all. That Amazon woman never lost her service game and seemed to have borrowed her arm from a Wimbledon star. Kyra, at five-foot-one-inch and one hundred pounds, was hardly a match for this bruiser of an opponent. Yet Kyra was fast and had amazing reactions. Her form was well-schooled, and what she lacked in power, she made up for in sheer deviousness: sneaky volleys in corners, drop shots, and killer returns aimed straight at the opponent's feet. Derek liked the subtle nastiness of it all.

Still, in this match, Kyra's tricks didn't seem to fool anyone. Kyra's partner, a long black woman who reminded Derek of Venus Williams, had a reach that would humble a basketball player. Yet this time she misjudged the bounce of the Amazon's next serve and hit the ball into the net.

"Kick serve. Awesome!" the kid yelled. Derek imagined what the boy would look like with his Popsicle shoved up his nose.

The clouds blew off and the sun returned. The players were blinded for a moment and Kyra's team scored a point. It had been like this all day. The clouds would part and then return. Rain was in the air, pressing on flesh, causing birds to scatter for shelter every half hour or so. Yet the sun managed to pull through. Derek felt the air pressure sinking lower; he could feel it in his temples, as if a monster headache were coming on.

He'd been trying to talk to Kyra about his trip west. All day he pulled back at the last moment, nattering on about New Mexico in general, or about Indian artwork, never coming to the point at all. Kyra just kept staring at him, as if willing him to make some sense. Finally, she announced she had a tennis league match to play. And Derek, true to his need to see more of her life, said he'd come and watch.

Now this. Kyra's team was losing. She'd be in a fine mood to hear that he was going off to Santa Fe without her. And if she heard about Sekhmet . . . .

Thwack! Another ace and Kyra's team was down, 3-4.

Derek's pocket buzzed. It took him a second to realize it was his cellular phone set to "vibrate" mode. He picked it up and spoke into the tiny mouthpiece.

"Yeah."

"It's me." It was George, on his cell, which he rarely used. He was much more likely to send e-mail or text.

"What's up?"

In the next row of bleachers, a large man with a bushy mustache was staring at him as if Derek were a cockroach. Derek knew better than to shout into cell phones when in public places, but this guy seemed to feel that any conversation was an intrusion of his personal space. Derek made his way out of the bleachers. "Double fault!" the kid screamed. Kyra was serving, and Derek wanted to wring the little monster's neck.

"Listen, I got something from Roger," George's voice continued, just audible. "I think I might have an idea what this is all about."

"Uh-huh." Kyra sent a decent serve into enemy territory, only to have it smashed back into an inaccessible corner. Love-thirty.

"Not on the phone. You need to look at it." George hung up with no further explanation, but Derek knew what was next: that stupid little park. He immediately called George back. Kyra served again.

"I can't," Derek said. Lob return right on the baseline. It bounced so high that Kyra couldn't reach it. Love-forty.

"Why not?"

"Kyra is . . . . "

"Listen, she can wait. This can't."

Kyra needed him and he realized for the first time that she was more important to him than a line of code. Just this once he had to shut George down.

Derek stood with his cell phone to his ear, staring at the atrocity that was taking place on the tennis court. Kyra had slammed a lightning serve wide to the edge of the service box. But the tall woman blew a perfect return right down the middle, surprising Kyra's partner, who had been primed for a blistering cross-court return. Game. This was known as a break game, because the server's game was "broken." Indeed, Kyra did look fractured. She blew air upward, fanning her damp bangs. She stomped over to the net and she handed over the balls to her opponents. One of them was over six feet tall. The other had linebacker shoulders.

"No," Derek blurted out, his heart reaching out to Kyra.

"What?"

"I'll deal with Roger myself."

This time it was Derek who hung up. He gazed at an open field beside him, not watching now as the serves whisked by. He heard the whack of balls swatted back and forth. He heard the kid scream "Match point!" He looked to the sky. Thunderheads had lumbered in from the west. Derek raised his eyes to catch the first sizzle of lightning. A drop settled on his cheek and then his entire face was bathed in a cascade. The pavement began to steam. Rain out.

He ran down and gathered Kyra in a hug.

"Ick! I'm all sweaty," she said. But she smiled in spite of herself. It was obvious she appreciated Derek's attention.

≈

"You have to be kidding, right?"

Kyra was demolishing a curry stew that Ravi had placed in front of her, while keeping a steady eye on Derek. Derek shook his head and answered.

"No, honestly. That's what the numbers spell out."

Kyra pulled a shrimp from her stew and bit off all but the end of the tail. She scowled. "Numbers from the dimensions of the Great Pyramid," she said, her voice betraying a smirk.

"Not just the dimensions, not just from the pyramid, but specific, verifiable, mathematical data. Much of it translatable to modern acoustical theory."

"Pyramid power? Like in the 1970s?"

"No, Kyra. Not at all. It's related to hermeticism, to sacred geometry."

Kyra shook her head and covered her eyes. Derek wanted to say that he was just kidding, that the code didn't say what it did. But he wanted her to know the truth about his trip to New Mexico. He wanted to explain the whole story. He had gotten this far into it and he couldn't get out.

Ravi approached the table to pour more chai as Derek stumbled for an explanation. Without waiting for an invitation, the young cook put down his steaming pot and cocked his head.

"Sacred geometry? You mean the Pythagorean discipline?"

Derek nodded his head, grateful for the interruption. Kyra looked up at Ravi, her expression at once devoid of sarcasm. She blinked and put down her fork.

"I had many years of study in this. It's an ancient science that most people do not take seriously," Ravi said.

"What is it?" Kyra said. She, who had been famished after her near-defeat, seemed to forget about her stew.

Ravi pulled up a chair, since there was no one else in the restaurant, and no diners were vying for his attention. He began to draw geometric figures on Derek's paper placemat. He explained the sacred qualities of numbers, the values of geometric forms, the puzzle of how to "square the circle"—incorporating *pi* into a two-dimensional figure.

"And the Egyptians figured that out. About 2,400 BC," Ravi said, off hand, ready to describe another figure.

"The Egyptians?" Kyra asked, looking fixedly at Derek.

"Oh, of course," Ravi said, drawing a giant pyramid on top of a circle. "The Great Pyramid of Cheops, or Khufu as he is more properly called. Divide the length of the perimeter of the base by twice the height and you get 3.144, too close to 3.142, *pi,* for a coincidence. If you draw a circle on the ground, using the pyramid's height as the radius, you would have the same perimeter as the square base. In other words, squaring the circle."

Kyra stared. Derek had been through this and about five hundred pyramid facts over the last month and a half—ever since Sekhmet dropped off that little packet on his Beetle. The Great Pyramid was so perfectly oriented to the four directions that even Greenwich Observatory in England is less properly aligned.

Its numbers contained *phi,* or the Golden Section, an esoteric but much sought-after number that indicated harmony in design.

"So what do all those numbers mean?" Kyra asked.

"When a structure is filled with sacred numbers it is alive and functioning," Ravi said. Kyra did not respond, but her green eyes widened.

"These are the numbers of the Hermetica, a sacred study that came down to us from the Egyptians," Ravi said. Even Derek was under his spell now. Who knew that the Indian mystic had studied so much, from cultures not his own?

"And so you see," Derek said, leaning into the table, "the magical numbers of hermeticism—handed down to us as alchemy, white magic and the rites of the Masons—were those of the Egyptian god Thoth. And Thoth's numbers were rumored hidden long before Egypt's first dynasty began."

Kyra tossed her napkin on the table and shrugged her shoulders. Derek moved back from the table. *Tough customer.*

"So what?" she said, pushing her hair away from the sides of her face. "Who cares about some long-lost numbers?"

"What if," Derek said, determined to win this battle. "What if someone fed those sacred numbers into a computer and discovered a formula. Not a magic formula, but a science-based technique, provable, something sought after by engineers the world over."

"A formula for what? I can't stand this anymore!" Kyra's face was flushing red.

Ravi nodded as if he were deep in meditation. He rocked slightly in his chair.

"The most ancient of secrets, the moving of mountains," Ravi said with a sweet smile.

"Using sound waves to move physical matter," Derek said, grabbing Kyra's hand. He looked into her eyes, trying to will away the disbelief. "As Ravi says, the power, literally, to move mountains."

≈

They walked up to Derek's door and, from the expression on her face, Derek realized that she was annoyed.

Derek unlocked the door and let Kyra sweep like a silent breeze through the portal. He cleared off a space on the couch and went into the kitchen. He came back with a beer left over from Boone's last visit. He placed it before her and took a long breath.

"It's not a bunch of roses, but I guess it will have to do."

Kyra crossed her legs and set her mouth, looking as if she would refuse. She pressed her lips together, tighter and tighter, scratched her shoulder, looked up at Derek—and burst out laughing.

"What?"

"For God's sake, Derek, you have no sense whatsoever," Kyra said, grabbing the beer and staring at it as if it fell out of the sky. "Thanks for the ancient history roundup, Derek, really. It was interesting. You're onto some really big game."

"But?"

"But why do you have to leave me at home on your trip to Santa Fe?"

"That's why you're pissed?"

"That's why. You haven't figured that out? I'm angry because I want to go with you." She tossed the unopened beer on the couch. "Bucky laid me off. I want to share some time with you. This is a perfect opportunity for you and me to spend time alone. So, why can't I go with you?"

"Because Boone is coming with me."

Kyra groaned and sank back into the cushions. After a few weeks of dealing with the big guy from Indiana, Kyra was nearly as exasperated as Astrid.

"A drive to New Mexico with Boone would just about do me in, but I'm willing to accept it to be with you," Kyra said. "I want to help and help I shall."

"But,Roger might message me and . . . " *Oh God, Roger. And that call from George.* "Hang on a minute."

Derek raced into his office and logged onto his computer. Sure enough, a message from Roger glowed onscreen.

To: D.Nils@bitjockey.com
From: roger@uchicago.edu
Subject: Re: George

They found him and the team. You better move.

Roger

Derek felt his stomach sizzle as if he'd swallowed live electric wires. He was about to yell for Kyra when he felt her leaning behind him over his chair. He reached over and touched her hand. Warm, alive, steady. She was there to assist him. He picked up his phone and pushed the listing for George.

"George?"

"Oh, hi." George's voice sounded distant, distracted.

"George, I'm sorry. I only got to the message now. Really, I'm sorry. I messed up . . . . "

"Oh, that's okay, my friend." George sounded odd. Drunk maybe. Or preoccupied. And what was the "my friend" bit? Derek's forehead began to sizzle.

"George?" Muffled noise filled the line.

"He's a little busy right now." The new voice was soft, conspiratorial, oddly familiar. Derek scrambled to reconstruct where he had heard it. The baseball game? A bar? With Boone?

"Ra!"

"We are so glad that you had time to read all that material from our goddess, Derek. But you didn't tell your partner much at all, did you?"

"No. I didn't. He doesn't know."

"But you do." The voice was snarling like a wildcat discovered in its lair. Derek imagined that bald head shining in the lamplight. "You haven't kept your end of the bargain, you realize. We want to know where you're going tomorrow. George doesn't seem to know."

"Only I know," Derek said. He felt as if he were leaping into a chasm. "Try and find me."

Derek hung up and looked at Kyra. He felt like a child who has just been caught breaking a picture window. He stared into Kyra's face, hoping for understanding. He tried to talk but could only let out a weak cough.

"We better get going fast," Kyra guessed, hugging him with empowering strength. So much life in such a little body. Derek drank it in, hoping he could live on this vigor in the days to come. He bolted up from his chair.

In preparation for his trip, he had offloaded important data onto the cloud and two removable disk drives. Then he had wiped his hard disk virtually clean. With the data removed, all Ra and his bullyboys would find would be e-mail from his mother. For the road, all Derek needed were the printouts, the atlas, and a few clothes. Kyra ran out of the office and came back with a duffel bag packed with jeans, t-shirts, underwear.

"We'll buy toothbrushes on the road, and I'll buy some clothes at any Target we pass by," she said. "Now we can hop a cab and catch up with Boone."

Derek nodded. She was already halfway out the back door, and Foo rode on her shoulders.

"Oh shit, who's going to take care of Foo?" he asked. "And these disk drives?"

"We are going to make a quick stop at Trevor's apartment. He owes me favors." She grabbed the bag of cat food, kissed him and turned to bolt down the stairs, Foo trailing after her.

"I still have a few things to lock down. I'll meet you at Trevor's place," Derek called after her. Then, for this run out west, what vehicle were they going to use?

CHAPTER THIRTEEN

Charlie was almost there. He trudged up the hill, feeling his thigh muscles flex and release. With every step, he felt himself getting stronger, more focused, more rooted to the earth. He closed his eyes and felt the warm tingle in his quadriceps. He knew he could climb all day and not tire. He looked ahead again and saw the cabin just coming into sight.

Elk Horn was right. The lights had started up again. Not like before, not a steady barrage of blinking and whirring. This time there were just seconds of glittering activity, but it was enough to awaken interest in the cabin again. Kids were coming up here, trying to get inside the shanty, hanging out and drinking beer. There was trash along the hillside, and Charlie stooped to pick up burger wrappers and empty pop cans. It wasn't like the Navajo nation to litter.

Charlie kicked aside a beer can and pursed his lips. He recognized a brand of beer that had appeared on the market after he stopped drinking. Antelope Beer, "microbrewed" in Santa Fe. It was all the rage with the hipsters and transplanted New Yorkers who migrated to the New Mexican capital city. Charlie never got to find out what all the fuss was about. But he knew that a taste of some damn, trendy beer wasn't worth it. Not after five years of blessed sanity.

He took a deep breath of the mountain air. It was dry, much drier than usual for early summer, but not arid enough for a forest fire. Charlie could smell the tiny hint of dampness clinging to the piñon tree needles, and he could pick up a trace of moisture in the atmosphere. Possibly, it would rain. Charlie had become adept at the Indian art of sensing climatic changes with his nose. And since he'd stopped drinking, he was amazed at how acute his senses had become. Rain was coming in from the east. He kicked the Antelope can again before putting it in his garbage bag. Something else was coming from the east too. It had nothing to do with weather. That was the ominous sensation that started when he got free of the booze—premonitions. And the damn sixth sense was always right. Charlie shook off his thoughts and moved ahead.

After Charlie and Elk Horn had learned to defeat the electronic locking system on the shack, they'd put a simpler combination lock on the door. This lock looked untouched.

A while earlier, Charlie and Elk Horn had brought a computer technician to look inside the shack. What the technician found was not overwhelming. There were basic white-box computers, linked to a modem. There were many gigabytes of data on the hard drives, but coding was too complex for decryption. Probably just a bunch of stolen credit-card numbers, the expert decided. Better to just leave it alone. Otherwise, the feds will be on top of you.

The computer guy scratched his wiry red hair and said the machines could keep running in their current set up for another few years or so without rebooting. He gave Charlie and Elk Horn some maintenance tips, collected his fee, and drove off. Charlie and Elk Horn decided to keep tending the shack, waiting for the day when the rightful owner came back to retrieve the data.

Charlie was convinced the mystery hacker was in jail. Elk Horn figured the guy was waiting until the world was ready for whatever secrets the computers held. The two were content to check on the machines from time to time, heading up the hill after a day of painting houses or fixing plumbing in reservation shanties. The hike never took more than ten minutes.

But now the lights blinked again. The gods were awake and the guardians called back to their duties. Charlie was now tending the cabin night and day, watching for vandals and thieves. Elk Horn sometimes camped outside, waiting for some kind of signal.

Charlie opened the front door and watched the main computer up close. It didn't look any different than it had every day of the five years he had been monitoring it. Once in a great while, the hard drive made a whirring noise, but mostly the box just sat there, a small light glowing in its base. He pulled a rag out of his pocket and wiped dust off the box. Then he produced a compressed-air canister and began to blast dust away from the controls and keyboard, just as the computer technician had instructed him.

His son, Derek, had owned one of these cans. Back when he was just learning about bytes and Unix. Charlie felt a small throb in his temple. He had heard that his son was now a computer scientist, with a master's degree from the University of Illinois. He hadn't attended the graduation. Why embarrass the kid any more than he already had? Someday he'd send a card, explaining how happy he was that Derek had made something of his life. Someday, when he was ready to face the rejection he was sure to get from his only child.

Charlie put the air canister down and clenched his jaw. Running away got him sober all right, but it still didn't settle accounts. Lots of work awaited him. Derek, Astrid, his old boss, a couple landlords he left high and dry, even old Boone. They all deserved amends. At least that's what Elk Horn had told him. You can't be free of the past until you face it. Charlie felt a shiver.

As he turned to go out the door, a name flashed through his mind. "Roger." He shrugged his shoulders. *Premonitions again.* He began to pull the door shut. Out of the corner of his eye, he thought he saw the modem lights blink. He gazed at the machine through the open crack, but nothing looked any different. He closed the door and locked up.

Roger. He didn't know anyone named Roger. But for some reason he felt he was supposed to.

≈

"Sometimes you're the windshield, sometimes you're the bug . . . ."

Boone slapped his hand on the steering wheel, adding percussion to the driving music.

"Sometimes it all comes together, baby; sometimes you're just a fool in love . . . ."

Derek let out a groan low in his chest and pushed his sunglasses back up to the bridge of his nose. They weren't out of Missouri yet and the damn country music was about to send Derek out of his mind. He watched the landscape roll by. Farmland had changed to green hills, which lolled about as far as he could see, draped with lush velvet upholstery. In mid-July, the greenery seemed out of place, but rainfall had been plentiful in the Midwest this year, blanketing the farm states with soggy heat. Out past Oklahoma, he knew the scene would change.

They hadn't talked much when he, Boone, and Kyra blew out of Chicago the night before. They had opted for Boone's pickup truck over Derek's Beetle. Boone's truck had two front seats and a rear bench seat—perfect for a person who wasn't driving to get some sleep. They put together a schedule of who'd drive, who'd navigate, and who'd sleep. They piled some sleeping bags, backpacks, and food in the back, and Kyra had her iPhone with earphones for music in her purse, but was warned not to use the phone for any calls. Too easy to trace their location. With a little adjustment, they were ready to leave. Boone had been planning for the trip and didn't lift an eyebrow over the sudden departure. He merely slapped Astrid on the back, thanked her for her hospitality, and hopped into the truck. Derek gave his mother a kiss and told her he'd find a way to call. Cell phones were too risky. He also slipped her Trevor's phone number, just in case. "A friend," he murmured as Astrid stared at the paper, nodding. She got the idea. Boone gunned the engine and they hauled out of town, Astrid leaning in the house doorway, waving like a small child.

"You know how true that is, don't ya?" Boone asked now, his eyes on the road, a huge grin on his sunburned face.

"Huh?" Derek scratched his hair, which was beginning to feel gritty. He wondered when his next shower might be.

"You know, about being the windshield or being the bug."

"Yeah. That's profound."

"You don't get country music, do you, boy?"

"Hate it."

Boone reached over and twisted the radio dial to off. Derek looked over to see if Boone was offended, but the big guy still had that slaphappy grin on his face.

"Well, it's no more profound than that shit you listen to."

"What? Mozart?"

Boone stopped smiling for a second and scrunched his lips into his quizzical expression. Before Boone had a chance to start expounding on modern music, Derek had caught him cold. Kyra let out a piercing laugh.

"Listen, Boone. When you did that big once-over of my apartment, you forgot to check out the music rack. Classical. I usually listen to classical music and Sinatra. Always have."

"Man, you sure didn't get that from Charlie."

"I'd like to think I got nothin' from dear old Dad."

Derek reached over and flipped on the radio again. He inched the dial back and forth, looking for another station. Static, farm reports, oldies, preachers spouting fire-and-brimstone sermons. Then, thudding rap rhythms pulsed from a St. Louis station. It would have to do.

Boone scowled, but whether it was in reference to the rap or the conversation, Derek couldn't tell. They fell silent for several miles, the urban music pounding softly in the background, Derek studying the map and its vast assortment of tiny towns with quaint names. Somewhere around Rolla, Boone snapped the radio off. Kyra, in the back, was tuned into her iPhone.

"We gotta talk about Charlie," he said.

"Why in the hell should we?"

"Because, my cousin, your mother has spent the last ten years of her life hating him. And she's poisoning you too. Charlie wasn't some kind of monster, Derek."

"Just another drunken bum."

Kyra popped up to listen to the conversation, but Derek shook his head. She took the hint and relaxed back in her sleeping bag.

"There but for the grace of God go I," Boone said and sucked his lower lip.

Derek didn't know what was worse, trapped in a pickup cab listening to hick music or lured into a discussion about his derelict father with a well-meaning relative. Hell, last year he couldn't even bring himself to tell that therapist he tried about Charlie. Better off to kill it, bury it, forget it. He gazed out the window. The green fields rolled head over heels, never coming to a stop. Rolling in Rolla, Missouri. Never having to explain himself to George, Kyra, or his mother. Never having to face up to anyone.

"You don't know what happened in the end, do you?" Boone asked, reaching into a bag of chips he'd opened back in Bloomington, Illinois. Derek shut his eyes. He couldn't stop this. Why even try? "They didn't tell you anything, I know. You were in college and they figured, what the hell?"

What the hell, indeed. Dad's leaving. Not saying goodbye. At least the place wouldn't reek of stale beer anymore.

"Do you know how hard it was for him to do that?"

Do you know how hard it was for him to hold a steady job? How hard he tried not to move off the couch? How hard he tried to shut everyone out? How hard he tried to leave his humanity behind?

"Derek, he did the AA meetings. He went to the hospital for rehab. He even took those damn pills that make you sick if you drink."

Antabuse. Big help that was. Dad puking his guts out because he had to drink anyway. Had to. Monkey was on his back and was never going away.

"He did the only thing he could. He told me about it. Called me up, Derek, and said he couldn't put you and your mom through the humiliation anymore. Said he was going out to the most desolate land he could find and just go cold turkey. He was desperate not to drink again, Derek. I've never heard a guy sound so scared." Derek continued to stare out the window. "He did it to spare you, kid."

"Good thing he did," Derek said, turning to look at Boone. He felt his eyes hot, itchy, angry. "He spared me having to look at his drunken ass one more day of my life." Boone crunched on a chip. Derek pointed at an exit sign. "Pull off here and I'll start driving. You could use some sleep."

≈

Outside Oklahoma City the rain fell. It sloshed on the pavement as if tossed from giant barrels in the sky. Cascades poured down, turning the highway into liquid glass. Then, as quickly as the rain came, it ceased.

Derek gripped the steering wheel with the force of sheer adrenaline. Kyra sat next to him as navigator, maps spread in her hands. Dawn was breaking behind them—he could see the pink glow in his rearview mirror—and he was barely able to focus. But the terror of trying to navigate through the sudden flood kept him awake and edgy.

Ahead was a truck stop, surrounded by big rigs. It looked like a mother sow, surrounded by bloated offspring, huge Peterbilt trucks with stinking loads of manure. The lonely building of steel and glass squatted in the midst of open plains and the empty stripes of highways and country roads. In a land as overpopulated as the United States, it was hard to imagine anywhere as desolate and forgotten as this spot, but here it was, an insignificant freckle on the wide face of the planet.

Derek spotted a pay phone on the side of the building. A pay phone in Nowhere, OK. What a find. He pulled off the highway and parked next to the telephone, hooded by a steel awning. He glanced over at Boone who was deep asleep in the back seat, burrowed into the pillow propped in the gap between the seat back and the headrest. He told Kyra he'd be right back and jumped out the cab door and fished in his pocket for coins. He dialed, his fingers steady and sure. When Trevor answered, the operator asked for $1.65 and Derek dumped in the silver. *How primitive is this?*

"Where are you?" Trevor sounded half asleep. and Derek, with an internal growl, remembered it was six in the morning and they were still on Central Time.

"I'm in Oklahoma."

"That was fast."

"Well, we didn't stop at the Holiday Inn or anything."

His friend was silent. Derek stared at the eastern clouds, watching the corals burn more brightly, turning to a robust orange.

"You okay?" Trevor said, speaking with uncharacteristic slowness.

"Fine. More worried about you. Do you know what they did to George?" Derek kicked the gravel under the phone. It looked blue in the thin light. "They haven't come looking for you, have they?"

Trevor said no, that he hadn't heard from any strange men with odd hairdos or Egyptian names. George was well, but shaken, he said. No bruises, just a broken sense of self-confidence. Foo was eating and looking happy, so Derek was not to worry. He didn't mention the flex drives. Smart guy.

Derek said they had a long way to go. He could only call on pay phones because anything else was traceable. But he would check in as often as he could. He was about to hang up when a scraggly, skinny guy walked out of the diner, reeking of whiskey and cigarette smoke. He had a lope like Charlie's and Derek felt himself gulp. At that moment, the tiny electrical wire tying him to Trevor became a lifeline, a tender, fragile conduit from one human being to another. He couldn't let go.

"Trevor. I haven't told you it all."

"All?"

"There aren't just the guys with Egyptian names. We are also running from Sekhmet."

"You mentioned her that night at Ravi's. Is that the woman who phoned your mom?"

"My *mother?*" Derek's voice rose too high. Boone made a mumbling noise in the truck. Kyra, who could hear through the open window, looked up in alarm.

"Well, we've been talking, your mother and I. I mean, you did give her my number."

Derek felt an uneasy pressure in his head. Yes, he was to blame. Of course, they were trading information about him. Who could blame them? He was behaving strangely; even he could see that.

"Uh-huh," he croaked.

"She phoned me late last night and said she'd gotten a curious call from some woman who was looking for you. Your mother didn't tell her anything and I said she did the right thing."

"Trevor," Derek said as he felt an artery pounding in his neck, just below the jaw line. He slapped a hand to it and pressed hard. "Watch out for my mother, will you?"

"Sure thing."

"If you get any calls like that yourself, please let George know. And maybe the cops if it gets bad enough."

"Of course. Take it easy, pal. Everything looks fine here."

≈

Back in the truck, Boone sat with his face red and puffy and his hand in the sack of potato chips. Breakfast in the wilds of Oklahoma.

"Got any coffee?" Boone said, crumbs on his lower lip. "Pump me full of caffeine and I'll drive."

"But it's Kyra's turn."

"No, I'll drive and you can sleep."

Derek hustled back over to the diner, bought two black coffees (he wouldn't be needing one) and jumped back into the cab. Too bad there were no double shots of espresso available in this hick strip. Kyra liked fine coffee. Boone was playing with the radio and tuned in the strains of Frank Sinatra. "All of You" boomed over the box.

"That okay?"

"Yeah. Maybe we finally agree on something," Derek said with a half smile. Kyra reached for the coffee and groaned. Guess she was not crazy about Ol' Blue Eyes. Boone grabbed the maps and set a course in his mind, screwing one eye almost closed as he pondered. Derek repositioned the pillow. As the truck moved forward, Boone sang softly. When he sang something half-decent, Boone's voice wasn't so bad. Sort of drippy and sentimental, but he carried a tune well.

" 'Cause I love all of you," he crooned.

Derek felt himself bouncing to the rumble of the engine and the strains of Frank and the Nelson Riddle Orchestra. Oklahoma, farewell.

≈

Somewhere near Amarillo, Texas, Derek woke up.

"Out here they've got a bunch of Cadillacs all sticking up out of the dirt, kind of like Stonehenge," Boone said.

"Stonehenge," Derek said with his eyes still closed. He'd been awake for about ten minutes and knew they were in Texas, but he didn't feel like looking.

"Yeah, honest to goodness. A bunch of Caddies with tailfins, all sticking up out of the ground. I think they call it 'Cadillac Ranch' or something like that."

Derek opened an eye and saw a flat field in the middle of nothing at all. It looked like more Oklahoma. "So where is it?"

"I heard about that from someone at home," Kyra said. "It's supposed to be a work of art. I want a look at it."

"They moved it down the road a bit. We'll come to it. I'll let you know," Boone said. "You'll have to look hard. It's the only nifty thing about this stretch of road. Boring as hell out here."

Derek couldn't argue. He wondered about the romance of old Route 66, which had cut through this same swath of rural emptiness. What kind of kicks were people getting from this lonely road? Derek shrugged off sleep and poked at the potato chip bag, now empty.

"Donuts in the back," Boone said, gesturing at the rear of the cab. Derek reached in the pink-and-white box and fished out a greasy éclair. Kyra squealed, "That's mine!" He moved onto another, simpler donut. He hated donuts, hated the oiliness in his mouth and detested the resulting lump in his stomach. But it would have to do.

"There it is," Boone yelped. He slowed the truck down and Derek leaned forward to see ten rusted hulks of automobiles planted nearly on end, half buried in the dry Amarillo dirt. From this stretch of the highway, where Route 66 joined the Interstate for a few miles, the Cadillacs looked more like leftovers from a Texas twister than a work of art.

"It is sort of like an ancient site, isn't it?" Derek said, gazing at megaliths of rusted steel.

"It's cool," Kyra said. "I want to stop and get a look at it."

Derek shook his head. "We're making good time but we really can't stop out here in the wilderness."

In defeat, Kyra shrugged her shoulders.

The Cadillacs were covered with graffiti, yet still had a dash of glamour about them. Derek thought of the days when taking a pink Cadillac convertible down Route 66 was the great escape, the icon of American freedom in the mid-twentieth century.

Then it was gone. They could have poked around the sculpture a bit longer, taking the pot-holed dirt road that led to the edge of the site. But there was no time for that, not as long as Sekhmet and company were on their trail. Boone picked up speed again and the scenery reverted to flat nothingness. He heard some thumping in his ears as if the air pressure in the cab were unbalanced. Fully awake now, Derek recalled why he felt so edgy.

"Sekhmet called Astrid," Derek said, licking chocolate frosting off his fingers. By now, Kyra had been totally filled in on Sekhmet and her devious ways.

Boone snorted like a caged bull. Derek shifted in his seat, waiting for Boone to say something. When the silence dragged on too long, Derek let out a low whistle.

"I guess you want to know how everyone got dragged into this mess," Derek said, squinting at a sign in the distance. Up ahead there looked like a good place to gas up the truck and grab a few burgers.

"You might say that," Boone said, leaning forward and peering at the same sign. "You just might say I'm mighty curious about that data—hot stuff important enough to drag in a whirly-bird surveillance team."

Derek looked over at Boone, not understanding. Boone jerked a thumb skyward in reply. Derek screwed his neck to the side to peer out the window—not easy from the back seat. Overhead a helicopter was keeping pace with the truck.

"Jesus, Boone! How long has that been on our tail?"

"Since the Texas border. He leaves for a while, then catches up with us. He just came back." Boone pulled out a pair of binoculars from under his seat. "Now that you're up, tell me if you can make out any insignia or anything. Kyra has had the binoculars but she can't make anything out."

Derek took the binoculars from Boone and wondered how he was supposed to know what the markings would look like—"US Spycopter"? He raised the binocular without a word, opened the window, stuck his head outside, and aimed the specs at the sky. He half expected to see the Ra-egypt.com logo on the aircraft's body, but nothing so spectacular was up there. The helicopter was yellow and black, sort of like a giant bumblebee. It resembled the traffic choppers TV news stations use at rush hour. But there were no station call letters on the side. No logos. Just two people sitting in the bubble-domed cockpit, looking back at him.

Derek pulled his head back into the cab.

"Well, now they saw me looking at them," Derek, yelled over the choppy racket. "That was a brilliant move."

"What do you see?" Boone was starting to sound snappish for the first time since this road show began. "Any military logos?" Derek shook his head. "Any sign that it might be a rented, local aircraft?" Derek peered through the glasses again.

"No," Derek yelled, frowning. "There's nothing on it at all but a few numbers near the tail."

"Private craft," Boone said, sucking in his lower lip. Derek pulled his head inside and Kyra shut the window. At least he could hear again. Funny that racket didn't wake him a long time ago. He must really have been out.

An exit appeared on the right and Boone swerved off the highway. He drove with his body squared behind the wheel like a linebacker ready to tackle.

"You, the girl, and I are going to get a little chow," Boone said with a bit of menace in his voice. "And you, computer nerd, are going to tell me just what the hell is going on."

≈

Derek was sure that places like Long Tex's Steak House didn't exist anymore. But here it was, a giant diner with pristine chrome and linoleum booths, vinyl-covered bench seats, plastic-coated menus, honey dispensers shaped like bears, and even little tabletop jukeboxes.

"Does this work?" Derek asked the waitress, fanning his hand up and down the front of the jukebox. The songs looked current. No golden oldies, unless you counted Tony Bennett standards—which he adored.

"Sure," the waitress said, staring over her notepad. "Gotta use tokens now, though. Quarter a play went out with Ronald Reagan."

Derek didn't know if she was making a joke or not, but couldn't stifle a silly laugh. These things looked as if they dated back to Eisenhower, not Reagan.

"How much are the tokens?" he asked.

"Forty cents a play, three for a dollar."

"Give me one. I have to try this."

The waitress slapped a quarter-sized plug on the green marbled tabletop. She jotted down their orders of burgers, fries, and cokes, repeatedly pushing an errant strand of straw-like hair behind her ear. Her nametag said "Ashley." When she slunk away, Boone stretched out on his bench seat, reaching both arms along the padded backrest.

"So let me tell you something else about the Cadillac Ranch," he said, picking up the conversation they had dropped twenty minutes ago. "I heard some interview with the guy who owns the place. He's a little eccentric, you know. Said he had them Cadillacs set into the ground at the exact angle of the Great Pyramid." Derek blinked. "That ring any bells, boy?"

Before Derek could answer, Ashley returned, slamming down cokes in plastic glasses.

Derek took his token and selected the Beach Boys from the list. Boone seemed soothed by that. But Ashley hadn't left.

"Yeah, I heard that about the Great Pyramid," the waitress said, fishing straws out of her lace-trimmed apron. She didn't seem aware that she was intruding on a private conversation. "The owner said he wants to send a signal to other civilizations. You know, if the cars are set at the angle of the Great Pyramid, then they weren't just dumped into the ground accidentally. Sign of an intelligent civilization." She shrugged her shoulders.

"What civilization? Who would be finding it?" Derek asked.

"I don't know. Aliens?" She lifted her brows and shuffled off.

"Aliens?" Derek asked Boone and Kyra. She giggled.

Boone sighed, leaning forward and jabbing a finger on the tabletop. The table jiggled, rustling the drinks, clinking the ice so the cokes sounded like muffled maracas.

"The point, buddy boy, is this: Why is everyone so damn interested in the Great Pyramid? Sekhmet and her crazy pals. Notes on papyrus. You babbling about secret numbers of the ancients? What the hell have you found out?"

Derek took a long slug of his coke and waited for the bubbly sensation to stop teasing the inside of his nose.

"I guess I've made a lot of mistakes," Derek said, trying to look away from Boone's fierce gaze. "I was trying to keep you guys protected . . . "

"Well, that worked real well, Derek, real well. They burst into your pal George's house and threatened him. They're calling your mother. And now a damn helicopter is following my truck." Derek nodded, feeling as if he were a toddler. But Boone wasn't done. He jabbed at the table, hard this time, so that the salt and pepper shakers rattled in time with the now furiously agitated ice cubes. Kyra covered her mouth in shock.

"It's not just this danger that you've attracted," Boone continued. "It's about you not being there, Derek. You . . . " The finger pounded and the table trembled. "You don't share. No one knows you or has any idea of what's going on in that over-stuffed brain of yours. You've got people all around you who love you, care for you—like that cute girlie of yours—and you don't give anything to anyone." Kyra blushed.

Boone eased back into the bench seat. Derek realized that he hadn't been breathing. Ashley hovered over them with their hamburger specials.

"Gotta get that table fixed," she said with a wink.

Derek felt his nerves strangling every little artery, vein, and capillary in his body. But he couldn't argue with a thing Boone said. It was his own damn fault that everyone he cared for was now vulnerable. He'd been keeping everything secret from George because he was too frightened of ridicule. Keeping Sekhmet secret from Kyra. Leading Boone on a merry chase cross-country without explaining what they were hiding.

What the hell was the matter with him? He hardly knew why he did it, why he sealed himself in his apartment, living online, avoiding the sunshine, expressing himself only to machines. Kyra was his only contact with the world of his emotions. He had to keep that line open.

Derek picked up a french fry and felt Boone's eyes on him. He didn't look up. He wondered if his problem was all because machines can't mangle your heart. They'll tear the hell out of your software or shred your data, but they'll never pick up and walk out of your life.

"Okay, Boone," Derek said. "What do you want to start with?"

Boone nodded. "After we eat, let's figure out how to dodge the 'copter out there." He chewed thoughtfully on his burger. "Then you can start with the Great Pyramid and work downward, so to speak."

He slapped the table and roared at his own joke. Ashley dropped the check on the table, touching Derek's forearm for a second before pulling her hand back. Kyra looked at her with fire in her eyes. Derek looked up into Ashley's smiling visage and felt his face burn. When had he given her any encouragement? Was she just sorry for him because Boone chewed him out?

Life was full of crazy little problems like this. If Ashley were a computer, he'd shut down the system and deal with it in the morning. No feelings of inadequacy. No second cousins hooting with laughter as you squirm in your seat. No angry girlfriend pushing you out of your bench seat. No need to toss out a five-dollar tip in order to cover your hasty exit out to the car.

CHAPTER FOURTEEN

Kyra took over driving and Derek started talking.

The Great Pyramid held Boone's attention better than a wrestling match on cable television. No wonder, for the massive structure on Egypt's Giza plain has fascinated mankind for four and a half thousand years.

"Boone, Egyptology is in a real flux right now," Derek said. "Interest is at a fever pitch with new theories and alternative thinkers. But the field of Egyptology is marked with traditionalism and resistance to change."

"You know I've heard all this before," Kyra said with a sigh.

"Well, this is for Boone's sake, so bear with me," Derek said.

For many years, Derek said, alternative Egyptologists and renegade scholars had been arguing that the Great Pyramid, estimated to have been built in 2,400 BC by Pharaoh Khufu, was far more than a simple tomb. In fact, many denied it was ever a tomb at all. No one ever found artifacts in the pyramid. Traditionalists attributed the bare walls to tomb raiders, but couldn't explain how robbers wiggled past expertly fitted granite plugs and slipped through a hidden entrance. No one could explain why no engravings of any kind had ever been found in the pyramid. Odd, when you consider this was supposed to have been a massive testament to one man's colossal ego. Even the only known markings that link the pyramid to Khufu—quarry marks found high up in "relieving chambers," or stacks of horizontal blocks, over in the so-called King's Chamber—were riddled with grammatical errors and anachronistic syntax. Some consider the quarry marks forgeries made by an egotistical explorer. Others accept them, but see them as no proof the pyramid was Khufu's tomb, just Khufu's renovation project.

"Okay," Boone said, nodding. "I could see that." Derek continued with his monologue.

There are many theories as to what the Egyptians intended for their pyramids: temples, initiation sites for mystery schools, keepers of records, power plants, outposts for aliens. Some of the so-called "pyramidiots" determined that the pyramid was a detailed foreteller of the future that predicted the coming of Christ and has set a date for the end of the world. Traditional Egyptologists have no trouble brushing aside such crazy claims. But a few ideas aren't so easily refuted.

One of the great mysteries of the pyramid, one of the most precisely engineered buildings of all time, is that it displays acoustic properties that scientists are just beginning to understand, Derek explained. The King's Chamber resonates at an exact pitch, vibrating at 16 Hz or an almost inaudible F sharp major. The pyramid's dimensions, construction materials and the "sarcophagus" inside the King's Chamber enhance, probably by design, any sounds in the chamber.

Derek shifted in his seat as he relayed the pyramid tales to Boone and Kyra. As he spoke, he peered into the sky, searching for any hint of the helicopter. It had vanished, probably at the Texas border.

"So, an acoustical engineer was inside the King's Chamber and discovered the room resonated to a specific musical chord," Derek said.

Boone, the navigator, had his eyes on the road, but his mind must have leapt thousands of miles away, to the Giza plain. Derek hummed the main notes of the F sharp major chord in sequence.

"Choir," Derek explained when Boone turned and shot him a raised eyebrow. "We had to learn to sight-read and memorize intervals."

"So what's so special about F sharp?" Boone asked.

"It's considered the harmonic signature of the Earth," Derek said as Boone's eyes narrowed. Derek rushed to explain. "Earth has a specific resonance frequency. Every object does. This has been documented. Some take this further and say that the Earth is tuned to a frequency that resonates to the F sharp major chord."

The tale got better. Derek told Boone and Kyra about the seventy-ton rafters in the King's Chamber—up there in the "relieving chambers" that were supposed to disperse the awesome weight bearing down on the room. The blocks also were tuned and served to further amplify the sound in the room.

"So the pyramid is a big tuning fork. So what?" Boone said, cutting Derek off mid-sentence.

"That means that the numbers contained in the Great Pyramid are more than the magical numbers of legend. They are keys to the scientific principal, acoustic technology. By subjecting mass to specific sound waves, the Egyptians could manipulate objects in ways we can only dream about."

Boone scowled at the flat, dusty road ahead of him. New Mexico was coming up and not much of anything had changed in the landscape.

"Okay, let me guess. Someone figured those numbers out, broke the code . . . . " Boone said. Derek grunted in assent. "The guy sent this code to this secret place in New Mexico . . . . "

"Seth Stonegate. But he's in jail."

"So the code is sitting in a box somewhere in the wilds, just waiting for someone to retrieve it. And that someone could be you or me or Sekhmet or heck, the CIA."

Derek coughed. Something made him uneasy now that he realized just how vulnerable the trove of data really was.

"Whoever gets it first," Derek said, "will have his hands on a secret that people have waited centuries to obtain. It's literally something to kill for."

≈

Derek fell asleep shortly after his lecture and woke to hear Kyra and Boone talking in the front seats. Boone was filling in Kyra on Charlie's alcoholism and its effect on Derek. Derek wanted to jump up and tell them to stop the discussion, but he pretended to be sleeping instead. He listened to the way Kyra asked insightful questions about Derek's dad and the effect the drinking must have had on his development as a young boy. Derek was touched that she cared so much and he felt guilty for not letting her in on this family secret earlier.

Night was beginning to fall as the road began to narrow. Santa Fe was still hours away and Boone was complaining that he could barely see anymore. Kyra offered to drive. However, Derek popped up, awake, and said he'd take over. He was eager to get off the road, out of the sight of any more helicopters. They were ahead of schedule anyway thanks to their efficient driving arrangement. So, an unscheduled stop for a little shut-eye couldn't ruin their plans, he figured. The sleepy New Mexican town of Santa Rosa, just off the highway, would do for a night's rest. Everyone agreed.

They rolled off the interstate on a narrow two-lane street, lined with taverns, drunks, and cheesy no-tell motels. They picked out a place with a long series of rooms joined together under a tiled roof, fronted with metal chairs that once were painted turquoise but now sat rusted in the evening sun. In front of the office was a giant stuffed rodent. A jackalope, in local parlance. It rose on a pedestal, one horn listing at a precarious angle.

"This will have to do," Derek said to Boone. "It'll get us off the trail for a few hours." Plus, he liked the jackalope. Who wouldn't? The poor thing, a jack rabbit with antelope horns, looked like a refugee from Frankenstein's laboratory. Or the Bates Motel.

Derek parked the pickup and they pushed through the doors to the front office. A hard-edged blonde with deeply tanned, leathery skin and a skinny frame looked up at them from a chair behind the front desk. On TV was a cable show about unexplained mysteries. She looked unsure whether to tear herself away from the discussion of psychic pets, but finally stood up.

"One room or two?" she said in a deep voice, nearly at a man's timbre. She leaned over to drum her pink fingernails on the countertop.

"Got one with two big beds?" Boone asked.

"Sure . . . " she started to say, but Derek interrupted.

"No, two rooms," he said, wanting privacy and remembering Boone's snoring in the truck cab. They didn't have to worry about finances that much—Derek had saved up a ton of money at home and left with a thick wad of cash. The idea was to get some sleep.

The woman lifted a penciled-in eyebrow and grabbed two keys off the rack. "Suit yourself," she said as she pushed the registry book at Derek. He fished some twenties out of his pocket. Without thinking, he signed a weak alias—Eric Nelson—and Kyra's real name on a line. Boone grabbed the pen and followed suit. Derek began to feel perspiration forming on his upper lip as the office lady read their names. Damn, if there only was some way to take it back, put down a better alias. All he needed was Sekhmet walking in here, following their trail.

"Nelson? Are you sure you aren't a Nilsson?" the contralto voice boomed. The woman lit up a cigarette and studied Derek up and down. He said nothing. "You sure do look like someone I know." Derek tried to shrug it off, but the woman stared right through him. "Numbers Eighteen and Nineteen," she said, handing out the keys. He felt her flickering eyes following him all the way to the door.

"Spooky old broad," Boone said, as he stood by his room. He paused, stepping back. "You know, I'm going to move the truck back, away from the road. Superstition, probably, but I'll feel better about it." Derek nodded, entered his own room and flopped on the chenille-covered bed without even taking off his shoes. The bed felt like a field of clouds. Fluffy and endless and silent, like millions of cuddly rabbits, with Kyra feeding them carrots. Soon he was dreaming of jackalopes, curling around him and nuzzling his aching head with their velvety horns. Or was that Kyra giving him a gentle massage?

≈

Derek felt himself entering a cave—or was it a temple? He peered into dark grottos illuminated by candlelight. In niches recessed into the stone walls were statues, most half-human and half-animal. Near Derek's elbow glittered the eyes of a falcon. They flashed so keen and bright they seemed to pierce his thoughts. Derek looked into the bird's face and it moved.

Derek stepped back. The falcon was alive, with its gaze trained on him. The raptor's beak looked sharp enough to split him open. But the falcon didn't leave its perch. It merely turned its head again, this time to regard the offerings of mice and rabbit left at its feet.

Horus welcomes you. Derek heard a voice speaking an ancient tongue, yet he understood the meaning. He peered across the gloom and spotted a man striding toward him. Or maybe it wasn't a man. His head alternately took on the appearance of an ibis and then of a clean-shaven, dark-visaged human being. It was then that Derek realized he was in a dream and powerless to pull himself out of it. He waited for the apparition to come closer.

"Thoth," Derek whispered, and the head remained human in aspect, dark and topped with coils of plaited black hair. The person looked like a Middle Easterner now, with skin the color of cinnamon bark and a narrow high-bridged nose. His eyes were sharp and deadly, like those of the falcon. He wore a simple white cloak rather than the linen skirt of the ancient Egyptians.

The Greeks call me that. But my real name is Tehuti.

Derek nodded. He knew this name from hours spent reading the myths of the Egyptians. In this complex religion, with gods for nearly every hour of the day, Tehuti was one of the most honored deities. A god of wisdom and learning, he brought writing to the Egyptians. Other than Osiris and Amun-Ra, Tehuti was the most vaunted god in the entire Egyptian pantheon. As the keeper of knowledge, Tehuti held all secrets. He hid his magical books from unworthy eyes for millennia. The fabled Numbers of Thoth, believed to be encoded into the Great Pyramid, were the goal of seekers from the ancient world to the modern-day Freemasons.

Tehuti looked at Derek and it seemed his gaze took in all directions at once. Derek felt fear ripple his spine. He wondered why he felt such awe for a god he didn't even believe in.

I was a man like you. Tehuti stretched his arm toward the Horus falcon. It flew to the man's forearm and perched there, its talons digging into the skin. But Tehuti did not bleed. *They made me into a god. The tales, the worship, the constant prayers . . . . I couldn't get away. I've been taken out of time and made eternal.*

He looked at Derek again with his bird face and he saw Tehuti as a human sailing from a massive flood, on a mission to bring knowledge to the world. He traveled the globe teaching building, technology, and writing of all tongues to dozens of cultures. His sojourn in Egypt was his last. Here he stayed; here he left mortality behind.

Derek tried to move but found himself unable to honor the simplest of his brain's commands. When he looked to the ground, he couldn't see that far. He might as well not have feet at all.

You have found my numbers. Perhaps this will free me. Your own world has no use for prayers—at least not to me. Maybe my reign will end. Derek felt the god's loss of time, cold and bottomless, and, with a shock, he realized that he also was in this eternal zone. He looked at his arms and saw he wore a linen cloak like Tehuti's. No t-shirt, no jeans. This subterranean shrine was a universe away from New Mexico.

I ask that the numbers will be used with wisdom, to continue the spread of learning throughout your time. Tehuti placed a scroll in Derek's hand. It was a scratchy papyrus, brittle and sealed with a wax scarab. *If the numbers fall into the hands of evil ones, the cataclysm that awaits will dwarf the one I lived through.*

Derek stared at the scroll and wondered desperately where to put it. He had no pockets. By the time he looked up, Tehuti was departing through a small door, changing shape as he stepped into the sunlight. For a second, he was a baboon, then an ibis, then he and the Horus falcon flew into the rays of the sun. As the door swung shut and darkness fell again, Derek remembered what he needed to do. Without words, Tehuti told him to expect a message from Roger. Derek looked to the papyrus again and saw it had turned to tiny fragments, floating particles of binary code.

≈

In the motel office, the radio was tinny and barely tuned to a talk radio show. Voices rambled amid the sputter and static, hashing over some local political scandal. The office lady nodded her head as the strident radio host railed on about "Nazi-esque tactics." She saw Derek enter and stood up.

"You could have just left the keys in your room," she said and took a quick slug of coffee from her mug. The morning light, not yet harsh, brushed over her features, dusting some rosy color onto the browned cheeks and softening the jowls. She looked almost attractive, standing there in her sleeveless bandana-print shirt with her thumbs hooked into the belt loops of her jeans. Might have been a cowgirl princess thirty years ago.

"We wanted to ask you about a better way to get out of town," Derek said, looking away quickly from her searching eyes. "Off the main drag."

"You are related to him aren't you?" the woman said, crossing her skinny arms in front of her nearly flat chest. "Charlie Nilsson's kin, as I live and breathe."

Derek stumbled back a step, only to collide with Boone, who entered the office in a bluster. Kyra must have been taking her time packing up belongings in the room, because she still hadn't shown up.

"You'll never believe who I saw out there on the street," Boone said, oblivious to Derek's discomfort. "Those two guys. The baldie and the crazy hair guy. Thank God I moved the truck last night."

Derek looked from the office lady to Boone. In the background the radio announcer was talking about a military maneuver near Los Alamos. Something about a search for a hidden structure in the mountain woods.

"Look, it's not fair to keep secrets," the woman said, holding out her hand to shake. "Name's Marge. Charlie stayed here once and we keep in touch. You're a dead ringer for him."

"Charlie?" Boone said, his voice booming in Derek's ear. "This is his son!" Boone looked out at the Santa Rosa 66 sign by the highway. "I guess it makes sense that he passed by here."

Marge smiled at Derek with an almost maternal softness.

"I knew it. That name on the ledger was bogus—I could tell the minute I saw it. Nilsson, yeah. Charlie doesn't talk much about the old life. I figured he had a family though." She tapped another cigarette out of the pack.

"About getting out of Santa Rosa . . . " Derek started to say.

"Don't change the subject, Derek," Boone said, winking at Marge. "How is the old guy?"

"Sobered up real good, if that's what you're asking," Marge said. "He even got me off the stuff." Derek blew out a puff of clear air and Marge exhaled a smoke ring. "Oh, who gives a shit? You're family. He takes me to meetings now and then. Bit of a drive, but once in a while he gets out this way."

She bent down and grabbed a map from under the counter. It was the kind the hotels give away to tourists. The Santa Rosa 66 Motel logo marched along the top, along with a cartoon of the jackalope. Derek couldn't help but notice that this time the fanciful beast had perfectly angled antlers.

"You want to get out of here fast and you don't want some old alkie tales," Marge said. "This road here goes up into the foothills but there are no steep climbs." She drew a red line along the state road. "Not too slow going and it's out of the way of snooping eyes. There are a few speed traps here." She marked a large X near one town. "And here." Another X. "But basically, it's smooth sailing to Los Alamos."

She blinked. Derek heard the radio announcer blather on about rumors of helicopters and secret troop movements. "I assume that's where you're going," she added.

Derek felt x-rayed and placed on a dissecting table. He didn't even try to lie anymore.

"Near Bandelier, actually."

Marge traced a few more lines, blowing smoke out of the side of her mouth. She handed the map to Derek.

"Can't keep you away from the military, but that's the best route you got," Marge said.

Boone thanked her as Derek attempted to duck out the door.

"Say hi to Charlie for me," she called after his retreating back. Derek bumped into Kyra, who looked puzzled and said, "How does she know about your dad?"

CHAPTER FIFTEEN

Charlie woke up, saw the ceiling fan come into focus and said, "I'm sorry." The words popped right out, gravely and wheezy, and didn't seem to have been formed by his conscious mind. They just shot to the ceiling, unedited. Charlie knew then that they were the purest words he'd speak that day.

He sat up and rubbed his forehead, trying to figure what to do next. Elk Horn wandered in, wiping his clean-shaven face with a towel.

"You say something?" Elk Horn asked.

"I'm sorry," Charlie repeated.

"About what?"

"About everything, I guess. I'm just sorry."

Elk Horn smiled and went back into the bathroom. Usually, he moved with vigor to get on with his busy day of fixing Quonset-hut roofs or repairing plumbing in the ramshackle homes on the reservation. But today, he walked as if he expected something to detain him.

Charlie disentangled himself from the sheets and walked toward his dresser. It stood next to Elk Horn's dresser, across from Elk Horn's bed. The room neatly divided in half with only a mirror shared by the housemates. He looked into the glass and ran his hand over his pasty blond hair and looked away. Something new and strangely sweet had invaded his soul. He couldn't place it, but it had to do with this sudden sense of culpability. Yesterday, he was a victim, a lousy drunk forced to run away from his life. Today, he was sorry, which meant he owned up to his part in the cosmic bargain. Sorry-ness wasn't necessarily a bad thing, he decided.

"I guess this means I have to do something about it," Charlie said, aiming his voice at the closed bathroom door. The toilet flushed. Elk Horn reappeared, nodding his head, attaching an elastic band to the end of his long braid.

"Yeah, that's the natural order of things," the Indian said. "Doesn't do much to feel sorry and not do anything about it, now does it?"

Charlie scrunched his lips and reached into the dresser for a clean t-shirt. This one bore a faded Chicago Bulls logo, a relic from the days of Michael Jordan. It was a lucky shirt, one that Charlie would wear until it was a rag.

"I called the computer guy again," Charlie said, knowing he was changing the subject, but unable to stop himself. Enough of this talk of seeking forgiveness. "That rig at the shack has been whirring for days now."

Elk Horn waited. Charlie grabbed a clean pair of jeans from another drawer, then socks and underwear. His thoughts were racing but he tried to get them in order, just like the clothing in his meager wardrobe. "I'm thinking that someone's trying to get whatever's on that hard drive," Charlie continued. "And I'm not so sure it's someone who should."

Elk Horn jerked a thumb in the direction of the front door. "Let's go over there now," he said. "I've got a bad feeling about it, too."

When they drove up in front of the cabin, it looked exactly the same and absolutely all wrong. They got out of the pickup and walked the perimeter of the small building, searching for footprints or other indications of intruders. Elk Horn narrowed his eyes as he ran a hand over the rough timber of the outside walls. He inspected the locking mechanism with his keen eyes for several long minutes.

Charlie looked up to meet the Indian's gaze. Deep in the black irises, Charlie saw a swirling fragment of concern. It was as much worry as Elk Horn ever displayed. Charlie felt his scalp sweat.

"Someone's been trying to open it," Elk Horn said, pointing to razor-thin cuts along the doorframe, next to the locked bolts. The combination lock, which was undisturbed, suited their purposes just fine and didn't require a series of complex maneuvers, one of which involved interrupting the power flow. But ever since troublesome events came to this part of the woods—helicopters in the night, strangers lurking in the woods, the increase in computer activity—they decided to lock the cabin electronically again. The combination lock remained on the handle, looking as functional as ever, so only a trained thief would start working on the more sophisticated system. The marks on the door were signs of a veritable safecracker at work. Someone was trying to find the electrodes by inserting a thin wire along the doorframe. In a couple places, the wire slipped and gouged the wood.

"Jesus," Charlie said, running a fingernail in the new grooves. He looked off into the pines, as if he might be able to spy the guilty party, hiding behind a boulder. A week ago, he'd been on the line with the electric company, attempting to discover who was paying the power bill for the property. The result was a puzzle.

The bill was pre-paid. Someone put down thousands of dollars in advance in the name of StarPortico Corp., based in New York City. StarPortico apparently was also the legal entity holding title to the property on which the shack stood. Charlie's attempts to locate StarPortico ended up in a blind alley. It was a sham corporation, set up with a New York City post-office box address, no reportable revenue, and no other property holdings. The company's CEO and chairman of the board was listed as S. Stein, with a bogus New Jersey home address. Charlie was pleased that Astrid's old reporting techniques, which he had learned second-hand, came in so handy. But even with all his snooping, he couldn't sniff out any more.

However, the electric company did provide him with one little nugget of information. The clerk let a little comment slip about the power use surging without notice after a long period of inactivity.

"Weird," she had said over the phone in a rare departure from corporate detachment. "It went from a tiny trickle of energy to big spikes in recent weeks."

That's when he decided to call Ned, the computer expert from Santa Fe. Ned arrived in a battered Volvo station wagon filled to the brim with cables, toolboxes, and manuals. He took his time walking up the slight incline to the cabin, wheezing like a couch potato of a man. Ned assembled and disassembled portions of the computer, muttering to himself about motherboards and circuit breakers the whole time. He said that no new data had gone onto the hard drive since he saw the computer last, so he disengaged the hard drive and put it in his box of tools.

"When you want it back, call me and I'll reinstall it," Ned said. "But right now, it'll just cause you a lot of trouble with people trying to access it on the computer."

Then he yanked out a piece of machinery, about the size of a thin paperback book.

"Hang on to this," he said, placing it into a translucent silver "static bag" and then in Charlie's slightly shaky hands. "It's a mirror drive. An insurance policy. Keep it safe. We might need it."

He pulled on wires and swore under his breath, something about the telephone connection.

"Telephone line?" Charlie asked, and Ned pointed out the door to a thin wire that extended past the electrical cables over to the telephone poles that serviced the reservation.

"It's a dedicated line," Ned said. "Unfortunately, I've broken off the connection. I'm sure the router dials in automatically to reconnect, so we may not have terminated the data flow. Whoever put this rig together planned on dropped connections."

Charlie tried to make sense of this information. Not much registered in his befuddled brain except one fact: if the connection was interrupted, someone might want to come poking around here to see what happened.

"Right now, the phone line being out puts an end to worries about break-ins," Ned said, chewing gum on one side of his mouth and speaking out of the other. On his wrist, he wore a black grounding strap to protect against static electricity. Around his neck, he sported cables, looking like a doctor wearing a stethoscope.

"Break-ins," Charlie repeated in a dull monotone.

"Kids, you know, hackers breaking into machines, putting nasty little viruses in there, screwing with boot files. You've heard of that, haven't you?"

Charlie shook his head. He'd been on an Indian reservation for the last five years, fixing toilets and replastering ceilings.

Even before he came to New Mexico, Charlie barely knew what the Internet was.

"Yeah, they've been coming in from all sides lately," Ned said, tapping little white command codes on an all-black screen. "FTP, Telnet, all over the freakin' place. Jeez, even a ping from a Milnet box; looks like Army." Ned pecked away at the keys and Charlie felt an ugly, metallic taste fill his mouth. "The crazy thing is that most of the traffic came in within the last two weeks."

"What would happen if they did break in?" Charlie asked. "Would we lose whatever is in there?"

"Theoretically, you could," Ned said, tightening up cables. "But whoever put this system together was no dummy. It's locked down tighter than NORAD headquarters."

"But there's a way to save the data, just in case?"

"There's a way to save anything," Ned said, winking.

Still, Charlie was worried as he stood now, staring at the electronic bolts. Elk Horn went through the procedure of freeing the locks and the door inched open. Inside, they saw the computer, looking undisturbed, one red light staring like a bleary eye through the dark, dusty air. Charlie walked back around the side where Ned had shown him the router, which connected to the phone line. The lights were blinking back there, which meant telephone connections were re-established. At least, there was one less reason for people to come snooping around. As Charlie traced the cables, looking for any telltale signs of meddling, Elk Horn squeezed through the dark space and clapped a hand on his friend's shoulder.

"Quick, out here," Elk Horn said and slipped through the cabin door as deftly as an antelope. Charlie pushed through the narrow gap to stand behind his friend, peering around his huge shoulder into the clearing. He saw nothing, but he knew better than to speak. Elk Horn maintained the vigil. The wind picked up, tossing branches about, scattering a dark flock of small birds. Then behind a scrub pine, Charlie saw it, a human figure in camouflage clothing, scurrying from a hiding place, creeping low in the direction of the road. How long the spy had been there was impossible to tell.

"We've gotten someone's attention," Elk Horn said, pausing to light a cigarette.

"Look, if it's all the same to you, I'm camping out here tonight," Charlie said, searching the woods for other interlopers.

"I'll go round the house and get a couple sleeping bags. One for you. One for me."

≈

"Truly, I didn't think we'd make it this far," Boone said.

The mountains of Bandelier National Monument rose about them, rugged and dry. These weren't the lush alpine snowcaps of Colorado or the painted red mesas of Arizona. Irregular and covered with dry brush and hardy pine trees, the New Mexican foothills stumbled one on top of another to form mountains. Somewhere, high in the piñon forest, the ancient Anasazi Indians left their cliff dwellings, and then abandoned them as the climate became too arid to sustain their numbers. It was rough country, savage and beautiful, desolate and rich.

Derek realized that he hadn't really expected to come this far either. The helicopters and rumors of government agents were daunting enough, but Derek was plagued by the idea of coming face to face with the data that had caused him so much worry, so much speculation, so much fantasy. Sometimes a thing is better when it is merely wanted, rather than achieved. Derek closed his eyes.

"Nope, I thought we'd have been shanghaied by Sekhmet and her friends long before we got here," Boone said. "And we might have been, if we hadn't gotten those directions from Marge. Damn nice lady she was."

Derek swallowed and opened his eyes again, trying to pick a direction to follow. Roger's directions had gotten him this far but now he was going to have to rely on sheer luck. The woods here were endless and it seemed little cabins peppered all the rambling foothill roads. Who'd ever think there'd be too many cabins to choose from?

"Aren't you gonna say something?" Kyra said, stretching from her nap in the back seat. She must have been listening to Derek and Boone.

"I'm trying to figure out where we're going, guys," Derek said, one hand shielding his face from the afternoon light. Boone snorted and Kyra let out a moan.

"Where *are* we going, Derek?" Kyra called out. "Do you have any idea? 'Cause getting lost in all this wilderness is getting me worried."

Derek searched the skies but saw no copters, only a lonely falcon sweeping from a high outcropping of rock. Derek watched the bird ride the thermal winds, sweeping close to the rock faces and then circling lazily over the brush below, eyes sharp enough to pick out the slightest twitch of a slumbering field mouse or the tremble of a jack rabbit's ears. One of the falcon's circles took him close to the highway and Derek caught a glimpse of the face—sharp, proud, the visage from his dream. Horus.

"Where's that bird headed?" Derek said, leaning forward in his seat, pointing at the sky.

"I don't see any bird," Boone protested, staring into the reddening sun. "I've got the sun in my eyes."

"Yes, yes, there's a bird," Kyra shouted. "A lovely one with strong wings."

Derek watched the falcon take a sudden loop to the north, picking up speed and plummeting toward the earth. *The falcon will give me Tehuti's message.* He must have found his dinner, here in the valley where the shadows lengthened. Ahead, a sign pointed to a turnoff: "Navajo Reservation."

"Here, turn here!" Derek shouted, almost seizing the wheel from Boone.

"Whoa, take it easy there, boy." They swerved on the dirt road and bounced over the potholes like kids at a carnival ride. Derek never took his eyes off the falcon. It was skimming over the ground now, its eyes focused on some unlucky rodent. It seemed to accelerate, lowered its talons and, with a mighty beat of wings, lifted back into the clouds, a struggling captive fastened in its grip. Derek felt sweat dribbling into his brows and brushed the dampness away. He saw the falcon soar up before tipping his wings perpendicular to the ground, right above a dead, charred pine tree. Then misty clouds swallowed the view and the falcon disappeared into his aerie home.

"That's it," Derek said, waving like a madman at the stripped and blackened pine. "When you get up to that tree—the one that looks like it took a lightning bolt—turn right."

"How the hell do you know there's even a road over there?" Boone said, navigating around boulders and broken branches.

"I just do."

The tree turned out to grow further up the road than Derek figured, a mile away easily, but when they got there, a smaller dirt road pulled to the right. They turned and headed uphill, as the sun slipped behind the mountains. Within minutes, they'd be in complete darkness, and Derek began to fidget in his seat, willing the truck forward at an ever-increasing rate. A cry in the woods made him turn and he saw exactly what he'd been looking for. A cabin, built of rough wood, its door slightly ajar. He'd dreamed of this old wreck for months now. He knew the smudged windows and the gritty dust on the floor.

"It's here," Derek said, his voice grave, his lips beginning to tremble.

"Then what's that up there?" Kyra asked. She pointed twenty-five yards north, where a twin cabin stood. It was the exact same shape, had the same dimensions. But this cabin had covered windows and wires attached to the power lines and telephone poles. A slight red light pulsed from one of the cracks in the wood frame.

"Bingo, babe," Derek said. "I knew you'd come through in a pinch."

CHAPTER SIXTEEN

It was too silent. Utterly, intractably silent, like a tomb sealed for millennia. Derek had imagined that once he found his shack in the woods, he'd face a live array of fantastic, state-of-the-art equipment, filled with whirring disks and blazing with busy, winking lights. What he encountered here in the dark was a locked shed, surrounded by chirping crickets and illuminated by the filmy light of a rising half moon. There was no sign of any kind of activity inside the cabin. When Derek aimed a flashlight through the tiny, smudged-up window, he saw nothing but the beam glaring back at him. But when he turned the flash off, he thought he could see the pulse of a steady red light, a pinprick in the deep black interior.

Electronic bolts secured the door, a precaution Derek expected. He'd researched ways to defeat such security, but wasn't too sure he was up to the task of safecracking at night. It might be better to see if someone else could do the work for him. Judging from the footprints in the dusty bare patches of earth, visitors had been in and out of the cabin—recently, too, he reckoned from the fragile marks under his flashlight beam. A good wind or a light rain would wipe these tracks out in a flash, so he figured they had to have been made in the last couple of weeks, or even the last few days.

Boone, who had been looking into the trees for the last few minutes, seemed on edge as he looked for spying eyes and hustled back to the truck with Kyra in tow.

Derek took the long way back, stopping for a quick peek at the twin cabin, the one with the open door and without electrical connections. It stood nearly bare, with a larger window, a space for a cot, and a rusted-out, wood-burning stove. It made sense. Whoever installed the computer equipment lived here while doing the job. It was good enough for temporary shelter—just a lean-to slapped together with plywood or some other kind of manufactured siding. Whoever built the shed wasn't on a budget or they'd have taken the stove.

Derek shuffled back to the truck, marveling at the sudden coolness of the air, which felt delicious after the long journey in the blinding heat of a fierce July sun. Just as he reached the truck's passenger door, a twig broke in the distance. Branches moved near the computer cabin. For one insane moment, Derek feared the claws of a mountain lion or the snarling jaws of a bear. Did they have bears up here? He wasn't sure, city boy that he was. He cast around with wild eyes but saw no sign of dangerous creatures. By the door of the cabin, two figures appeared, one long and lean, the other tall and solid. Derek crouched, although he could tell the people weren't looking his way. He was pleased that he, Boone, and Kyra took the precaution of parking downhill, behind the cover of trees. Through the foliage, Derek watched the men jiggle and enter number combinations on a metal pad on the cabin door, which eventually swung open with a mighty squeal of protest. The skinny guy lugged in two lumpy parcels and the door closed with another loud shriek.

Derek wondered if they had locked themselves in. Did they leave some clues about how they unfastened the bolts? The only way to find out was to creep up and take a look. Derek scurried over to the driver's side door of the truck and tapped on the window. Down it rolled, Boone's face hanging out, blanched and shaken. Derek put his fingers to his lips.

"Somebody went in there," Derek whispered. "I've got to check it out."

"You nuts?" Boone asked. "It might be Sekhmet and her pals."

"This wasn't them, believe me," Derek hissed. "I just want to take a look at the locks."

Boone looked into the distance and scrunched up his lips as if he'd gulped down some rotgut whiskey. "I don't know what I'm so spooked about, anyway," he said. "I came along as your bodyguard, right?"

"Huh?"

"Well, that's what I was thinking, even if I didn't tell you. So here I am cowering in the car, like I'm afraid of some girl." Boone shook his head in apparent disgust. Kyra gave him a little punch in the arm.

"Kyra, you stay in the truck," Derek said.

"Why do I need to hover here like a little girl?" she argued.

"Look," he said. "I want you to stay safe from all the creepy things that are going on around here. Not to mention the panthers and bears."

"Bears? They have bears around here?" she said with derision.

"Probably not," he admitted. "Just keep down and out of sight and I'll be back in a flash." She said she would keep her eye out if she were needed.

Boone grabbed his own flashlight—a nice big industrial model—and hopped out of the cab. He held it as if it were a cudgel. "Okay, let's get over there."

They crept over to the trees near the computer cabin, listening in the dark, trying to pick out anomalous sounds. It was a tricky business for Derek, born and raised in the city, unused to the calls of nocturnal birds and the rustle of tiny, foraging mammals. Everything sounded wrong. Yet, it seemed still enough. The interior of the cabin glowed with soft light, but nothing seemed amiss outside the door. Derek inched forward, out into the open.

Boone nodded his head, taking up sentry position near the edge of the trees. Derek shambled his way to the edge of the cabin, pausing to catch his breath and get his bearings. A lone coyote—or was it a wolf?—let out a harsh yelp in the distance. Derek stood frozen to the ground, looking around for any sign of trouble. He slipped to the door and took a quick read of the bolts. The door was unlocked but he couldn't tell immediately how the bolts were disarmed. Derek began to study the wires, looking for places where the current was interrupted, when a swishing sound caught his ears. He stood upright, senses afire. The whoosh sounded exactly like fabric, silken fabric, sweeping against human skin. Derek turned a millimeter at a time, but saw nothing in the distance. He looked over toward the trees for Boone's reassurance, but the big guy had disappeared. Someone was coming his way; that much he could figure out.

Derek leaped back, ready to return to the shrubs. His feet felt paralyzed, yet he urged his body to run. Just as he planted his left foot in the dirt, ready to sprint for cover, the cabin door opened. The creak wailed overhead and the wood whacked Derek in the back, throwing him off balance. He staggered sideways, then tried to right himself, pushing forward and smashing into a man stepping out into the dark woods. Derek wheeled and hands grabbed him about the shoulders.

Derek steadied on his feet and stared straight into the face of Charlie Nilsson. His runaway father. Charlie had his mouth open, ready to shout at his captive. But in the instant he made eye contact with Derek, he bit down on his lip. He relaxed his grip and, bit by bit, let go, using one hand to wipe the blood that started beading at the side of his mouth.

"Goddammit," Derek snarled.

Charlie stared, his familiar blue eyes clear and alive, even in the dark. There was pain in his eyes. But what was Derek supposed to do, hug the old bastard? Here he was messing up the greatest job of Derek's life. This was Derek's shack, and no one was going to mess up his chance. Screw Charlie.

"What the hell are you doing here?" Derek said, trying to keep his voice from turning into a scream.

"Well, how about you?" Charlie asked, voice low, concerned, and far too reasonable. "I thought you were a prowler, someone trying to get in here. Turns out you're my own son." He paused a bit, blotting the blood again with his fingertips. "Derek. It's good to see you."

"Oh, please, spare me the emotional reunion," Derek said, spitting out the words. He really didn't want to sound so savage, but something was roaring up out of his guts now, an energy that made him want to rip off heads, ambush small villages, lay waste to this entire countryside. Damn it, damn it. He could hardly stand still. His chest vibrated. Damn it to Hell.

"Well, it is," Charlie said, looking down at the ground. "Good to see you, that is."

"Look, Dad," Derek said, flinching inside at the teenage brat sound in his voice. "I don't know what you're doing in that cabin, but I've been tracking that computer data for months, actually more than a year. And I've got to get at it. Or else someone else will beat me to it."

As he spoke, a large shape appeared at the door and Derek was at a loss for words. A large American Indian man, one built for football, filled the entire doorframe. His needle-like gaze searched Derek from the ground to the ends of his hair.

"Who is this?" the man asked Charlie.

"This is my son, Elk Horn," Charlie said with a broad smile. "My son Derek in this, of all places."

"He doesn't sound happy to see you," Elk Horn said, nodding Derek's way.

"Well, under the circumstances, I guess it's understandable . . ." Charlie started to say.

"You did leave without a word five long years ago," Derek said, finishing the sentence. He turned abruptly, gazing at Elk Horn. "If you don't mind my asking, sir, I really need access to the data in there," Derek said. Elk Horn smiled.

"So do a lot of people, it seems," he replied, not moving an inch from the doorframe.

They stood at an impasse, Elk Horn peering through the dusk with no hint of emotion, Derek so electrified he felt able to run an Olympic sprint at a second's notice. A feminine yell and Boone's shout in the woods pierced the quiet and Derek was off in a shot, dashing for the scrub pine, searching for the place where Kyra's shout emanated.

Derek searched the golden grasses and the green pines, hearing his breathing and nothing more. A hand clapped him on the back and he turned around, expecting to see Boone's moon face. He stared instead into the eyes of Ra. The tubby guy from the Milwaukee bar with the bald head, leather coat, and pretentious name was someone Derek would never forget.

"I figured I'd see you here," Derek said, keeping his voice steady as his heart slammed in his chest.

Ra only smirked. He took his hand from Derek's shoulder and made no further move to restrain him. Derek lifted his shoulders as if shaking off a bug.

"Where's Kyra, my girlfriend?" Derek asked. "I heard her yell." Ra stepped back to reveal Kyra, stepping out from the trees.

She was standing unharmed, although shaking under the feeble light of the half moon. Boone stood next to her and pointed shakily to his right. Derek then realized what had so rattled Kyra and the big guy from Indiana.

She stepped out of the trees, the fabric of her black pants swishing as she strode. She walked with a swagger more befitting a man than a woman. She was average in height, no more than five-foot-six, but she carried herself as if her presence were enormous, expansive, and royal. She had long black tresses that fell in waves almost to her waist. In the dark, it was nearly impossible to see her sneering face. But Derek knew who she was.

"I've been looking forward to this meeting," said Sekhmet, her voice cool and smoky at the same time. She came closer to Derek and regarded his face. Her eyes were black, yet luminous as the starlight overhead. Her face was smooth like a young woman's, but her voice and self-assurance hinted at more mature years.

"What did you do to Kyra?" Derek said, marveling that he could still find his voice.

"Kyra? Is that your name?" Sekhmet said in a smooth, mellifluous voice, glancing over at Derek's lady love. "Such a pretty girl."

Sekhmet fingered a Horus-eye pendant around her neck. "Have you never met a goddess before?"

"Boone couldn't believe you were really a woman," Derek said. "He thinks everyone on the Internet is a fraud."

Sekhmet let out a soft snort of derision, then turned to Ra.

"What's going on up there?" she said, pointing at the cabin. "I saw some kind of argument. Maybe they couldn't get in."

"Maybe they couldn't," said a deep voice several yards away. Derek turned to see Elk Horn standing like a sentry, legs apart, hands on his hips, directly between them and the cabin. Charlie scurried over to Elk Horn's side, checking out the newcomers.

Sekhmet smiled before sauntering up to Elk Horn, without a hint of temerity. Ra followed. From out of the shadows sprang skinny Salim, who tailed behind, his braids jerking with each step. Derek went to put his arms around Kyra and had difficulty hearing what transpired between the big Indian and the sultry

Sekhmet, who spoke in hissing whispers. She moved in close to Elk Horn's body and flicked her hair. Once she laid a hand on his muscular forearm. From the look of Elk Horn's rock-like stance, Sekhmet might well have been attempting to seduce a statue. Meanwhile, Charlie looked from face to face, following the discussion. Derek noticed how, even in the dim glow of flashlights, Charlie stood straighter than he had before. He had some meat on his bones and walked with sure steps. Not the staggering semi-skeleton Derek remembered from Chicago. Their voices began to rise to an audible level again.

" . . . protecting it for the Navajo nation," Elk Horn said so all could hear. Sekhmet let out a shrill laugh laced with her scorn.

"We all know this isn't Indian property," she said. The rest of her speech was garbled, leaving Derek frustrated. If this wasn't Indian property, what was it? Didn't the sign say Navajo Reservation?

The conversation droned on until Sekhmet pulled something out of her pocket and held it to Elk Horn's face. For the first time, he moved. He considered the object for a second and stepped back.

Sekhmet held something to her lips as a jackrabbit scurried from one tree to another. There was a slight sound of an arrow rushing through the air and the rabbit stopped in its tracks. The animal was stunned, wobbling slightly on three legs, before dropping to its side. The back legs jerked for what seemed an eternity. Foam and blood issued from its gaping jaws. Derek felt his stomach churn as the rabbit went through death throes.

"You should see what this blowdart laced with poison can do to a dog, or a bear," Sekhmet said in a loud voice. The rabbit still thrashed.

Sekhmet brushed past Elk Horn and strode toward the cabin, Ra and Salim skulking behind.

"What are you doing?" Derek yelled, taking his arms off Kyra and racing toward Elk Horn. With each step Sekhmet took, Derek could see his treasure slipping further away. "Why did you let her go?" When he reached Elk Horn, the Indian merely shook his head, arms crossed over his chest. Charlie held a hand up to restrain Derek.

"Cobra venom," the Indian said. "There's no antidote for miles. Probably not even in Albuquerque." A blood-curdling cry came from the rabbit's direction. Derek had only heard a rabbit scream once. It was something he never wanted to listen to again.

"Don't worry," Charlie said.

"Don't worry? Don't worry? We can't let her get it, we can't," Derek said, pushing past Charlie and racing up to the cabin. When he reached Sekhmet, she turned and smiled with a triumphant glow.

"You're just what I need," she said. "Someone to extract the data. To make sure there are no booby traps."

"You're dreaming," Derek said.

"Like the little bunny back there? Don't fool yourself, Derek. I won't hesitate to use this on a human."

Sekhmet opened her hand and displayed a golden scarab, carved in the form of a small pillbox. "It's fast acting and totally paralyzing. Poor Cleopatra. She thought the asps were painful."

Derek attempted a brave expression. She wasn't fooled by it.

"So much neater than gunfire," Sekhmet said, wrapping her long, dark fingers around the beetle. She pointed at the computer inside the shack, indicating that Derek should get to work. He looked from face to face, trying to figure a way out of his dilemma. Sekhmet could be bluffing. She was good at creating a mumbo-jumbo mystique that could baffle even the most rational of human beings. Maybe she held a simple poison that only worked on small animals. Still, anyone who killed innocent animals just for fun can do just about anything.

Derek turned to the computer and looked for the first time at the object of his quest: a couple of simple boxes with monitors, a modem and a router—all uncommonly dust-free. How could these electronic gadgets have been sitting unattended for years in this remote location? He looked over at Elk Horn.

"Have you been taking care of them?" Derek asked.

"I have," said Charlie. He puffed out his chest and stared at Sekhmet. "And you can forget about forcing my son to give you the data. We erased it."

"You what?" Sekhmet said, her kohl-rimmed eyes narrowing.

"It's gone. Look for yourself."

CHAPTER SEVENTEEN

Something stank about Santa Fe, Derek decided. The sheer, unfiltered sunlight cooking his brain by day, the chill mountain winds raising goosebumps at night. The way gravity seemed to take hold at all the wrong times, such as now when he wanted to run like a tornado, yet stayed locked onto the cheap linoleum sheet flooring of this claptrap cabin. He looked from face to face and wondered why things had gone so impossibly wrong.

Sekhmet stood with her beautiful face pressed into a frown, flustered for the first time this night. Elk Horn tipped his head to the side as if asking a question. Ra and Salim stood at the ready, eager to start a fight should their leader command one. Kyra, standing near Elk Horn, sending Derek a questioning look. Boone, last up to the cabin, just kept staring in disbelief at Charlie.

Charlie, of course, was the problem. Every time, without fail, he managed to screw up some element of Derek's life. First, he messed up Derek's boyhood. Then he deflated Astrid by taking off without warning. Now he had just ruined the greatest opportunity of Derek's career. What would he do next, that useless bastard? Derek looked at Charlie, who stood unperturbed, hands in the pockets of his jeans, wearing the Chicago Bulls t-shirt he bought Derek on their one and only father-son sports outing. The jerk took the shirt away, too, when he left town.

Derek's gut squeezed and he felt his muscles tingle with electricity. His hands lifted of their own accord. Then he flew on top of Charlie, pounding his old man on that snorting bull logo, beating the hell out of a festering old memory.

"Why didn't you stay out of it?" Derek yelled, pulling back, this time taking a swing at Charlie's chin. He just missed. "Why the hell couldn't you get lost and stay lost?"

No one moved. Charlie stood, breathing heavily, but making no move to defend himself. Boone began to step forward and then, glancing in Sekhmet's direction, seemed to think better of it. Derek stood his ground.

"We were guarding the cabin, Derek . . . " Charlie began. But Derek felt a screaming sound in his brain.

"You couldn't just watch the data, you had to destroy it," Derek barked. "Do you have any idea, any at all, what that data meant? She knows." He pointed at Sekhmet, who continued to scowl. Charlie shrugged.

"We didn't know what it was, we only knew someone was after it," Charlie said.

"So you just annihilate it, the way you annihilated my childhood, and all the people you loved?" Derek said, no longer able to stop himself. "You must really enjoy shattering dreams, because you just did it again." As he spoke, Derek felt strength fill his body, strength to lift a hundred men. He raced at Charlie again, punching hard this time, reaching up to his father's face and making contact over and over again.

It felt good, pummeling him like that. Beating out the pain of nights spent crying in the dark, smashing the hurt of losing his mother to a zombie state, pummeling the memory of midnight arguments and howling fights. He hit and hit, felt people rushing about him. He heard Kyra scream. Then hands pulled him away.

Boone hauled Derek outside, propped him up against the cabin wall and wiped off his face with a bandana. He clapped Derek on the shoulders, tacitly ordering him to get a hold of himself. People pushed and shoved their way out the cabin door, disappearing into the woods. Derek twisted his neck to the right and the left, trying to feel and release the tension that kinked his muscles. He made out the huge form of Elk Horn, who was once again quiet and emotionless. Kyra stood next to him, tears running down her face.

"You better move on, Derek," Elk Horn said, with a trace of kindness in his deep voice. "I'll clean him up." Derek looked down at his fist, which was covered with his father's blood. Derek nodded to Elk Horn.

"The others, they disappeared," Elk Horn said, pointing out into the darkness. Clouds had begun misting over the moon, and the landscape was impenetrable.

"Come on, Derek," Boone said, leading his charge toward the truck. "I think you made your point." Kyra put her arm around Derek's waist and helped lead him away from further trouble.

≈

The next morning, they found the cabin cleaned out from top to bottom. Derek and Boone stood at the foot of the hill and discerned yellow tape winding round the shack, the unmistakable mark of a police search. Sure enough, as they reached the building, they saw the letters on the tape "Crime Scene/Do Not Cross." A glimpse through the crack in the paper-covered window yielded no little red lights, no sign of anything at all. The electronic bolts were undone and the door, loosely shut, looked as if it would pop open with the slightest gust of wind. No more computer, no more Pyramid Project, no more hope.

If someone had seized the computers as evidence, then the machines must be connected to some sort of crime. All Derek could think of was Seth Stonegate, sitting in a Club Fed, where they put all white-collar computer criminals, escaping, and then high-tailing it to Santa Fe to pick up his information. The brilliant idea to transfer data to this shack nearly worked out. But now things had gone haywire.

"Well, look at it this way," Kyra said. "At least Sekhmet didn't get it."

Derek sighed. It was a small consolation, but he had to admit it was true. Who knew what she had planned for the secrets of sonic levitation? Was she going to sell it to terrorist governments? Create a weapon of her own? He hardly imagined her using the technology to create useful inventions to better mankind. He remembered his dream of Tehuti. He warned Derek of letting the program fall into the wrong hands. But was the government any better than Sekhmet?

He felt like such a chump. He should have saved his punches for Ra and Salim. With the aid of Boone and Elk Horn, they easily could have subdued the self-styled Egyptians. But then, what was the point of that? Charlie had erased the data.

Derek turned away. His insides were gone. He was nothing but a walking shell, a pretend human being. He couldn't really feel the ground each time he put a sneaker to the red earth. "Let's get some breakfast."

On the way, they stopped to refuel and Derek went over to another rare pay phone he spotted. After piling in coin after coin, he finally connected with Trevor.

"We were wondering," he said, his voice detached.

"It's all gone to hell, Trevor, the whole damn thing."

"Did you get a chance to see your girlfriend?"

"What? Kyra is my girlfriend. She's right here." Derek ground his molars together. His stomach was knotted up. Kyra looked at him with suspicion . . . .

"Trevor?"

"I went over to get the medicine for Foo's hairball problem., and I found someone had searched your place. I looked in each room to check out the damage. Papers everywhere. And then I saw her picture on your filing cabinet."

"That's Sekhmet," Derek said, as if that explained everything.

"How nice for Kyra."

"No, no, Trevor. That's the woman who's been after the data. She sent me that picture and I just thought it was an elaborate come-on."

"Which worked."

"No, I mean, it wasn't a come-on. She actually looks like that."

"I don't know what your intentions are out there, Derek."

"Look, Trevor, she's an evil bitch. She killed a rabbit with cobra venom and then she was going to use it on us. I mean, Trevor, cobra venom. She'd do anything to get her hands on the data. She's been on my trail since Chicago, and now that the data is lost I'm hoping she goes away."

Trevor was silent for a few seconds. "It's lost?"

"Gone. And it looks like federal agents seized the computer."

Trevor exhaled a long stream of air. "What are you going to do now?"

"Probably come home. I was involved in a scuffle at the cabin and I don't want to get arrested if the g-men investigate too closely."

Derek heard the blast of a car horn and saw Boone leaning against the truck, his hand through the open window, pressing on the steering wheel.

"Look, I've got to go, but I'm going to call you the minute we get settled at a hotel. It's really crazy. My father showed up. My long-lost father." Trevor didn't answer.

"Why did you get me involved in this crazy mess?"

"Sorry, man, we'll be home soon."

He looked over at Kyra who was still regarding him as if he were a rattlesnake.

"It's nothing. Trevor didn't know we were running from Sekhmet."

Kyra kicked dirt on the ground, sighed, and turned around to go back to the truck.

≈

Derek stood under the warm water, breathing in steam, reveling in his own semi-solitude. After days shut up in a truck cab with Boone and Kyra alternately crammed in the back seat, Derek had nearly forgotten what it was like to simply hear the soft hiss of running water and no constant commentary.

There was no reason now why Derek, Kyra, and Boone couldn't splurge and find a decent hotel—two rooms with a view. With the data destroyed, Sekhmet wouldn't be tracking them anymore. They didn't have to cover their tracks. Heck, Derek could even use the hotel phone to check on George. But the minute he began to think of George, Derek felt his mood darken. How was he going to tell his best friend that everything they had dreamed about for the last few years had slipped away? How could he even begin to explain that Derek's own father was to blame?

What of his future? He had planned to take BitJockey's free vacation and never come back, because he was planning on becoming a rich man holding world-shaking, valuable data. July was almost over. Did he have to crawl back to Bushy for his programming job?

He rinsed the shampoo from his hair, turned off the water and stepped out into the air-conditioned bathroom. Wrapping himself in the fluffy white towel, he reached for the dial that controlled the heat lamp. He flicked it on, waiting for the chill to dissipate, realizing that his solitude had turned to wretched loneliness.

He called for Kyra on her cell phone and got no answer. *Where could she have gone off to?* Derek pulled on some clean clothes and wondered if he should just burn the jeans he'd been wearing since he pulled out of Chicago. Shuffling out to the bedroom, he stared at the night sky, full of more stars than his city-bred eyes had ever seen. It had been days since Derek stared at a computer screen and he was beginning to observe things he had never noticed before. The stars. The flight of the falcon. The lump that bobbled up and down in Charlie's throat when Derek told him to go to hell.

He looked down on the nightstand and saw a note from Kyra. She had gone down to the hotel store to get a few non-grungy items of clothing. She also said she took a knapsack of clothes down to see if she could find a hotel laundry. She ended the note with the words, "We need to speak about this whole thing with your father." Her too. His shoulders slumped.

The phone jingled by the bedside, but Derek didn't pick up the receiver. Kyra wouldn't call, she'd just come up and use her key. Instead, he lay down on the cool, queen-sized bed and covered his head with a pillow. Too much starlight, too many thoughts.

≈

A soft pecking rapped away at Derek's consciousness like a woodpecker hammering at his brain. For a few seconds, Derek dreamed of the woodpecker—five feet tall with a bill of solid steel—until he began to come back to the real world. Someone was knocking on his hotel room door. He almost yelled at the visitor to go away when he heard the distinctive sound of Boone's muffled bellow.

"Come on, Derek, what's the problem?" said Boone through the solid door.

"Hang on," Derek shouted, slipping off the bed and shuffling across the deep-pile carpeting. He reached the door, turned the handle and came face to face with Boone and a woman. She stepped toward the hallway light. Black hair, dark eyes, a maddening magnetic pull. It was Sekhmet. Derek stared, unable to find his voice. Boone jumped into the breach.

"We've been talking," he said, pushing past Derek into the room. "Miss Sekhmet here's got some interesting news to share." Boone smelled like a brewery and Derek instinctively retreated. Sekhmet moved past Derek without a sound. He let her pass; he wasn't sure how he would have stopped her anyway. *Where is Kyra? What if she walks into this tableau?*

Boone kept babbling as Derek continued to stare at his unwanted guests.

"She's misunderstood, that's all," Boone said, reaching over and chucking Sekhmet under the chin. "She wants to work with us, not against us. And she thinks the data is still stored somewhere . . . ."

"Forget it," Derek snapped. "The data's gone. Charlie was too stupid to create a backup. He doesn't know how. Anyway, the feds seized the machines."

"And I know where they are keeping them," Sekhmet said, her voice like warm chocolate syrup.

Derek looked at Sekhmet, illuminated by the incandescent overhead light. Her smooth skin was the color of café au lait, the features graced with Arabic accents. He thought back to his research on the ancient Egyptians, to the fact that they were a mixed-race people. Black Nubians mixed with tan Semites and white Mediterraneans to produce a population of many colors. But, in paintings, most of the ancient Egyptians were like Sekhmet: dark tan, black hair, slender build, and average in height. Around her eyes, she wore thick eyeliner of kohl. On her neck, she wore the Horus pendant. But instead of the Egyptians' white, pleated linen dress, she wore a black silk gown, cut low in front and slit up one side from her ankle to the thigh.

Derek noticed something else. There was nothing ancient at all about her. Her beauty was so radiant he almost forgot to keep breathing.

"Stealing impounded evidence?" Derek said. "That's trouble I don't need."

Boone laughed and sat down on the bed. He swayed a bit as he giggled.

"Well, there's stealing and then there's borrowing," Boone snorted. "We'd just take a little old peek." As he spoke, he fell back on the bed, chortling to himself. Within seconds, he was asleep.

"You got him drunk," Derek said, fixing Sekhmet with accusing eyes.

"Yes," she said without a trace of contrition. She walked over and sat on the other bed, crossing her legs so the split skirt fell open. Her skin looked like melted caramel, sweet and creamy. "Anyway, it was easy."

Derek stood with his arms crossed defending his torso and stared at this provocative interloper. He felt absurd, trying to look macho when inside he was a panicky teenager. He needed to get her out of his—and Kyra's—room.

"You got him drunk so you could get in here with me," he said. "What are you up to?"

"Now, Derek," Sekhmet said, tilting her head at a fetching angle. "I'm not all that bad, am I?"

"Obviously Boone doesn't think so," Derek said. "What did you promise him?"

Sekhmet laughed, tipping her head to the ceiling and shaking out her long, abundant hair. "Just a kiss, actually. That's all it took."

Derek wrinkled his nose in disgust. The woman was a cliché. Her every move looked copied from a Mata Hari movie: the cooing voice, the back stretches, the lowered lashes. Boone was a sitting duck for Sekhmet and God knows how much information had spilled out while Derek had crashed out on the hotel bed.

Yet, for all the contempt that played in Derek's brain, a disturbing desire was creeping through his body. First, his skin sizzled when Sekhmet brushed by him at the door. Then his knees became wobbly and unreliable when she spoke. Now his heart wasn't quite beating the way it should. The arrhythmic pounding in his chest started when she fluffed out her hair.

"Well, that's not going to work with me," Derek said, arms still crossed, feeling belligerent. "So just tell me what you want and then get out."

"After I tell you what I know, you won't want me to get out," Sekhmet said. She leaned back on her elbows and fixed him with a puzzling sense of familiarity. "And you won't want that girlfriend back either." She chuckled. "Do you know of Seth Stonegate?" she asked. Derek nodded. "He and I worked together for a time."

Now she was talking his language. Derek sat in the small desk chair across from the bed, ready to listen as Sekhmet wove her story.

Seven years ago, Stonegate was a young coder much like Derek himself, Sekhmet said. But young Seth was into trouble early, noodling around, stealing credit-card numbers, breaking into top-secret government boxes. Kid stuff. Far beneath his skills. He had become a true "hacker."

Things changed the day Stonegate read *The Lost Books of Thoth*, a wildly speculative best seller by an amateur Egyptologist. In the book, Stonegate learned three key facts: that Thoth supposedly built the Great Pyramid, that Thoth hid his secret books of knowledge, and that, according to legend, the pyramids were built by the lost art of sonic levitation. Stonegate figured this ancient technology would be in the hidden books and that all he had to do was find them. Unlike most Egyptologists, New Agers, and Atlantis seekers, Stonegate assumed the books weren't actual volumes at all but encoded mathematical data. After all, Thoth invented math.

He flew to Cairo, took a tour of Giza and eventually ran into Sekhmet. She'd been tailing this computer nerd much the same way she tailed Derek, she said. Her modus operandi the same. She targeted him via e-mail, met him in person, and then lured him in. She knew that if Stonegate had any hormones at all, she would win him over to her side.

The reason she needed him was simple. Sekhmet was a brilliant mathematician, but she still required an encryption expert to help her decode some ancient carvings. She insisted traditional Egyptologists wrongly interpreted them as funerary decorations. She showed Stonegate some photographs of wall paintings and carvings, all featuring repeated geometrical shapes, angles, and proportions. Stonegate saw the patterns immediately and was intrigued. She promised to show him the "books" of Thoth if he'd swear to share the knowledge with her alone.

"Where was this? I thought the Great Pyramid had been investigated from top to bottom," Derek interrupted.

"Even in Giza, which is crawling with self-styled archeologists, there are secrets," Sekhmet said. "Adventurers still find tunnels. Someone found evidence of a cavity below the Sphinx and they are searching there now for a subterranean chamber."

"You found something under the Sphinx?"

Sekhmet only shrugged her shoulders, making her breasts rise and fall. Derek, trying to ignore the distraction, knew she would only divulge just so much.

The story continued: Sekhmet enticed Stonegate to her secret subterranean grotto and revealed the walls engraved with mystical writing and lavish painted scenes of gods and goddesses. Preserved by the arid climate and hidden from the bleaching effects of the sun, the artwork was in pristine condition. Sekhmet and her spellbound partner spent two days taking photographs and making wax rubbings of the carvings.

Stonegate lived for the next two months holed up in a seedy Cairo hotel, sifting through the dimensions and geometrical angles. Sekhmet, as skilled at reading hieroglyphics as she was at mathematics, compared her notes with Stonegate's. The Egyptian text spoke of a room, or space, alive with sound. Stonegate found repeated proportions that could be used in constructing a room. Oddly, the proportions matched those of the King's Chamber in the Great Pyramid, a space with noted acoustical properties.

The hieroglyphics went on to speak of the "song of the gods." Stonegate discovered what could only be interpreted as tonal frequencies or notes tuned at precisely determined intervals. The final text involved the god Osiris and his soul ascending to the stars in the region known as the Duat. Here, there were no calculations possible, only cryptic pictures of Osiris' mummified body floating at a forty-five degree angle. Sekhmet and Stonegate were stymied at this point and couldn't fit the whole picture together.

Then Sekhmet stumbled on the answer. In her "funerary" artwork, there were similar pictures of puzzling objects also floating at forty-five degree angles. One of the articles was a pyramidion or Benben stone, a pyramid-shaped object that was said to have fallen from the heavens, a shape that determined the form of the pyramid—and an ornate copy of the Benben once capped all of these ancient monuments. Here, the Benben was floating in a precisely aligned chamber, with the notations of specific tones all about the picture. Sekhmet hadn't seen the significance before, because the calligraphers inscribed the hieroglyphics with only design in mind. They didn't follow a simple left-to-right or right-to-left pattern. The characters could proceed in any direction, even from top to bottom, as long as they framed the picture correctly. Up until this point, Sekhmet had no idea the "song of the gods" had anything to do with the floating Benben. But it did. The song played in the chamber made the Benben rise toward heaven.

Stonegate and Sekhmet realized that what they had were formulas for raising and lifting mass by the power of sound vibrations alone. Not only was there a formula for the Benben stone, but adjustments for mass of various sizes. All Stonegate had to do was to isolate the core mathematical formula. He returned to New York with a suitcase full of numbers and proceeded to work out formulas for various types of objects, carefully matching tone to mass size and the volume of the acoustical chamber. He devised an encrypted code and transmitted the data back to Cairo.

Sekhmet took the numbers he sent her and tested them. Under the auspices of the dummy Ra-Egypt Corporation, she paid engineers to experiment on real objects. After several defeats, they reached the point at which small objects, about the size of marbles, were levitating on sound waves. Then, the numbers stopped flowing from New York.

Sekhmet flew to the United States to find her partner, only to discover that he'd been arrested. Stonegate, it seemed, couldn't get the habit of raiding banks and credit-card companies out of his system. Or so the coppers said. So, he was tried and convicted, landed in the federal penitentiary, his computers were seized by the government, and Sekhmet thought she was out of business.

"That's where you came in," she said to Derek, holding up her empty wineglass that Derek had produced from the mini-bar.

"You found out what George and I were working on," Derek said, pouring her more wine like an obedient servant.

"Well, you put up a line of encrypted code on the Hacker Haven social network page," Sekhmet said, pausing to take a sip. Her lips glistened. "I recognized it instantly. Stonegate's signature. I realized that Stonegate was too smart to let the data die. He'd hidden it away somewhere. And you were the answer." She grabbed his arm before he could return to the hardback chair and urged him to sit next to her. "You still are," she said with a purr.

CHAPTER EIGHTEEN

She smelled like earth, like something untamed and forever fecund. The scent had a spiritual note, too, reminiscent of a touch of frankincense or myrrh or something from an incense pot at a high mass. There was nothing floral about Sekhmet, just an aroma of amber and musk, of power and lust. Derek moved closer to breathe it all in.

She rolled her head along her shoulders, as if loosening the muscles in her long, slender neck. Derek had a fierce urge to touch the dark tangles of her thick hair and pull a strand to his nose, his eyes, his open mouth. He resisted, knowing he was in jeopardy getting so close to her, but he needed to know just who this woman was. From a distance, she seemed too seamless, too strong, too much like a true goddess—whatever that meant to him. Up close, where he could see her perfect skin, Sekhmet was only more divine.

Her eyes were wide open, pulling in his gaze. The onyx pupils and amber irises made her look cat-like, as if the eyes were gathering all available light before pouncing on a gentle bird. For all the smoothness of the skin surrounding her eyes, what was inside her gaze was older than anything Derek had ever seen. In the depths of her eyes, she was primeval, with memories of the first days on earth etched within the retinas. Derek felt a tremble work up his back.

"How old are you?" he asked, still staring into her eyes. Sekhmet laughed, throwing off the spell, becoming merely human again.

"That's an extremely rude question to ask a woman," she said, taunting.

"You're not what you seem," Derek said, persisting.

She smiled as if she were dealing with a small child, and took another swallow of wine. "Derek, I came here to ask if you would like to take Stonegate's place."

Derek squinted, trying to figure where she was going with this line of thought. "The data's gone . . . " he started to say.

"I don't think so," she interrupted. "First of all, I have a great deal of the original data in Egypt. Second, I think you are bright enough to recover something from the erased disk."

"That the feds took."

"Which I can get back."

Derek blinked.

"Trust me, Derek," she said, running her hand up his forearm. The hairs stood up in shock, and bits of electricity hit his groin.

"You threatened us with cobra venom, for God's sake! Trust you?" he said, standing up, unsteady on his feet.

Boone snorted on the other bed, rolling over and beginning to snore like a cartoon bear. Derek knew the sound. It meant Boone was having trouble breathing and would soon be awake.

Sekhmet shot up and grabbed Derek around the waist, pulling him close to her so that his face was just inches away. Her breath smelled like sage leaves. Her eyes gave off a dark light. Her breasts burrowed into his rib cage.

"Listen, Derek," she said, her soft lips forming the words the careful way a singer creates sweet notes. "I had to get you to listen. Guns are not my style. The Native American understood."

Derek swallowed, trying to loosen her grip. She pulled him even tighter. Her sexuality, the full force of it thrust in his face, pressing into his body, scared him more than he wanted to admit. His mind jumped from thoughts of Sekhmet naked, to worries about his own skinny body, to a panicky memory of Kyra. He wished he were dreaming. Sekhmet kissed him, her soft mouth pressing hard into his. She didn't so much kiss as penetrate him, her passion burning into his cells, erasing everything he knew, breaking him down. Her body etched itself into his, insinuating its warmth into his bones, stripping his last vestige of resistance.

"We'll make a nice pair, won't we?" Sekhmet said, pulling back at last. Derek nodded, despite the protests of his screaming brain.

"Let's get out of here before he wakes up," she said, releasing him and gesturing at Boone. "I'll show you what I want you to do." She grabbed Derek's hand and pulled him to the hotel door. Boone made a wheezing sound and rolled over onto his stomach.

Kyra was still missing.

≈

The night was dry and dusty, with pollen on the breeze. Charlie sniffed through his bruised nose and considered the smells. No rain tonight; it must have been blown off course. He'd be safe at his lookout point all night if he wanted to stay here.

For hours now he had been hiding near the trees across from a hotel parking lot, waiting to catch a glimpse of his son. It hadn't been hard to find the hotel Derek, Boone, and that lovely young woman checked into after the incident at the cabin. Charlie figured he knew Boone's taste well enough to limit his search to chain hotels. Boone didn't like any surprises, especially not the kind that fussy bed-and-breakfasts might afford. On his second try, Charlie found a Boone Sandstrom registered at the Best American hotel just outside downtown Santa Fe. Across from the fast-food restaurants and strip malls and within easy walking distance of a liquor store, the hotel had Boone written all over it.

Neither Derek nor Boone were easy to pin down, however. When Charlie tried calling them at dusk, neither one answered their telephone. Charlie figured his son had to return eventually, so he staked out the outside window that corresponded to the room number and waited in the wooded area near the car lot. Sure enough, the lights came on in Derek's room a little after nine. From the look of the figures in the windows, Derek had a guest.

Charlie gazed at the shadow play for a long time, wondering how he would put things to his son when he finally had the nerve to approach him. Charlie had expected anger. But the depth and power of his son's frustration sent Charlie into a tremble. A bloodied nose was not a huge price to pay for his alcoholic sins, but Charlie did not know how to account for Derek's unfettered rage. How do you apologize to a swirling vortex of fear and agony? How do you make peace with a tornado?

But it must happen, that much was clear. Elk Horn spelled it all out: you make restitution with your past, explain your complicity, seek to do right, and don't look back. You make amends, Elk Horn said, then you put your memories down and walk on, unencumbered. Marge said something else about the process of owning up to one's wrongs: "No regrets. Make amends and the past doesn't exist anymore."

Charlie taped Marge's maxims to the inside of his wallet and looked at them whenever he could. He was sick of lugging his guilt with him and was more than ready to let it go. But it meant facing the whirlwind, and a twinge of fear played in his empty stomach.

Slowly, he backed away from the branches and moved into the parking lot, watching the figure of his son moving across the large window, carrying something. It looked like a small bottle of wine in his hand. Charlie winced, wondering if his son was living out the same nightmare he had escaped. The disease ran in the family. Charlie began to run, as if to outpace the evil thoughts that threatened to overtake his mind. He entered the hotel.

In the hallway, outside room 105, Charlie hovered, pacing back and forth in an attempt to appear casual. He approached the door two or three times, ready to knock, and then backed away, unsure of his voice, convinced that he was dressed like a bum, afraid his courage would fail. This time, he crept up and heard footsteps inside, coming closer to the door. Charlie knew his moment had arrived and reached up with his fist to knock.

Then Charlie lost all control of the moment. In an instant, the door swung open and Derek stepped out, nearly knocking Charlie over. Not knowing what to do, Charlie lurched back and took a deep breath. He spoke before focusing on what stood before him.

"Derek, there's something important I have to tell you," he said.

His son stared at him, his eyes wild, his hair rumpled, face as pale as birch bark. Behind him was a woman—that same woman from the cabin last night. She moved away, scowling, then walked quickly down the hallway. Charlie, not knowing if he were breaking up a tryst or intruding on a quarrel, decided to go for broke.

"It's about Roger, Derek," he said, ignoring the woman. "I have a message for you."

≈

Boone sat up in bed, squinting, eyes the color of cotton candy and one half of his face embossed with the quilted texture of the hotel bedspread. Derek and Charlie sighed at the same time.

"It's about time you went to bed in your own room, Boone," Charlie said, his voice even and tender. "Can you manage by yourself?"

Kyra appeared at the door with a few shopping bags and a knapsack full of clean clothes. She had a look of astonishment on her face when she saw Charlie. Then she saw Boone.

Boone blinked his bleary eyes several times before attempting to stand. He stood on two feet, not like the Rock of Gibraltar, but not tipping over either. "Yeah," he mumbled. He started shuffling toward the door. Before he grabbed the handle, he turned to Charlie and stared.

"You're supposed to be her," Boone said. "You know, the babe." Charlie cocked an eyebrow.

"Right, Boone," Derek said. "Nighty-night."

Kyra rushed in, dropping her bags and knapsack on the bed. "Those two bullyboys, *her* friends, tried to detain me downstairs," she said, blowing the perspiration off her forehead. "But I'm here now."

She looked from Derek to Charlie and back again, her eyebrows set at a quizzical angle.

"Kyra, meet my dad, Charlie," Derek said. "Dad, this is Kyra Van Dyck, my girlfriend, whom I love very much." Derek had never said that before and felt sudden joy. Kyra had a shocked look in her eyes. Charlie smiled at what he considered Derek's good taste in women. Kyra shook Charlie's hand with grace.

"Help Boone get to his room, would you, Kyra?" Derek asked. She looked at Derek for a long minute, nodded, and zipped out the door, pulling Boone's hand.

The door slammed, and Derek and his father were alone for the first time in five years. Derek thought about sitting on the bed and then decided against it. He shoved his hands in his pockets and kicked at the dust ruffle on the bed Boone had vacated. He felt twelve years old at the most. Something was required at this moment, so he rushed in to fill the void. Sekhmet, Derek realized, did her usual disappearing trick when Charlie showed up at the door. At least he didn't have to explain her presence.

"I've got to say I'm sorry, Dad. About the nose and everything," he said. "That was really childish."

Charlie just shrugged and waited for more.

"Well, I'm still pissed as hell, goddammit. With you leaving and everything. I meant to read you the Riot Act about what happened to Mom after you left. She's in a constant state of depression, got forced out of her job. You missed my whole education. Dad, Dad . . . then I just started punching like a little lost kid.

"But now I look at you and I don't see the same man I remember. You seem decent somehow. When were you planning to show us this change? This sobriety?"

Charlie reached into his pocket and started to cough a bit. He began to pull out a piece of paper before Derek looked at the door and said something that stopped them both cold.

"Thanks, by the way."

"Thanks?"

"I was just about to do something incredibly stupid and you just happened to hang out there in the hallway," Derek said, trying to find the right words.

"Sekhmet?"

"Yeah."

"Well, she sure took off in a hurry." It was Charlie's turn to scuff his feet on the ground. Derek knew that explaining what had just gone on with Sekhmet would have been impossible. Let Charlie think it was just another sexual adventure. Too scary to contemplate the truth.

Charlie finally pulled out a sheet of paper from his pocket. He looked at it for a few minutes and then seemed to reconsider, putting it away.

"You mentioned Roger," Derek said. "Remember?"

"Yeah," Charlie said, fishing for the paper again. He stopped, his hand quivering near his pocket, and then sat down on the bed. "Oh, shit. I can't do this right."

Derek sat next to him, waiting. For some reason, his ire tempered, still there, but on simmer. Now curiosity burned in his chest. Could this quiet man really be his father? He sat so thoughtful, so calm. What had the old Charlie been like? Derek looked up front at the nose he had broken and again felt hot waves of shame work through his body.

"I have the data," Charlie said, staring at the wall. Derek nearly jumped to his feet.

"You what?"

"I didn't want anyone else to know," Charlie said. "Only Elk Horn is privy to the information and I trust him with my life. In fact, if it weren't for him, I wouldn't have a life." Derek waited, his heart doing gymnastics in his chest, while Charlie got up and paced. "Is that Egyptian woman definitely gone?"

Derek went to the door and looked into the hallway. Nothing but silent doors as far as he could see. No one stood outside, but he couldn't be sure just how safe his room remained.

"I don't see her, but maybe we should find a private place to talk," Derek said. Charlie nodded. "I don't want to get paranoid about being bugged, but you never know."

"This Roger, you see, sent a message the last time we checked the drive and I was supposed to deliver it to you," Charlie said, taking the paper out of his pocket. "But there's also a message from me on there too."

He handed the smudged sheet to Derek. It looked as if it had been folded and re-folded about fourteen times. On the top began a standard e-mail message from Roger. No new information. On the bottom a handwritten list added to the missive.

Amends for Derek:

1) Leaving you when you needed me.
2) Missing your childhood.
3) Arguing with your mother.
4) Cussing, stinking, and puking.
5) Forgetting to tell you every day how much I loved you.

CHAPTER NINETEEN

Boone didn't look much better at breakfast. Weird, Derek thought. People celebrated the guy for always holding his liquor. In all those years of *jul* parties, Derek never remembered seeing Boone so much as slur his words. Yet, one night—heck, a few hours—with Sekhmet turned him into a queasy mess.

Boone ran his hand over his blond hair, then looked at his hand as if it were not attached to him.

"I swear I can't feel my own head," he said, when he realized Charlie, Derek, Kyra, and Elk Horn were staring at him.

"That's probably a good thing at this point," Elk Horn said.

Boone moaned and grabbed for his black coffee. Everyone else ordered full breakfasts of eggs, toast, and pancakes. All Boone could face was coffee.

"What did you have last night?" asked Derek, although Charlie's eyes were telling him to cease and desist.

"That's the hell of it," Boone said, driving a fist into his brow. "No more than I've had a thousand times before. A couple beers. And then she talked me into a couple martinis. And when I say a couple, I mean just two." He held up a pair of fingers. They were shaking.

"Did you actually see the bartender pour the drinks?" Kyra asked. Boone stared at her, considering the question. A dim light shone in his bloodshot eyes.

"You mean, did Sekhmet . . . " Boone said, stopping to think. "Come to think of it, she brought those martinis over from the bar."

Kyra nodded, tapping the end of her fork on the table. Derek nodded too. They looked from Charlie to Elk Horn.

"You see what we're dealing with," Derek said. "She said she doesn't like guns. But she sure knows her potions."

They finished their meals in silence. Derek picked up the check, plopped some bills on the table, and pointed his chin toward the door.

"Time to get started," he said, looking at Charlie. "How far do you think she's gotten?"

"She's surely in Los Alamos by now. That's where the government is likely to hold the evidence they've seized," Charlie said. He looked toward Elk Horn. "So we are going in the opposite direction."

"As far in the opposite direction as possible," Elk Horn said.

≈

Things were different in the truck cab with Boone. As Derek drove and Kyra plugged in her iPhone music again, the big man remained silent on the trip to Albuquerque, not even trying to interrupt when Derek told the story of Charlie and the mysterious resurrected data. Charlie had hired a computer maintenance man to look after Stonegate's box, Derek said. But when he saw too much interest in whatever resided on that hard drive, he decided on a bold plan. The computer man found a mirror drive on the computer—a standard safeguard when vital data is present. They simply removed the mirror drive and erased the main hard drive. The tech guy disengaged the hard drive and put it in his box of tools. Then Charlie took the mirror drive and hid it. That's what Charlie never got to explain in the cabin, because Derek hauled off and hit him.

Now Sekhmet stood ready to break into a heavily guarded facility to grab a disk that she figured had data on it somewhere. Meanwhile, Charlie would give Derek the mirror drive to take home to Chicago.

"It's brilliant, isn't it?" Derek crowed.

"What's brilliant?" Kyra called, ripping off her earphones. Derek summarized what they had just been talking about.

"Your dad is just fantastic to have saved that mirror drive," Kyra said, giving Derek a thumb's up.

Boone merely shifted in his seat, staring at the brown landscape. Derek's foot lay heavy on the accelerator and he felt as if they were about to take off.

"I thought nothing Charlie did was right," Boone said, not looking at Derek.

"Oh God, Boone, I didn't tell you," Derek said, realizing that Boone was slumped over dead drunk when Charlie appeared in the hotel room. He never knew about the apology. Didn't see Derek break into tears and embrace the old man. Didn't know that Derek began starting to think that a second chance might be possible. "I mean, you were right. All along, you were right."

"About what?"

"About change and the human spirit."

Boone laid the back of his head on the headrest and closed his eyes. He reclined in such silence that Derek was afraid he'd drifted off to sleep.

"So you finally stopped acting like a brat and gave your old man a break," Boone said, opening one eye.

"Yeah," Derek said. "I got sick of the act anyway."

"There's hope for you yet," Boone said. He smiled for the first time that day.

≈

In Albuquerque, Derek pulled off at a gas station. Elk Horn's truck pulled up alongside and Derek leaned over to the nearby passenger window. Charlie leaned out.

"Gotta make a phone call before I leave," Derek said and jogged over to the pay phone (another fortunate sighting). By now he had become used to the amount of change he had to pump in before he could make a connection. He'd be happy when this antique ritual ended. But this time, the distant ring tone provided no answer. Trevor's recorded voice piped over the line, sounding tinny and distant, as if he were receding into the New Mexican dust.

At the tone, Derek left a message. He'd be home that evening. Come meet him at the airport. Tell George. Something fantastic has happened. The voice mail beeped again and anything more to say disappeared in silent space.

≈

At the ticket counter in the Albuquerque airport, just half an hour before the boarding call for Sun Country Flight 505 to Chicago, Charlie realized that he stood ready to buy a ticket, too, to accompany Derek and Kyra.

"Make it three," he said to the ticket agent, fishing a shiny credit card out of his wallet. Elk Horn stared, looking bug-eyed at the plastic money. Charlie shrugged his shoulders. Derek knew he lived on the cheap at the reservation. Probably no one had ever seen Charlie pay on credit.

"I always kept enough to get home," Charlie said, fidgeting with the torn edges of his wallet as he avoided Elk Horn's black eyes. "And the card's still good, even though I last used it maybe three years ago."

"Better be good," snapped the ticket agent. Her sharp eyes told Charlie that she didn't joke. Times must be rough for Sun Country Airlines.

"It is," Charlie said, fishing his driver's license out of its tight plastic pocket. He also produced a fishing license and motor club card. The woman scribbled on a piece of paper and punched computer keys vigorously. The machine spit out his ticket, which she handed over with slight reluctance.

"You got a window seat, middle seat, and an aisle," she said, as if challenging them to argue with her. "Gate 15C. Have a nice day." The last comment sounded like a curse.

Derek let out a soft snort and stepped away from the counter. He surveyed the tidy new airport, homey, and festooned with colorful restaurants and shops selling Indian artwork. So different from the cold, angry inefficiency of O'Hare International Airport, their destination.

"What are we going to do for half an hour?" he wondered out loud. "Even before we go through security, there's time to kill."

Charlie pointed at a small café. The group wandered over and grabbed the first available table. They ordered cokes and sandwiches. Boone attempted to get a hair of the dog, but Charlie stared him down. Boone had a coke with the rest of them.

"Why are you doing it?" Derek said to Charlie, breaking the edgy silence that had fallen over the small group. Boone and Elk Horn looked up with interest. Charlie coughed and fished an onion off of his bun.

"Well, you know," he said, stalling. He looked at Elk Horn, who nodded slowly. "Astrid. Amends."

Boone squinted, but before he could speak, a voice announced boarding for Flight 505 to Chicago. Charlie stood up and crumpled his napkin onto his plate, then shuffled off to bus his tray. Derek fussed with his pockets, searching for his ticket. Boone fished the document off a cafeteria tray and handed it to Derek, who let out more of a whistle than a laugh. Good old Boone. Kyra laughed and took hers out of her purse.

They hurried to the security line, each lost in thought. Derek stopped in the line, ready to file in with the masses, and let his gaze wander from Kyra to Boone to Charlie. Still close by, but on the other side of security, Elk Horn and Boone stood shifting their weight from foot to foot, as if eager to be off. Boone had decided he would make that drive back to Indiana by himself and said he didn't mind, but Derek felt a bit guilty about his own need for speed. He couldn't think of a thing to say that didn't sound simpering or foolish. Take care? Attaboy? Could he be just using Boone?

Elk Horn broke the silence.

"I'll take care of Boone," he said, putting a burly arm around the Swede's shoulders. "I'll keep him out of trouble."

"You better," Boone replied, starting to laugh, then narrowing his eyes in a slight wince.

"Well, you know the way home," Derek said, meeting his second cousin's blue eyes. How often had he avoided this simple act? Meeting Boone's gaze, approaching him as equal to equal. Derek felt as he gazed into those unguarded portals that there existed no more shame between them. Derek was flawed, so was Boone. But they were family, joined by culture and blood and history. Derek lowered his eyes.

"I think I'll stick around here a while," Boone answered, jerking his thumb toward Elk Horn. "This guy's pretty cool. Maybe he can teach me a thing or two."

Charlie smiled—too broadly, Derek thought.

"You won't return to the reservation," Elk Horn said to Charlie. He issued a statement of certainty.

"Probably not," Charlie said, as a TSA worker urged them forward.

"Go. Do good," Elk Horn said, then turned on his boot heel to go. Boone fixed Derek with a sudden wild stare.

"Get that disk home, Derek," he said, sotto voce. "Don't stop until it's safe."

He rushed after the retreating form of Elk Horn. Boone's hunched shoulders strained the seams of his denim jacket.

≈

Getting into the personal space of strangers on an airplane felt unpleasant enough, but this time Derek felt the close quarters almost unbearable. Derek folded his long body into a middle seat since he gallantly gave the window to Kyra. He was jammed next to skinny, quiescent Charlie—the father he barely knew. When the flight attendants wheeled their rumbling drink cart down the aisle, Derek had a strong urge to call for a double Scotch. His nerves were blasting red-alert signals to every corner of his body. But Charlie ordered an apple juice and Derek, in deference to his dad's new lifestyle, asked for a cola. Kyra just had water. The harried stewardess, surely a twin of the ticket agent, handed them plastic cups. He examined the level of actual brown liquid in his plastic cup and determined he was enjoying seventy-five percent ice.

His gaze drifted toward the neighboring seat and alighted on Charlie's carry-on bag, scrunched into the under-seat compartment. Inside, the mirror disk lay hidden, unceremoniously wrapped in t-shirts and underwear. Derek and Charlie had argued about ways to transport the precious data. The one thing they had agreed upon was the need never to become separated from the disk—it must be carried on board. Charlie had wanted Derek to slide it into his inner coat pocket, but Derek pointed out the issues posed by walk-through metal detectors. Everything is scanned, in your pocket or not. Derek would have to take it out of his pocket, put it in a spare-change tray, and explain what the darn thing could be. God knows how long the whole process would take—if they ever were cleared at all. Better to leave the disk in the duffel bag. It would get x-rayed, but chances were good that the worker running the baggage scanner would ignore the whole thing. Heck, a disk doesn't look like a weapon.

Sure enough, that's exactly what happened. The bag flew through security clearance without earning so much as a second glance. So far, so good.

Derek kept staring at the beat-up luggage, a duffel made of leather. It had a history as a former luxury item, probably worth several hundred dollars, but now the leather had become, in the parlance of fashion, "distressed." Where else had Charlie carried the bag? Derek wondered. He could see it lying beside Charlie underneath a highway overpass, or stashed in the overhead bin of a cross-country train. Derek realized that he knew almost nothing of the way the bag had gone from burnished to dilapidated. He had little idea of how Charlie had lived between the time the old drunk left his neat suburban home and when he ended up a spartan teetotaler doing odd jobs on an Indian reservation. Where had Charlie's epiphany taken place? Could it be real?

Derek closed his eyes as the plane took off and he offered a silent prayer that he, Kyra, his father (and the disk) would make it home in safety. He held Kyra's hand. She gave his a squeeze. As they headed northward, he imagined the jet trails leaving puffs in the sky over Los Alamos. He dreamed that Sekhmet turned her bronze face skyward, shading her keen eyes with one bejeweled hand and homing in on Derek's plan. Then he imagined her in the air, in a private jet that drafted in the commercial jet's wake, dead on track to intercept Derek in the air. Derek let out a groan.

"Derek," said Charlie, poking his son in the arm. "You don't want to miss dinner."

Derek bolted alert, amazed that he managed to drift off like an infant. He thought that nothing could take his attention away from the disk sitting right next to him. He resolved to maintain better control of himself.

"Probably just peanuts," he muttered. He pulled the tray table down as a steward slapped a bag of pretzels in front of him. He sighed and handed the snack over to Charlie, who practically inhaled the food. Nothing goes to waste on the reservation, Derek remembered.

"What happens when we get home?" Charlie said, tossing the wrapper onto his tray.

"What do you mean?" Derek mumbled.

"What if she shows up?" Charlie said.

"I doubt she'll get to Chicago before we . . . finish our business," Derek said, wishing Charlie would take a little care to keep the conversation private. Not that the lunkhead in front of him was concentrating on anything but the inside of his eyelids. But still.

"But she will show up," Charlie said, nodding into his apple juice. "What do you think she really wants? Not the usual stuff: not just money, not just power. Something else. What is it?" Charlie looked out the window into the distant clouds.

That dangled in the air as more than an idle question. Derek felt a chill. He thought back to the moment when he looked deep into Sekhmet's eyes and saw more than he expected. What secret did she hold? What would satisfy that gaping hunger behind those soulless eyes?

"Worship? Devotion?" Derek searched for words. "She seems to think she's a genuine goddess."

"I think she wants magic. Wizardry over time and space. How else do you convince people that you are divine?"

"Magic." Derek tested the word in his mind. What could be more magical than moving objects through space, hands-free? The stuff of sorcerers—and witches.

"Don't expect her to go away any time soon, Derek. If she can stalk you by computer, she knows everything: your address, your bank account, your health records, where Astrid lives . . . " Charlie broke off, his eyes unfocused.

Derek swallowed but said nothing. He knew Charlie was right, yet he'd been so busy running he hadn't had time to think the whole mess through. Stashing the disk in a safe place became mandatory. And then what?

The familiar pilot drawl boomed over the public address system, informing them that the weather in Chicago loomed ugly in the upcoming miles. Lightning had struck the control tower, he said, so they would touch down in St. Louis "for a spell," until conditions were safe again at O'Hare International. A single groan erupted from the passenger section. Derek joined with a small sound of protest. He hated that airport in St. Louis more than he detested O'Hare. A few hours in that barn, reeking of fast food and piled sky-high with St. Louis Cardinals memorabilia, assaulted his brain as more than his tense nerves could take.

He gazed over at Charlie who merely pressed his feet to either end of his battered duffel bag. Charlie looked back with a smile on his tanned face that shone as good as a promise, Derek realized. That duffel wasn't leaving Charlie's side. Derek stared nakedly into his father's face, open once again to the old man's care, hoping that this time he would not squander his trust.

≈

As Charlie held down the fort at Gate 59, Derek, followed by Kyra, ran to the only pay phone at the St. Louis gate. He tried George and got no answer, not even a voice mail. Trevor's line rang four times and Derek felt a streak of anticipation rocket through his chest as he waited for the voice mail to kick in. As Trevor's recorded voice droned on, Derek felt a sudden urge to turn around and collapse into Kyra's arms. He needed this beautiful, warm woman to steady him for just a few more hours.

"St. Louis base here," Derek said to Trevor's machine. "The Eagle has not yet landed. Expect a delay." No sense giving any details. He'd figure it out. He replaced the receiver and gazed into the distance.

Beyond the telephone kiosk, crowds pulsed, moving like swells of fluid coursing through the long tunnels and moving walkways. Heads bobbed at various altitudes, some blond and puffy, some slick and bald, some topped with ball caps. One head jerked up and down along with the current, snaky braids popping up with each step. The wild plaits seemed to leap out from the anonymous mob in a moment of heart-stopping clarity.

Salim. Who else had hair like that?

"Did you see that? Crazy braids? Sekhmet's bully boy?" Derek asked Kyra. She shook her head. Derek refocused on the crowd and tried to pick out the braids again, but the moment dissipated. All he could see was a faceless blanket of surging humanity. Yet, he hadn't imagined it. Far from it. He determined that Salim poked through the throng from the direction of Gate 59.

Derek broke into a jog, pulling Kyra along, making a beeline for a recently emptied gate, reaching it as a desk clerk pulled a sign off the wall. As she placed it under the desk, he could just make out the letters " . . . querque."

"Did that flight just arrive from Albuquerque?" Derek asked the agent, who reached up to smooth flyaway hair from her perspiring brow.

"Yeah, they were re-routed," she said, pointing down the hallway. She fixed Derek with her tired eyes. "Did you miss someone? Most of them were continuing to Chicago on Flight 505."

Derek stared. The agent raised her eyebrows.

"Okay? Or do you want me to page them?" she asked.

"No, it's okay," Derek said, barely meeting her eyes before he and Kyra charged full-force back to Charlie's side.

CHAPTER TWENTY

The drive from St. Louis to Chicago took less time than finding the car to get there. Once Derek grabbed Charlie by the arm and hauled him out of the airport, Kyra trailing along, it became apparent that the Nilssons weren't going anywhere under their true names. It hadn't taken Derek long to see those strange, grim-faced men stationed at the newly re-assigned airport gate. Little microphones in their ears. Identical haircuts. FBI. If they weren't looking for him now, they would be soon, just as surely as they were tracking Sekhmet and her errand boys. Who talked and got him involved? He suspected Ra.

It looked easy enough to bail out of the airport without being seen, but finding alternative transportation to Chicago lurked ahead as risky. Amtrak was hopeless. They'd need identity cards for even a simple ticket across the river to Alton, Illinois. Renting a car presented the same dilemma. Derek would have considered hitchhiking if it weren't for that precious disk in Charlie's carry-on bag. And he thought of Kyra's safety too. He couldn't take chances like that.

When Charlie suggested walking, Derek thought his old man had lost his marbles. But Charlie just chuckled in his clucking way and ambled out the terminal doors, along the walkways, past the parking lots, past the freeways, coaxing Derek and the tiring Kyra along.

"I would have worn sneakers if I knew I was in for a hike," Kyra complained. Derek put his arm around her and let her lean on him as she navigated any difficult terrain.

Soon enough, they were in the outskirts of a working-class neighborhood. The entire walk took all of twenty minutes. Kyra rubbed her ankles.

Charlie pointed at a gas station.

"There ya go," he said, indicating a humble array of fuel pumps and a small convenience store. Derek and Kyra stared at the crumbling building without comprehending what Charlie suggested. A trip to the bathroom? A coke? A bag of chips?

"Here!" Charlie said, shuffling up to an aging Audi, parked under the large Mobil sign. The small sedan sat amid blowing newspapers and discarded cigarette wrappers—a throwaway in a vicinity where possessions weren't tossed until they were exhausted.

The Audi shone a burgundy color, which disguised corrosion in a devious fashion. But Derek could see the iron oxide inside the door hinges and wheel wells. Not a rust bucket, surely, but anything but pristine.

"They want $800 for it!" Derek said, pointing at the sign in the window.

Charlie continued to inspect the car, as Derek ranted on. "How are we going to pull that together? You can't take that much of a cash advance on your credit card. And we can't use plastic now, not with the, you know, those government guys on our tail." He looked at the car's tires. They had decent tread. Derek scratched his head, while Charlie gestured toward the gas station's office.

"We can make a deal," Charlie said. "My gut tells me it'll make it to Chicago. Then we can turn it around and re-sell it. Probably for more."

"How's that possible?" Derek looked frantically at the office door, where a paunchy man in a stained blue attendant's shirt hopped outside ready to make a sale. Charlie gave Derek a soft punch on the arm.

"Remember Ivar and the Viking Traders?" Charlie's blue eyes twinkled in the setting sunlight.

"The guy who sold those junk heaps all over the North Side? You said you'd never buy a car from him."

"Oh, but I'd sell to him, especially if I were bringing up a car from St. Louis. One with medium mileage, decent condition and a popular body style."

Charlie kept chuckling, a little rumble in the bottom of his throat, as he stepped forward to meet the squat gas-station manager. Derek shrank back, hanging next to the beater, loathe to get too close to the negotiations. Kyra questioned Derek about what was going on, but he could only answer with an exaggerated shrug.

Up near the office, gestures filled the air as the lies flew. Derek retreated to the sidewalk and Charlie and the manager advanced on the Audi and opened the hood. The men waved their hands in an argument about the spark plugs, and the man pulled one out to demonstrate that it sparked as new. Charlie demanded a new air filter and the man shrugged his shoulders in defeat. They continued their civilized rapier fight as Derek leaned lopsided on the signpost. Kyra sagged down to sit on the curb. The haggling seemed to delight Charlie, who glowed by the time he shook hands with the seller. The two negotiators looked as pleased as if sealing a Mideast peace agreement. Charlie slipped into the office and re-emerged five minutes later with keys and a title.

"How much?" Derek ventured as Charlie opened the Audi's passenger side door for him.

"Three hundred and a percentage of what Ivar gets for it," Charlie said with his cheeks in high color. The old man had always loved getting a deal. It seemed to light his internal engines. "Turns out he knows Ivar from high school days."

"Yeah, sure," Derek said. "More like he knew Ivar from the Illinois state pen." Kyra laughed.

Charlie whistled as he turned the engine over. The engine hummed and the dash lit up like the instrument board of a finely tuned jet. "Yeah, that's probably closer to the truth," Charlie said with a cackle. The "license applied for" sticker was applied to the rear window and they were legal for travel.

"And I can't believe you bought the car without a test drive first," Derek mumbled.

"You complaining?"

"Let's just get out of here."

Before nightfall, they were in the Illinois cornfields. A couple hours after that, Derek spied the lights of the most remote Chicago suburbs. He rehearsed what he'd say to Trevor when they stopped at his apartment door and required refuge.

The rain started at nine in the evening, around the time Derek pulled off Interstate 55 to make a telephone call. He fished out a heavy load of change from his pockets and dialed Trevor's number. He longed for the convenience of his apartment telephone or at least a cellular phone. He listened to Trevor's line ring several times and then, once again, the voice mail delivered its message. Derek spoke quickly, telling Trevor there had been a change of plans, that he should expect him later that night, and not at the airport. He replaced the receiver with a heavy sense of defeat pressing on his shoulder blades. Maybe this is what made old men sag, he thought.

He turned toward the Audi, watching the sheets of rain pulse between where he stood and the safety of the car. This morning, he'd woken up filled with a sense of purpose. He started the day thinking he'd be bringing Stonegate's hard drive home and expected to arrive as a conquering hero. He'd outfoxed Sekhmet, ran around Stonegate's data traps, even steered clear of the government men who lurked around during his entire southwest trek. He felt he returned home with the prize. But there was no way to explain it to Trevor or George.

Meanwhile, Sekhmet still snaked behind him on his trail. The Bureau guys had caught his scent. The mirror drive, sitting in Charlie's beat-up satchel in the trunk of the Audi, was never more vulnerable. Derek had no idea if it would be safer to show his face in his own apartment building. It seemed doubtful. Kyra was under strict advice to not use her own cell phone, even for music now, lest someone track her signals. Homecoming wasn't what people cracked it up to be.

Charlie waved from within the car, urging Derek to return. Derek realized, for one electric second, that bringing his dad home to this cops-and-robbers show wasn't the brightest of moves. Who could predict how Charlie would act? Could Derek count on him to stay quiet? Where would the old man stay? Would he be tempted by the old haunts, the familiar bars? Lightning struck a nearby tree and Derek's brain lit up. He realized he needed someone to hide that hard drive—and hide it well.

Derek urged himself forward and shot through the rain, which stung his skin like the attack of a hundred wasps. He yanked the car door open and hurled himself in, then lay gasping on the sticky vinyl seat. The roof drummed as if pummeled by an army of mad pixies. Charlie fiddled with the radio.

"Listen," Charlie commanded. At first, Derek could only hear a few squawks and the tail end of a sentence or two, but eventually he made out a newscaster's voice droning on about the economy. Derek shot Charlie a look of impatience. Charlie held up a finger. The announcer began a new story.

"Also today, two men were taken into custody at Chicago's O'Hare Airport as they disembarked from a flight originating in Albuquerque, New Mexico. The two suspects were arrested for allegedly breaking into a secure US military research facility at Los Alamos, New Mexico. A third suspect, a female, is still at large."

Derek turned to Charlie and searched his father's face for a hint of emotion. Charlie nodded and smirked, covering half his mouth with one bony hand.

"We got off that plane in the nick of time," Derek said. Kyra sighed and agreed. Charlie continued to bob his head up and down. Derek drummed his still-dripping fingers on the dashboard. He looked back at his father and squinted. "How did you know they were going to do that report?"

"They announced the headlines while you were staring into space out there." Charlie shoved the gearshift into drive and started up the windshield wipers. They did nothing to improve visibility, but that didn't stop Charlie from inching forward.

"Well, your timing was good," Derek admitted. "It makes a few things pretty clear. For instance, we know that Sekhmet got away, and soon she will be lurking around Chicago somewhere." Derek kept chattering as his mind worked, even though his deductions were only half worked out. "But the goons, Ra and Salim, were arrested. So, we only have Sekhmet to worry about. That makes it a little better."

"Yeah, only Sekhmet," Charlie said and let out a sharp whistle. Kyra shivered. Derek said nothing and the car nosed through the storm to merge with the crawling traffic bound toward the heart of a drowning metropolis.

≈

They wound up sitting cross-legged on the enormous Persian carpet in the middle of Trevor's loft. For all of Trevor's design sense, he had precious little furniture, and certainly not enough for a crowd of four. Everyone made do by lounging on the carpet, some lying on their sides, others sitting with knees akimbo. Charlie sat perfectly balanced in the corner in a modified lotus position. Derek wondered idly if Charlie had been meditating out there in Santa Fe. It certainly would help him fit in with the New Agers. Derek's mind stuttered at the idea of Charlie as a post-hippie seeker of Eastern mysticism. There still remained a great deal he didn't know about this man who was his father, and about the journey that had delivered him from addiction.

On this Sunday night there had been nowhere to go except Trevor's place. He was the only person who hadn't been tailed or stalked by some creepy agent—whether that be a devotee of Sekhmet or a faceless government operative. He hadn't appeared on the radar screen yet—but it was only a matter of time before Trevor, too, fell under surveillance. This was the gift Derek brought all who touched him.

Trevor cleared his throat and said they shouldn't try to go to Kyra's apartment. Government agents had stopped by, FBI.

"What?" Kyra cried. "How do you know?"

"They left their calling cards," Trevor said and produced two business cards. One for an agent Rock and the other for an agent Stone. Kyra looked over them in shock.

"Try calling your voice mail. I bet they left messages," Derek said. She raced over to Trevor's phone, dialled, and spent the next few minutes listening. After enough time, she placed the receiver down and looked at Derek.

"They were looking for you and thought I might know where you were. They said they knew the plane was delayed and wanted to know if I was going to meet the re-routed flight. Then they gave up trying. Lucky that Trevor has a landline or I couldn't get my messages from voice mail without tipping them off about the location of my cell phone."

"How in the hell did they get your phone number—your landline?" Derek blurted. He seized on the idea, in a clumsy fashion, that the messages were the FBI's way of finding out if Kyra sat at home. His mind muddled too much to make sense of the whole of it.

"Come on," Trevor said. "It's the FBI."

"You notice they didn't ask about me," Charlie said. "It's as if I don't exist. So they don't know everything."

Derek nodded, considering his father's valid point. Surely they knew Charlie traveled with him, but they hadn't linked Charlie—the bearer of the hard disk—to the data. Still, it would be only a matter of days, or hours, before everyone Derek knew and loved fell under the watchful eye of Big Brother.

"Well, we are completely in the dark," Kyra said. "And what do you think is going to happen to Boone?"

"He's safe out there at the reservation," Charlie said. "Believe me, the government has nothing to do with the Native Americans. They just don't care."

Derek started telling Trevor and company the story from the moment he left Chicago, filling in his audience on the auto trip, the helicopter surveillance, the discovery of the cabin and the appearance of Sekhmet. Derek glanced at Charlie when he came to the part of the story where he attacked his own dad. Derek shrugged and glossed over the facts, mentioning that he and Charlie had "a difference of opinion." His dad merely nodded in the corner like a simpleton. Derek wondered if he even were listening.

There were other landmines to step over. Derek delicately danced around the subject of Sekhmet, who starred in his story as more of a witch than a seductress. If Charlie didn't approve of the spin Derek put on this fairy tale, he couldn't tell. His dad continued to sit like some Tibetan lama, closing his eyes now and then and smiling at some private pleasure. Derek wondered idly if the old dude cruised on some sort of drug—mushrooms, herbs, prescription tranquilizers. If not, Derek wanted to sample some of that natural high that Charlie appeared to trip on.

Derek did mention Sekhmet's little love scene with Boone. It was important to explain the Mickey Finn that Sekhmet slipped to Boone, the big guy's subsequent remorse, and his sudden experiment with sobriety.

Competing thoughts crowded what little gray matter Derek had left for rational discourse. He sweated out the final bits of his story. When he got to the part about the St. Louis airport, he ran out of steam.

"You can probably put the rest together," he said, shoulders sagging as the impact of the tale's pathetic end tanked his mood.

Kyra should have been consoling him about this time, giving him a compassionate hug. Instead, she sat alone in a corner, visibly distressed by the calls from the FBI.

Derek changed gears. "How's Mom? I'm worried about her. Boone's worried. He gave me a royal tongue lashing for putting her in danger."

Trevor sat up straight. "She's okay. The bullyboys broke in when she had stepped out. Ripped off her hard drive, and a few papers. I took care of things for her."

"They took her hard drive?"

"Well, George didn't have anything, so maybe they got desperate. Don't worry; her homeowner's insurance covered the theft loss. She didn't lose anything important—just e-mail from her friends and budgeting software. All her writing had been backed up on the cloud."

Derek breathed with relief. At least he had told his mom about the benefits of off-site cloud storage. Astrid loved it. As she said, all writers are paranoid. That manuscript existed as all she lived for these days. If Sekhmet had taken that, she might as well have gouged out Astrid's heart. Derek jumped up and paced as he mulled this over, making more connections. His feet danced under him as his inner anxiety grew. Forward, then back. Still. Shift of weight. He knew he had screwed up in ways he could hardly imagine. He ran to Trevor.

"What if they knew you had my flex drives? You could have . . . . I can't believe I . . . . "

Trevor smiled and flipped back his long hair. "I don't have them anymore. They're in a storage locker. I'll give you the key."

Derek stared at him, feeling weight lift off his shoulders

"And Foo?"

"I'll bring her to you," Trevor said, smiling with delight for the first time that night. "But I have to warn you. The two of us are bonding. She might not want to return to your digs."

≈

Charlie started edging toward Trevor's front door.

"I guess I'll be going now that everyone is pretty much settled," he said with a nervous cough. "Derek, I'll be with Ivar at the Viking Traders." He handed Derek a small note. "There's the phone number. Call me whenever you need me."

Derek suddenly felt off-kilter with his father taking off so fast. "I'll walk you down to the car," he said. He and Charlie negotiated the stairs in silence, went out the front door and stood by the Audi, kicking at the concrete. The rain had stopped.

"Son," Charlie said. "I know I messed things up horribly between us. I'm hoping we can, you know, start over or something."

Derek looked at his dad—thinner, balding a little bit, shifting his balance from leg to leg, looking like a humbled schoolchild who'd been punished by the principal. He felt a lump rise in his throat when he thought of the courage it took for Charlie to write that note of amends. He couldn't just let him go like this.

"Derek . . . I . . . . "

Without thinking, Derek threw his arms around Charlie's shoulders in a way he had only done when he was ten years old. He hugged him a long time and came up only to find his cheeks were damp with tears.

"Dad," he said, choking a bit. "There have been too many years of anger and mistrust. I just want to welcome you home and love you now. I promise to call you every day."

Charlie raised his eyebrows and stared as if not comprehending.

"What I mean is the punch in the nose was my catharsis and now all that's left is an open space that I'd like to fill with forgiveness. And if you want me to go to AA meetings with you, just for support, I will do that," Derek said, aware that the tears were still falling.

Charlie leaned over and patted Derek's back. "There now, son. I understand. No more hard feelings."

Derek swallowed and nodded. He wiped the tears off his face.

"We need to put that mirror drive in a storage locker," Derek said, ashamed to bring the subject up. Charlie agreed and handed him the drive, hidden in a folded up t-shirt that Charlie said he didn't need anymore. He didn't act insulted at all, just sure that Derek was making the right decision.

"I just want you to know that I completely trusted you with that mirror drive," he said. "I completely trust you with everything. You're a completely new man to me now."

Charlie smiled slightly. "I've put a lot of work into that. But having my own son forgive me and take me back—that's the best thing I can hope to achieve."

"Well, you did it," Derek said. He turned towards Trevor's door. "Don't be shy about calling. I want to talk to you a lot, until all this sinks in."

"Of course, Derek," Charlie said in a soft voice. He got in the Audi, put his leather bag on the passenger seat and started the engine. He gave a long, slow wave goodbye as he started the car down the street to Andersonville.

Derek felt that knot in his stomach dissolve.

CHAPTER TWENTY ONE

The next morning, after Derek deposited the mirror drive at a local U-Store-It, he hurried off to George's place. When answering the door, George acted as if Derek had merely stepped out for a donut—and stayed away for three weeks. He asked about Boone and the trip west, but it appeared obvious he had already heard the story from someone else early in the morning. George nodded his head as Derek seemed to confirm the facts already assembled in that brimming Esterberg brain. He had already determined that Derek was hiding out at Trevor's place for a while, but he wanted to know where Charlie had gone. When Derek told him about Charlie's old Swedish pals in Andersonville, George gave a thumb's up. He didn't ask about the hard drive, but Derek held up a U-Store-It key before those glittering blue eyes. George nodded, and Derek slipped the key back in his pocket. They'd talk about it later.

George strolled over to his desk and filled Derek in on the night of the ugly break-in, when Ra and Salim and few other toughs decided to pay George a late-night visit. They had followed a pizza-delivery guy through the outer doors, then pushed their way into George's apartment when he answered their knock. They immediately stationed themselves at George's computer array, searching for any links to the missing data. When they didn't find what they wanted, Derek placed the fateful call to George.

"It really wasn't as bad as it sounded," George explained, pointing at his workstation. "They had no guns, no real muscle. They simply outnumbered me."

"It scared the hell out of me," Derek said, running a hand along the side of George's Mac desktop, feeling where the plastic was shredded in the crude effort to extract the hard drive. It took some expertise to dissect an older Mac properly and the Egyptian crew wasn't up to the job. "They sure butchered your hardware."

"Well, they didn't get anything," George said, shrugging. "I can't understand why they didn't check out the computers at the university. That's where I do most of my work."

"They do what Sekhmet tells them to do," Derek said. "She determined the important e-mail issued from here." He indicated the Mac. "The next stop was my place." Derek didn't need to add that the university hardware remained far too secure for a few rowdy ruffians to compromise.

"You left in such a hurry, I'm surprised you had time to lock the door," George said with a snicker. He reached into a file cabinet and started to pull out a stack of mail. "Meanwhile, look what accumulated," George said. He slammed a thick white envelope on top of the pile.

Derek knew he'd be coming home to an avalanche of unpaid bills, but he hadn't expected to confront paperwork at George's place. It seemed incredible, but he and George together needed to make decisions on plenty of computer issues, from maintenance on domain names to monthly charges from the university server. There were piles of the usual junk mail, offering big deals to the webmaster, not-so-obvious pitches from loan companies, and now this letter from a law firm in New Jersey.

Derek picked up the letter, immediately noticing the heft of the envelope, the substance of the stationery. It didn't feel like a ruse from an ambulance chaser. "R.P. Black, Attorney at Law," read the return address, spelled out in expensive, engraved letters.

"So, what's up with this?" Derek asked, turning the letter over in his hand. "Are we being sued?"

"Read it," George said, delight playing at the edges of his lips.

Derek let out an exasperated breath and pulled the letter from the envelope. The vellum nearly unfolded on its own. Derek squinted at the writing, forcing himself to comprehend:

> Dear Messrs. Esterberg and Nilsson:
>
> My client, Seth Stonegate, has informed me that he would like to speak with you regarding certain

> computer data. He is currently incarcerated at the Federal Correctional Institution in Milan, Michigan, where he is working with me on the appeal of his computer theft conviction.
>
> He requests that both of you meet with him at the prison, at your convenience. I will be pleased to put you on his visitors' list, if you will kindly telephone me at my office.
>
> Regards,
> Riff P. Black, Esq

Derek read the letter twice before looking up. He couldn't seem to make the black letters mean anything to his scrambled brain cells. His eyes met George's.

"Riff?" Derek said, laughter exploding from his gut. "His lawyer's name is Riff?"

"Riff Presley Black." George's eyebrows danced up and down with each word. "I called already. The guy filled me in on everything. He's a long-time friend of the Stonegate family. He's the product of hippie parents, a Deadhead lifestyle. They did the pilgrimage to Graceland and drove a VW bus. They named him Riff in honor of Eric Clapton and Presley for you-know-who." George folded his arms and suppressed a giggle. "And, oh yeah, he's Stonegate's lawyer."

Derek threw the letter back on the overflowing desk. "It was an internationally famous case. All the news reports featured it. And he had a lawyer named Riff?"

George scooped the letter up and returned it to the envelope. "Well, he goes by R.P. Black in court. That's how he'll argue the case if it goes to the Supreme Court." George tucked the letter into a file cabinet by his knee. "He's the real deal. Anyway, we have an appointment at 4 p.m. Saturday with Stonegate at the Club Fed in Michigan."

"What?" Derek felt the amusement draining away. What could Stonegate be playing at? The only way he'd even know that George and Derek existed was if Sekhmet had tipped him off. If

Sekhmet still communicated with Stonegate, Derek doubted she put a positive spin on his latest activities in Santa Fe.

"Look, it's no biggie," George said. "I'd have gone myself if you hadn't turned up. Riff said Stonegate knows we have the data. He's aware that the feds are never going to let him get it back. Legally obtained or not, that data sat on confiscated computers. He's more likely to get his Lexus back than those hard drives."

"So what does he think he's going to get out of this little interview?" Derek wasn't enjoying this news. He didn't feel an inner thrill that Stonegate knew about him. He had a wobbly feeling in his gut.

"I'm sure he wants us to throw him a bone," George said, his thin lips pressed together in a sly smirk. "But look what we can learn from him."

Derek felt his shoulders slump as he leaned back against his chair. The truth hit him. There were more questions about that data now than there were before the encounters with Sekhmet. Derek had no idea if her story had the ring of truth. He had no idea if Stonegate had made the formulas work. Who else had scrambled after this treasure trove of bits and bytes? Stonegate could shed a floodlight of lucidity on the whole murky affair.

"How can we trust him?"

"He's in federal custody," George said, rolling his eyes. "It's really a lot harder for him to trust us."

"Okay, it's your call," Derek said, standing up and shaking out the nervous energy in his legs. "But it feels bad. Like walking into a black widow's web."

"Wait until you walk into the joint. That'll feel even worse."

≈

Derek next stopped back at Trevor's to hide the key in a place not likely to be searched. As he was putting the key in an Altoids box, Kyra reminded him that he forgot something when he went chasing after his father. Kyra opened the door to a bedroom. A delicate pink nose sniffed the air near the hinges.

"Foo," Derek called like a doting father, dropping to a knee. "Here, little Foo girl."

She pressed her side along the door as she stepped out. Derek now got down on all fours and tipped his head to the side.

"Foo, girl," he intoned. "I'm home."

The calico approached like a ballerina executing precise pointe steps—soft, strong, balanced. She glided in a wide circle around Derek, nose picking up what must be an aromatic potpourri of clues. Satisfied, Foo came along Derek's right thigh, pressing her face against his jeans. Derek reached over and enfolded her in his arms. She nuzzled his face and let out her familiar throaty purr. Derek continued rubbing his cheeks against her dear face, stopping when he felt her fur was damp. The wetness, he realized, was from his own tears. *Tears again. What is happening to me?*

He looked up to see Kyra biting her lip. There had been no way to hide his sudden outburst of emotion, but he felt no shame. Kyra, too, looked a little emotional. She looked like she was feigning an itch and rubbed her forehead, hurrying her hand across her eyes.

Foo sniffed the legs of the sofa, slid alongside and behind it, and then disappeared on a detective mission. Foo, they decided, would stay with Trevor until Derek could feel safe enough to move back to his apartment.

In the meantime, he directed an invitation to Kyra.

"I want to take a little drive with you. The Oriental Institute at the University of Chicago," Derek said. "You'll love it. Then we'll lunch downtown."

Kyra screwed up her mouth in the peculiar way that Derek loved. It meant that she didn't want to but would be game to try.

"Will we be, you know, out of the public eye?" she asked.

"Look, it's impossible to say that we'll never be followed, but Trevor gave me his car keys. And we'll be in a crowd of students at the university. It's safer than any place else I can think of."

"I guess."

In the day since they'd returned from New Mexico, she ruled out almost every setting where he might feel comfortable: her apartment, his place, George's flat, or even Ravi's restaurant. Kyra even insisted that he meet his own mother at some dingy coffee house near Wrigley Field. Derek couldn't blame Kyra for being scared, but her panicky sense of precaution put a huge damper on intimacy. Since they came back to Chicago, all he'd been bestowed were hugs, a hurried kiss and a hand-squeeze from her. A quick trip to the South Side might be just what they needed to loosen up.

She shrugged on a windbreaker and they went down to the street.

On the ride down Lake Shore Drive, Derek talked about Charlie. By the time he got to the father-son reunion in the hotel room, when Kyra was walking Boone to his room, Kyra had fallen silent. Did she know what parts he left out? He pressed on with his story.

He didn't know why he felt compelled to spill his guts about dear old Dad, but he couldn't stop his mouth from moving. A dam had broken, he thought, but it hadn't yet been repaired. He endured the effects of a flood, an emotional overrun. If Kyra didn't want to listen, he couldn't tell. She sat there, after all, a captive audience.

He glanced over at the passenger seat. Kyra seemed to hear him, but Derek could discern that she acted distracted. She kept tapping at the side window, staring at nothing visible in the middle distance between the side mirror and the cars in the next lane. She told Derek he needed to learn to trust his father again, that total transformation couldn't happen in one night. He wanted to say that it did, but held off contradicting her.

He decided not to tell her of his tearful moment of reconciliation in front of Trevor's door. This wasn't the time.

Derek felt his focus reemerge on the present as he began to look for a valuable city parking place. His long lapses in concentration scared him. He'd been driving for a good ten minutes on autopilot and could not remember how he ended up in Hyde Park. He clutched the wheel with an iron grasp and circled several blocks before he found a place to curb Trevor's fancy ride. The two-seat sportster stood out amongst the simple sedans of students and professors. He might as well have been driving a limo. As Kyra moved to get out of the parked car, Derek swooped around to the passenger side to guide her up the sidewalk. Kyra, surprised, smiled like a baffled teenager.

They slipped through the heavy Gothic doors of the Oriental Institute's small museum, a dark, cathedral-like set of rooms with thick stone walls, ironwork on the windows and little natural light. No one seemed to bother whether they came or went, so the couple slipped into the Egyptian gallery after Derek tucked a couple bills into the bin for voluntary donations. The museum was far from empty, but Derek still felt conspicuous, as if the milling visitors recognized that he appeared as a university interloper.

"Some guy who works here supposedly can help me with the information I have on this Egyptian data," he told Kyra in an unnecessary whisper. Somehow, the setting seemed to call for low voices. "Sekhmet sent me a picture, an engraving of a pharaoh raised in a specific angle as he ascends to the eternal stars. Or something like that."

"Are you sure the picture is here?"

"No. She wasn't exactly forthcoming. She said some of the important pieces she studied were here and at the Met in New York."

"The Metropolitan Museum is awfully big, Derek. It could also be in the British Museum, or Berlin, or Cairo."

"I called London and Berlin already. New York, too. I checked the Web on Trevor's computer. It's not in any of those places. New York suggested the O.I., where a curator should be able to give me some leads."

The small gallery was clean and smartly redesigned, with impressive signage and optimum lighting, but it still emitted the musty, crusty aura of age that all fine museums exude. Mercifully, there were only two mummies on display—wrapped in their desiccated linens and hiding in their sarcophagi. All the relics, from the scribe's tools to the tiny amulets, were buffed by millennia of wear. The carvings, the stelae, even the fifteen-foot statue of Tutankhamen bore a fine coat of ashen antiquity.

Derek searched the carvings closely. He compared them to some hieroglyphic symbols, found in a textbook, that could possibly be the writings Sekhmet referenced. But since Derek couldn't read Egyptian writing, the task proved monumental. It was like looking for a Rumi poem in lines of untranslated Arabic. He moved away from Kyra who stared in rapt attention at the case containing protective amulets and papyri of magical spells.

As Derek bent over, scrutinizing the etchings of ibises and papyrus stalks and extravagantly designed eyes, he came nose to beak with a sharp black countenance. Peering keenly at him stood a four-foot-tall Horus falcon. The obsidian bird had a beak of gold and its eyes, although carved out of flat stone, glowed from within.

"It's not here," a voice said. Derek looked at the bird and felt his blood pound in that sensitive vein in his left temple.

But the bird never moved and Derek was convinced he was hearing things again.

He found a guard and asked for the name of the curator. The guard indicated a small man standing next to a showcase of some Egyptian pottery and scrawling notes in a leather notebook. Derek introduced himself and asked about the drawing of the king raised at a forty-five degree angle.

The curator shook his head. By the time Kyra caught up, Derek was shaking his hand and apologizing for bothering him.

Kyra looked quizzical and Derek admitted the carving was in Cairo.

"We wasted the afternoon for nothing," Kyra said with a long face.

"Not necessarily," the curator said. "I can translate the hieroglyphics you've written down." He looked at Derek's pad of paper. Derek moved it closer to the academic's perspiring face. "Yes, delightful," the man continued, pressing his fingers together.

"Well?" Derek demanded.

"Quite straightforward. 'Raised on sound.' Although the glyphs for sound could also mean singing."

Derek sneaked a glance at Kyra. She regarded the curator with wide eyes.

"Would you know where I might find more information on this odd arrangement of words and carving? The pharaoh rising at an angle? Are there any other similar plaques?"

The man shook his head with a look of defeat and handed over a business card. "You'll find everything you want to know in this book," the short man said, indicating a publication on a bookshelf of tomes for sale. "It's got the information you need on the dead king 'lifted by sound,' as the hieroglyphs say. But this author isn't mainstream. Not by a long shot. People around here laugh at him."

Derek looked at the title: *Serpent's Song* by Darryl Driven. He had never heard of the guy. Inside the book was a flyer about an acoustics demonstration coming up soon at a remote site in Connecticut. Derek showed it to Kyra and they both exchanged puzzled glances. He bought the book anyway.

"Are we done here?" Kyra asked, taking in the length of the gallery.

"Well, I am," Derek said. "And I'm surely not going to catch the next flight to Cairo." He shrugged. They emerged from the caverns of the Oriental Institute to the busy urban sidewalk. They picked their way between cars and students to a small campus coffee shop. Unlike most spaces in this antique-chic, neo-Gothic setting, the coffeehouse shone in chrome and glass, as modern as the next spaceship to Jupiter.

Derek looked at the business card the curator had given him before he left. He turned it over to read the front:

> Horace Petrie, Ph.D.
> Harold Lawn Professor of Ancient Languages
> Hilary Peats Professor of Egyptology
> The Oriental Institute of the University of Chicago

"The guy has two endowed chairs?" Derek mused, handing the card over to Kyra. She looked at the card and tossed it on the table with disgust. Dr. Petrie's name was on that flyer for the sound demonstration out East.

"One for each cheek," Kyra said, standing up. "If his grant proposals are full of that much bullshit, the guy is probably rolling in money."

≈

As Derek and Kyra rolled northward on Lake Shore Drive, they began to slow as traffic thickened. The late July sun still burned brightly in the western sky, but rush hour was nearly upon them. Soon they'd be sitting at a standstill amid irritated motorists. Once they crossed the Chicago River, the vehicle flow became a trickle, and Derek pulled off to cruise the Streeterville neighborhood.

It wasn't hard to convince Kyra to grab an early dinner. A restaurant squatting in the basement of a three-story storefront advertised a raw bar with fresh shrimp. Kyra and Derek dove inside after handing Trevor's car to a valet parking attendant. The minute they sat face to face in the quiet restaurant, Derek knew he had plenty of explaining to do.

"So," Kyra said, tossing her hands in the air. "Here we are. You're back and still chasing remnants of a lost world, with the FBI on your trail. And I'm waiting . . . " She broke off and grabbed her glass of water.

"You're waiting for me to stop tap dancing around our relationship."

Kyra didn't answer, but Derek knew he hit the vein. The trip to Santa Fe had hardly been a success and Kyra was left out of much of the action, but not out of the danger.

"There's hope for me yet," Derek said. "Please believe that. I've got more on my brain than computers." He took her hand and looked into her red-rimmed eyes. "I was right when I introduced you to Charlie. You are my girlfriend and I love you very much. Kyra, I'm not too good with words—numbers, yes, but words, no. I waited too long to tell you how I felt about you. But believe me, truly, in my heart you are all I ever wanted."

Kyra looked down at the table and mumbled, "I almost cut this relationship off several times."

"What kept you going? I know I deserved to be dumped, many times."

"It was the look in your eyes when you talked to me—just to me and not Boone or George or anyone else. I felt you found sanctuary in my soul."

Derek coughed so he wouldn't cry. "It's true. I have felt that way."

Kyra looked as if she might start blubbering and rubbed her nose with fury.

"That Sekhmet came on to me when you were detained by Ra and Salim," he ventured. "But it was nothing. A temptation. It made me realize you are a greater treasure than I ever knew."

The check blew around the table, propelled by the breeze of the ceiling fan. It made several lazy circles as they stared at each other. When she slipped over to give Derek a hug, the bill landed in Derek's lap.

"You're forgiven," Kyra said. "We will make this work."

He plopped down cash and they hurried into the twilit city streets to find the valet.

CHAPTER TWENTY TWO

Saturday arrived before Derek came to his senses. He awoke on Trevor's sofa bed and stared at the high loft ceiling, filled with painted ductwork and pipes. It took him several long minutes to figure out where he had slept. But once it came back, Derek felt swirling depression in his head. He swallowed back a bitter aftertaste from the night before. He had let loose with some risky admissions at dinner with Kyra and he knew Kyra was taking it well, but the malice of Sekhmet hung over Derek's every thought.

Every minute, Trevor annoyed Derek with his ever-present helpfulness. He offered his apartment, a shower, even an uncompromised computer where Derek could check a website or two. Trevor had always been a good guy, but why was he all at once so indispensable?

Derek pulled himself out of bed with a mighty effort, coming to grips with the idea that he didn't consider himself ready for a tête-à-tête with Stonegate. The hacker stood as an icon to a whole generation of computer geeks. When Derek labored in graduate school, he had a roommate who maintained a Free Seth web site. Stonegate's picture was plastered all over his tiny Urbana apartment, almost the way images of the Virgin Mary abound in Berwyn bungalows. Stonegate, save us from the evils of Big Brother.

I'm really losing it now, Derek decided as he grabbed a clean shirt and some khakis off the side table. Trevor must have picked it out. Here lay the perfect attire for a prison visit, a nice white polo shirt with a tiny American flag embroidered on the left front. Derek fumbled his way into Trevor's kitchen and found the coffeemaker brewing a full pot of fuel. Derek slipped a cup into the stream and collected his morning manna.

"Early," said a voice from the rear of the loft. Derek turned to see Trevor standing back near the bathroom. Wearing a bathrobe and glistening slightly, he appeared as if he had just stepped out of the shower.

"Yeah, it's a good few hours to drive out there," Derek said. "It's almost to Detroit."

"Why would they pick Michigan?" Trevor said, walking toward the kitchen. "For the prison, I mean."

"According to the map, it's in the middle of nowhere," Derek said. He placed objects at various spots on the counter. "Detroit's here. Flint there. Ann Arbor there. And there's nothing here. So that's where they stuck him."

"I hear he can't use the phone lines, except to call his lawyer—then they watch him like he's under a microscope." Trevor reached for his coffee mug. The coffeemaker switched off and exhaled a puff of steam. As if on cue, Trevor picked up the urn and measured out a cup.

"Other than talking to his lawyer, that's about it. They're too afraid. No computers, no e-mail, no faxes. It's like putting Harry Houdini in a locked box."

Trevor reached over the counter and seized a set of keys dangling on an oversized chain. He placed them in Derek's hand.

"Go ahead and take my car," Trevor said.

"If it's all the same to you, I'd rather take the Audi before Dad puts it on the block. No plates, but a 'license-applied-for' sign, an out-of-state vehicle. It's perfect."

Trevor nodded as Derek returned the keys to the counter. He chugged down the remains of his coffee and mimed a thumbs-up. *Where was Kyra? Probably asleep on the couch.* No need to wake her. Derek slipped out the back door and down the alley. Traffic had picked up already, roaring when George picked him up to take him over to the Viking Traders and the beat-up Audi. With a cheery wave to Charlie, they then headed across the Chicago Skyway to Indiana and points east.

≈

Derek figured he'd spend some time waiting at the prison. After all, bureaucracy ruled this place. But sitting in the thinly furnished waiting room for an hour wore away at his nerves. The linoleum squeaked under metal chairs, the air conditioning rumbled like an ancient garbage truck, the public-address system droned with dead static, and the same fly had been playing kamikaze at the window for the last twenty minutes. A leaden aroma of industrial-strength pine cleaner made Derek's sinuses fill up.

"Lotta good old Riff did putting us on the list," Derek mumbled as George played hearts on his iPad. "We might as well have walked in off the street."

"What street?" George said, gesturing toward the window. Open acres rambled in every direction. Out near the highway loomed a guard tower. George refocused on his iPad, touched an area of his screen and began to crow: "He took the queen!"

"He is not real," Derek said, staring at the clock on the wall. "Your opponent is computer software."

"I love beating that guy," George said with a smirk. Derek covered his eyes with his hands, but looked up on cue when he heard footsteps echoing across the room. A beefy guard with a gray crew cut appeared in the doorway. He held a battered piece of paper in one hand.

"Esterberg and Nielson?"

"Nilsson," Derek said, keeping his voice even.

The man gestured for them to follow. They went through a dingy beige hallway that emptied to two small chambers. The man pointed to the left.

Another guard, who'd been standing against the doorframe, snapped to attention. "Any guns, drugs, contraband of any kind?" he asked, looking the visitors up and down.

"Just this," George said, producing his trusty iPad. The sentry squinted at it. "Trust me. They don't want me to bring it in there," George continued.

"Sure, whatever," The guard tossed George's toy into a small cardboard box. He walked over with a metal-detector wand and waved it over their limbs and torsos. Then the guard asked them to empty their pockets into a small tray. The guard sifted through spare change and key chains and pulled out a small prescription bottle. He shot George a questioning look.

"It's for my allergies," George explained.

"It goes in the box," the guard retorted. He tore off a ticket from the container and handed it to George. "This is your claim ticket. Don't lose it."

Satisfied that they were clean, the sentinel let Derek and George into a large room with long tables down the center. Plexiglas cubicles divided the tables into visiting areas: inmates on one side of the clear window, visitors on the other. Live, manned television cameras focused on the tables from all four corners of the room.

"Table Four," the guard said. "You have forty minutes. No swearing, spitting, or loud conversation."

Derek and George squeezed into the narrow steel chairs in the cubicle and stared at the telephone receivers before them.

"I thought he couldn't . . . " Derek started. A figure at the electric gate broke off his thoughts. There lurked a presence as familiar as any from Derek's life. A tall man with a beak nose and large glasses. His once lavish mop of dishwater blond hair now reduced to fringe around the ears. Searing brown eyes glowered under hairy brows. Stonegate.

Derek felt his insides shrivel as Stonegate strode through the buzzing gates. A guard mumbled something and Stonegate turned toward Table Number Four. The gates snapped shut with another electrified blare. Up close under the blue-tinged fluorescent lights, Stonegate looked less like the legend of Derek's school days than a bored, middle-aged library clerk. He had developed a stoop to his shoulders and his skin had taken on a pale cast, as if he hadn't been out of doors in many years. But, then again, maybe he rarely saw sunlight when he lived as a free man. He was a hacker, after all. The best.

The lanky computer legend stopped in front of the table and squeezed himself into the steel chair. His gaze was directed at the desk. He picked up the phone. George and Derek grabbed their receivers. Finally, Stonegate's eyes swept up, the bear-brown pupils fastening onto the interlopers who dared to wander so close to his presence. Derek felt those eyes penetrate his skin. He was relieved about the minimal protection of the Plexiglas. Static sizzled for long seconds on the telephone line. The silence of the room pressed on Derek's skull.

"Thanks for seeing me," came the voice—deep, and, to Derek's surprise, soothing.

Derek looked into Stonegate's eyes, searching for sarcasm but found no hint of ill will, just that feral, amoral stare. His vocal cords frozen, Derek nodded at the prisoner. George followed suit.

"I don't want to beat around the bush," Stonegate continued. "I know you have the data."

Derek felt his throat squeeze shut but fought against the fear. There was no reason to lie now. Sekhmet had blown everything into the open.

"Yeah," Derek croaked. "I guess everyone knows now."

"Even the Bureau," Stonegate said, leaning back into the unyielding chair. "You've got to know they have you in their sights. They know you're here, too. In fact, they probably want you here—to see what you'll do next."

George tapped on the desk with his fingers. He looked as if he were studying the peeling black paint. "That's our problem. The question is, what do you want?"

Stonegate let out a soft chuckle. "You're kidding, right?"

"You know they'll never let you get the data back . . . " Derek started to say. Stonegate waved away the rest of Derek's comments.

"Sure, sure. That's obvious," the prisoner said. "I want to know how you found it."

George breathed a small sigh of relief and began relating the story of the telecom internship, the one-way data flow, breaking into the table of contents, following the signal to New Mexico. Stonegate nodded in appreciation, his dark eyes glittering.

As Derek listened, he began to imagine Stonegate younger, free, full of vigor and ideas. That gleam in the eye told the whole story of his ambition and his greed. Derek saw Stonegate in Egypt, peering at carvings with Sekhmet, breaking down the ancient code. And then his mind fixed on the image of Stonegate, alone with the Egyptian siren. Derek's head began to squeeze and he realized with horror that he had been seized by a jealousy so powerful that he wanted to thrash the man bloody with the telephone receiver—even though that was impossible.

He blinked and realized Stonegate and George both were staring at him. They must have asked a question—yet Derek couldn't get the idea of Stonegate entwined with Sekhmet out of his mind.

"Who is she?" Derek heard himself spit out.

"Well, that's a non sequitur," George started to sputter. "We were talking about the condition of the hard drive and asked . . . "

Stonegate cut him off with a cough. He gazed at Derek, his fierce eyes softening. "Who is she? Or what does she think she is?"

"Both," Derek said, peering with intent through the smudged partition.

"She's a viper," Stonegate said. "She's utterly cold. Completely calculating. Never for one minute does she have her mind on anything but herself."

"But what does she want?"

"To be worshipped."

"So she really is . . . ?"

"Sekhmet? No." Stonegate chuckled and leaned forward. "Do you know how much I've read here in prison on Egyptian gods? I've practically got my own PhD in Egyptology.'' He scratched the two-day growth on his chin. "Sekhmet existed as a kind goddess. She had the maternal instinct, cared for others, nurtured, and showed eternal love and devotion."

Derek tried to listen, but his mind kept lurching through memories of the woman's skin upon his, her honeyed voice, endless gaze, and full lower lip.

"The more I learned, the more I realized that this woman might have taken on the evil guise of Sekhmet," Stonegate continued. "But she is something quite different. Perhaps she is more like the lion side of Sekhmet. You know of her?"

"The lion goddess," Derek said, recalling a page out of his reference books. "The flip side to cat goddess Bastet."

"More or less," Stonegate said, a mirthless laugh escaping from his mouth. "When the earth had been born, Sekhmet had the taste for human blood. She'd go out at dawn on feeding frenzies, reveling in blood. After a few days, she had nearly devoured the human race. Then someone put out beer colored with pomegranate juice for her at night. She thought it looked like blood and lapped it up, became drunk and fell asleep. Thus, the salvation of the human race."

Derek became aware of George's eyes boring into his temple. There was no way to explain this bewildering digression. George simply had to deal with it.

Stonegate continued, peering intently into Derek's eyes. "Make no mistake, Derek Nilsson, she's certainly as dangerous as the lioness Sekhmet. You've come in contact with her, so you know." The prisoner closed his eyes and, for a few seconds, seemed to age several years. "You know. She doesn't just lure people to her side; she sucks them dry. Pulls out their energy, their vitality, their intelligence. Drains them."

Derek remembered the weightless feeling of falling into Sekhmet's gaze, the sense of wandering into a foreign magnetic field, of losing bearings, fragmenting.

"Derek," Stonegate said, his eyes almost melting the plastic divider. "You've got to find out what she can do with the knowledge, the data. If she gets it away from you, I fear for more than myself."

George cut in, his voice tinged with irritation. "Do we even know if the data works?"

"I'm pretty sure it does. I didn't get much testing done before . . . this." Stonegate gestured at the prison walls. "The important thing is that Sekhmet has all the knowledge to make levitation work, just not the ability to control it. My data worked out the ratio of sonic waves to the mass of the object for lifting. Without this knowledge, she's operating in the dark. But now Sekhmet has been contacting people from rogue governments, even the absurdly named ISIS or ISIL. Daesh is the better name for them, kind of an Arabic slur. Third World people are interested. People who'd pay a great deal for power like that. And you can bet she'll be doing her own testing soon—on a massive scale."

"Without the actual numbers, what can she do?" George countered.

"Enough," Stonegate said. "Enough to get a petty despot interested. Energy for nothing is a rather popular concept."

"And they'll all be gunning for us," George said.

Derek tried to formulate a question, but a guard walked up to announce that time had almost expired. Derek held up five fingers and the guard nodded. What were five more minutes with a nonviolent computer geek?

"She's got a legitimate argument. The data is half hers. And half yours. And none of it's mine," Derek said.

"It doesn't matter. Don't let her get it."

"What do you want?" George asked.

"When I get out," Stonegate said, with a budding smile, "it's likely I'll be a new man." George smiled. "With a lot to offer the computing world."

"As a new man."

"Indeed."

Stonegate shifted his gaze to Derek. "Three tips. And then you're on your own. Number One: Her ego is her weak spot. Two: Stay ahead of the guys in the plain black suits. Three: If the data really works, you'll never hold onto it. Just try your best to keep it in good hands."

"So what do we do then, wise guy?" George broke in.

"Use it," Stonegate said. "In a way she'd never think of. It's the only way." He signaled to the guard and hung up the phone.

Five million questions swirled inside Derek's head as Stonegate stood and waited for the guard to walk him back to his cell. Before the steel grid let out its electronic bleat, Stonegate turned to look at Derek. One eyelid lowered with a hint of menace. *Do it,* Stonegate seemed to will across the empty space. *Stop her.*

Derek inclined his chin—the barest hint of assent—and Stonegate vanished.

CHAPTER TWENTY THREE

In one week, the mood of the city hit a downbeat. The celebratory aura that prevails during Chicago's summer—a season of lakefront festivals, outdoor concerts, and ragtag street fairs—seemed to evaporate like a brisk shore breeze. The beginning of August was near, pollen filled the air, and kids walked the streets with leaden steps as they began to dread those obnoxious back-to-school ads. For Derek, it felt as if a blur of panic flitted through the still air. He needed to move, get out of town, hunt down answers, but he didn't have the slightest idea how to begin.

He called BitJockey.com, now TechStar Industries, and told Bucky he needed some more time off. Just a couple weeks, he asked. Inside, he hoped he'd never have to show his face there again.

After a week of hiding at Trevor's loft, suffering daily the sense that Trevor might also be dubbed a traitor, Derek became a nomad. He'd crash one night on George's floor, another on Astrid's living-room couch. Once, he spent a blissful night with Kyra, who had gone home because she couldn't stand Trevor's place anymore. The tenderness never left their embrace, but Derek worried mightily that he still wasn't doing enough for her. He was still running away from Sekhmet and the feds, trying to keep the acoustic information safe. How could he be concentrating enough on Kyra? Until he did something, until he made some essential move to end this acoustics nightmare he wandered in, Derek could never make enough space in his life for what Kyra needed. And he needed her, because he had fallen so deeply in love. What she required was nothing less than his full attention. Derek wondered if he had focused on any human being with that kind of devotion. Computers, yes. People, probably never. It was time to learn to turn that around.

So far, Derek had been lucky in his current peripatetic lifestyle. There had been no sign of Sekhmet, or tails by stiff-shouldered goons—federal or private. He wondered, if the feds really wanted him, wouldn't they have picked him up by now? Still, he worried. The flat humidity that rolled off the lakeshore did nothing to abate his edginess.

He'd read the book that Dr. Petrie mentioned. Once he saw a copy wedged between the paranormal and UFO volumes in a New Age bookstore in Hyde Park, so that reminded him to page through it. Sure enough, it detailed information on movement by acoustics, translated hieroglyphics that supposedly related to acoustical dynamics and even had an illustration of the plaque Derek had been searching for. But, as he suspected, the book rambled off into mumbo jumbo that appalled him—even by occult-book standards. The author tied the whole phenomenon to settlers from Mars, or did they come from the Pleiades star system? Somehow, the author latched onto decent data and then used it to hitch a ride to his own mental fantasyland.

Stymied, Derek decided to risk a visit to George's office at the university. He really needed to get his hands on a computer again. Being away from a keyboard for this long frayed his nerves to the breaking point. Just looking at George's Mac gave Derek a case of the shakes. Together, they cooked up a plan to spoof a new user name that would allow Derek a chance to use the university system. Out in the public media room, he could research and dump information completely undetected. But he had to work with diligence.

They pushed open the glass doors to the ice-cold computer room in the middle of a summer day. It was packed with students, most of whom were so grim-faced and hyper-focused on their work that they didn't give Derek a second glance. For the last week, he'd been doing subtle things with his wardrobe to disguise himself. Today, a bandana covered his hair, and he had sprouted two-days growth of beard. The goatee was ancient history. Now he had dusty brown stubble all over his jaw line. He looked like a kid who had eaten too many chocolate donuts.

"Skid row," George mumbled. "Why don't you complete it with Bermuda shorts and black socks?"

"Maybe a better disguise would be a banker's suit," Derek grumbled as they slipped behind a bank of screens. No one looked up. He reached for the keyboard and logged in as a new person, then carefully zipped over to his old cyber haunts. The old crowd at the Hacker Haven social media site, where he became "Guest Luser," had completely forgotten that Derek had existed. Sekhmet hadn't posted there since June. Over at Derek's old e-mail account, all attempts to retrieve the spool of old e-mail failed. "Over limit," said the warning window.

Not that it mattered. At least it bounced the spam.

He slipped into a few websites where he retrieved more details on acoustics, archeology, alternative history, and Dr. Petrie, the Oriental Institute curator. On the Web, the effusive University of Chicago Egyptologist didn't appear in the legitimate world of academics. Indeed, a quick scan of the U. of C. online archives showed that Petrie had never worked there. Somehow, Derek wasn't surprised. But when visiting *The Shrouded Truth*, a website created for alternative interests of all types—flying saucers, alchemy, archeology, linguistics, Atlantis, and ghost hunting—Derek hit pay dirt. There, under a story headlined "The Case for Acoustical Engineering," flashed a picture of Petrie with several other people in expedition gear. Derek had even heard of one of the pictured men—Fox Hammersmith, an English author who had stirred up a monstrous controversy with his theories of an advanced ancient civilization. Hammersmith didn't qualify as an academic, but he certainly carried weight in the world of journalism and was never considered a wild-eyed crazy. If Petrie stood in his company, the strange little man couldn't be a complete nut case.

The Web article billed Petrie as an "outlaw academic" who did a radio show on the East Coast, wrote for underground journals, and organized tours of ancient digs. This year's "Ancient Acoustics" event stood on the calendar for early August in rural Connecticut. Petrie planned to prove that ancient architects moved large boulders with the use of acoustics. The unnamed author of the Internet story used a slightly bemused tone to describe Petrie's theories, indicating that even the alternative community considered Petrie a tad strange.

Derek printed out the page, planning to show it to George later. Then he did a quick search for other mentions of Petrie's name. He found posts from Petrie on several Usenet newsgroups devoted to Egypt, Atlantis, and other arcane subject matter. He also discovered more references to continuing arguments between Petrie and academics on commercial newsgroups and mailing lists. The guy got around on the Net, always using the moniker of "Dr. Petrie," although Derek never found any reference to an actual doctorate degree anywhere.

"About ready to log off?" George asked, coming up behind Derek and breaking his mesmerized state. "Have you checked your e-mail?"

"Funny joke. You know everything's bouncing back by now. No one's writing me at my old account."

"Well, I established a new one at this server for you," George said with a deadpan expression.

"Oh, okay, I get it." Derek moved aside to let George log into the university's e-mail server. He let Derek choose a password and then Derek checked his In box. As Derek expected, he found a welcome note from George.

"Thanks," Derek nodded as he deleted the item.

The In box blinked. "One more item remains," it read.

"Spam already?" George mumbled.

Derek opened the message. It loomed voluminous, at least two screens worth of tightly packed words. Roger signed it.

≈

"I'm telling you, the only person who could have done that must practically live on the university system," George said when they moved outdoors, pressing his palm into his sweating forehead.

Derek hunched on a bench near the campus midway, holding a perspiration-soddened printout of Roger's e-mail. He had read it three times, but still could make no sense of why this message came to him now. George had been jabbering at him nonstop, trying to dream up some explanation for an e-mail that dropped into an account activated only five minutes earlier. Derek didn't really care how it took place, he only knew it meant someone must have been watching him. He felt acid eating out his stomach.

"So that would mean he's got to exist somewhere here, a student or staff member," George fretted, now twisting his index finger as he spoke. "Maybe he even saw you walk in. Who was in that room?"

Derek broke into George's monologue with a tired voice. "Can't the FBI break into the university machines? Can't someone like Sekhmet?"

George stared with his chin jutted out ready to defend his security systems. Then he lowered his head just slightly. "Maybe I'd have a better clue if I knew what the damn thing said."

Derek handed the printout over to his friend. He wasn't sure what George would make of it. The message brimmed full of the usual spiritual gobbledygook that Roger always sent—messages about forgiveness and trust and "learning experiences." Derek no longer suffered embarrassment about sharing Roger's guru guidance with outsiders. Roger remained a cipher, but he had proven useful in the past. Maybe he had provided a clue Derek could use. He endured such ennui, not caring whether Roger meant good or ill. Now all he needed was a finger pointing in a definite direction. At the least Roger's latest message achieved that end.

George skimmed the e-mail, shrewd eyes glossing over the section where Roger expressed remorse for losing track of Derek in Santa Fe, and then reassessed the moral progress of the journey west. Derek winced when George reached the part where Roger lectured him about Kyra. The words burned in his chest: "The lesson of shared experience still eludes you. Enlarge the heart."

George rolled his eyes as he continued to the second page, then narrowed his lids as he reached the nitty gritty. Roger had written that he reached Derek just in time. The data remained safe, but only barely. The time raced ahead, straight to their very being, to face Sekhmet down and establish ownership of their precious, dearly acquired information. Don't let anything hang in the balance, Roger wrote.

George spoke the last lines in a whisper, "Go to Connecticut, meet Petrie, and get the proof you need. The legitimate heir will win the trial."

"He knows just about everything, doesn't he?" Derek said, handing George the printout of Petrie's acoustic exhibition. "I was alone with Kyra when we met this guy." He pointed out the sandy-faced, portly Petrie on the printout. "I hadn't even had a chance to tell you about him yet."

"Who is that guy?" George asked, peering closely at the photo. "I've seen him hanging around here, but not at the Oriental Institute. He's been on my turf at the computer center."

"For how long?"

"The last couple weeks, that's all. You notice a guy like that. He has that kind of air of self-importance."

"The kind of guy who'd carry something like this around?" Derek asked, pulling Petrie's business card out of his wallet.

George read the inscription and let out a hoot. "What a jerk. Two endowed chairs."

"One for each cheek," Derek mumbled, staring off into the distance, trying to shake off the sensation of being scrutinized by malevolent eyes.

≈

"Okay, get ready," Kyra cautioned as Derek cringed before a mirror. He saw himself clean-shaven for the first time in several years and that proved shock enough. But the larger transformation was on its way. Kyra ripped the towel off his head and began rubbing furiously at his hair. "Voilá."

He stared at the blond man in the reflection. He blinked several times and felt a smile creeping along his lips. Maybe he could deal with this new face. The new golden hair color enhanced the blue of his eyes. The sunless tanning cream that Kyra had applied a few hours earlier had already gone to work, changing Derek from a pasty-faced techno punk into a Nordic sun god.

"Damn," said someone behind them. Penny, Kyra's college pal, had lent them the after-hours use of her salon station and had been checking up on them every fifteen minutes or so. Now she stood behind them with a relaxed smile.

"Is it too light?" Kyra asked, eyebrows squeezing together.

"No, no," Penny said, standing back with crossed arms, looking Derek up and down as if he were a Mr. America contestant. "It's quite fine. Quite fine."

Derek coughed. Women did not talk about him this way. He remained a geek, remember? He started wondering why he had suggested a change of appearance to Kyra when he first posed the idea of zipping off to the East Coast for the acoustical experiment. He'd need new identification papers, he had fussed. And he'd have to find some method of transportation that even Sekhmet wouldn't think of. He remembered how Kyra lit up when he talked about needing a disguise. She called it a "makeover," but he had no idea how much of a metamorphosis she had in mind.

"So where are the outfits?" Kyra asked, gesturing at the shopping bags at Penny's feet.

"I scored big," Penny said, reaching into the paper wrappings with relish. "For less than two hundred dollars I got you the stud, adventure-photographer look." She pulled out khaki shorts, vests, denim shirts—every item replete with multiple pockets. An Australian bush hat and some topsiders completed the fashion spree.

Kyra smiled as if she had never doubted Penny's ability to find discount items. She turned to Derek.

"So here's the deal, you are a freelance photographer. And a handsome one at that. You have a new name," she said, slapping a new Missouri driver's license in his left hand. "And you are shooting the SANS Institute's Internet high-tech security conference at UCONN for *Great Escape* magazine." She plopped a fake press card on top of the pile.

"Who . . . ?"

"Your dad and his pal Ivar took care of this," she said, indicating the phony ID. "And your mom created this on her Mac." Kyra picked up the press pass and dangled it from its recycled plastic casing. Kyra had used Astrid's old press-pass chain from her newspaper days to make the whole thing look official.

What a family I've got, Derek thought, turning the fake driver's license over in his hand. He took a short breath and touched Kyra's hand like a child testing the fur on a new kitten. Gently, but wary of a sudden bite.

"Where's your new identity?"

"I don't need one." Her shoulders tensed and she drew her head back.

"Well, sure you do. I'm not making this trip without you," Derek said, slipping his hand around her waist. "You made the last trip a delight—with Boone and all the distractions."

"Oh boy," Penny said, throwing up her hands and backing toward the door. "Count me out on this make-over."

CHAPTER TWENTY FOUR

Charlie kept plunging down the soggy streets of Andersonville, ducking behind dumpsters and sidestepping discarded motor parts, hauling a battered duffel bag as he ran. Sometimes he paused to breathe or switch the load from hand to hand, but no more than a minute at a street corner elapsed before he plunged forward again, off on the side streets, avoiding the betrayal of streetlights.

The last time he had lived in Chicago, Charlie couldn't have run a city block. Living in New Mexico taught him how to crawl. Life with Elk Horn transformed him into a skilled mountain hiker. Now, home on his own turf, Charlie was like a marathon man, ready to run the race of his life for his son.

Charlie flew up an alley, just catching sight of a garbage crew getting to work on the morning collection. He'd be out of danger by dawn. Up at the corner a bus idled on busy Peterson Avenue. Charlie waved at the driver, who held the door open a few seconds longer than normal, time enough for Charlie to leap aboard, draw out his radio-signal city bus pass and pay his fare. Two middle-aged women sat in the middle of the vehicle, staring straight through Charlie. He nodded anyway and took a seat at the fore, perching at the edge the seat, his knees bobbing up and down as he counted the blocks. At Rockwell, he disembarked, stumbling up the residential streets as he tried to read addresses in the dawning light. He stood before the right apartment building, the one with the yellow bricks, the funny gargoyle on the left molding, and the vines creeping halfway into the gargoyle's mouth. When he recognized the building, Charlie knew he had arrived too late. No light on in the bedroom annex, also known as the computer room. No sign of life.

Derek had disappeared. There was no way to warn him of who could be on his tail. He couldn't telephone. It was too risky.

Not familiar with his son's neighborhood, Charlie poked down Devon Avenue, looking for the first place where he could find a decent cup of coffee. A smiling Indian man stood at the door of a small shop, having just turned over the "open" sign and unlatched the door. Something about the Asian fellow and this simple restaurant filled Charlie with a sense of coming home, although he had never seen the establishment before. He smelled cardamom, an Indian spice his mother used to mix into the batter for her best Swedish coffee cake. The aroma soothed his tired muscles and dissolved the trench between his brows.

He pushed open the door and plopped down at a table, at once aware of how many miles he had run. He wasn't surprised when the Indian man gazed at him with familiarity as he handed over a menu.

"You a Nilsson? You look just like him."

"Like Derek."

"Yes. Derek, my good friend."

"I was just looking for him, but . . . . " Charlie spread his hands on the table in exasperation. He had no idea why he shared such touchy information with a complete stranger.

"He's gone. I know. I'll bring you some coffee and we'll have a good, long talk," the man said. He began to make his way to the counter and then turned back. "I'm Ravi. Derek often came here at this hour." Charlie looked into Ravi's liquid eyes and felt an inward surrender. *This is good. Go with your gut.*

≈

The guys who had busted up Ivar's place weren't just a bunch of hoods, that part was obvious. They were professional, solid, strictly business. As Charlie had hidden out in the back of the car lot behind a rusted Jeep with his duffle bag at his side, he watched Ivar's office windows. The men with impassive faces grabbed files, smashed open the office safe, and opened drawers. Then they stepped outside and pulled out the floorboards of certain sedans. These jamokes knew what to look for: contraband, drugs, hidden dough of any currency.

As a rule, hoods smashed and grabbed. These guys were too sure of themselves, too methodical. They left the obvious goodies, including car radios and airbags, but hung onto manila envelopes, keys and small items that Charlie couldn't make out in the dark. Only two kinds of tough guys acted this way. They were either muscle from the Outfit or employees of the federal government. Even though Charlie had kept his nose clean during his lost years of boozing, he'd seen enough of Ivar's deals at the Viking Traders to know all about law enforcement—or mob enforcement.

The families from the West Side usually left the Swedes alone. Hell, one crazy Viking bastard on the North Side hardly cut into their lucrative chop shop business. The feds usually considered Ivar beneath their scope as well. But there had been misunderstandings, nonetheless.

Somehow, Charlie knew things were different now. Ever since he saw those dark suits at the Saint Louis airport, he knew his trail had heated up. Hiding out with Ivar made sense for a while, but soon Charlie got the feeling stalkers were behind him. Getting rid of the Audi didn't help much. Right after that, Ivar received a visit from a government pair with the absurd names of Brick and Clay. They were looking for a Swede named Nilsson, but Ivar spread his hands wide, exclaiming that Nilsson had gotten himself lost in Injun land about ten years ago. They shrugged, unimpressed with Ivar's acting, and left. But they never really stayed away. That dark blue Dodge Intrepid parked outside on Clark Street too many times, and no one, especially the FBI, pretended it was a coincidence.

When Derek's cute little girlfriend showed up at the back door, asking about a way that Derek could get out of town undetected, Ivar's creative juices started flowing. Nothing like creating fake IDs to put the crusty Swede into such a jolly mood. Only creating counterfeit twenties got him more excited. Ivar, his face rosy-pink to his blond roots, got busy, meeting with some of the Latino posse down the street, making deals and bartering auto hardware. The phony ID business became so complicated that

Charlie could barely grasp it, but it came down to a car for the Hispanic guy who paid off a city worker who had an affair with a secretary at the Immigration and Naturalization Service. Somehow, new papers arrived for Derek—and later, for Kyra.

No matter how many changes the US and state governments made in their official documents and currency, the boys in the back rooms had equally efficient ways of beating the safeguards. Holograms? No problem. Light-sensitive paper? Piece of cake. Watermarks? Old stuff. Bar codes? You have to be kidding.

Ivar exulted as the happiest man in the Windy City the day he re-created Derek and Kyra in the federal database. They were now Scott Vanderbruck and Nancy Thorsten—two nice kids from the St. Louis suburbs. Charlie enjoyed this little game, but also realized that Ivar operated too close to the surface. The periscope had been turned on them for weeks. The feared reprisal came without warning on a Sunday night.

Charlie had been ready. He retrieved the mirror drive from the storage locker in one hour (he had the duplicate key Derek made for him), packed up his faithful duffel bag with t-shirts and sneaked halfway off Ivar's property when the bust-up gang jumped out of their large urban assault vehicles. Ivar, who smelled danger like a wild animal, was conveniently not home at the time and all his hiding places were miraculously cleaned out, but Charlie watched from his filthy bunker as a few simpering Viking Trader employees underwent impromptu "interviews."

Before he fled, Charlie looked in the direction of the Intrepid. G-men. Had to be. The family guys did not dress with so little regard for appearance and there was this funny plump man watching from the back seat. He appeared dark like an Arab, with a pointed, birdlike nose, and sported a ludicrous comb-over hairdo. Charlie had a feeling he'd see that weirdo again.

≈

Later, Ravi listened with barely a change of expression. Then he poured more coffee, settled into a chair and told his story to Charlie. Derek had stormed in one night, demanding from Ravi if anyone had been looking for him. Ravi related the list of strange stragglers who had stopped in for coffee and nosy conversation: a couple of tough neighborhood punks, a well-dressed couple in dark clothing, a sweaty professor, a nervous computer student from the U. of C., and "a most beautiful lady."

Charlie straightened. "Exotic lady?"

"Exotic. You mean foreign, huh? Not quite as brown as me," Ravi said, eyes dancing. "Long black hair, all dressed in silk. Lots of eye makeup."

"With the oldest gaze you've ever seen?"

"That's her."

The two fell silent. Charlie stirred his coffee, even though he hadn't added any sugar. Ravi shuffled off to attend a pot on the stove. He returned with an aromatic brew in a brown mug.

"Try this. You'll like it much better," Ravi said, presenting the steaming drink as if it were a royal gift. "It's chai. Derek's favorite."

Charlie sipped the beverage and let a smile touch his lips. No one who made tea this well could lie about Sekhmet.

"What did you tell her?"

"The lady?"

Charlie nodded.

"That he'd left for the west some weeks ago and I hadn't seen him since, which was the truth. At least it was the truth at that time."

"And the truth now?"

"Well, he rushed in a few days ago with Kyra and asked all those questions. They came across as panicky. They wanted me to walk by his apartment building every night and check to see the windows were closed and that the place looked secure. He said he was leaving again but wouldn't say where." Ravi twisted a dishtowel in his taut hands, looking worried.

"They can't drive, not with that lot after them."

"Trains are too . . . "

"More than slow. You can't make a quick exit from them."

"Can't fly," Ravi added. "Not these days with security so tight."

Charlie mused over the new IDs, the changed appearances, and the photographer ruse. It might work, but the feds (if they were still looking) might be too smart. Then he snapped his fingers. Unless his son thought small—really small.

"Ravi, do you have anywhere safe I can put something important? The people chasing Derek aren't far behind me, I'm sure. I've got to travel light. I don't know whom to trust anymore."

"My sister lives in a two-flat a block from here," Ravi said. "Come on. As long as no one else is in the place, let's duck out now." Charlie finished his tea and slipped out the door, while Ravi locked up. They sprinted a short way to the home of Jyoti and Chitra Sinharoy, sister and cousin of Ravi. After a great deal of discussion in fluent Hindi, the women led Charlie upstairs to the dining room. In the corner stood a chest, finely inlaid with ebony and rosewood. They opened it and the scent of fine jasmine flowers sailed into Charlie's nose. The chest held silks and taffetas, embroidered and finely woven, layered with tissue paper and aromatic herbs. Charlie handed Jyoti the small mirror disk, looking so angular and spare in its silver anti-static bag. A much better spot than a storage locker wrapped in an old t-shirt. Jyoti's long fingers tucked the disk deep within the layers of rich fabric.

"The dowry chest," Ravi said, his chest puffing as his eyes gleamed. "Only a cad would dare look in there."

Cads are what we are up against, but odds are against them thinking of this hiding place, Charlie thought. He bowed low to the women, who giggled at his gallantry. He bid farewell to the long-limbed, elegant women with a promise he would return within two weeks.

Ravi gave him a gentle pat on the back. "No worries, my friend. It's as precious to me as my own treasures."

Time to bolt again. Charlie felt his legs fly under him, back to the bus stop. He rushed off to the suburbs, ready to take another long bus ride.

CHAPTER TWENTY FIVE

Blue expanded in three directions: north, east, and south. To the west rambled rows upon rows of glass-eyed structures, all glaring and winking in the dawning sun. Up here, where the wind roared like the wrath of Thor, Derek felt no tie with the Earth whatsoever. Up here at three thousand feet, making a lazy turn southward over the lakeshore, Chicago looked like little more than a town made of cardboard miniatures, an architect's model, a ruse exactingly constructed by aliens to resemble a real world.

He'd never been in a light plane before. It felt like the top of his head was lifting off his brain, melding with the fiberglass roof of the cramped craft. He thought he ought feel a twinge of fright, but instead the lights and maps on the instrument panel fascinated him, as did the voices broadcasting from control towers at various airstrips, and the rasping static on the earphones. He hardly noticed the small updrafts of wind that sometimes sent the floor rising to his knees and then back down. He could have been in a gondola, hanging between twin mountain peaks, or on the upward track of a roller coaster. He could be anywhere but thousands of feet above his native city. For some reason, he felt safer from Sekhmet here than he had on solid earth.

"Pretty amazing, huh?" came Kyra's voice over the headset. She turned around to wink at him, as he sat crammed in the rear section of the four-seater aircraft.

"It's pretty cool now," Derek yelled—unnecessarily, he realized—into his microphone. "But how cool is it going to be all the way out to Bradley Airport?"

"You wait, you'll see," crackled the pilot's voice. "Weather's perfect from here to there. No fronts. No rapid air pressure changes. So, I doubt we'll get any noticeable turbulence." The pilot broke off as the tower gave him instructions to ascend. Derek looked to his left and saw a large jetliner bound for O'Hare Airport. His plane would ascend and the passenger plane would lower with the grace of a clipper ship coming to port. The whole operation materialized with such elegance that Derek felt goose bumps prickle on his skin.

"No big deal," the pilot continued as the heavy jet began to sink under them into the western sky. "Nope, our only concern is making good time to Erie, PA, where we'll refuel."

Derek pressed himself into his leather seat and watched the landscape alter. The toy city faded, replaced by squares of suburban homes and swimming pools, then the entire view flattened and spread out to nothing but amber cornfields and brick-red silos. Chicago had become a memory and they were officially on their way.

He had never envisioned getting to Connecticut this way. Ever since Roger's e-mail arrived, Derek had been busying himself with plans to drive George's car to the East Coast and then change to a rental car, but Kyra suggested a better idea. The big airports were too risky, she conceded. The train existed as a lumbering steel trap. Driving such a huge distance would wear everyone out before they had a chance to encounter Sekhmet. Why not take a private plane and avoid the hassles? she proposed.

Derek thought she just popped off wild ideas until she got on the phone and rang up her brother, the AAA baseball jock. Pace Van Dyck wasn't just a crafty pitcher, he'd made some important fans in his career. One owned a light plane at Chicago Executive Airport, which he'd rent to friends for a modest fee—providing they used a pilot he liked. Kyra agreed to pay for fuel and the pilot's fee (with Derek's money, of course), Pace finessed the deal and they were booked out of Chicago within twenty-four hours.

The scheme fit their needs seamlessly. Security hardly existed at the little airport in the northwest suburbs. They flashed a driver's license, signed a passenger manifest, walked through a metal detector, and ambled out to the plane. Drub Carraway, their pilot, was a wheezy, middle-aged Texan who looked like Clint Eastwood if you caught him at the right angle. But there were no Dirty Harry antics for Drub. He just wanted to make it to

Bradley before Saturday so he could sit back and catch the Dallas Cowboys preview opener on Sunday and drink Lone Star beer at the only sports bar that carried the brand.

Out on the tarmac, Drub looked over the plane with exacting specifications. He'd flown it hundreds of times for Milt, its millionaire owner who didn't seem to have a last name. Drub chattered about the weather and baseball while draining a pet cock here and tapping a half-closed panel there. When the bird stood gassed up and ready, he ordered the two passengers into their places. As soon as the tower radioed "clearance for takeoff," the Cirrus came alive, racing down the runway and then pulling its nose away from the earth.

Drub showed them the map on his big display screen. He indicated the airstrips at Waukegan, Milwaukee, Rockford and Ann Arbor. He showed them the weather radar and chatted nonstop about the Cirrus' many features, including a built-in parachute designed to save the whole plane in the event of engine failure. But Drub closed right up when Derek asked a few gentle questions about Milt. Derek sulked a bit after Drub's rebuff, but later he had a chance to riposte when the pilot asked too many questions about where he and Kyra were headed.

"Let's say we're not sticking around for the Cowboys game," Derek said with a stone face.

"What's in Connecticut, huh?" Drub asked.

Derek didn't miss a beat. "Lots of getaway houses with pools and lots of land. Tennis courts too."

That killed the conversation for many miles. The last thing Derek remembered was Kyra offering him a bottle of fizzy water. Erie was still miles away.

≈

The stars appeared in the east windows as tangerine fire sank away in the west. It seemed far too early for the sun to start setting. Derek began counting hours and calculating miles. He stared at the pinpoints of light and felt his concentration begin to dance. The stars were no longer suns billions of light years away, but peepholes for the gods hidden beyond the impenetrable blackness of nowhere.

Then they pulsed until they broke out into five-pointed bursts—five rays emanating from one, unseen center. Derek rolled his head on his shoulders and remembered the pictures on the ceiling of Queen Nefertari's tomb. An eternal parade of five-pointed stars. Orderly, peaceful in their regularity.

He looked eastward again and his gaze rested on a tiny speck surging toward him. As it grew larger, the form became proud and strong, borne on wings of long, multi-colored feathers. He moaned as the figure coasted closer to the aircraft, so close that its face peered into the passenger window. Sekhmet.

Her merciless, cat-like staring eyes probed him through the glass and he struggled with his body, trying to force himself to look away, to warn his fellow travelers, to open his mouth and scream. Instead, he froze in her glare. He realized then that he found himself wound in a dream that would not release him.

The moon shone on her features, which didn't move in the high winds outside the plane. Her hair hardly rustled. Her golden headdress never tilted. Without provocation, she let out a sharp laugh, shattering Derek's will to pull away.

So you see me truly now. I wondered how long it would take.

Derek shivered.

I haven't forgotten about you. I'm not about to let you run away.

He remembered Stonegate's words about Sekhmet's place in Egyptian history as a kind, maternal goddess. The sweet model of fertility and womanly beauty.

Yes. It was that way.

Derek's bare feet touched sea spray and he lifted his eyes to view the remains of Menouthis, one of Cleopatra's pleasure cities off the coast of Alexandria. In the distance, a building lay in ashes and disgrace, columns toppled into the briny mud. Painted murals of sunshot color drained their lifeblood into the rack of rain, seawater, and wind. He knew without knowing that this signified the end of the last remaining temple of Sekhmet, the goddess.

It was 414 in your CE dating scheme. Christian mobs burned it. The followers of Muhammad would finish their work.

Sekhmet stood next to him, robed in white linen, one breast exposed in the style of the Middle Kingdom. She stood next to

Isis, another goddess representing purity in love and maternal devotion to her child, Horus.

The end of the Egyptian empire filled Derek with depression. Thousands of years of glory toppled in one day by the arrogant Octavian. After Cleopatra VII committed suicide, her entire culture perished bit by bit.

Some died. Sekhmet pointed to a shattered statue of Hapi, the god of Nile flooding and fecundity. *I chose to live on. There is always a place in your world for a powerful woman.*

The waters wore at the temple steps and Derek felt remorse for a crime he did not commit. He wanted to rage for the loss of Sekhmet's realm. He felt her sharp-edged bitterness slice through his body, and then he felt nothing at all.

He and Sekhmet flew together. She again took to the winds as a winged human with Isis and Horus at her side. They sailed over the pyramids, which still rose like mountains from the desert plain, despite wars and countless earthly disasters. Sekhmet, too, had found a way to outlast history. She held out her hand, expecting a tribute. Derek felt weight in his hand and saw that he held the sought-after mirror drive, silver within its envelope, a barely fitting gift for a queen. It floated mere inches from her grasp, but he jerked his hand back with a harsh cry. He began to plummet to the ground.

"Why?" he screamed to the night. "What difference does it make? What is it you want?"

The answer spread across the heavens. *Worship. I demand it.*

Derek continued to fall until Kyra shook him sharply in his seat. They were on the ground in Erie, PA., and he shuddered like a boy.

≈

Roger once asked about strange dreams in one of his invasive missives.

"They are not dreams, you realize," Roger had written. "The reveries are your window into their world. This is where they live. And your life is a dream to them."

At the time, Derek filed Roger's advice away as more inscrutable mumbo-jumbo. But now he pried open the memory. First, there had been his vision of Tehuti and now of Sekhmet.

Derek looked up and saw that in real existence, it was only late afternoon. Drub busied himself getting fuel for the next part of their journey. Derek quaked inside, feeling the authenticity of the dream of Sekhmet in the night. Why did he feel that night hid behind a curtain of sunlight in Erie, cleverly disguised to the unseeing public? He turned quickly and followed Kyra into the tiny airport, hunting down a bathroom and then snacks. He felt desperate to tell her about the flying Sekhmet and Roger's message, but he couldn't get past the frankness of her gaze. Dreamy meanderings weren't going to mean much when she frowned in this kind of mood.

They sat on an uncomfortable cement bench in a silent hallway, munching on salty cheese crisps and sharing a soft drink. Kyra stared into the distance and spoke to the clock on the wall.

"How much longer before we get to Bradley, I wonder?" she asked.

Derek pulled out a map and pretended to make calculations. He sat in confusion, as lost as anyone else. "It's gonna be a late one," Derek said. "It's only a four-hour flight, but we didn't exactly rush to get started." Then he began re-folding the map with elaborate precision.

"What were you dreaming when your lights went out up there?" Kyra asked, licking the salt off each finger. Leave it to Kyra to throw him off base before firing the big question.

"About them." Derek smashed the rest of the map together and stuffed it in his pocket.

"Her?"

"Yeah, her."

Nothing moved for several long minutes. Derek traced the pattern on the floor tiles as it slithered from square to square. Someone had laid the blocks so that it looked as if the rock patterns were continuous. He heard Kyra's breath, her exhalations staccato and forced. Footsteps clacked in a distant room.

"Roger says I have to face her down to end this thing." Derek stared at his knuckles as he clutched the edge of the bench. They were silvery white. He thought he could see bone through the cellophane skin. "Trouble is, I don't think she can . . . that she will . . . just go away."

Kyra looked at him and ran a tired hand through her newly blackened hair. With her white skin, she looked like a Goth queen.

"So what are we going there for?"

"I think we're supposed to kill her." Derek felt himself swallow as if he were trying to take back the words. Kyra's face froze.

Drub stomped down the hall, hollering something about getting a move on. Kyra rose, her shoulders quivering a tiny bit under her Cubs t-shirt. Derek put his hand about her waist and they walked on to embark on the second leg of their journey.

≈

"Boone, you old dog." Derek hopped up and down like a terrier as he yelled into the phone. "Gotcha on the first ring."

They had just landed. Derek was calling on a cheap "burner" phone with pre-paid airtime. They were less traceable and no bills would be arriving for him in Chicago to alert all the interested folks who monitored his mail and bank accounts. Plus, those phones were supposed to work anywhere. Maybe. Why he never thought of this for the New Mexico trip, he couldn't understand.

"Tell him to meet us . . . . " Kyra whispered, but Derek jumped on it, already on top of things. Car travel in Connecticut promised to feel dicey if Derek hadn't covered his tracks well enough. A burly escort would certainly boost their confidence level.

"We're in Windsor Locks, CT., now and will spend the night. Yeah, that's right. It's an airport hotel near Bradley International. And then off we go tomorrow to a rural location near a tiny town called Hebron." Derek held his hand over his free ear and squinted.

Drub pushed through the door and tapped his watch, miming that he had to leave them. Derek repeated his cellular phone number into tiny holes that served as a mouthpiece. The signal dropped and Derek babbled at static. Then he and Kyra ran to the private plane to get out their belongings before Drub took off.

Boone, still off the charts as far as the feds were concerned, had no trouble hopping a jet in Albuquerque. He landed at Bradley the next day. He found them at a popular chain hotel that Derek mentioned, registered under the name of Scott Vanderbruck.

Boone left the feed shop still in the care of his patient partner, and the pickup truck in the trust of Elk Horn and the Navajo reservation. For the big guy the entire trip sailed like a soft wind. He rented a car at Bradley and whisked off to get Derek and Kyra in record time.

"Wouldn't have recognized you at all if you weren't with Kyra," Boone boomed when he grabbed Derek for a bear hug. "Blonde as me and you look like you even gained a few pounds."

"All illusion, I assure you," Derek said. "And keep it down. People are always listening."

"In this place?" Boone's laugh thundered again.

Derek and Kyra made a beeline to the door.

Once in Boone's rented car, Derek talked. He became a ventriloquist's dummy, mouth chattering with no apparent control on his part. He explained to Boone about their aborted flight from Santa Fe. He described the mysterious Petrie, and Roger's warning. He discussed why George had to stay behind to tend his summer classes. He yakked about Charlie and how the old man covered their tracks, found them new IDs, and stayed away from Astrid. He blathered on about Astrid's slow recovery and how her son's latest adventures could be threatening her newfound stability. He filled Boone in on Foo's stay at Trevor's home. He even mentioned the dreams.

That's when Boone stopped him.

"You said the goddess was flying? With those long-feathered wings?"

Derek croaked an assent. His voice, he realized, began to sputter.

"That dream won't leave me alone, either," Boone said, frowning at the two-lane road ahead. "She keeps asking me to come over to her world, her queendom or whatever. And it's weird, Derek. There's something so blasted real about those dreams. They are more true than actual life, I swear to God."

"I know."

"That's why I had to come here."

Derek nodded and could think of no more to say. The sun felt like it was melting the dashboard through the windows. They found their rooms and planned to meet up at breakfast. Boone, Derek noticed, sat there in no hurry to get a beer. Elk Horn, he decided, must be some sort of Zen master.

CHAPTER TWENTY SIX

When Boone, Derek, and Kyra decided to eat at the grill, they found a shabby affair with wire chairs that cut into your back and tables that all refused to stay level. They ordered chicken strips and talked about covering the high-tech security show at UCONN (their cover story) the next day. They heard a loud "harumph" in the background.

Derek looked around to see a slight blond man with florid skin and deep dimples in each cheek. He had a large head and barrel chest carried by stick legs, reminding Derek a bit of a giant Popsicle. When Derek stared gape-mouthed, the man hurried over to explain his presence.

"I'm Fox Hammersmith, a journalist. I wondered if you're here for that acoustics event. I'm co-sponsoring the experiment with Dr. Petrie."

"Wow, I didn't recognize you," Derek stammered. Here stood the writer whose work he admired so much. Of all the alternative historians, Hammersmith appeared to be the only one who did his homework. "Yes, we . . . " he looked for Boone and Kyra and recognized that they were both sneaking off to the bathrooms. "We are here for the demo, yes."

"A little early, aren't you?" Hammersmith said with a gap-toothed smile. "Bunch of others arrived ahead of schedule as well, including Petrie."

"That's what I hear," said Derek, narrowing his gaze. He spied Kyra and Boone and waved them over. "Do you know where we go?"

"That's why I'm here, to pick up arrivals. I'll shuttle you over to the site—as it were. You can look it over before things really get going." They waited until Boone and Kyra returned. Hammersmith led the way to a beat-up VW bus. Derek felt as if he were heading to a Grateful Dead concert.

"I'm Scott Vanderbruck, freelance photographer doing an assignment for *Great Escape* magazine," Derek said, offering his hand, which Hammersmith pumped with vigor. "This here is Nancy Thorsten. She's writing the story." They displayed their phony ID tags, but Hammersmith didn't even take a glance.

"Lovely. And this would be . . . ?" He gestured at Boone.

"Meet Bo Sandstrom," Derek said, reverting to Boone's original Swedish name. "My cousin and a pretty good traveling companion."

Hammersmith offered his hand again, and Boone shocked Derek by behaving exactly like a true Swede. He shook the hand as if accepting a chilly fish, nodding forward as he did so. He muttered a greeting in a heavy accent and stepped back in polite deference. Derek had to smother a guffaw.

As they climbed into the bus, Derek arranged things so he could sit next to Hammersmith.

"Tell me about Petrie," he said, as Hammersmith pulled out of the hotel area. "How did you get to know him?"

Horace Petrie mystified Hammersmith almost as much as he tantalized Derek. Petrie started showing up on Hammersmith's website, posting long and thoughtful theories about the relative age and sophistication of the Egyptian civilization. He knew a great amount of detail, more than any amateur Egyptologist that Hammersmith had ever known, so the writer accepted Petrie as a scholar. The thing that amazed the Englishman was how much Petrie appeared to know about the daily life of common Egyptian citizens. Archeological digs often confirmed many of Petrie's comments.

Hammersmith explained how fascinated he became with Petrie's theory of acoustical engineering. He had puzzled for years over the problem of megaliths. In just about every ancient society, from Tenochtitlan, Mexico, to Göbekli Tepe, Turkey, prehistoric peoples were somehow able to lift and position multi-ton boulders into precise formations. Many of Hammersmith's books puzzled over how the ancients achieved these feats, and he wasn't convinced by the tales of teams of men hauling slabs of rock with levers and ropes. Most engineers said the ramps would have to have more mass than the Egyptian pyramids themselves.

Right from the start, however, Hammersmith felt a buzz of skepticism about Petrie. The man claimed to have a doctorate, but never revealed where he had earned the degree. Petrie associated himself with the University of Chicago, but Dr. Adam Wechsler, who remained friendly if not in agreement with Hammersmith, claimed to never have met Petrie. Derek nodded as Hammersmith spoke, mentioning that Petrie didn't exist in the U. of C. database.

Still, when Petrie announced the great experiment in Connecticut, Hammersmith admitted to just accepting Petrie. The chance to experience a huge scientific and anthropological breakthrough, or to expose a fraud, lured Hammersmith to come see for himself. How does a journalist miss out on the biggest story of the new millennium? Hammersmith offered to co-sponsor the event, getting clearance from the state government. He'd sponsored events before and had experience in dealing with the paperwork.

"And if anything goes wrong, it will be all on my head," Hammersmith finished with a deflated tone, as they pulled up to a huge boulder known as Prophet's Rock. "My reputation is shaky enough. If Petrie makes a mess of things, I'll be bankrupt."

≈

Prophet's Rock existed as a tourist site—and for good reason. The thing was massive and probably bigger than any of the Ice Age megaliths that dotted the countryside. Boone got out of the vehicle and ran his hand over the ancient boulder.

"This thing looks like it weighs several tons," Boone said, still speaking like an off-the-boat Viking. "And you say the glaciers moved them down?" Boone's new pal Hammersmith nodded.

"There are plenty more of these where they are going to do the experiment, which is miles from here in the countryside," Hammersmith said. "These are littered all over New England."

"Well, okay," Derek said aloud, raising his hand to Hammersmith in a gesture of peace. "We're just going to poke around out here. Is there some way to get to the main rocks from here?"

"The site? Come back to the hotel and I'll give you a handout with a map and everything," Hammersmith said, his eyebrows dancing mid-forehead. "You possibly could walk from here. But there's nothing happening now. It's all set for tomorrow."

They headed back to the hotel where Hammersmith parked himself at the bar. Boone plopped next to him. Derek stomped over and glared at Boone, who accepted an amber-colored liquid from the bartender.

"It's just ice tea," Boone said in that odd foreign-sounding voice.

"I asked him to try the local beer from the micro-breweries," Hammersmith said, smacking the bar with the flat of his hand. "You Swedes are all too reserved. Live it up!"

"Don't push him," Derek said with a hint of a snarl. Hammersmith's eyebrows reached nearly to his evaporating hairline. Derek leaned over and mumbled in Boone's ear.

"What would Elk Horn say if he saw you here?"

"Elk Horn can't see me."

"So that makes it okay? You can see yourself. And you'll have to live with the consequences if you slip."

"You don't have to tell me. I know." But Boone wore an expression of regret rather than resolve. His blue eyes flickered down to the wooden bar. His mouth drooped and his massive limbs went slack. He looked like nothing more than a man backing away from a fight.

"Listen," Derek said to Hammersmith, "where is that map and the brochure? We're just going to go poke around out there. We'll use Boone's car."

"We just want to see things without the crowds," Kyra said, cool and professional in her new guise as Nancy. "You know, background color." She jammed a reporter's notebook and pen in one of her cargo pockets.

Hammersmith opened his satchel and pulled out a map and a brilliantly colored "Acoustic Wonders" brochure. Then he inscribed something on the back of his business card. He handed both items to Kyra.

"This," he said, indicating the business card, where he scribbled "approved for two" on the back, "should get you in if they have guards posted already—protecting their precious acoustical equipment."

He lifted his beer in a jolly salute. Derek and Kyra shuffled off, leaving a jumpy Boone with the joyfully beer-imbibing Englishman.

CHAPTER TWENTY SEVEN

When Derek and Kyra crept up to the acoustical test site—which stood in the middle of nowhere—all they could see were trees and plenty of giant rocks. A cheap wood-and-wire fence ran a ring around the whole area, about a half-acre in circumference—but didn't look capable of keeping anyone out. In fact, when they got to the makeshift opening that served as a gate there was no one there to challenge their entry. Yet people milled about the greens, setting up sound equipment and wires.

They crept along the perimeter of the fence to try to get a good look at the scene. Derek expressed puzzlement at the lack of big machines and sound equipment, which he knew would be necessary for a test run like this.

"All I can see are trees," he whispered to Kyra. "How are they going to move rocks by sound with all this forest in the way?"

She shrugged and dared to move a little closer toward the center, still looking for some kind of clearing or even a solitary boulder. They nosed around, trying to not to snap too many twigs or crunch fallen leaves. Then Kyra let out a gasp.

"There!" she said, pointing dead center in the middle of the circular field. There stood a multi-ton boulder that was swerved inward as if it once stood next to a tree, but only a stump remained there to mark the tree's former presence.

"That's like rape of the land," Derek said. He stood still and glanced around to see what stood next to the rock. Nothing. Then some intuition made him look up and he saw what he was searching for. Speakers and sound equipment were tied up and secured to the nearby tree trunks and also in some large branches.

Like a panther, he crept up to a tree to look at what perched in its limbs. Big, powerful speakers, with power lines that stretched out to a power source. Even out here, people needed electricity.

Pretty clever location, when you considered the constraints of the situation, he thought.

"Listen," Kyra whispered in his ear. He searched for a sound and then found it. Static buzzed from a few trees. The speakers were already on, and the demonstration wasn't scheduled until tomorrow. Curious.

"Let's get Hammersmith," Derek whispered back. "I don't think he knows this is going on." It looked like the experiment was poised and ready to go. But as soon as Derek turned around, he walked straight into the imposing figure of Dr. Petrie, who wore a scowl on his face.

"Got here early did you?" he asked, not fooled for one minute by the pair's disguises. "Well, you might as well go up to the grandstand. Sekhmet will want to know you're here."

"Sekhmet?" Derek said. "How do you know her?"

≈

They were lead to a makeshift seven-foot-high stage that was created out of sturdy boards with stairs up the sides and back. It looked like a platform where many people could assemble. There was a microphone on this "stage." Underneath the main flooring was a veritable labyrinth of boxes, sound equipment, and other pieces of junk that created multiple places to hide. Sekhmet, in all her smoky glory, stood behind the stage. She was too busy to look at Petrie and his unwelcome guests, so Derek decided to make a break for it.

"Get down!" Derek called, extracted himself from Petrie's grasp and pulled Kyra with him behind some straggly shrub. Petrie started running for them, lost them in the greenery and then slunk away, distracted by a noise of snapping twigs. Derek and Kyra peeked through the branches to see people walking back and forth around the field, setting up more equipment. They even saw some horn players out in the woods. The giant limestone block sat in the middle of it all. Derek didn't know how he did it, but he and Kyra made a hard-scrabble dash through scratchy branches and low-hanging bushes until they were somewhat near the gate and hidden from Sekhmet. Petrie was nowhere to be seen.

≈

As they crept farther north, Derek realized that a small crowd had gathered in the bushes on the other side of Sekhmet. Dressed in Arab gear, looking like ISIL and Al Qaeda members and toting fearsome guns, they stood around with video cameras and cell phones at the ready. Then further away he spied a slightly tipsy Hammersmith.

Derek ventured out from his hiding place and waved a hand in Hammersmith's direction. The writer held a firm finger to his lips and then beckoned with his other finger. Hidden by dense undergrowth, the couple duck-walked through toward Hammersmith, trying to keep a low profile to the workers' field. It was hard work. Breathing like bulls, they finally made it to Hammersmith's side.

"Not playing quite fair, are they?" Hammersmith whispered as they drew close. "Setting up is one thing, but it rather looks as if they want to prepare for any, uh, poor outcomes."

"You mean that if the experiment doesn't work tomorrow, they are going to make it work?" Kyra whispered.

Hammersmith nodded with such vigor it looked as if his oversized head might roll into the brush. "I was tipped off that this might happen. Don't like the looks of it at all."

"I want to get a closer look at what they are doing," Derek said. "I have some knowledge of what the data, er, the directions dictate."

"Well, the stage area is shoddily constructed and full of places to take cover," Hammersmith said. "We could sneak up on them easily. The entrance can't be more than fifty feet in front of us. C'mon," the Englishman urged. "I'll go with you. I want to see what Petrie's up to myself."

He dashed toward the stage and Derek had no choice but to run with him, Kyra following behind. They reached the wooden edifice, edging along its gritty back side with frantic fingers, searching for the small openings in the dusky light that marked a stairway. At first, the edifice appeared unassailable, but Hammersmith crouched along the base, eventually waving them over to a little gap between more rocks and the wooden structure.

Even though they were still in an open field, the makeshift platforms that Petrie, Sekhmet, and company had cobbled together gave Derek the feeling of being inside a structure.

"Let's try it out."

Hammersmith squeezed his fit body into the slit between the rocks. There was barely room for him. A potbelly would mean no entrance.

"Yahoo," Hammersmith said with a sound almost whispered, his voice muffled by stone and layers of dust. "Come on in."

Derek sucked in his breath and slipped through the crack, pulling his cameras in with him. Kyra jumped through with barely a struggle. They were in a little enclave behind the stage, which gave them a clear view of everything that transpired.

A footstep at the edge of their hiding place shocked them into action. Derek and the journalist jumped to the left, scampering up behind Sekhmet and her celebrity guests. Kyra cut to the right before Derek could grab her. Within seconds, Kyra slid into another rocky hideaway, while a large guard seized Derek and Hammersmith by their collars.

"Sneaky, sneaky," said an eerily familiar voice. Derek winced as he tried to turn his head. He caught sight of a young man with sweat streaming off his bald pate. There stood Ra, apparently escaped from US custody. Salim couldn't be far away.

Ra shoved his captives forward, coughing to get Sekhmet's attention.

"Not now, son," she said with irritation in her voice. "Can't you see we're making the final adjustments for our guests?" She waved her hand at the group of ragtag thugs from various Third World countries. Derek imagined that every rogue nation had sent a representative to scout out Sekhmet's enticing new technology.

"I think you'll like this new development," Ra said, his voice oozing self-satisfaction.

Sekhmet whirled about, her black hair swishing like a satin scarf. Her exotic features rearranged themselves from an expression of arrogant scorn to one of bemused excitement. She smiled without showing her teeth, so smug that Derek wanted to reach out and slap her. And still, he realized, she made his knees weak.

Tipping her head to one side, she called to Petrie.

"Look at this, Horace. What better gift could we receive?"

"Yes, I caught them before, but they are slippery little devils. Lost them the first time I had them."

Petrie lumbered about and leveled his avian-looking black eyes on Derek, who trembled in spite of the heat. Petrie's expression didn't change, but he inclined his head. Neither Sekhmet nor Petrie paid Hammersmith the slightest regard. They deliberated over Derek.

"Just the person we need," Sekhmet said, strolling forward, reveling in her good fortune. "I thought we'd have to wait until tomorrow. But today will do. It will do just fine."

She reached forward and pulled Derek close to her. Her hands were claw-like, icy, completely unlike the silken-skinned seductress he remembered from New Mexico. She wasn't particularly strong, but he could sense that breaking her hold would not be an easy task. Petrie stood immovable at the side and Ra protected the rear exit from the stage. And in front of him lurked the boulder.

On the ground and up in the trees, workers aligned sound equipment. They also positioned an array of hundreds of long-necked trumpets. Derek took a steadying breath and closed his eyes. He tried to shift backwards, but felt Sekhmet's hand at his back. She hissed in his ear.

"Think I'd hurt you?"

Derek thought indeed she might and tried to control the banging heart inside his chest. He mumbled in assent and Sekhmet let out a shrill laugh.

"No, I don't think so," she cried. "What a waste that would be. You are the key. Without you none of this would work."

A rustling sound surged behind Derek, like the wind scooping up a hundred maple leaves on a brilliant autumn day. Derek cringed and tried to drop to the ground for safety, but stumbled backwards instead. He opened his eyes and discovered that everything had changed outright. In front of him was the landscape he had just gazed upon, but now the sky teemed with incomprehensible objects; giant beetles as large as helicopters, cranes and ibises, an eerily familiar falcon and, in front of him, a huge vulture with a human head and body. The Sekhmet of his nightmare hung in the sky before him.

He wheeled wildly, searching for Hammersmith. The journalist stood bound next to two guards, one of whom was Salim—who had an odd serpentine look, as if he was ready to coil himself on the ground. Hammersmith wailed, miffed at his imprisonment, but hardly astonished by the sight before him.

"Don't you see that?" Derek screamed. Hammersmith shrugged and Salim cuffed him on the shoulder. Derek spun around again, looking for Kyra, but saw nothing. The men holding the trumpets remained the same, but everyone else in Sekhmet's party mutated into bizarre beasts—many half-human. Derek struggled to regain his hold on reality and not succumb to the hallucinations that Sekhmet was sending him, but all he could hear in his head was the dream voice of Tehuti. *They wouldn't let me die.*

Sekhmet grinned like a harpy in front of him. "Are you ready? We're about to begin."

"I don't have the formula and you know that," Derek called out to the monster with Sekhmet's voice. "You know no one's tested any of those numbers that you and Stonegate extracted. The ones I found have never seen the light of day."

Sekhmet responded with a shriek of glee.

"You should have known I'd figure it all out," she said. "What was missing was the sound of the human voice—and you are going to provide that."

She lofted into the air and then descended to a perch next to him on the wood and stone platform. "The numbers we can extrapolate. What matters is you."

Derek's vision blurred and he felt Sekhmet slip her hand in his. He heard the wings of a falcon and sensed Petrie pressed close to his other side. He clamped his eyes shut, trying desperately to think clearly. Hammersmith doesn't see this. The musicians aren't running around in a panic. This is just me. The waking dream. While Derek tried to maintain focus, Sekhmet began to chant in a language he had never heard.

Her voice had a mellifluous cadence, clear tones like ringing bells in the air. She sang a tuneless ode, syllables repeating and changing in hypnotic fashion.

"Kheper-ee-kheper-u, khep-um, khep-um, kheperet," she intoned, her voice humming with the vibration of deepest earth. "Her-u, heru-akhty, heru, eheru-um . . . . "

Derek blinked, remembering something from his research. Heru, the falcon. That was the original Egyptian name, or one of its versions, before the Greeks changed it to Horus. He opened his eyes and looked to his left to see the ersatz professor, Petrie, standing in casual attire, looking for all the world as if he had never sprouted wings.

"Horace. Horus," Derek said, fastening Petrie with his eyes. "How could I have missed that?"

Petrie looked over with sparkling spectacles. "You see what you want to see, my friend. You should know that by now. We have always been the same."

Derek looked to his other side to see Sekhmet, glowing in her guise as a young woman. She chanted the litany of the gods in their original names, in a language that had not been heard by human ears in nearly two thousand years.

"Aset," she said, announcing a favorite goddess's name. The trumpeters put their instruments to their lips. Drummers seated at their feet began to beat the same rhythm set by Sekhmet's chant. The speakers began blaring strange, unmusical sounds. Derek felt strange rivulets of energy working through the stone, as if the pulsing sound redirected the atoms themselves. He braced himself by setting his feet apart. *Will this wooden stage hold?*

"Khalkhlak, Khalkoum, Khiam, Khar, Kroum, Zbar, Beri, Zbarkom, Khre, Kariob, Faribour. Aaaaaaaaaaeeeeeeeeeoooooo oooooouuuuuuu . . . . You see how the words of power hold magic in their very vibration. You see why we didn't share the vowel sounds with outsiders." Sekhmet snorted faintly. "But none of it works with we gods only. It takes a non-god, a mortal connection, to make the power find its way to earth."

She moved Derek forward and signaled the trumpeters to begin. They let out a wail that didn't resemble any kind of music. First whining, then blaring, they created a wave of oddly resonant sound that refracted off the edges of the forest and bounced against the rock. The waves felt like small eddies at first, bouncing and drifting, but soon the movement felt palpable. The tiny hairs on Derek's knuckles stood up and danced in the waves. He saw with horror that the boulder placed dead center in the middle of the field began to vibrate.

"Now, *you* will utter the sounds that will make the whole thing work," Sekhmet said and snatched him by the shoulders. He stretched airborne, clutched in her talons, as she wailed a magic spell into the shimmering air. She brought Derek down, in front of the boulder, which trembled like a child ready to run. Derek tried to wriggle from her grasp but she held on, part bird, part human, all goddess.

"I don't know the words!" he screamed.

"But you do. I taught them to you."

Of no accord of his own, Derek heard his shaky voice repeating phrases Sekhmet had sung in his ear. The boulder tilted to one side, one edge raised into the air. It wriggled and shivered, longing to free itself from gravity, and Derek felt his blood nearly shooting out of his arteries. He made one last effort to scream, when the boulder fell with a thunderclap back onto its platform.

Someone pulled at his hands, trying to wrench him from Sekhmet's claw. The figure leaped into the air, hacking at the talons with a small pocketknife. The rescuer struggled to wrench Derek free, but fell back to earth before the job could be finished.

"Kyra, get out of here," Derek cried. But Sekhmet clamped onto her before Derek had the phrase out of his parched mouth.

"The paramour," Sekhmet said with scorn. The goddess had returned to human form. She gestured to a servant who manhandled Kyra, tying her to a chair in an empty part of the south of the field. "We'll make her part of the experiment. That ought to end this rivalry."

Kyra was on the chair, the target for the rock to land, Derek said to himself, *This experiment can't work. I've got to get some dissonance going.* Before he had time to think, the hum started again, the drums thudded, the trumpets whined and Sekhmet put the words of transformation into his mind. He tried to change them, to shape his mouth into the wrong shapes, to splay his tongue against his teeth, to belch. It didn't work. The stone rose again, and Derek tried to convince himself that he was suffering from some arcane hallucination.

As a last-ditch effort, he sent out a strangled word he had never heard before and the rock leaped from the earth, hovering like a UFO.

"Move it," Sekhmet said with a roar. "Use your mind." She strutted in front of him and began to mutate from woman to shimmering proto-female to a slobbering, ravenous lioness standing nearly twelve feet tall. Derek did try to move the rock with his mind—but he pulled the rock toward himself, and this hideous beast that had been Sekhmet. Sound roared in his ears like a whirlwind, sucking all life from the landscape, making the sultry air as chilly as the inside of a freezer, and the rock began to roll in the air, first twisting toward Kyra, then reeling in Derek's direction. As he prepared to call the rock to crush the life out of himself, Derek let out one more dissonant shout, but another heart-stopping wail caused the rock to spin out of control.

Derek gyrated to see a bulky man leap toward Kyra, pulling her to the safe ground, screaming something that made the rock shudder. The yell came again. "Nej!" the voice wailed (sounding like "nay" in English) and the large runner, screaming the Swedish word for "no," headed straight for Sekhmet with his arms out, ready to tackle. Out in the field, the boulder quivered, rocked, leapt, and then plummeted to the ground, squarely on top of a rampaging Boone.

As it slammed to the ground, the megalith shattered, with boulders and shards blasting out from all sides. The trumpets and drummers ran for cover, of which there was none. Screams filled the air, and Derek felt a rock graze his leg like a piece of shrapnel. It bled and hurt like hell. He fell flat to the ground until the rumbling stopped. He heard Kyra calling and he dragged himself in agony across the ground until he reached her side. She screamed Boone's name and bled from her left arm. Derek found a discarded bandana and wrapped her wound.

"Look. Now," she said harshly, with the last extra breath she could manage.

Derek craned his neck to see Sekhmet and Horus, now returned to feathered form, ascending into the sky and wheeling straight into the setting sun. They spiraled in the red glare and then were eaten by the light—gray streaks of dust on the sun's bloody face. They had returned to Ra, the original Ra, the governor of their universe . . . .

"That woman . . . "

"Flew away, I know," Derek said, shaking his head at the ground.

"No," Kyra said, shaking. "She didn't do that at all. She ran away, along with that Dr. Petrie fraud." Kyra stared at Derek as if one or both of them were losing their sanity.

Derek looked back over at the boulder, taking in the bloodied forms on the ground, hearing the groans of the wounded, and smelling the sickening scent of fresh blood. His entire chest sagged.

"One thing we do know. Boone didn't make it."

CHAPTER TWENTY EIGHT

The disastrous experiment boomed across the landscape, like a retreating thunderstorm. It was a colossal failure and it wouldn't be long before the local police arrived to investigate Boone's death and the myriad injuries. As he and Kyra tore towards the park's exit, Derek felt a pang of panic about abandoning Boone, but he knew the big guy was beyond help.

Without bothering to rest their weary, wounded limbs, they flew past the gate and nearly barreled into a man. He looked up, eyes slightly unfocused until he finally recognized them. It had been a ruinous afternoon for Fox Hammersmith.

"Get in your car and get out of here," Hammersmith said. "Get out of Windsor Locks, this rural area, and the whole area. Leave this place now."

Derek patted his pockets to check for his wallet. Still there. Kyra nodded her assent. She also must have stowed money and her notes in those big cargo pockets in her safari shorts. They began to run for Boone's rental car, but stopped short when they realized that the Englishman wasn't following them.

"Aren't you coming?" Kyra yelled.

Hammersmith shook his head with a remorse-filled sigh. He had a basset hound's sad eyes. "Can't. I've got to clean up this mess. Remember?"

"You can't be serious. Petrie was just as much to blame," Kyra said.

"He just walked off with Sekhmet. You saw them," Hammersmith said. "I've never seen a woman do that before. Shrank and aged into a codger in front of my eyes. Completely took my focus off Petrie. When I came to, he had vanished."

Kyra nodded, clearly sharing Hammersmith's view of Petrie's disappearance. Derek decided to say nothing about his version.

He knew Hammersmith wouldn't be meeting Petrie again, but didn't know how to warn him. Derek felt time closing in on him.

"Fox, he's not going to share the blame," Derek said. "Come with us while there's time."

Hammersmith shook his head again and shooed them away with his arms.

"I'll meet up with you near the Connecticut shore. My office number is on my card. My assistant will get you in touch with me." He turned his back and returned to meet his fate.

They were just ahead of the police, who must have heard the clamor from miles away. Derek fingered the rental car keys in his pocket, lowered his head as he spied the remains of the central boulder, which now stood as a tombstone for Boone. *The price was too dear. It wasn't his fight to lose.*

≈

Against all odds, the piña coladas were working. Derek felt the cool buzz of spirits and fruit juice sizzling through his organs and leaned back in his chair. Relaxation—or just exhaustion?—permeated his muscles for the first time. He and Kyra had discovered a sweet little bed-and-breakfast tucked next to an untrafficked section of Rhode Island known as Misquamicut. There was an outdoor bar built over the water's edge, with a view of the marina. The lodgings included a diner with wi-fi, so the inn was perfect for their needs. The plan was to stay put until they heard from Hammersmith, who would be in Misquamicut in a few days, according to his London-based assistant.

The escape from the killing field in the Connecticut boonies had put both of them in a blue mood, so deep and trenchant that they hardly talked to each other during the entire car ride. It wasn't until they arrived at the picturesque beach—a compact stretch of land—that Kyra came back to life. She had suffered a nasty array of cuts and scrapes, not to mention the wound to her arm, but an emergency care clinic nearby found nothing that required stitches. Bandages and disinfectant balm put affairs aright and a few aspirins slowed the throbbing pain. Derek's leg checked out as just a flesh wound and he sported a large bandage.

Derek knew how lucky they had been and promised, deep within his thudding heart, that he'd make it all up to Kyra.

Now he gazed at her grave face, just visible above a fluted pineapple slice on her towering beverage. She caught him staring and managed a wan smile.

"Looks like Carmen Miranda's hat." The old sparkle was still in her eyes, even if her body language was silent.

"Yeah. More than your daily requirement of Vitamin C."

Kyra played with the straw and opened her mouth as if to speak, then seemed to reconsider and stared back at the flowered tablecloth.

"Come on, out with it," Derek teased.

Kyra tried again, leaning towards him at the table, almost as if she were sharing a secret. "What exactly were you planning to do out there? I mean, if things went the way you wanted?"

Derek felt a nascent shout of amazement erupt from his throat and almost choked trying to keep it down. After launching into a massive coughing fit, he sank back into his chair, avoiding the stares of neighboring bar patrons.

"You're kidding, right?" Derek choked out. "I had no freaking idea what I was doing."

"None?"

"Absolutely zilch," Derek said, a grim laugh slipping past his mental censor. No need to worry now. He had screwed up big time. Kyra caught the tide and joined in with him.

"I thought you had a plan. Some idea how you were going to tangle with her, that Sekhmet being, whatever she could be."

Derek took another sip of piña colada, considering an answer. *How do you explain that you can't battle a goddess?* The dreams convinced him on the trip to Windsor Locks that any direct confrontation with Sekhmet would end in utter devastation. But before the showdown, he did prepare a bit of a scheme. He figured he'd better share it now, for it wouldn't be right to let his girlfriend think that he had no plans to protect her.

"Well, there's the principle of dissonance," Derek began. "You see, the whole idea behind sonic levitation requires resonance, lots and lots of it, building in waves. Enough resonance and you can move matter."

"Thinking like a scientist again, weren't you?" She still laughed.

"Lot of good that did me, I admit. The idea was to introduce dissonance into the mix. I thought that if we scoped out their set-up, I'd see an opportunity to pump noise into their symphony. I didn't have any time. They sneaked in early and events just took off on their own."

"So, if you had a loudspeaker and played, say, hip hop at high volume . . . ?"

"That would have put a crack in their reality." Derek felt his laughter wilt within his chest. "Instead they cracked mine."

Kyra didn't speak for a second or two, watching some yachts sail down the shore. The view seemed to soothe her. She turned back to Derek with a soft gaze.

"What was she really? A shrunken hag or a beautiful babe? What kind of hold did she have over you?"

"Kyra, if I told you what I saw, you'd leave me on the next plane to Chicago. Stonegate knew. He warned me at the prison. He called her Sekhmet, the lioness." Derek shook his head, aghast at the content of his own speech. "Or you could just say a woman out of her time. Someone who should have died a long time ago." He paused again, presuming he sounded a bit more rational now. "And what did she want? Well, that part is obvious."

"To sell the technology to those assassins and thugs?"

"Of course not. That was all show, to scare us. She wanted something simple." He paused and crumpled his brow. "She wanted to be worshipped."

Kyra's eyes had a peculiar glaze, as if she too were trying to see into the world Derek had glimpsed. Maybe those ancient Egyptian words were chanting inside her head, maybe she also smelled the myrrh and amber. She put down her drink with a thunk as if reassuring herself of the solid table surface.

"Well, she got away. Who's to say she can't come back and demand it again?"

He pondered the question and remembered his vision of the sun devouring the goddess and her follower. It didn't look as if she were resurrecting any time soon. The ignominy of total failure remained too great, even for a goddess. Still, Kyra's question stood as a fair one. He touched his empty cocktail glass and gestured for another to the waiter.

"If it's not her, it will be someone else," he said, not realizing where the words were coming from. "There's always someone who will risk everything for the power of a god. History tells us that."

He looked into the sunlight, which had a peculiar glow. Curious, clear and refreshing, as if the light had been renewed and replenished. The sun god, Derek thought, had had a fine meal.

≈

Using the diner's wi-fi, Derek sent two messages under his own name. As far as he was concerned, "Scott " was as dead as Boone. One message went to George, the other to Roger. Both read: "It doesn't work."

That told the whole story, really. George would know enough to alert the people who needed to know. Roger, well, he seemed to know everyone and everything. The FBI would lay off its investigation. Three words should just about cover everything. Before he pressed the send button, he decided to add two more words to Roger's message. "Cousin lost," he wrote. When he sent the mail, he felt as if he had personally ushered Boone's soul into the afterlife. Somehow, Roger would inform people. Derek felt a pressing ache below his collarbone as he imagined Astrid hearing the news.

He paid up, turned to Kyra and tilted his head. The cash on hand was dwindling, but there was enough in Chicago and plastic was safer now. It was still warm in the Great Lakes states, but who knew what fall would bring? Rhode Island's ocean sparkled a rich royal blue with golden reflections, and Kyra had never looked more sunlit than she did in this brilliant moment.

Derek knew there had to be a way to get over this monstrosity of a trip east. He also knew he had to make things right for Kyra, whom he seemed to disappoint more times than not.

"Let's take a break and do a little soul-searching on the beach," he said to her as she plodded beside him.

Kyra threw back her finely chiseled chin and shook her hair in the breeze. "I think you're right," she said. She grabbed his arm and they strolled along the sand until they found a spot where they could be alone to do some introspection in the sunshine.

CHAPTER TWENTY NINE

Little reached Derek in this blue-and-white retreat and he reveled in the simplicity. There would be time enough to face consequences. Now was the opportunity to luxuriate in the salty tang of seaside margaritas and the sultry sweep of sea winds.

He crawled up the sand sideways to Kyra, who was lying on her stomach reading a novel. He crept as close as he could, like a tiny crab inching closer to a fine meal. Then, as close as he dared, he took a sudden swipe with his tongue at the back of her reddened ear.

"Yah!" Kyra said, rolling on her side and dabbing one hand at her sloppy earlobe.

"Umm, salty," Derek said, licking his lips. He inched forward again and pressed his face closer to hers, seeking the kisses that would release him from blame. Kyra's body eased into his arms, allowing him to meld with her delicate frame. Tangy, thirsty kisses, one urging on the other, took over. After weeks of bittersweet regret, careful consideration, and well-chosen words, this one moment left the two lovers unchained. For Derek, it was as if the sunshine lifted the shadow of Sekhmet forever, allowing him to adore Kyra completely for the bright, luscious, selfless person she was.

"I *do* love you, you know," Derek said, pulling her freckled, sand-speckled body closer than before. She glistened like a Bond girl from the movies.

"I think this time I believe you," Kyra said in a low growl, her eyes teasing. A momentary pulse of blue flicked through the green field of her irises, like an emotion running for cover. Her gaze fell over the sea.

"What's wrong?"

"Nothing. I guess," she said, her voice lowering to a pitch only sea creatures could hear. "Boone. The thought of how he went." She gulped and faced Derek. "Also I really, truly want to believe you."

Derek held her right hand as if lifting the finest pearl from its shell and held it up to admire. The tiny blue veins were like roadways, speeding around hundreds of freckle towns. The arteries were deeper, but just as vital, taking express routes to her deepest senses. He kissed her hand and sent a wave of his passion along, urging it through the avenues to her heart.

"You can believe it, Kyra. This experience has taken me through a transformation—whether I wanted it or not." He was silent for a second, trying to regroup his swirling maelstrom of thoughts. "Out there," he gestured in the direction of the woods, "I learned something. Boone tried to warn me earlier, but I didn't see it then."

She looked into his eyes, searching for signs, but he didn't say any more. She squeezed his hand, urging him to continue. A puff of air ruffled the beach sand, tossing the pages of her book. She let the pages, like the plot of her own life, blow wildly out of control.

"He said I couldn't live my life without sharing," Derek said, throat tightening at the idea of recalling Boone's presence in that beat-up truck cab. "He told me everyone has connections, whether they want them or not. I only had connections with my pizza man and my motherboard. I was hurting everyone close to me by shutting down."

Kyra's lips stretched into an inscrutable smile, the kind that expresses more pain than amusement.

"He was certainly wiser than anyone would have thought—anyone judging by first appearances," she said. "When I met you, you were as remote and peculiar as that guy in federal prison."

"Stonegate."

"Yeah, him. I'd read about him and wondered about that kind of life. The difference is that you are free to walk around."

"Why did you bother with me?"

She reached down, scooped a handful of sand, and considered. "I really don't know." She let the grains slip between her fine fingers as a sweet breeze swept over the beach. "I guess it was as much of a challenge as anything else. You certainly weren't like the jock boys I knew before."

"Well, consider your challenge met. You released me from my penitentiary."

She rolled into his arms and they were swept by something stronger than a tsunami. They tossed and rolled across the gritty carpet, grinding their bodies closer together. Derek's blood vessels filled with new life. He was, indeed, out of his cold fortress, and eager to seize this moment with a willing partner. They pitched about in the sand, stopping when they hit a rather large rock at the water's edge.

We aren't doing a tawdry remake of a Hollywood film.

"Grab your book," he sighed in her ear. "The maid just changed the sheets."

≈

The lusciousness of Kyra's slender body never failed to amaze Derek. Compact and well muscled, her form betrayed no softness at first glance. She had a warrior's body, full of quickness and mercurial temperament. But unclothed and pressed against sunlit cotton sheets, her breasts and thighs were sexy and soft. Today, after succumbing to Derek's love play, she looked more enticing than he ever remembered because, just before she fell away from him with a sated swoon, she shouted out her love for him.

He stroked the fine hairs on her forearm, listening to the surf, lost in the memory of the last few minutes. If Kyra loved him too, he had a future to consider—something brand new for him. It would no longer be he and his computer hacking the world. Someone else had saddled up for the ride. It felt unnerving, but infinitely better than months on end of loneliness.

Kyra had asked what he was thinking about, a common female question that usually drove Derek wild when he actually woolgathered over an algorithm or the Cubs' home-win record. But this time, he only pulled her tightly in his arms with no more guilty thoughts.

"I'm wishing that I hadn't failed back there."

"Failed? Where?"

"At the forest. I wish I had come away with a technology that worked. So I would get rich and provide a fine life for you."

Kyra rolled away a bit and then reached to tousle his hair.

"The roots are growing in," she observed. "But I rather like you like this. You'll be a funky CEO."

"CEO, sure. I'm coming back with nothing to show for two years of struggles. Two years of decoding and a national chase down the drain. Oh yeah, and letting down my best pal, too."

Kyra shook her head and giggled. "Wrong, wrong, wrong. All that hacking proves that you and George, above all the other computer geniuses, were the ones who could break into Stonegate's treasure chest. When word gets out about that, you'll be the two most sought-after encryption experts in the world."

Derek swallowed. He hadn't considered that angle at all. He and George did defy the odds by cracking Stonegate's box. Even Stonegate gave them props for that.

"The technology does work," she continued. "Sort of. You saw that boulder rise into the air?" Derek nodded. At least they could agree on that vision. "All it needs is control. More research. Even if we can only move small objects with sound, we're onto some valuable knowledge."

Derek sat up and scratched the stubble on his chin. Kyra had something there. Maybe he could sell George on the idea. Maybe there grew a germ of a business venture here. And since everyone else, FBI included, thought it failed, he'd have some wiggle room.

"CEO, indeed," he crowed, grabbing Kyra in a fierce hug and dancing her around the bed with him. "And you will be the best marketing director on the planet."

"Chairman of the board, please," she corrected, then gave him a long, probing kiss that made Derek's knees weak.

≈

Hammersmith blew onto the beach like a sun shower, just as he promised. Hammersmith's assistant, Nilesh, an Indian graduate student having the time of his life in London, had promised that the peripatetic journalist would make it to Rhode Island by that weekend.

"After what he's been through, don't expect a publicity tour," Nilesh joked. "He'll be staying below the radar."

Sure enough, Hammersmith called and arranged a meeting at a humble burger joint far from the beach. Just as Kyra and Derek found a clean table, the Englishman pushed open the door, squinting as he tried to make out the occupants. He'd altered his appearance. Instead of dressing like a high-tech safari leader, Hammersmith could have passed as a vacationing insurance salesman: broadcloth button-down shirt rolled up to the elbows, khaki pants, and brown loafers. The only concession to journalistic insouciance in his sartorial presentation was the chili pepper tie he wore in place of a normal cravat. After he blinked his large eyes a few times, he picked Derek out of the paltry crowd. He raised a hand in the air like a politician.

"Scott," he barked. His face was reddened from the sun. His eyes gleamed abnormally white in the dim restaurant. Derek walked up and took his proffered hand.

"It's Derek. Scott's long gone," Derek rumbled in Hammersmith's ear.

"Well, sometimes a fiction's worth maintaining. You still have to get home, you know." Hammersmith walked over to the table where Kyra pulled out a chair, but he greeted her by her proper name. The writer's shoulders were compressed more than Derek remembered, although that improbably large head still bobbed about. Hammersmith plopped himself into a chair and started babbling about his trip to Hartford to explain the mess in which he had participated.

"Fox," Kyra interrupted, "what happened to you when we left? Why did you have to go to Hartford?"

While Kyra spoke, Derek scrutinized the table rather than take in the pain in Hammersmith's face.

"The government, you know," Fox said, with a dull shrug. "I owed them an official explanation. After all, they gave me express permission to put that show on. There were six dead, eighteen injured, mainly Connecticut residents. All hit by flying rocks that flew off the main megalith. It looked horrendous."

Derek looked up. Before he could find the words, Hammersmith answered his tacit question.

"Boone's remains were pulverized. There really wasn't anything left to identify. A bolder that size dropping at that much velocity. . . . Well, there wasn't even enough dental matter."

"Did you give his name, anyway?" Derek asked.

Fox pulled out a driver's license from his briefcase. "He gave me this at the bar at that cheesy hotel. Wanted me to hold on to it in case he did something stupid. I had no idea what he could have been babbling about. I told the state police this person was unaccounted for. Not much more I could do, really. They took notes and returned the license to me. Not really interested, I guess."

Derek received the card. The photo showed a toothy blond man named Bo Sandstrom. His eyes looked into the distance, wistful, full of unfulfilled dreams. He had stood at the midpoint in life with barely a thought of mortality. Derek flipped the license on the table. His throat constricted at the thought of explaining Boone's death to Astrid, and to the relatives in Sweden.

The fidgety group sat in distracted silence for a second or two until the waiter slunk over and plopped tumblers and a sloppy pitcher on the rickety table. "Miller time?" he inquired. Derek nodded without a thought and the man slipped away. Kyra busied herself with the refreshments, pretzels and beer nuts, while Derek fumbled in his pockets for money. Hammersmith stared at them with a softening glow in his bloodshot eyes.

"Look, Derek," Hammersmith said, touching the young man's wrist. "When Boone ran out there like that, it wasn't out of desperation. I'm sure he wasn't drunk. He was like a warrior out to save Kyra. I'd say he died with more than a shred of dignity attached, which is all I could hope for any of us." Hammersmith pulled his mug toward his chest, coughed, and gulped down half a glass of beer.

"You're sure?" Derek pursued. "When you left him, he lounged at the bar. He could have been half blind with drink by the time the accident happened."

Hammersmith winced, bringing a bushy white brow almost over one eye. "No, I'm quite sure he followed right behind me. After you two became suspicious of the sound experiment, I too became cynical of Petrie's motives. I left, he followed me, and I saw him at the site, skulking from rock to rock."

Hammersmith fell back into his seat, as if settling on an important fact. "You know, he seemed to operate in a trance. Muttering to himself about a flying woman and that damned Sekhmet. It wasn't me he followed. It was the lilt of her mystique."

Kyra played with water rings on the tabletop, mentally pasting the facts together. She licked her dry lips before addressing Hammersmith.

"She infected, poisoned really, both Boone and Derek. What they saw out there mesmerized them like a multi-dimensional hologram of what you and I experienced, Fox. Derek couldn't help what he did any more than Boone. They were drawn to her, attached to her by a psychic web. But something made them stop her."

Derek nodded, and Hammersmith, with a look of interest, polished off the rest of his glass. "You might be right. Yet, even those walking in the wild know right from wrong, Kyra. Boone knew what he had to do. His choice was inescapable to him, if not to us."

The waiter reappeared for his payment, placing more pretzels and beer on the table with an apologetic half-smile. Hammersmith nibbled on one end of a pretzel and his face soured. Derek felt a dull squeeze in his throat.

"Connecticut doesn't like you anymore," the writer said, rubbing his lined forehead. "The heat's going to lean on you soon. Too soon. My fortunes there are mixed at best. I talked my way out of culpability and blamed it all on Petrie, whom no one can find. Anyone new they can pin this catastrophe on—well, you don't want to lollygag long enough to see any troopers."

Derek tried to apologize for what he had put the journalist through, and even took out his wallet to make amends, but his patter went nowhere. Fox wasn't in the mood for cajoling.

"You have tonight. Do you have money?" Derek and Kyra nodded. "Good. You can fly home on a commercial jet and then you can drop the Scott nonsense. At least no one knew your real name at the experiment site. Go and get on with your life and maybe we can forget this whole thing ever happened."

"Little chance of that," Derek said. However, he stood up and shook Hammersmith's hand as the journalist got up to exit. He felt on the verge of tears, but hugged the man instead of showing his face. Derek had no doubt, as he watched Hammersmith's slightly bent, retreating back, that he'd see this friend again.

CHAPTER THIRTY

The traffic light must have changed about five times, but the cars and buses weren't going anywhere. People cursed behind their steering wheels, and a Muslim woman in a black garment simmered in her dark cover-up at the corner bus stop. Charlie sat on the molded seat in the bus shelter wondering why, for the first time in years, his own life had slowed to a crawl.

He could have been in a car. Hell, the Viking Traders gave him a new one every week to get the hunker off the lot. But he decided to try the bus this time and sat outside on Devon Avenue sweating, losing color and probably shrinking in size and dimension. Memory frayed along with the tempers, and Charlie couldn't remember what it felt like to walk, run, and be chased. When had all that pursuit ended?

There had been that day in August. He recalled it clearly so that he could hear the cicadas singing in the trees and smell the grasses gone to seed. George discovered him sleeping on some Swedish pal's sofa in Andersonville. George, that friend of Derek's with the receding blond hairline and the frozen expression on his perpetually confused face. Yes, on that August day there were two remarkable changes. George looked at Charlie as if he were mentally deficient and mumbled something about the data being dead. Forget about the disk, George instructed. Nothing of any value existed on it anymore. Charlie didn't pay any attention to that command, of course. He promised his son only.

Then that navy Dodge Intrepid stopped driving around. No more visits from strange agents with names such as Harley and Davidson. No more moonlight chases through the alleys of Foster Avenue. And, most amazing of all, no more raids on Ivar's chop shop. Charlie actually felt safe going back to work there over the last few days. They were off the radar screen—and no one knew why.

Yet, at the same time, rumblings in the emotional atmosphere hinted at something terribly awry. Charlie didn't understand why, but every time he looked skyward at an airplane, he felt his guts squeeze into quantum-sized fragments. He'd be walking down the street and swear that animals were talking to him. Not wild chatter. No lottery numbers or anything like that. But a cat that he stroked expressed sorrow. Charlie was sure he heard it in his mind, although no one in the small alley heard a thing. Sometimes, at night, a tear would fall, and he would thrash about, thinking of his traveling son. But, no. Derek couldn't be in trouble. This knowledge he felt deep in his heart. But someone, someone close, was not just hurting, but lost.

Ivar liked to poke around the Internet and discovered some bad news from New England. Massive boulders had been blown up and there were ghastly reports of a person smashed beyond recognition. The writers blamed it all on an English journalist, however the Connecticut state police felt that a mysterious missing professor figured as the real villain. Charlie read the stories with deep interest, knowing that his son had ventured out east. But he found no mention of Derek or anyone else he recognized. All that didn't relate to the odd heaviness he felt in his heart, Charlie figured.

Another story caught his eye for no apparent reason. Some super hacker, a cyber villain named Stonegate, had been released from federal prison after a successful appeal. The man's history sounded remarkably similar to Derek's. As Charlie studied the grainy picture on Ivar's antiquated computer, he thought he recognized something about the man. He thought he'd seen the guy's picture in Derek's college apartment long ago. Why would that have been?

Another plane flew overhead and he heard an Indian man exclaim, "I should have taken a bicycle, for God's sake." The traffic stood hopelessly gridlocked and Charlie was going nowhere. He got up and gave his bench seat to a lady who might have been pregnant—who knows these days?—and meandered down the street somewhere in the direction of the last place he parked his car.

≈

After so many high-voltage years, Charlie's old house in Evanston looked as serene as a sea yacht, framed by the blue of Lake Michigan and shining with brilliant paint. Who did the upkeep while he'd been gone? Surely not Derek, who was about as handy with household tools as Charlie was with a computer mouse. The yard, too, smelled of a recent mow, and the front shrubs looked razor-trimmed.

Charlie stopped at the front stoop and felt a momentary shyness, as if he were a salesman arriving unwanted at the front door. Heck, no one came in that way anyhow. He went around the side and tested the other door. It opened silently and he sidled back inside the mudroom. He stood still for a few dreamy moments, smelling the cedar paneling, hearing the sounds of a washing machine, sensing the emotions that rammed at him from every direction.

He crept around a pile of laundry next to the washer and slid into the kitchen. Astrid wasn't there, although a lemonade pitcher stood sweating on a bare counter. In the dining room, he confronted the big table from the old days. He touched the polished surface and hunted for a wedge-shaped gouge. There it glowed, near the edge, patched and varnished over with a carpenter's pride. He rubbed a thumb over the smooth surface, remembering more than twenty years ago when Astrid came crying to him with a big carving knife in her hand. He had thought that she cut off a finger or something just as horrendous, but she had only slipped while carving a turkey, slicing a trough in the dining room table—the table Charlie had crafted by hand.

He remembered kissing her, slipping the knife out of her fingers and whispering in the hollow of her ear below her blonde curls. He'd fix it. Nothing broke that couldn't be repaired. Nothing of any value had vanished from their lives. And Astrid let out that blubbery laugh that one has when trying to will away tears. She allowed her strong body to become relaxed and fluid in Charlie's expert grasp.

He padded out to the living room, and then climbed the stairs, avoiding the steps that squeaked. Or did someone fix the squawks? He found no Astrid in the silent, rearranged bedroom. He slipped downstairs, to the back of the house, and finally caught sight of her in the backyard, sitting at the patio table. She propped her feet on another chair and tipped her head back to receive the late summer sunlight.

Charlie opened the sliding screen door without a sound and approached as silently as Elk Horn stalking deer in the forest. Astrid breathed softly, her rounded breasts rising like baking bread with each intake of air. She appeared heavier than he remembered. Her upper arms were padded with a light layer of doughy flesh and her waist looked thick, straining at the buttons where her dress fastened on the side. Her skin didn't wear the golden shade she once glistened with at the end of summer. She looked as if she had been dusted with ash. Her hair no longer dared to out dazzle the sunlight. It was still blonde, but no longer a sweet mix of amber and gold.

Charlie took a long, silent breath. To him, she was flawless. As the azaleas rippled with a tiny puff of wind, and the purple coneflowers nodded their thorny heads, Astrid's perfection infused the garden as incense works its way through a cathedral. The daylilies and zinnias genuflected in her presence. The tall hollyhocks along the back fence whispered her name. The bees sizzled overhead, protecting her, blessing her.

She was all that Charlie would ever have. And she remained a prize he would never regain, because he'd hurt her to the quick. How long, he wondered, had he thought of this moment, the time when he teetered on the edge of yet another discovery? How often had he rehearsed things he'd say, practiced how his face would look, what sort of flowers he'd bring to her? But, of course, the flowers were already here, brought to this time and place by a power greater than Charlie.

Go, Elk Horn had said, do what is right. Charlie let out the breath. He stepped forward, loud enough for Astrid to hear.

"I heard you were here," she said without turning around.

"Sorry for just barging in like this."

"You took your time. I was expecting you sooner or later."

She still hadn't moved, and Charlie stood on the balls of his feet at the edge of the pavement. It didn't matter if he had rehearsed this moment to perfection; this reunion struck him as a disaster no matter what tack he took. He took two steps forward and his mouth took over.

"No one had any right to hurt a human being the way I hurt you," he said. At once he was sorry he spoke. Why didn't he start with something light? Ask about the lemonade on the table? Joke about how tall Derek is? Something less confrontational. Less to the point.

Astrid still didn't turn to him. She merely put a hand before her eyes to shade the sun. Charlie let the silence work through the landscape and breeze through his heated mind.

"It hurt like hell," Astrid said at last.

"I know. I feel it now. I didn't then."

"No. I guess you wouldn't have." Astrid started to move, bringing her legs to the ground and smoothing her skirt as if to stand. Seconds elapsed, and Charlie practiced his Zen breathing. Then she dropped her arms by her side and sank deeper into the chair.

"I didn't come here for forgiveness," Charlie said, moving with care now, circling the table, arriving at her side like a courtier.

Astrid let out a sour laugh. "Well, that's a good thing," she said, frowning. "What did you come here for?"

"To hear myself say that I acknowledge your pain," Charlie said, looking into her eyes for the first time. He felt his hands shake but stayed with the moment. Go. Do what is right. "To tell you I see what I did to you. To tell you that I can never fix it or make it right. But I can tell you I can see clearly today. I can feel like a man again. And your pain is real to me."

Astrid tipped her head sideways. "It was the booze that made you that way," she said, whisking her hand through the air as if dismissing the whole course of Charlie's disease. "I know that."

"More than that. Not feeling. That's what made me that way," Charlie said. He felt urgency. He wasn't going to get off with that old excuse. "When a person is senseless and brain dead, it's amazing how much damage he can do."

Astrid forced a tense smile, and then covered her mouth with a hand. But her eyes still emitted a twinkle of life. "You don't want me to forgive you?" she asked, her eyes opening wider, the blue emerging from a secret hiding place.

"Only God can do that."

"I thought you people talk about a Higher Power."

"I call it God."

"Okay, have it your way," Astrid said as she sat up straight in the chair. A thin leaf skated over the surface of the table. "And you don't want me to welcome you home with open arms?"

"Not unless you want to. I came to tell you I behaved badly. I came to hear myself admit my part in that horrible duel . . . . "

"That we called our marriage," Astrid interrupted. A tear gathered in the corner of one eye, but she wiped it away. "Well, I'm sorry, too."

"Why?"

"I'm sorry that I thought we'd never have a moment like this again."

Charlie took her hand and guided her to her feet. The air rippled ripe with pollen, fragrance, and the heaviness of late-summer life. So different from the light, dry freedom of the desert air. Charlie would need to relearn the landscape.

"Come on," he said with a sure sweetness in his voice, a sound he hadn't heard in decades. "Let's have some of that lemonade I saw in the kitchen. I won't be staying long."

≈

The phone line buzzed "busy" for about twenty minutes, so Charlie busied himself at Viking Traders by getting his files organized. Amazing what a mess an FBI investigation can make—and then when the mess sits there for a couple weeks, well, it's hard to tell an invoice from an invalid license application. Now that Ivar and his buddies were in the clear, maybe it was time to put affairs in order.

They needed to toss a yard-high pile of paper, and Charlie had only begun filling the trash basket. He picked up a file titled "June Receipts" and tossed in a few likely looking stubs with June dates on them. He thought about his old Victorian home in Evanston. Could there ever be a way he could make a home there again, where trash didn't heap on the floor and motor oil didn't soil every bit of exposed flesh? He looked at his grimy hands and decided not.

He reached for the phone and dialed again. This time a familiar voice came to life on the other end. Elk Horn's baritone nearly boomed all the way from New Mexico. The man's phone existed as the sole one for many residents on the reservation, so the delay getting a connection made sense. Charlie thought they'd chat for a while about how their lives were going, but Elk Horn got right down to business."

"You heard about the experiment?"

"Connecticut?" Charlie had to search a few ragged brain cells before he recalled Ivar's Internet report. Flying rocks at a wooded site with glacial-era boulders. Yes, he had heard. Wait a minute, it was on the news, in the newspaper. Everybody heard about the disaster in Connecticut. Charlie's brain was slow, but he got things eventually.

"Did you know Boone was there?" Elk Horn continued, his voice turning somber.

"Derek didn't say a thing about that. Just Kyra and he were going. They were going down to meet some English guy. No one would really tell me much, so I'd have nothing to tell the feds or whatever . . . "

Elk Horn interrupted Charlie's ramble. "Boone took off to meet them there." He paused. "But you know what really drew him. That Sekhmet. She lured him with her spells. Once he entered her domain, there was no way out."

"So what are you telling me?"

"Listen, Charlie. No one's heard from Boone in a week. You either. Derek reported that he and Kyra are safe and on the way to Chicago. And some of the dead at that Connecticut disaster are unaccounted for."

"Which means what?"

"My heart tells me Boone has moved on to another state of being. Only your son knows more."

Charlie stared wildly at the receiver, wondering what more to ask.

"Thanks for taking care of Boone," Charlie choked out. "When he needed help . . . . "

"He had a mission. I'm sure he fulfilled it well. The rest is out of our hands."

Charlie felt like running, but didn't know where to go. "Stay well, Elk Horn."

"Always, my friend. Our own missions continue."

He hung up and realized where his feet longed to fly. He needed to phone Derek. He had a trip to Evanston to make. Again.

CHAPTER THIRTY ONE

Candles oozed amber light in nearly every room of Astrid's house. From the street it looked as if a grand party were in full sway, filled with tipsy guests and fashionable North Shore bores. But no laughter escaped from the open casement windows.

As Derek emerged from his red VW Beetle—which had still been parked where he left it on Peterson Avenue—he knew what cathedral he was walking into. Astrid had staged a memorial of her own design. Derek felt his throat catch as he wondered if she had gone overboard in her grief. But how did she find out? He'd only been home a few hours and it looked as if Astrid had not only heard what happened to Boone but was going to throw herself on the funeral pyre.

He crept along the side of the house and keyed open the side door, not smelling any house flames. With all those candles, you never knew. He passed an arrangement of lights in the kitchen—all propped in sensible, nonflammable candleholders. The votives licked inside their glass containers and the long tapers dripped onto their silver candelabras. Astrid wasn't going to burn the place down, he thought to himself, and stepped with a little more assurance through the hall into the living room.

That's when he realized who had beaten him to his unhappy job. There sat Charlie, the image of the uninvited guest, perched at the edge of the velvet sofa cushion. At his side sat a ridiculous cup of tea in a bone china cup, poured as if for a neighbor's social visit. It must have long gone cold. Charlie's mission wasn't of good cheer. He sat wringing something in his hands. When Derek approached, the old man looked up through the soot of candle flame waving across the coffee table and met his son's cool blue eyes with his own. In the father's lap sat the duffle bag he schlepped all the way from Santa Fe.

"Where's Mom?"

"I'm right here, darling," said a warm voice behind Derek. He turned to see his mother, dressed in black, but healthy and in high color. She came forward to embrace him tightly, closer than she had in many years. He gestured at the light show and tried to speak. She shook her head the way she used to when he launched into some elaborate story.

"Your father told me. Just tonight," she said, glancing at Charlie without a hint of anger or blame. "We thought this would be our little rite of remembrance."

Typically Swedish, Derek thought. Just about every Swede he ever met was an undeclared agnostic. A little head dunking for a baptism, splendid weddings, and a consecrated grave were all the church stood for in that secular society, and transplanted Swedes were even more independent than their forebears. To the Nilssons, this candle memorial had more meaning than a hundred Italian novenas.

Derek nodded and slid down on the couch next to Charlie. He looked from father to mother and tried to make calculations. Together again? Just cordial? Tolerating each other for the sake of the dead? Charlie said nothing for several long minutes, still worrying the bag in his lap. Derek finally leaned over to touch his dad's knee.

"It's okay. The data doesn't work. Whereever you put it is fine."

"I was going over to get it, but I'm still not sure, Derek. The feds aren't looking anymore, but I have a bad feeling."

Charlie stared into the candlelight as if trying to read a thought there. Astrid hadn't been listening. She moved toward her son and took his left hand in hers.

"You saw him die?"

Derek nodded. The thoughts started flooding back and he lowered his eyes before they gave away a hint of a tear.

"Whatever he died for, it was for a cause, a reason," she continued. They all bobbed their heads in silent agreement. Charlie let his hands go slack. Astrid lowered her head in individual prayer. Derek let his memory play back to the time Boone held him shoulder high at a local carnival. *Show me everything, Boone. You're so big, you can see it all.* A shudder worked through his breastbone and ended in a long, nearly silent howl.

Eventually Derek spoke again, his voice earnest and hushed.

"I brought back his driver's license. It's too long a story to explain why anyone would have it, but it was given to me. I thought we could put it together with a nice engraving and hang it somewhere as a memorial."

"Where? He never went to church," Astrid said.

"I thought here, in your home. It was as sacred a place as any to poor Boone."

"That's a sweet idea, Derek."

"I'll take care of it. It will say Bo Sandstrom and give the dates of his birth and death, and I thought I'd add 'may he rest with the angels.' "

"He always like the idea of angels," Astrid said. "Maybe now they will have pity on us and relieve some of the pain we feel."

"Let's say a prayer for him," Charlie volunteered. Mother and son looked at him in shock. In this home, a prayer never was recited.

"I don't know how to pray," Derek said, perplexed.

"Like this," Charlie said, and started intoning "Our father who art in heaven . . . . " Derek and Astrid joined in automatically. Derek was surprised he remembered the words. When they were finished, Charlie noted that they had just held a memorial for Boone. With that, Derek walked over and gave his dad a bear hug. Somehow the pressure was gone, and they all could let Boone go. No big church service could have been a finer send-off.

≈

He stayed at Astrid's that night, calling to make sure Kyra stayed safe in her apartment. Charlie slunk off at some point, but no one asked where he went to sleep. Morning arrived only a few hours later. Derek jumped up to check that nothing had burned down.

The entire house smelled like a New Age Tarot emporium with a malfunctioning chimney flue. Derek opened a few casement windows and a tart wind blew in from the east. Late summer waned and soon the weather would veer from torpid to brisk. Derek felt a letdown in his stomach every time another summer died away.

After presenting his mother with a basket of seashells from the Atlantic, he kissed her cheek. He noticed her eyes were clear blue and he smiled inside himself. She's hanging together. He said he'd be back to check on her soon and jumped into his Beetle and swung by to pick up Kyra for breakfast. After a quick muffin and coffee, they headed south to see George.

Derek's meeting with his broken family had been easier than this confrontation. George paced in a fury from one end of his apartment to another, taking in the story of Derek's travels. The part about Sekhmet's lure he could understand. He'd heard enough about the goddess to know what a dangerous vixen she could be, but George felt galled that everyone deemed the data faulty. He couldn't accept that it didn't produce optimum results.

He argued with Derek about the numbers, the proportions, the angles of the speakers. To George's mind, Sekhmet just didn't get things accomplished in a proper fashion. By nature she couldn't be orderly or scientific. The numbers, George pronounced, had to work. Stonegate said they did, and that was good enough for him.

"I know it works. I have my sources," George said, pursing his lips like an angry politician.

The rest of Derek's tale about the dreams, Sekhmet's mutable qualities, the mysterious, disappearing Petrie, the snake-like Salim, all of it fell on George's ears, but it was obvious he understood none of it. George didn't believe that the experiment didn't work. He wasn't going to accept it and figured that everyone had gone mad.

"Look. What we basically have is intellectual property, right?" Kyra asked. George looked at her as if he never realized she was participating in this conversation. "But this material has no clear ownership. The government thinks it owns the data, because it seized Stonegate's computer. Stonegate really does own it, but he's a con and no one believes the data is worth anything anyway. And you two think you have dibs by the law of Finders Keepers."

George and Derek looked at each other and nodded.

"If you just sit on the data," Kyra continued, "no one wins. And anyone can make progress on it, if it really does work." She said the last line with a pointed look at George. "But there is a way to release the data to the world and still get what you want."

"And what would that be?" George said.

"Publicity. Lots of it. You would be the men who broke the Pyramid Program."

Derek sat staring at his thumbs, while George's mouth worked without sound.

"Derek's mom could be a big help with all her contacts in the communications business," Kyra continued. "And if we spin the story just right, the government won't dare step in. Once the story's out, it's too late."

Derek nodded. Kyra's idea made sense to hear, but George still scowled, wanting sole ownership over the material they had worked so hard to obtain.

"I'm not giving up anything to anyone, including Stonegate," he said.

By the time the group parted, the participants were barely making eye contact. Derek promised to bring back the mirror disk that Charlie had protected for so long.

"Oh forget that. I think he destroyed the thing," George said, his eyes flaring.

"No. He still has it hidden somewhere—even from me."

George's eyes opened millimeters wider. "Well, someone still believes then. Someone is still loyal to the cause."

Derek and Kyra slipped out the door. Derek wondered how, for once in his life, his father stood as the only person accused of faith and honesty.

≈

Moving back into the abandoned apartment on Rockwell Street went by in fits and starts. First, Derek showed up day by day to clear up the papers and files that Sekhmet's tough boys left strewn around the place. Then he did some serious backups and re-builds on his computers, which—in light of the whole monstrous affair—hadn't been too damaged.

By week's end, Derek had brought in food, the all-important coffee, decent towels and shower niceties, including a new curtain for Kyra. After a long visit with Trevor, he brought home his little calico Foo. He owed a lot to Trevor for caring for her all those weeks. He let go of Foo somewhat reluctantly, Derek thought. Maybe he let Foo stay there a bit too long and Trevor truly bonded with the cat. Derek thought about picking out a cat at the nearest shelter and giving it to Trevor as a surprise gift.

Derek and Foo re-entered their old home with a can of tuna for the cat and grocery store sushi for the human. After a glass of water, Derek fell exhausted into his old bed. Foo, after a leisurely period of inspecting all corners of his room, jumped onto the mattress and curled at his feet. It was almost like old times.

≈

Foo's eyes stared unblinking into Derek's. Nose to nose, the two regarded each other in the dim morning light. Too groggy to register fright, he attempted to focus on the feline face, which appeared alarmingly leonine at this range. Foo nuzzled closer and Derek sighed. He'd been dreaming of this tête-à-tête. His reverie had been of itching and soft, wet tickles. He didn't have allergies, just a bad case of affectionate cat. He moved Foo down on his chest to give his eyes a break. He stroked the fur behind one of Foo's ears and she began to rumble loudly.

In his head, he began to run through the errands he'd need to do to fill up his day. Kyra's whole idea of publicizing his disaster was taking a while to sink in, but Astrid would be eager to use her news resources to help. Even George had warmed to the idea of landing a lucrative contract with a company that needed some crack cryptographers. Derek thought it was better than going hat in hand to BitJockey.com and sucking up to Bushy. They figured that by opening up the source code, they could show how Stonegate got such spectacularly secretive results.

What intrigued Derek the most was George's insistence that the sonic data really did work. If they got some sound technicians to do more testing, they might have real gold. Or maybe not. He still didn't know where Charlie had stashed that mirror drive.

Foo leapt off his chest with her characteristic suddenness, bouncing to the floor as if she had wasted far too much time on this silly human. Derek pulled himself out of bed and ran his hand through his hair, feeling the hair growing out, dark roots with blond tips. In vogue and so unlike the Bohemian he lived as, or used to.

He shuffled to his bathroom, then pulled on a pair of jeans, eventually finding a t-shirt on the floor and heading to the kitchen. Something didn't look right beyond that giant Plant from Hell, which still lived, even thrived, in the living-room window. Taking a step to the side, Derek peered around the plant at the living-room couch. There sat a visitor.

Seth Stonegate waited patiently for Derek to say good morning, a cup of fancy coffee in his hand.

Derek hardly paused, nodded hello and stomped into the kitchen to retrieve coffee from the auto-timed coffeemaker. He expected his heart to pound, but he felt sane. He had heard that Stonegate had been sprung from the pen and expected him to show up sooner or later, although not at such an early hour.

Derek lumbered back into the living room and squeezed into a litter-strewn chair across from the newly freed hacker.

"Well, I suppose anyone who can hack into the International Monetary Fund is not going to have a problem with a Chicago apartment lock," Derek said, after he swallowed a hot quaff of coffee.

Stonegate smiled and slurped from his paper cup. "I thought you'd be pissed off."

"Well, the thought crossed my mind."

"I couldn't waste any time going through formalities. Is your phone even hooked up?"

"I didn't pay any bills for a while," Derek said with a smirk. "But it should be back up by now." Derek leaned forward in his chair and studied the man he once idolized. Just as he did in the prison, the computer renegade looked like a man with a secret. Nothing appeared quite genuine about this easy-guy demeanor. Derek continued, "I thought you were hinting that the feds were going to let you go."

"I'm off the hook," Stonegate said, his eyes shading a long, complicated explanation.

"George tells me that all the dark suits went away."

Stonegate nodded and drank some more joe. "My acquittal," he said with fingers indicating quotation marks, "was all preplanned. They let me out on a technicality: they had no warrants for some of the computers they swiped. We knew they'd let me out eventually. I'm too valuable to them."

Derek shrugged. He should have figured as much. So many hacker "criminals" have ended up with new identities, working for the Department of Defense or even the NSA. At least that was the mythology that pervaded the nerd world.

"But they wanted that sonic data badly and were willing to coop me up until I spilled everything. That's why you were being tailed like a skunk at Tiffany's. But I couldn't rat on you and I had no way to turn in the data. Plus, how could anyone explain Sekhmet?" His eyes met Derek's, and the two shared a palpable chill. "So I was trapped . . . until the news flash arrived saying that the experiment didn't work."

"I figured my e-mail would shut everything down."

"It sure did. That mess in Connecticut was the best thing that could ever have happened to you and me."

"Well, not for everyone." Derek stared past the plant to the gray sky outside the window.

Stonegate stirred, seemingly unused to discomfort in others. He stood and began to pace, looking like a man who was familiar with stalking confined spaces. He thrust his hand into his pockets and turned on his heel.

"Look, it sounds nuts. I never knew that Boone guy at all. Never met him. But because of his contact with Her, well, I feel I knew the exact time he died. I felt it. Like an avalanche pressing the air out of my lungs."

Derek had no reason to doubt him. Anyone who'd been kissed by Sekhmet was part of the fraternity—and a fraternity it was, since she had no effect on women.

"I really came over here to thank you," Stonegate said, striding the length of the room again. "You stopped her and I really despaired that anyone could. But something still remains. It's not done yet."

Derek swallowed in anticipation, thinking the ex-con was gong to tell him a new mini-Sekhmet was running around, gathering new data. He must have looked heart-stricken, because Stonegate let out at barking laugh.

"No, you dweeb, she's not back. Who knows about that dimension of hers anyway? They come and go, but I think she's given up on this particular puny plane of existence. No, no, it's not that. It's that the data works."

"Some people believe that."

"That means double trouble. We've got to find a way to capitalize on it, but we can't let anyone know until the time is right."

A bizarre new reality started dawning in Derek's foggy brain. He stood up and looked at Stonegate, who lurked like a gremlin, a brilliant one, in the middle of his living space. He realized that he and this shady computer jockey were working together. Partners. No way out.

"Yeah, I'm in," Derek said. And he walked over and clapped Stonegate on the back. Stonegate put out his hand for Derek to shake. Derek took it. Flesh upon flesh. The deal was done.

"Let's get on with it," Stonegate grumbled, before pulling open Derek's front door.

CHAPTER THIRTY TWO

Gauzes, taffetas, cotton sateen clouds and embroidered linens fell about Derek's feet. Jyoti, dressed in a sari of finely pleated floral cotton, smothered a giggle behind a mocha-toned hand as she pulled piles of lush textiles from the inlaid wooden box. Charlie stood off to the corner of the room, pointing with enthusiasm when he spotted a square mound of white silk. The other Indian woman, Chitra, picked up the package and began to hand it to the elder Nilsson. But he gestured instead to Derek.

As the scent of coriander, cardamom and anise swirled around him, Derek could think of nothing but to bow deeply when Chitra presented the parcel to him. He unwrapped the fabric with deliberate care—the material was so flawless it seemed to have been woven of invisible silk threads. Inside were the hard edges of the silver mirror-drive cover. Amid such luxury, it looked like a piece of odd translucent material, but inside was the black and silver mirror drive. Derek turned to Charlie, then to Ravi, questions written all over his face.

"Dowry box," Ravi said, and Jyoti giggled again. She and her cousin were busy re-folding and re-packing the sweet-smelling box. The soft rustle of fabrics nestling into place soothed Derek's jumpy nerves. This had been an excellent hiding space.

He looked over at Charlie, amazed that the old man kept the faith, when every one else had lost it. He only hoped now that he wasn't going to break that band of trust by delivering the drive straight into the hands of their old enemy, Stonegate. They needed to approach Stonegate with care and supervise the data that was on that mirror drive.

As they bid the Indian cousins adieu—princesses they looked like in their glowing saris—Derek tucked the mirror drive into his inner coat pocket. He chattered a bit about his trip to Connecticut with Ravi, but the chef seemed to know everything already, even about the fate of Boone. But Ravi had plenty of new tales about excitement in the neighborhood, including police surveillance and FBI sedans parked in front of Derek's apartment. Charlie started telling the accounts of keeping himself out of sight of Chicago's Finest.

While they reminisced, Derek pondered his next moves. He and George had come to an accord over the last few days. After some verbal dog fights, they decided they wanted to go through the publicity show that Kyra suggested. There was nothing wrong with getting a couple of good jobs for their labors. George also realized that a partnership with Stonegate was impossible to avoid, but wanted this unholy alliance to stay in the background.

While Derek mulled the future, Charlie was firmly rooted in the present. "Where does the hard drive go now? The junk heap? A museum?" Charlie said with a chortle as they made their way back to Ravi's shop. Derek looked at him as if he had just returned from a trip to Mars.

"Just because the data doesn't work doesn't mean that we can't fiddle with it," Derek said in a low voice. Ravi nodded like an advisor.

"It didn't stay in the dowry box because it was useless," Ravi said, head bowed as he unlocked his door.

"But the heat's off," Charlie exclaimed as they pushed open the restaurant door. "No more FBI. Not the mob. No international cartel." His shoulders were so relaxed; he looked like a kid at play.

Derek merely mumbled and shook hands with Ravi. He gave his father a slap on the back.

"You'll see. You did a lot better service than you can possibly know."

Derek slipped out onto the street before his dad could ask anything more.

CHAPTER THIRTY THREE

The next few months went by with blinding speed. Announced as the men who broke the famous Stonegate code, Derek and George's photos flashed on the pages of every type of newspaper from freebie shoppers to downtown broadsheets. Derek had been chattering as an interview subject for weeks, interacting with so many people it made him dizzy. Ever since he worked with the reporters from Astrid's old newspaper, and their story hit the business front page like a cannon blast, Derek and George had become high-demand feature subjects.

As much as the days were taken up with interviews—and calls from prospective employers—the nights were full too. They belonged to Stonegate. He and George weighed the options of investigating the veracity of the sound data and could find no reason not to test it. They discovered a small acoustics lab in a Chicago suburb where a sympathetic technician helped them set up late-night experiments when the lab was vacant.

Results, duly tabulated and charted, went to various computers, one an anonymous box in a teenage boy's room. The kid got a small stipend from Stonegate, who paid another kid to whisk by each night to gather printouts from the first kid's windowsill. Really low-tech.

As far as the government knew, the acoustical data was dead. After springing Stonegate from the pen, they put him to work during the day to do Department of Defense decryption. They were interested in what Stonegate did during his off-hours, but they didn't stop to think that acoustics were on anyone's mind after the Connecticut catastrophe. To the entire world—the government, the press, other nations, and academics—the sonic levitation material was as much of a non-issue as cold fusion.

For some weeks, results from the sonics lab were disappointing. The technician could only keep a pea-sized stone afloat for about thirty seconds. But one night, Stonegate himself pushed his way into the lab and loudly began arguing with the mild-mannered sound guy. Stonegate felt the physical setting was wrong, that the objects were not placed in exact positions. Exasperated, Stonegate ripped open the sound chamber and shoved speakers, bringing them closer to an invisible reverberation wall similar to the one Derek experienced in Connecticut.

"Now try this," Stonegate said with a hint of menace in his voice. The technician hit the switch and the speakers began to hum. A stone the size of a child's block began to twist and wiggle. It seemed to do a dance on its pedestal. The sound man then applied the higher pitches, similar to the horns Sekhmet used in Connecticut. The block tipped, rose and then plunged forward a good five feet before hitting the ground. It was the closest thing to success they had seen.

Watching this minor miracle, Derek wondered if there was a chance he could remember the song and words of power Sekhmet had channeled through him that day in the wooded field in New England.

"Give me a minute or two with a keyboard, a piano or something," he asked the surprised sonics worker. Derek fought with his memory to regain the melodic lines. They sounded odd, atonal, and even grating, but there was something familiar about the way they hit his gut. He finally took a long breath and allowed relaxation to enter his body. He didn't will it, he simply allowed it to happen, forgetting Stonegate, George, the lab and everything around him. He thought of nothing except Roger's old instructions to listen to the infinite. And a series of notes issued from his fingers to the keyboard.

"Record that," he commanded the surprised sound technician. And Derek repeated the sounds. "Now, let's do the test again, this time adding this line just after the horns." Stonegate watched him with a look of hunger on his lean face.

The experiment resumed, replicating the previous elements, then, just as the block was about to rise, Derek's sound line mixed into the acoustical blast. Derek's mind was at once back in New

England when he heard the sounds, the words that Sekhmet uttered. Some were words he recognized from his occasional study of hieroglyphics—names of the gods. Others sounded like little more than gibberish, rhymes, and plays on syllables.

Sound, so integral to solid matter. Sound, the vibration of molecule against molecule, quark against quark. Sound. The beginning. He saw the connection in a flash. As he jumped up in surprise, the block spun and hovered in the air. The technician found that as he played the overlaid theme, altering speaker directions, the stone would flip and spin and dip, as if on command.

Eventually, the experimenters ended the test, settling the block on its pedestal. All was quiet as it came to rest.

Stonegate walked over and put his hand on Derek's shoulder. There was a great deal of room for fine tuning, but now that they could control movements of the blocks, they were steps away from reclaiming a secret known only by the ancients. Meanwhile, that mirror drive held all the calculations Stonegate had made for large masses to move. No one said a word as they locked up the lab, but the future path was spread out for them. Derek, George and Stonegate held one of the most valuable secrets in the world. And they planned to market their knowledge, when it was ready, to every construction company willing to pay the price.

Filthy lucre, Derek thought. But at least it won't fall into the hands of those thugs Sekhmet planned to benefit.

≈

"I don't think so."

Derek turned to Kyra with clumsy speed, nearly missing her arm as they breezed down Michigan Avenue.

"But you'd be perfect. Those wonderful press kits you put together with Mom. They were a journalist's dream. No wonder we got so much coverage. The way you talked those producers into getting us on their shows. You're the reason George and I got our fancy consulting gigs."

Kyra waved her hand, unconcerned, and then paused to look at an intricate garment in a shop window. As far as Derek was concerned, she was on a shopping trip in some other universe.

"Kyra, the dream. It's still alive. We're going to do this thing. And I want you as an integral part of it."

"It's your dream, Derek. Always was." A brisk breeze pressed in from the lake and she pulled her sweater closer. October had already begun, and the Michigan Avenue planters were now filled with asters and mums. A few maple trees had already turned scarlet and blazing ginger.

To get out of the wind, the couple slipped into a large mall complex, looking for a sedate place to talk and be alone. All they could find was an isolated table at a food court, surrounded by fast-food restaurants. At least no one paid attention to them there.

Derek went to get coffee. When he returned, a large brochure lay centered on the table. The only words he could make out were "ancient art." Kyra beamed.

"What's that?"

"They've offered me a job," Kyra said, pushing the thick booklet over to Derek's side of the table. "It's unheard of for someone in my situation, someone with no MFA in art. They offered me an interesting position with a future, a small staff and a nice budget. And here's the kicker: they contacted me."

Derek stared at the booklet. The Marz Museum of Ancient Art was one of Chicago's tiny cultural gems. Boasting a permanent collection donated by a wealthy businessman from the area, the museum was only ten years old, but already enjoyed an international reputation. For someone like Kyra, it would have been untouchable, because the Marz usually only hired people with advanced degrees in art history.

"They called and asked if I had put together the press kit on you and George, and I explained that Astrid and I were responsible," Kyra said breathlessly. "It turned out that their marketing manager is a good friend of your mom's."

Derek looked at the name on the cover sheet. Shawanda Jones. Of course. He'd met her a thousand times at parties and newspaper events.

Kyra rushed on, her features flushed with something that looked like love. Derek imagined it was passion for him, but he knew he was kidding himself. "One thing turned to another. I explained my situation. They needed a press director who understood art. My lack of classical art education posed a problem, but get this . . . . " She leaned over and gripped her coffee cup with both hands. "They said they will sponsor me for a masters in fine art. I'll have to do it in my spare time, but, well, who could say no to that?"

Derek's stomach sank. "So you told them yes?"

"What do you think you'd do?"

"But Kyra. I thought we were in on the sound technology thing together. It won't be the same working without you."

"Lots of couples work at different jobs. Don't be ridiculous."

"Well, I'm glad for you. I'm amazed. And happy my connection—my mother—helped you."

"Oh, Derek, you helped in more ways than that. I impressed the hell out of Shawanda by translating some hieroglyphics. And I was pretty knowledgeable on Native American art, which didn't hurt either. I wouldn't have known any of that if it weren't for you and the trips we took."

He tried to smile sympathetically, but under the table, one of his feet was wiggling like a newly caught fish. He visually scoured the mall as Kyra gushed. There was a kid trotting by, hugging an oversized teddy bear that still sported a dangling price tag. Couples glided along, wedding rings on their fingers. A man bent down at a pie shop, pointing with excitement at just the slice he fancied. A pair of women, eyes alight with fashion wisdom, carried bags of shoes from a posh department store.

Choices. Everyone looked pleased with the ones they made that day, especially Kyra. Derek sat wiggling his whole leg now, pondering the decision he had cast for his future. By hooking up with Stonegate, he might have moved away from any real future he could have with this woman he adored. He imagined Kyra was beginning to slip away now. Day by day, she'd enter a circle of art friends, losing the togetherness she shared with Derek on a moonlit beach on Rhode Island's shore. It was only a matter of time before he mentioned the one word that would drive Kyra away forever.

≈

"Stonegate."

"Stonegate?" Kyra's fork seemed to float abandoned in midair as she stared at Derek's burning face. "Seth Stonegate? The creepizoid? The jail bird?"

"Yeah. But it's not like that . . . " Derek began to mumble. "It's a lot more complicated."

"I'll bet it's complicated, if you risked your life, mine, and sacrificed Boone's existence to experiment on his data. He's the guy you tracked for years, until you nailed his machines in New Mexico." Kyra put the fork, laden with lobster, down with disinterest. "If he's so nifty, why didn't you just walk up to him a long time ago and ask, 'Please, sir, may I have your data?' "

"It's not like that, Kyra. Yes, he was in jail, but he was a sort of hacker poster boy. We grad students considered him a bit of a hero, standing up to the government, defying the rules of encryption."

Kyra's eyes danced around the room, and Derek knew he was losing her attention. He thought he had prepared for this moment with such care. It started out when she called and said a big celebration was in order. Derek had to guess the occasion—their birthdays were still a week or two away. Kyra sounded like a kid at Christmas when she blurted out that she won the North League Tennis tournament. She won at singles, not her specialty, and earned a big trophy to put on her fireplace mantel.

So, they booked a table at one of the best restaurants on the North Side, dressed for the occasion and talked of nothing but their glamorous new futures. Hers with her new museum job. Derek's with consulting and, um, this guy interested in sound experimentation.

Nice scenario but, in reality, all hell broke loose. While Kyra leaned back slowly into her chair, he tried to explain Stonegate's role in the entire caper: prison martyr, evil collaborator with Sekhmet, sudden turncoat, and ultimate government mole. There was no simple side to this man, Derek tried to explain. And as long as he and George felt there was something to gain from the acoustics material, Stonegate was their main man.

Kyra pressed her back, nearly bare in her shimmering sateen halter dress, into the rattan weaving of the dining chair. Then she crossed one arm over the other. Derek could see the compression bandage on her arm, where her tendon still ached. This was Kyra's big victory dinner, but he could see who really had won. Not Kyra. Not Derek. Not Stonegate. The genuine victor was Sekhmet, dead perhaps but living on in many a man's libido. It was obvious that Kyra had been fighting the Sekhmet spell over Derek for months, most desperately in New England, when she dashed nearly to her death to pull him from Sekhmet's side. The idea that her man was partnering with another Sekhmet devotee made everything clear as glass. Kyra gazed with anger in her eyes as Derek tried to extricate himself from the mess.

"So you go back to hacking at nights, ordering pizza, and hiding from life?" She spat out the words.

"No, Kyra. We have had incredible success already. We are ready to incorporate. We're putting together the staff now. It won't be long before we are able to work with construction companies—small ones—and build a big business."

Kyra nodded, unimpressed. "I saw that horror in Connecticut. I can't believe you're trying to make something out of nothing. Unless you're trying to bring back a dream."

Oh boy, here it came. He knew exactly what Kyra was talking about, and grabbed her hand—the left, uninjured one—with desperation.

"Listen, Kyra, my darling one, you are not a dream. It's you I think about day and night. For you, I want to build a successful business, make tons of money, buy you Tiffany diamonds and designer clothing. I want you to have the chance to go pro at tennis if you wish. Or be a full-time art historian. It's for you."

She took a half breath and returned an unconvinced gaze. Derek continued at a frantic pace.

"That's why I wanted you to join the company. Be part of the magic." She flinched and Derek slowed down. He'd better watch his choice of words. "If it wasn't for you, where would I be? Some geek in a brownstone, tapping away at a keyboard until dawn. No life. Worse yet, no connection. You, Kyra," he pulled her arm closer. "You helped me learn to close the gap, to touch, to caress, to reach for another's light."

Kyra looked down as a waiter came by to scoop up dishes. He offered to pack up Kyra's nearly untouched lobster. She nodded, expressionless.

Derek gulped. He knew he had changed. Kyra had started it, but others helped. Boone talked him out of his self-sufficiency. When he hit Charlie that one day, he punched out of his own glass enclosure—the one that insulated him from feeling—and began to breathe a true, fresh atmosphere. The more he breathed, the more he knew he could never suffocate in a dark, remote apartment again. He could no longer count only computers as friends.

But he also knew Kyra could read his passion. And she never could match that past devotion to Sekhmet. As Stonegate often said, Sekhmet never left you. Even dead—or wherever her spirit led—she tainted the men she kissed. Could anyone ever shake her off? Would Kyra even want to try?

"Kyra," he said, his hand trembling as he touched the tiny hairs of her forearm. An electric shock went through his tendons as he remembered the nights on the beach. "Making the connection is only part of the lesson." She made no reply, but she did not move away from his touch. "The feelings, the whole range of them, the pain, the stretching of soul. It's what you do with them that counts."

He felt he was crazed, jabbering like a maniac, yet Derek knew no other alternative than to pitch forward, continuing down this mad avenue. He closed his eyes and tried to remember what dreams had informed him in the night.

Kyra kept her eyes focused on Derek's. On her neck, she wore a charm, delicate and intricate, that they had bought on their journey to the Field Museum. It was a tiny image of a falcon, crested with the double crown of Lower and Upper Egypt. The Horus god, the true one, which hovered before him, was stretching its wings with the promise of rebirth, daily renewal with the sun. The falcon that led him from the mists of illusion to the larger reality, would it lead Kyra back to his heart?

After dessert—Kyra's favorite, creme bruleé,—she began to calm down. Derek stopped his frantic banter and simply talked about Kyra's tennis victory. Eventually, she put her spoon down and looked Derek deep in the eyes.

"Lots of couples have separate jobs and they manage to keep their relationship close," she said, with a warm smile. "Maybe I'll even learn to like Stonegate. The point is, my new job shouldn't keep us apart."

Derek beamed and felt that fresh Rhode Island air blowing again in his memory. They were still in love.

CHAPTER THIRTY FOUR

"What are you doing here?" Derek said, putting his cup of chai back down on the countertop at Ravi's diner.

George stood grinning self-consciously, a sheaf of papers in one hand, and a cell phone in the other. He slipped into a stool next to Derek and set the papers down with a loud whomp.

"Oh, this guy told me I'd be likely to find you here," George said, jerking a thumb in Ravi's direction. Ravi smiled like an icon of Buddha. Derek looked from Ravi to George for an explanation, but didn't learn anything from their casual body language. George continued to smile like an insurance salesman. Ravi offered nothing, standing with his arms folded. They were in cahoots.

"Sonic technology," Ravi said with a wink, and turned back to the oven, where he checked on browning pastries.

"But he's a mystic, a Hindu philosopher, not a computer wizard," Derek protested to George. His buddy shrugged.

"The two aren't mutually exclusive, you know," George said. He pointed at the papers. "Here's why I'm here. More gold-mine material. It gets better." George thumbed through the reports until he found a page for Derek to read. The document bore the title *Successful Application of Sound Technology on Large-Scale Objects.* Derek skimmed the copy, dry as dust, until he found information on moving bricks and large cinderblocks. It was from Stonegate's work with Sekhmet.

"The tricky part is the manipulation," George continued, jabbing an insistent finger at some photos of bricks wobbling in the air at bizarre angles. One looked ready to settle on an engineer's head. "Once they get that part down, no mistakes, we can go to market. Small scale." He spread his hands apart as if apologizing.

Derek looked in wonder as he regarded the simple equipment: loudspeakers, a sound chamber, regulating equipment. All told, it added up to less than he might find in a suburban living room. A gold mine, indeed. It simply couldn't be this easy.

"The trouble is, we always need a sound chamber," Derek said. "That limits how it can be used outdoors. So that rules out using it in building applications."

"Not so fast," George said, producing another photo. "All it takes is a series of reflective panels, which must be aligned at exact angles. Then it works outdoors. How else did they build those pyramids?"

"That's what Sekhmet tried, and we all know what happened there."

"Any problem can be surmounted."

"Uh-huh." Derek's thoughts were trailing back to Kyra and how she regarded all their work with a jaundiced eye. *Damn, her birthday is tomorrow. Better start looking for a present.* He was aware he wasn't answering George but the distraction was too great.

"Kyra again?"

Derek figured he must look like a lovesick dog. He nodded.

"Well, you know. She'll get used to it. We've got some good people. I thought all the mistakes ended after Connecticut."

"Yeah. Didn't we all?" Derek felt his guts settle again. George was only trying to get everything back to normal. Derek appreciated the gesture, but knew George had no idea what was going on in his love life. George never did.

"Ravi, I'll catch you later," George called out, tossing a five on the countertop. Derek gulped down his chai and followed him out the door. Ravi waved amiably. As Derek turned to pull the door shut, Ravi gave Derek a knowing wink.

"How do you know him so well?" Derek sputtered as they stepped back into the press of busy foot traffic. George looked into the sun and squinted. Or was that another smile?

"I'm thinking about hiring him," George said, hugging the papers to his chest. "When we get moving, that is."

"For what? Short-order chef in the company cafeteria?"

"Derek, Ravi is one of the most brilliant students I've ever had," George said, his bald spot shining in the sun, making him look older, more professorial than his tender years would suggest. "He graduated last year—adult night school—with a masters. We stayed in touch."

"When were you going to tell me about him?"

"I only found out recently that he knew you, through your father," George said, eyes glowing. "Derek, the point is that he's perfect for the job of technical manager, a real genius when it comes to applying theoretical engineering," George said, getting back his former vibrant energy. "Damn, that guy could program. The only guy in the whole school who could create sound files that were undetectable. Made it sound as if the computer was talking to you."

CHAPTER THIRTY FIVE

In early autumn, Cartouche, the company that George, Stonegate, and Derek founded, was beginning to hum. Derek, George, Stonegate, and Ravi learned how to move giant slabs of rock up two stories or more, earning them contracts for fancy buildings in Chicago's downtown. Things were looking up and even Kyra was excited. Derek moved from his dinky apartment to a giant skyscraper downtown.

Stonegate had jetted off to a hacker's convention in Las Vegas. It was a slightly seedy affair that attracted computer devotees from industry intelligence technology companies to crafty kids fashioning gambling software. Some of the attendees were operating within the law; many were not. The bad-boy cachet was just too much for Stonegate to resist. He'd gone to Vegas every year, when he wasn't in prison, and he wasn't about to miss out this time.

He was leaning over a robotic mine sweeper display when two Arabic men cozied up on either side. They asked him to walk down a nearby hallway to discuss business. They looked harmless enough—unarmed, anyway—so Stonegate slipped out of the conference hall with them. Once away from the crowd, they presented Stonegate the finest of puzzles. They were self-described revolutionaries, allied with no religion or party (but probably with the Islamic Brotherhood), who wanted to return Egypt to its former glory. To achieve their goal, they needed the brand-new Grand Ethiopian Renaisssance Dam to disappear. But they wanted the job done slowly enough for local residents of the Nubian area and Sudan to get to safety. Cartouche offered a far better alternative than dynamite.

Stonegate, out of jail now and aware of his image, pretended not to take the bait, but he continued to listen to their "de-construction" scheme, and to the reasons behind it.

For millennia, the urgent Egyptians said, the annual inundations of the Nile River deposited Lower Egypt with rich soil perfect for agriculture. The Nile had been the country's greatest asset from time out of mind. Then in the mid-twentieth century, President Gamal Abdel Nasser took charge with a fervent desire to drag Egypt into the modern age, no matter what the cost. Stomping on traditions and ignoring archeologists' pleas, Nasser insisted on a dam to cut off the Nile in Upper Egypt to produce electricity for his nation. No more floods in Lower Egypt meant more control over the land, he reasoned.

Nasser fought an uphill battle for years. Ignoring the advice of his predecessors, he insisted on creating a huge lake in Nubia, named after him. To create it, thousands of priceless artifacts and tombs would be drowned. The British and the Americans refused to help, finding the project financially and ecologically flawed. Eventually, in the midst of the Cold War, Nasser secured funding from the Soviet Union.

The Soviets moved in with brute force, and it was only due to the intervention of the United Nations that such masterpieces as the Colossi of Ramses the Great and other treasures of Abu Simbel were saved. Everything else succumbed to the flood.

Stonegate, listening with his eyes narrowed, barely remembered these events from his scanty load of university history classes, but he did remember the forty-million-dollar project to move the Ramses statues. The Arabic men didn't let him dwell on that subject as they rushed on with their plea.

The dam did more than destroy history, they said. It also changed the Nubian climate from arid to unbearably muggy. A variety of disease-bearing mosquitoes and snails lived in the water and became a curse throughout Egypt, spreading through the once-life-giving Nile. Even the fertile silt sank to the bottom of Lake Nasser, forcing poor farmers to use artificial fertilizers. Salinity levels were rising. To Stonegate's prospective clients, the Nile was dying. Solar energy could replace the energy lost from the dam, they insisted.

The addition of a dam in Ethiopia meant that a significant amount of water would be cut off from lower Egypt. Many felt Egypt would go dry. The Ethiopian dam, located in the high Blue

Nile area of Africa, would cause havoc when it went full scale in a few years.

"Only you can get rid of the dam," hissed their leader in the corners of a frigid hallway. "In one night, you could start a trickle, a leak. Then the whole thing will crumble. And we take Egypt back to its days of glory."

Stonegate took their card, shook hands and left Vegas on the next plane. Cartouche stood to make millions from this bit of terrorism disguised as ecological improvement. The promised money was astronomical; it was so high a number that it was doubtful the dissidents could come up with half the promised sum. It certainly was tempting, for Stonegate and Derek were united in a dream of Egypt—the golden land of the gods. All thanks to the influence of Sekhmet.

There were manifold arguments against the project, the instability of the Middle East being the greatest danger of all. The most worrisome jeopardy was tipping off Interpol, which had never stopped spying on Stonegate.

After the hacker's convention, Stonegate attended several clandestine meetings. They downloaded architectural plans and global positioning system coordinates. Cartouche was to send sonic equipment to secret warehouses. Although the dam looked sleek and solid from afar, there were individual blocks that made up the structure. All they needed to do was to press a button and move the correct blocks to cause a huge breach. This should take place at the precise beginning of the ancient Egyptian solar year, which was the traditional day the Nile began to gush downhill from Nubia. It was the day Sirius rose with the sun.

When Stonegate arrived home and spelled out the caper to his business partners, Derek reacted with alarm. Was this the reason he had gone into business? To aid in eco-terrorism? He wondered if the secretive Egyptians really could rescue citizens from the surging waters of the Nile. Were they serious about creating enormous amounts of solar energy to power an entire country? Could Cartouche count on secrecy? Most importantly, Derek wondered if he was sliding down a slope away from respectability, and forever away from Kyra.

"Nevermore," pulsed a voice from the computer. Derek looked for the e-mail from Ravi. The guy kept Derek's hours now and readopted the habit of sending cryptic advice and audio jokes to his old pal. Derek opened Ravi's e-mail. It was a graphic of a falcon in full flight. It bore an uncanny resemblance to the carved bird that Charlie gave to Derek, which now rested on a shelf over the media station. Silent. Except when Ravi wanted it to liven things up.

The keys clacked and Derek formulated a response, something about ravens being a different species.

"But, 'Nevermore' is the right word," he wrote to Ravi. He called a meeting of Cartouche the next day.

When the group was assembled, Derek started a long speech about the software they had inherited from Stonegate and how important it was to make clean use of it. "Buildings and useful structures, yes. Destruction and an aid to terrorism, no," he said in a loud voice. Stonegate looked shocked and gazed at his shoes, a contrite expression flooding over his face. Ravi nodded his head in agreement. But still Stonegate objected.

"And what was it you told us at the prison?" Derek asked Stonegate. "Keep the data safe from Sekhmet. Make sure it's only used for good? Something along those lines. Don't you think Sekhmet would love this little Egyptian adventure? If we do this one job we'll soon be doing work for every malevolent organization on earth."

Stonegate dropped his jaw.

"That's right," Derek said. "Sekhmet would be doing the same thing. I say we put the kibosh on this or we dissolve the whole company."

"No, no," George rushed in. "We can stick together. Just take no jobs that walk on the side of evil." Ravi nodded. Stonegate mumbled something about money and then got up and walked to the door.

"You don't need me anymore," Stonegate said. "You think you're so high and mighty."

"Without us, you'll go nowhere," George called after him.

Stonegate said nothing more and slammed the door on the way out. The other three breathed a sigh of relief. The next day,

George sent word that the deal was off and the Arab conspirators were furious, sending threats, even vowing to find Cartouche's headquarters and blow it up. Over time, they got over it. Or so they thought.

≈

Tonight, as clacks from the keyboard resonated like a ticking clock, Derek sat in front of the triptych of 30-inch plasma screens. He was working on a downstate building that wanted Cartouche's signature "big rock" look. It had become all the fashion in architecture in the last year.

Kyra was asleep in their bedroom. Derek had asked her to move in a couple months ago.

Now the taps and clicking from the keyboard were for a wholesome architecture undertaking. In the near silence of a winter's night, Derek entered a three-key code in a window and the left plasma monitor came to life. A three-dimensional display of moving boulders spun and nestled into the shape of a wall. Tap. Derek adjusted the graphic equalizer and the audio coming through his wireless headphones pounded with bass-heavy thuds. To the right, a collection of graphs pulsed and shifted. The boulders settled with less nimbleness. Click. The settings returned to normal.

After settling the simulated boulders into line, Derek typed a new code and they arranged themselves in a four-sided pyramid. Then he made adjustments for one boulder to move into a place marked by a square in the middle of the circle. With great intent, he touched each boulder with his mouse and they began assembling themselves next to each other to create a great platform. He leaned into the screen, listening to the ancient symphony of sounds pounding through his headphones. Foo lay in his lap purring like a windup toy.

He rolled his neck and gazed outside the window. The view, illuminated by streetlights far below, reminded him of living inside a huge cotton ball. This must be what they called cocooning. There were disadvantages to being on the sixty-eighth floor when the air pressure was this low. Rain and sleet actually fell below Derek's living room. His view was straight into the heart of a cloud. He felt as if he were wrapped inside yards of polyester fluff.

As the images danced on the video screen, Foo came awake, yawned, and sat up. She stared at the rectangular shapes that were slipping along the screen and raised a paw to the monitor, ready to leap at this new prey. Her pupils dilated and her irises were the size of teaspoons. She sprang to the desk and began to bat at the screen.

"No, Foo, down," Derek said before Foo could get her claws onto the screen. He picked up his calico pal and cuddled her into a bear hug, then leaned back in his chair, petting the cat, while deep in thought. The problem was that his client wanted the next set of boulders to stack on top of this platform, and more would be added on top of that. It was a puzzle for Derek to figure how to get the few rocks that were designated for the top to rise to the apex. He rose to his feet, still holding the rumbling cat, and headed for the kitchen, trying to empty his mind. He grabbed another Wild Ram caffeine drink from his brushed steel refrigerator, drained the tart contents, and let his mind wander.

He was building another pyramid. His client was a rival of the man who owned the Golden Pyramid house in Wadsworth, IL. It was out in a rural area—horse country really. The Golden Pyramid was a curiosity that people came from miles to see, but it wasn't really any great size and it wasn't built in the exact dimensions of the Great Pyramid of Giza. This new client wanted a bigger pyramid, based on the angles of the Great Pyramid, and it would be placed further downstate in some farmland the client had acquired for a song.

Cartouche had already performed some flashy construction projects with their sonic energy techniques. But nothing compared to this undertaking. The client wanted a building that would be world famous, if they could just get it right. Burnishing all the details to be exact was bedeviling Derek.

Well, at least this project was for the good of all, Derek thought and gave Foo a gentle squeeze. They had the chance to make new Egyptian history right in their home state.

But now Derek faced his current problem of stacking one megalith on top of another.

In the middle of the project, Derek's cell phone rang.

It was George. What he had to say made Derek start to tremble. He could have uttered millions of things. But all that tumbled out of his mouth was, "Uh-oh."

CHAPTER THIRTY SIX

Derek ran over to George's apartment even though it was the middle of the night. As he rang the doorbell, he reviewed what George had told him. Sekhmet was back. Stonegate (who still was on speaking terms with George), let it slip that she showed up at one of the meetings for the Ethiopian Dam project. Stonegate said he himself was pretty disturbed because he knew only she could turn the project into something truly evil.

George opened the door and let Derek in. They both stared at each other speechless for a while until George went into the kitchen and returned with two beers.

"I think we're going to need this," he mumbled. Derek took a long drink.

"The first thing we have to do is find out how far along they are on the project," Derek said.

"Not very far, Stonegate says," George replied. "When we pulled out, they had lots of adjustments to make. Then Stonegate showed up again. But he doesn't have the equipment we have and it will take some time to order the speakers and partitions."

"Why did Stonegate go over to them anyway?" Derek asked, frantic. "He listened to everything I had to say against that project? What did he want?"

"I think Stonegate is so rock-solid convinced that his numbers work that he wanted a large-scale project like that to test just how great his discovery is."

"And what do we make of . . . " Derek shuddered. "Her?"

"Yeah. It was only a matter of time before she heard of it, I'm sure."

"But George, I saw her fly away into the sun. She left this plane of existence."

"Listen, Derek, I don't think you are crazy, but you and Stonegate are the only ones who believe in this goddess stuff. Everyone else thinks she's just a clever and dangerous rogue."

Derek stood and peeled the label from his beer. Kyra was asleep and he wasn't going to bother her with this, but what about Ravi? Could he shed any light on how they should prevent this disaster?

"Let's call Ravi," Derek said. "He'll have to know eventually."

"Let's just schedule a daytime meeting to get all our ducks in a row," George replied.

George got on his computer and sent out a group e-mail stating that they'd have a meeting at noon tomorrow. He looked at Derek for confirmation. Derek nodded. Noon it was.

≈

Derek climbed into bed, leaving his construction project unfinished on his computers. He slid in next to Kyra, who mumbled something and reached out to hold his hand. He grabbed it as if grabbing a lifeline. Foo came in and settled between them, purring softly. Falling asleep was nearly impossible, but Foo helped, and some time around dawn, Derek slept without dreaming. At ten in the morning he was up and ready to make the Cartouche meeting.

In the kitchen he ran into Kyra who was enjoying a day off from her job. Some kind of national holiday. One that Derek never paid attention to anymore. Presidents' Day?

"Kyra," he said, encircling her waist with his arm before she could grab another cup of coffee. "We need to talk."

Her eyes opened wide. "Is it about us?"

"No, no," Derek said, giving her a kiss. "We're just fine. It's about Cartouche. Come over to the couch."

They plopped down together overlooking Lake Michigan, which had ice along its shoreline. This winter was a mild one, but not mild enough to keep the huge lake from showing signs of some bitter nights.

"Kyra," Derek said, getting her to look into his eyes, "Sekhmet is back."

Kyra jumped to her feet and let out a loud, "What?"

"Sit back down. I have more to tell you," Derek said, leading her gently by the hand. "You don't have to worry about her bothering you again, but she somehow came back from the dead, or what I thought was death, and is working on that Ethiopian Dam project."

Derek spoke about Stonegate and how he left to work with the terrorists. Kyra's eyes said, "I told you so." He then described how Stonegate recognized Sekhmet at one of the meetings. Derek tried to keep the discussion as logical and low-key as possible, but Kyra still stared out of bulging eyes, looking both frightened and enraged at the same time.

Derek reassured her he had a plan to get rid of Sekhmet. She let out a huge sigh and said she hoped Derek knew what he was doing. Then she picked herself up and went back to the kitchen to finish getting some coffee.

≈

George was already pacing the floor when Derek got to the Cartouche headquarters. Ravi sat looking meditative. Nothing ever seemed to upset his cool demeanor. When George saw Derek coming through the door, he ran over to ask a question.

"Stonegate wants to talk to us. Should we invite him?"

Derek looked at George's taut, pale face and nodded his head in the affirmative. "He wanted to stop Sekhmet too, if you remember the conversation at the penitentiary," Derek said.

George nodded. "He said to stop her anyway we could," he remembered.

"Actually," Derek said, "Stonegate may be essential to getting this Sekhmet problem out of the way. He understands her, how she wants to be worshipped. He and I must have some way of figuring how to deny her what she needs."

Ravi looked up and said, "You ought to research how to kill a goddess. Or at least make her go away permanently."

"I had a dream or a vision when I was on that light plane that Kyra commissioned for us," Derek said. "I dreamed I saw Sekhmet's last palace and the ruins the Romans made of it. She told me that all the gods went away because they were no longer worshipped and prayed to. She said she continued because people still believed in her."

"So how do we get people to stop worshipping her?" George said, a smirk on his face. He wasn't buying the "goddess" line for a minute.

"I think I have a pretty good idea," Derek said. "I'll see if Stonegate agrees."

They sat around eating grilled cheese that Ravi made on their toaster oven until Stonegate burst through the door. He had a look on his face that could make a whole room of terrorists fly.

"You heard it," Stonegate said. "What can anyone do about it?"

"First, tell me how far along the project is going and then we'll get to how we get rid of Sekhmet," George said.

Stonegate first explained that he never would have gotten into the Ethiopian Dam project if he knew Sekhmet would return. Derek rolled his eyes and told him to get on with it. Stonegate admitted that things weren't much past the talking stage.

"When Sekhmet first showed her face, she started talking about how she could get a hold of all the materials the terrorists—who now call themselves the Nile Liberation Front—needed," Stonegate said. "They fell all over her as if she were—well, a goddess. As far as I know, she is now appropriating speakers, panels and all the things she needs."

"Well, the panels are made only for us by one manufacturer," Derek said. "Let's find out if they got any requests for more orders."

The group nodded, and came up with several other things they could do to see if materials were being shipped off to Ethiopia. Then Stonegate got up for the door.

"I've got a meeting with them in two hours," he said. "I'll report back as soon as I know anything."

"Hey wait a minute," Derek said, squinting at Stonegate's lanky figure. "Whose side are you really on? Are you still working with them? Or are you now a spy in the middle of their works?"

Stonegate looked stunned, but formed an answer. "They will think I'm still working with them. But I solemnly vow that I am working against Sekhmet and will do almost anything to stop her."

"Good enough for me," said Ravi. The rest gave curt nods, and Stonegate beat a hasty retreat.

George cast a dark gaze over at Derek. "Do you really have any idea how to stop her? Besides not worshipping her?"

Derek looked up with a gleam in his eye. "Yes, I have a solid idea of how to stop the project cold. But we'll have to wait until the project is almost off the ground. It's going to be dicey. But just before they start, I can ruin the sonic technology in a minute."

George looked impressed but still tense. "Well, we'll go over the idea you have. Right now, I think we need to put a pause on the projects we are working on. Derek, is that pyramid you're building done?"

"The plans are done," Derek said. "We'll just tell them we can't implement them right away because an emergency has come up. They'll wait. No one else can do the work for them."

CHAPTER THIRTY SEVEN

As the weeks went by, Derek stayed in touch with Cartouche's suppliers—Charles Manufacturing. He checked in with Stonegate on how plans were going with the Nile Liberation Front (NLF for short).

For almost a month there was no news to ring the alarm bell, but Derek was uncomfortable and antsy. He'd speak often to Kyra about this to calm himself down. Kyra kept telling him he would brave out this peril in the making.

Then Stonegate stormed in one afternoon at Cartouche headquarters and said Sekhmet had reappeared at the Ethiopian Dam meetings.

"She says they have their equipment on order," Stonegate said, eyebrows pinched and eyes squinting. "But can't she just make the panels and sound devices appear? She is a goddess, you know."

Derek laughed. "She can't create machinery," he said. "Her magic is limited to that of sound."

"And passion," Stonegate added.

Derek picked up the phone and called his suppliers to find out if anyone was ordering equipment on the scale that Cartouche would use. He discovered that an order came in the day before for giant sound panels and speakers similar to what Cartouche bought.

"Do you finally have a competitor?" asked the manufacturing agent.

"A fledging one in Ethiopia," Derek answered, scoffing at the idea that anyone could best Cartouche.

"That's where the stuff is going—Ethiopia," the man confirmed.

Derek thanked him for the tip and decided to call a Cartouche meeting that evening. But beforehand, he conferred with Kyra.

"I found out that Sekhmet's coming back soon now," he told Kyra in their kitchen. "They ordered equipment and everything."

Kyra's eyes were wide, but she maintained a cool composure. "You know how you're going to foil her plans, right?" she asked.

"Of course. But I have to do it at just the right time," Derek said, crossing his arms and looking out into the distance. "That's the difficult thing to figure."

"I guess you'll get there around the time they are setting up their project . . . . "

"Actually, I'll come in at the last minute with my disruption plans."

Kyra raised her eyebrows, but nodded and walked off to the living room. She looked confident. *So why do I feel so shaky?*

At the meeting it was decided that Stonegate would jet off to Ethiopia as soon as possible to join the NLF gang, while George and Derek stayed in Chicago out of sight.

"I'll meet you there when you think they are just about ready to set their plans in motion," Derek said. George would help with the equipment Derek needed to foil the Ethiopian plan. Ravi would keep the day-to-day business running at Cartouche—basically keeping people at bay who wanted to order new construction.

"I'm only worried about her," Stonegate said. "What if she gets in my head again?"

"I can only tell you to fight it," Derek said. "I broke away from her once, so it can be done. Just keep remembering I'll be coming to destroy their plans and run her out of this world for good."

Stonegate looked agog. "You're going to do all that? How?"

"Remember what she wants? Worship? We are going to give her the absolute antithesis of worship."

Stonegate raised an eyebrow and whistled. He didn't ask for details, but seemed to know what Derek meant. The meeting broke up.

≈

Derek looked every day at Stonegate's texts sent from Ethiopia. The terrorists were making rapid time, getting Derek more and more nervous. They had set up their sound equipment around the dam. Soon the huge sound panels would be coming and Stonegate said they had bribed some local official to set up the panels as boosters for cell-phone towers. Derek wondered how they got away with that far-fetched explanation, but it hardly mattered.

Derek was being devious. No huge speakers for him. He had assembled a large array of piezoelectric speakers—tiny things that fit into a crevice of a rock and turned the entire boulder into a broadcasting object. No problem getting the speakers over the border. They packed neatly in his suitcase and looked like bluetooth speakers.

When it looked like the Ethiopian Dam was two weeks away from starting to run, George took off to work with Stonegate on the sly. Shortly thereafter, Derek would show up with the piezoelectric speakers and find ways to put them in secret places throughout the Ethiopian Dam. He had to figure how to get himself to Egypt at just the right time to thwart Sekhmet's plans.

He asked Kyra if she wanted to accompany him but she said she had to work. She looked genuinely disappointed, but mentioned that at least Sekhmet wouldn't get any more ideas about squashing her beneath a rogue boulder. Derek laughed and held her close.

"I'd never let her get her claws into you again," he murmured, kissing her face, her hair, her neck. "You're too precious to me to squander on a trip like this. I'll take you on a vacation to Giza and see the pyramids when this is all over."

Kyra mopped her eyes, which had let out a few tears, and told Derek that his job was to take care of himself. He promised to come back in one piece. Then Foo came over and sat on Derek's lap, meowing softly. She was adding her two cents. She wanted Derek safe also. Derek petted her soft fur and listened to the purring begin to rumble.

Just as they were settling down, Derek got a text message on his phone.

"Sekhmet recognized me," Stonegate had written. "Of all the people working on this project she zoomed right in on me. Now she wants me to be the lead man on the project."

Derek figured this would happen. Sekhmet would never forget anyone she'd worked with—or kissed. Still, Stonegate was in no danger.

"Just keep up the pose that you are working with the terrorists," Derek tapped back to Stonegate. "She has no idea what I'm up to. And please don't mention my name or any knowledge of my whereabouts."

He waited a few seconds and the reply came back. "She hasn't asked about you and she doesn't recognize George."

Kyra looked curious and Derek just told her that Sekhmet had finally poked her nose in their business.

"But no worries," he added. "She has no idea what we are going to do."

CHAPTER THIRTY EIGHT

Derek was at O'Hare International Airport a week before Stonegate said the Ethiopian project was set to go off. He got on a plane to Cairo, then connected to one to Khartoum. Then a bus trip to the dam area up in the low country before the highlands of Ethiopa. He alighted with just one checked bag and a carry-on with an old-style CD player and recordings. He made sure to stay at a hotel that Stonegate had not mentioned.

He got a look at the land, which was impressive and spacious. Housing was located on the lower part of the land, far away from the water jets shooting out from the dam. The building itself looked like a giant slide made of marble, but on closer inspection, Derek could see the blocks that made up the structure. Derek knew he could defeat the NLF easily.

He got out his "burner" cell phone and called Stonegate, who was fortunately free.

"How's it looking?" he asked his old co-worker.

"We've installed the speakers amid the ground-level rocks and the rocky landscape. If you take a look around you'll see the sound panels on either side of the dam."

"Any idea of how I'm going to get down there and install my anti-Sekhmet device?"

Stonegate had no idea what he was talking about, so he promised to meet him at a site downriver and explain his plan.

In the meantime, Derek took a walk about the warm and picturesque landscape. The water was still and sweet-smelling, until you approached the dam. The air was breezy and the temperature in the seventies, which was a nice break for Derek in the winter. All around were palms and other exotic plants.

When he met Stonegate, he wasn't ready for the panic-stricken look in the other man's eyes.

"We have to keep you safe," Stonegate said. "If she sees you, we are all cooked. I even have a sixth-sense feeling that she knows you're here already."

"Just keep her focused elsewhere," Derek said, pulling out a roll of paper. "These locations are where I'm going to place piezoelectric speakers. Tell me if the locations are too close to her speakers."

"Piezoelectric speakers! You are a genius," Stonegate said. He then looked over the schematic and showed Derek where a couple speakers couldn't go, and then suggested better locations for them. Sekhmet's speakers were going on the ground, aimed up at the sensitive slabs. Derek's could go anywhere up higher.

"But what are you going to play on the speakers?" Stonegate asked. "Are you just going to drown her out?"

Derek shook his head and said it was a secret that he didn't want Sekhmet to drag out of Stonegate, but he did say that when the dam refused to break, he wanted Stonegate and everyone else to join in an uproarious recording of laughter that would follow.

Stonegate looked confused.

"You'll get the idea," Derek said. "What's the opposite of worship?"

Stonegate closed his eyes and chuckled. "Derision," he said. "She'll be a laughingstock."

Derek explained that he'd wait until Sekhmet started her evil project and then would push a button that would activate his smaller, but more powerful speakers. Everything would work wirelessly. Stonegate got the concept instantly. Even if Sekhmet spotted Derek, he'd still have that button in his pocket to push. George would have a duplicate button in case something went wrong. Sekhmet's magic could not overcome the simple physics of Derek's plan.

They parted, with Derek scheming to plant the tiny, undetectable speakers throughout the dam at night. Stonegate said Sekhmet would distract the guards

"How do you know the guards will truly stay out of our way?" Derek said.

"Remember her kiss?" Stonegate asked, looking mesmerized. "Do you remember what it did to us? Well, this time, she had us gather the guards together and one by one she gave each one a kiss. Then she tranced them so they would stay away from the dam."

"I know her power," Derek said. "She'd easily be able to pull that off."

"I haven't seen a guard around here for days and she only kissed them last weekend."

Stonegate and Derek shared a laugh, and then, embarrassed, looked at the ground. Derek, for one, didn't want to be affected by Sekhmet like that again. He guessed Stonegate felt the same.

≈

He slipped in and out of the rocks and tall pillars of the dam, finding the going a little difficult as he looked for footholds and handholds. Yet there were numerous places to put his speakers. The security lighting made it easy to see where he wanted to put the speakers, but there were ominous shadows everywhere. Midway through his inserting one tiny speaker in a crevice, he almost thought he was caught by Ra, who naturally would be around Sekhmet on any of her projects. Derek slid into a partition next to the pillars and Ra walked right past him. Derek's heart hammered for long minutes after that, but he was able to finish his job, drenched in sweat, in twenty more minutes.

He was up early the day of the event, and Stonegate texted him a rundown of the itinerary. Derek needed to put the tiny CD player in a place where it couldn't be found, but not too close to the speakers, as he was expecting possible fragmented rock and rubble to fly in the air. They found the place outside the cordoned-off area that Sekhmet had set up days before. They set the device on play and it would respond wirelessly. It would turn on the minute Derek pushed his secret button.

Derek was marking down the hours until noon, when the Ethiopian project was supposed to go off, and he walked along the top of the dam, looking for where the terrorists had put their speakers. He thought about the houses downriver below the dam and shivered, thinking of how the people in them would be caught in an instant deluge and probable immediate death if the NLF plan worked.

An unexpected text beeped on his cell phone and he took a look. Stonegate had warned in all capital letters:

GET OFF THE TOP OF THE DAM. WE ARE WORKING ON THE BOTTOM ON THE BOULDERS. SOMEONE IS GOING TO SEE YOU UP THERE.

Derek put his phone in his pocket and started to make his way down one side of the dam when he felt a pull on one of his arms. It was Salim.

"Going somewhere?" Salim hissed. "I think we need to bring you over to Sekhmet."

Not this again. Just like last time. Caught because I was in the wrong place at the wrong time.

He tried to break free from Salim but couldn't loosen his grip. They went down a long sloping trail until they arrived at the bottom. Once again Sekhmet had set up a stage of sorts near the lower edge of the dam. Stonegate stood there, compromised by his double-agent status, unable to help Derek.

"I should have known I'd see you again," Sekhmet said. This time she wasn't wearing black silk or anything seductive. She was dressed as an ancient Egyptian in a linen sheath, wide collar necklace, hair done up in braids and an elaborate crown on her head. Her makeup was heavy with wings painted on either side of her eyes.

"Thank you so much for improving and fixing the technology over the last year so that it works now," she said with an imperious air. "You and Stonegate get my highest appreciation. And to show you just how much I appreciate it, I'm going to let you call out the magical words, just as you did before."

Derek squirmed in Salim's grasp, saying, "You don't need the words anymore. We improved it so that they are unnecessary."

"Fool. The words are what make it magic. Come over here and stand by me."

She pushed Derek up to a microphone. He gazed at his watch and saw it was nearly noon. Still, he wasn't worried. He had the means to ruin her plans.

She also reached over and brought Stonegate to the microphone and said they would cooperate. Then she smirked. Stonegate looked at Derek with a wide-eyed gaze, but Derek stayed calm. The endless seconds counted down until the sounds started blaring from the speakers near the dam.

"Now," Sekhmet said. "Now you start. She began to coach them in the ancient Egyptian words as she sang along." Derek had no idea what he was saying, he just parroted Sekhmet. The panels on either side of them began to shake as sound bounced off of them.

Nothing happened for a long time, since the job was so big, but soon Derek saw a stone move and then shake. Stonegate nodded to him. Just then Sekhmet grabbed Derek's left hand and told him to hold his other hand with Stonegate.

The button in his pocket! How was he going to get to it? And without his phone handy, how was he going to tell George to push the alternate button? Derek started sweating. He couldn't just break the link of hands without Sekhmet noticing. The rocks were shaking, and one began to move a couple feet. They sang on and the blaring increased.

Sekhmet began to wail in glee as she saw her plan beginning to work. She yelled and said that all of them should hold their hands linked high in the air. This was going to be her moment of glory.

This was just the break Derek needed. On the upswing, he dropped Stonegate's hand and shoved his hand in his pocket. Then he did a roll to get away from Sekhmet's grasp.

Once the button was depressed the piezoelectric speakers turned on, blaring something loud and raucous. Most people looked completely clueless until they recognized the signature beat of rock and roll. Stonegate looked astonished and Derek, now running for cover, just laughed. "Dissonance," he shouted. "You can't make sonic levitation work with dissonance breaking up the sound waves." The dissonance was the loudest, most obnoxious noise Derek could imagine.

In seconds, it was a shambles at the reviewing stand where Sekhmet stood. The rocks had stopped moving and instead the dam became a wall of primitive rock and roll sound. She yelled at Ra and Salim. She screamed at the terrorists, but no one could tell her what was going on.

"What's playing?" Stonegate yelled to Derek.

"Rage Against the Machine!" Derek said. Stonegate laughed with glee. The name of the band fit the situation perfectly.

And as surely as they broke through the top 40-hit charts, Rage Against the Machine was breaking up Sekhmet's sonic levitation scheme. The combination of noises all turned into random noise and screaming, and Sekhmet had her team turn off their speakers. Then the rock music ended. Immediately, a recording of uproarious laughter followed.

Derek and Stonegate made sure to laugh along. George came out of hiding and began to laugh too. The sound was so infectious that some of the terrorists, and even some curious area residents on the riverbank, laughed too. They made it obvious that they were laughing at Sekhmet, pointing at her and doubling over with deep breaths.

A goddess who needed worship at all costs was being made sport of. She was humiliated and derided. She began to shake and moan.

"Got enough worship?" Derek shouted to her, but she made no reply. Instead she began to shrink. She ran to hide behind a rock, and made no sound. After five minutes or so, Stonegate went to check on her and grabbed Derek to look.

There behind the boulder, the once great and mighty Sekhmet was little more than a tiny Egyptian statue. When the laughter reached its peak, she broke into pieces, and then into grains of sand. The wind blew. She was gone.

Ra and Salim were never seen again.

The dam stayed perfectly strong and solid as the day it was built, and the terrorists all made their getaway in jeeps. Downriver residents never had any idea how close they came to annihilation.

Derek, George, and Stonegate dug out the piezoelectric speakers, packed up the CD player and were gone within an hour. Before they left, they let loose the guards who were penned by chains in an area by the riverbank. They blinked and walked out as if they had been in a trance. Derek thought perhaps they had been tranced.

CHAPTER THIRTY NINE

When they arrived at O'Hare, Derek, Stonegate, and George were met by Ravi and Kyra, who brought balloons and whooped and hollered. People nearby stared, but no one gave them an explanation.

"Heroes!" yelled Ravi.

Behind Ravi, Derek could spy some extra greeters bearing microphones, cameras, and notebooks. They crowded around Derek, George, and Stonegate, asking a myriad of questions.

"Wait a minute," Derek said to Ravi and Kyra. "Who called the press?"

"It was me," Ravi said, smiling like a madman. "This is a big story." He held out the *Chicago Star* and showed them the story headlined "Sonic Levitation Firm Defeats Ethiopian Dam Terrorists."

So, the Cartouche buddies turned and smiled for the camera and gave a brief sketch of what had happened in Ethiopia, leaving out the subject of Sekhmet.

"Will you return to talk with the Egyptians and Ethiopians about ways to protect the waters of the Nile?" one reporter asked.

"That's a job for diplomats," Derek said. "But I would like to go to Egypt and get a good look at the Nile down there."

Kyra looked up at Derek with love in her eyes. "Could you take me?"

Derek gave her a kiss, dutifully recorded by the press. Kyra beamed. Derek started pushing through the throng.

"Let's get our baggage and let these guys,"—indicating the reporters—"get to work."

Kyra gave Derek a subtle nudge and whispered in his ear.

"They have to get to work making you a hero."

ACKNOWLEDGMENTS

This novel never could have come about if it hadn't been for my husband, Brad Blumenthal, PhD, who spent may hours typing on his computer late into the night. Although he is nothing like Derek (he's friendly, open, handsome, and as good with small talk as with erudite discussions), he still inspired my protagonist. That's because his love of computers equals my fictional character's. He also helped with plot development and copy editing.

I owe great gratitude to my expert group of test readers. Carol Luce and Virginia Voedisch read my first version of "The Kiss of Isis," (when Isis was not a bad word and geopolitics hadn't changed so suddenly). I decided the book needed a rewrite and new ending, and a new title! Thanks to readers Renee James, Libby Hellman, and Penni Sibun for pointing out all my mistakes and all the outdated technology that remained from version number one. Sibun also gave me great information about rural Connecticut.

There's no way to offer the sheer amount of thanks that must go out to my writers group: Susan Van Dusen, Traci Koppel, Al Manning, Renee James and Lisa Sachs. All pointed out many goofs and we spent a lot of time discussing how much techno-babble was too much for this novel.

Thanks also to the writers who ponder such imponderable things as sonic levitations for the late magazine *Atlantis Rising*. I poached many ideas from the many sources.

Of course, I must honor my Swedish relatives, who provided so much background for the story. Many of them are gone now, but I'll always cherish the experience of growing up in a Swedish-American family.

And many thanks, as ever, to publisher Lou Aronica for believing in me.

ABOUT THE AUTHOR

Lynn Voedisch is a Chicago writer who had a long career as a newspaper reporter and worked for many years at large metropolitan dailies. She wrote for the *Chicago Sun-Times*, the *Chicago Tribune*, the *Los Angeles Times*, *Dance* magazine and many other publications. She also worked as a writer and editor for an online news service. She lives with her husband and two cats in a suburb close to Chicago. Her son, an attorney, lives and works in the city. She is a member of the Society of Midland Authors and the Association of Journalists and Authors.